# THE EMERALD QUEEN RISES

I0712856

## MAEGWEN SALLEY-MASSIE

MAEGWEN SALLEY-MASSIE

An imprint of Green Ferns Publishing House
Copyright © 2025 Maegwen Salley-Massie
Cover copyright © 2022 MiblArt. Cover designed by MiblArt.
Second Edition, Original Copyright date 2022

All rights reserved under the International and Pan-American Copyright Conventions. No part of this book may be reproduced or transmitted in any form or by any means, electronic or mechanical, including photocopying and recording, or by any information storage and retrieval system, without permission in writing from the publisher

Library of Congress Cataloging-in-Publication Data
Salley-Massie, Maegwen
The Emerald Queen Rises / Maegwen Salley-Massie
489 pages.

Summary: "A queen and an outcast, two enemies meant for something greater. They will have to face the dark powers and hope that the queen's choices will awaken the ancient magic to save her people."
—Provided by publisher.

ISBN 979-8-9870525-7-0 (paperback), ISBN 979-8-9870525-8-7 (hardcover),

Subjects: Fantasy—Fiction. Love—Fiction. Adventure—Fiction.

Printed in the United States of America

This is a work of fiction. Names, places, characters, and incidents are either the product of the author's imagination or are used factiously, and any resemblance to any actual persons, living or dead, organizations, events, or locales is entirely coincidental.

Warning: the unauthorized reproduction or distribution of this copyrighted work is illegal. Criminal copyright infringement, including infringement without monetary gain, is investigated by the FBI and is punishable by up to five years in prison and a fine of $250,000.

To my husband, Kyle, who was the key to unlocking my magical world.

To my family and friends, who helped inspire and motivate me.

To my Clear Pond Book Club, who encouraged me and were my wonderful beta readers

The Gelida Seas
Glatania
Sacharo Lagoon
Vichinos Channel
Havas
Melting Water Seas
Dragon Cove
Stoltland

The Snaer Seas
Ten Nove
Elysium
Golden Lake
Hostile Channel
Emerald Lagoon
Korpam
The Margyger Seas
thlantian Seas

# TABLE OF CONTENTS

# CHARACTER NAME PRONUNCIATIONS

Adalina (ad-ah-Leen-ah)

Adma (Ad-ma)

Adomin (a-Doe-Min)

Aellizzabelle (Ale-Liz-ah-Bell) aka Lizz

Aerrick (Air-Rick)

Alon (al-on)

Anabeth (Ah-na-be-th)

Anadelvia (an-ah-del-vee-ah)

Audayia (Aw-Day-ee-ah)

Barm (B-arm)

Bip (b-ip)

Brandle (Bran-Dill)

Brenna (Bren-nah)

Briar (br-eye-ar)

Brielin (Bree-Lynn)

Char (Ch-Ar)

Cian (See-an)

Cidreek (see-dri-k)

Corentine (Coer-en-teen)

Dinyelle (din-yell)

Doebromir (Doe-broe-meer)

Drystan (Drih-stan)

Ebbalee (Eb-bah-Lee)

Elmond (el-mon-d)

Ezen (Ee-Zen)

Faith (Fay-th)

Favien (Fae-Vee-in)

Finn (Fin)

Finnley (Finn-Lee)

Graelynd (Gray-Lind)

Haedon (Hay-don)

Herb (h-erb)

Hueweyn (Hui-When)

Jace (Jay-ss)

Jashun (Ja-Shoo-n)

Jdru (Droo)

Jem (Gem)

Jesh (je-sh)

Karis (Care-Ris)

Keket (Key-ket)

Kolt (Colt)

Lulana (Loo-La-nah)

Madilina (Ma-di-lee-nah)

Maekel (May-Kel)

Marin (Mar-Rin) Araelien (ah-RAY-lee-in)

Max (Max)

Melaina (mel-ae-na)
Menry (Men-Ree)
Micdoeclaven  (mic-Doe-
clae-ven) or Mic
Mimby (Mim-bee)
Miola (My-O-La)
Norella (Nor-ell-lah)
Oren (O-re-n)
Pamme (pae-m)
Phyre (Fire)
Pinx (Pin-X)
Pyry (Peer-Ree)
Quenton (qu-en-ton)
Quinten (Quyn-Ten)
Raquel (Rah-Kell)
Rav (R-av)
Rayn (Rain)
Redone (Ree-doen)
Rielen (Ry-Len)
Rivers (Ri-ver-s)
Royce (Roy-SS)
Runihura (Ru-ni-hur-a)
Ryker (R-eye-ker)
Araelin (ah-RAY-lee-in)
Ryland (R-eye-Land)
Saeth (Say-th)
Sakul (Sa-Kool)
Saven (Say-Vin) Dovinus
(Doe-Vin-us)

Sealyn (See-Lin)
Siany (See-On-ee)
Song (S-on-g)
Sorcha (Sore-Shah)
Stawyer (St-aw-y-er)
Stev (St-ev)
Svagon (S-vae-gon)
Tahbert (Ta-h-ber-t)
Temm (Tem)
Tilmond(t-IH-l-m-uh-n-d)
Toven (Toe-Vin)
Trey (Tray)
Trit (Tr-it)
Tybalt (Ti-Balt)
William (Wil-lee-um)
Zedvonair (Zed-Von-air)
Zuri (Zur-Ree)

# PROLOGUE

You could smell death. You could cut the fear in the air; it was so thick. But most of all, chaos was now king. Brother fought brother. Sister killed sister. Sons betrayed fathers. Mothers sacrificed daughters. Everything that was promised was a lie.

The twelve crouched low in between the rocks and trees. They could hear the soldiers surrounding them. How do twelve fight an entire army? The answer is—they do not; they die, but they die with a purpose. They were there for a reason. They were there for the promises. They still believed in them.

Sweat dripped from the leader's nose and landed on a dirty blade of grass. Three sleepless nights had gone by. They had survived on muddy water, snails, and worms. Their bodies could take no more. Their hearts ached for a miracle, the miracle that their King Novaedon would fight against the curse instead of embracing it. How could their king fall for the lies? The Second Chance happened only months ago. He should have been able to resist such a calling.

They were the last stand against the wishes of the curse on Elysium. If they did not rise, then who would? They needed their deaths to matter. They needed a lasting ripple effect to prevail for eternity: one last battle, one last try.

The leader, bleeding from his ears, nodded to his comrades. This was it. Rise and fight. They sprung up from their hiding places and charged the green-dressed soldiers from Elysium. Their voices roared with their strides. With bodies and swords colliding, the Battle of the Twelve commenced. They did not fight to win—they fought to take as many infected down with them.

Swords slashing through bellies and necks, the twelve killed more than King Novaedon anticipated. The final three had their backs to each other, fending off the traitors. Their faces were covered in blood, and even more, was dripping out from where their bodies had been stabbed and scraped. The last three almost did not look like men anymore, rather dark creatures of the night. A stab to the shoulder, a dropped sword, and a slash to the leg made the remaining men drop to their knees.

They heard the king yell, "No mercy!" They held each other's hands and saw a large shadow pass over them. They looked to the sky to catch the final glimpse of the Green Phoenix. The Elysian soldiers raised their swords and jabbed their blades through the hearts of the last of the twelve.

And just like that, the purest blood of all seven kingdoms was spilled. All twelve died a martyr's death. With the last breaths of the three, the giant phoenix disappeared. The old magic died that day, waiting for someone new and pure to awaken it.

curses have a way of infecting the next
generation worse than before. with each
new babe, the claws of the curses sink
deeper. only the light can dissipate the
darkness of old. three. the curse must
be washed three generations over. this is the
antidote. but if the first ever begins, then
the world is doomed. what bloodline can
resist the powerful calling of the curse?

i have failed. i have failed my people, my
kingdom. they are here to destroy us. i saw
the light but was not strong enough to resist.
now, my children are infected. hope for breaking
our bondage is lost. i can only fight against our
mortal enemies, but not the calling. i hear
its voice and bow. i am a weak king like the others
before me.

i write this letter hoping it reaches the fingers
of the one who has the heart to unlock what
was lost. though it will be buried six feet
below, i believe the purest bones will protect
it and call to the one our land needs.

king perdon belfron

7704

KING RYKER

# Chapter 1

Because he dared to believe in dreams, dared to believe one person could change the world, King Dovinus created the first ripple to unlock magic and all the chaos that would follow. In the year 7930, nearly six thousand years after the Second Chance, King Saven Dovinus tossed and turned under the night sky, feeling the rough terrain underneath his blanket. The tall, dark-haired king was a bold warrior, renowned for his strategy and tenacity. His men were tired of battles, tired of this never-ending war. He sensed his age in his bones and prayed Creator would grant him sleep, but more than that, he asked for a plan because Saven was out of ideas.

On the eve of the final battle, Saven dreamed of a giant green phoenix soaring above his men. The mythical phoenix soared through the air effortlessly before perching among the treetops. It glared down at the enemy's camp. The phoenix lifted its head, its yellow eyes fixed on Saven, and then let out a loud screech that roused him.

Saven gazed at the light green haze obscuring the blue sky. His heart raced. He would send his army into battle today. Saven felt weary of fighting; he was exhausted by the curse, the curse that plagued all lands. He recalled his dream and wondered why the legendary creature had chosen to visit him in sleep. What was the phoenix trying to convey? He studied the treetops swaying gently in the breeze. Wait.

Saven sat up straight and snapped his fingers. The treetops! The phoenix had settled on the treetops. He now had a new strategy to pursue.

Saven ordered his best climbers and archers to the treetops. They would attack the campsite from both the trees and the ground. This was meant to be a battle he could not win, but perhaps his new plan would give them the edge they needed. He had to save Elysium from falling under Stoltland's rule. It felt as though they had been battling Stoltland for what seemed like eternity.

His men were positioned; it was time to end the prolonged war. The ground soldiers struck their swords against their shields, stirring the enemy camp.

Falling into the trap, the black-armored soldiers charged from their makeshift tents toward the emerald-bannered Elysian army. As they fended off the Stoltland soldiers, Saven signaled for the treetop warriors to attack. They descended behind the enemy, stabbing their backs and necks. Shock and confusion filled the enemy's veins with fear. Saven's men sliced through the dark soldiers' flesh with brutal force; crimson stained the forest floor. They were no match for the surprise tactic. Saven watched the last soldier surrender, and a wave of relief rushed over him like a tidal wave. It was finished. They had won. As custom, Elysium left only one enemy soldier alive to carry the severed head of their leader back to Stoltland. Saven watched him leave with mixed emotions.

With a long exhale, Saven gazed out over the blood-soaked forest, bodies piled on top of each other. War was ugly, but it was over. They had won the necessary battle to end the prolonged war. Soaking in the great victory, Saven felt the urge to cleanse the land of the curse. Many other kings had tried and failed, but it was time for him to rise and confront the curse head-on.

He understood this would be challenging. He might not even witness the entire land healed in his lifetime, but he could chart a course for his family to follow because the generations to come would bear the heaviest burdens of the curse.

Elysium was consumed by envy, affecting the hearts of its people; only a handful resisted the curse's allure. Upon returning from battle, Saven resolved that creating character laws—the first of their kind—would instill discipline among his subjects. He also created Reformation Rock for those who had given themselves to the curse. This remote island would provide those consumed by darkness with the isolation necessary to prevent their influence on others, while also offering hope to pull them out of their enslavement to jealousy.

Strangely, the air began to clear, and the olive haze that had once filled the skies started to dissipate. A bright, colorful, and lush land began to flourish. Flowers, thought to be extinct, blossomed. Animals that had been hiding stepped into the light. Elysium was finally on a path to freedom, but it was now time to align the next generation.

Picking a successor was crucial to cleansing the land. King Saven and his queen had four dark-haired children worthy of the throne. They had to choose carefully—one who could resist the curse, one with a pure soul.

Princess Graelynd, the third child, was a princess with a heart of such genuine goodness that some claimed she glowed as a child. Everyone always said her eyes mirrored her father's, with golden specks sparkling in a sea of deep green; they seemed to shine against her porcelain, ivory skin. She could always be found serving the less fortunate on the streets and playing with the farmers' animals. She loved painting murals around the city's walls and hallways of the palace, knowing her drawings brought smiles to everyone who passed them.

Saven knew who needed to rise. Princess Graelynd, embodying love and selflessness, would be able to resist the curse and lead their people towards breaking it one day, so the people had their heir, their new queen, to rule them. And with Graelynd on the throne, the curse continued fading, almost as if it was just a bad dream—almost.

The crown needed a strong military leader to keep their drooling enemies at bay. Each time the crown was passed, there were attacks on their borders from Korpam. Korpam's curse would one day consume itself—Saven hoped. Thankfully, Saven had fought alongside a gallant man who had even saved his life several times, and since his brave comrade had four sons, he chose Lord Marin Araelien's family to find a match for his daughter.

Saven had seen Lord Marin's third son, Ryker, fight in several battles. Even at a young age, Ryker displayed exceptional skills and a mind capable of outsmarting any human. He would be the ideal match for his daughter, but more importantly, he could be the potential father to nurture another hope for Elysium.

Ryker was a dashing young man with light brown hair, sparkling dragon-green eyes, and a voice that could calm the fears of any man before battle. Leading armies to numerous victories, he was a true hero in every sense of the word. The people loved this match for their kingdom.

The two fell madly in love: a marriage for the world to mirror and some to only dream about. The second generation of leaders established a strong path to scrubbing their land of darkness. Mythical creatures that had not been seen for hundreds of years started reappearing, but none of the old magic. Ryker and Graelynd had hoped their union and continuous fight against the curse would have unlocked the lost ways, but something was missing, or perhaps something had not happened yet.

Wonderfully, their vibrant marriage produced two stunning daughters, which leads us to where this story actually begins: the time to choose the next heir, the third generation.

The weight of a Crown is not easily measured.
A crown itself is light, but the responsibility's weight is that of a graveyard.
You can not simply weigh the bodies of the graveyard, for they are heavier than scales will tell you.
They are weighed in the grief of their loved ones, in decisions of the crown, and in the results of battles.
How does a scale measure this? It cannot.
This is why the Crown is more like a curse than a privilege.

King Ryker Araelien

7983

# Chapter 2

King Ryker and Queen Graelynd chose to take their time with the decision, as their empire was precious, and they did not want to succumb to the fall like the other kingdoms.

Pacing around their sitting chamber, Graelynd pondered how many tough decisions they had made as king and queen of Elysium. They had sent soldiers into battles, banished people to Reformation Rock, and faced creatures the curse had unleashed from other kingdoms. Still, this decision weighed heavier than any of the historical obstacles. She wanted the best for her daughters and her kingdom. With the rumors their spies delivered, her heart ached for what one of her daughters would face as the new queen.

Graelynd patted one of her peacocks' heads as it gave a tiny squeak. "My love, we must choose cautiously," she sighed. "Who we choose will face adversities we've not yet seen." She placed her hands on her hips, shaking her head.

Her crown twinkled against the candlelight. "I don't want to make the wrong decision."

Sitting on a deep green, velvet couch, Ryker sipped his lemon-lime juice, embracing the sour tang. He crossed his ankle over his knee. His polished boots reflected the crease in his brow. "We won't. We'll make the best decision for our people and the future," King Ryker announced proudly, trying to sound convincing.

Queen Graelynd had tears in her eyes. "I hope you're thinking of what lies ahead, especially what has happened beyond our borders. Which one of our girls can handle such strife?"

The majesties began their process of assessing each daughter. Princess Siany, the firstborn, was a straightforward, easy choice. Her brilliance was highly evident in her royal studies and her work ethic, which surpassed that of most commanders. She perfected sword fighting, outmaneuvering all her age. Siany didn't like taking much time in the beautifying rituals of a royal; instead, she would spend most of her days either in the library reading, on the training grounds, or in the schools volunteering. Her gingerbread-brown hair melted down her shoulders, giving her a natural portrait look. Her stature was shorter than many, with broad shoulders and a bust that would make most blush, not to mention the rear of her being, as one correctly says, "Noticeable."

She had sparkling jade eyes that held innocence and wisdom. Sweet freckles embraced her ivory skin, and she had a natural talent for the piano, which her grandmother often begged her to play. Orchids were her favorite flower, which meant her room was filled with every color.

The king and queen noticed early that Siany was a well-mannered child, obeying their every word, which continued throughout her adulthood. Siany's passion was educating children. She believed knowledge would help keep her kingdom strong, so she focused on teaching the children what she had learned. The king and queen knew Siany's heart was with the people of Elysium; she would be a wise and healthy choice. With her credentials, they did not feel they needed to review their other daughter, but they considered their youngest out of respect.

The youngest daughter of Ryker and Graelynd was very different in spirit from her sister. Unpredictable was the best description of Princess Sealyn. Her beauty was known across the seven kingdoms and spoken about in every court. She had chocolate-brown hair with hints of auburn and gold that poured down into thick locks, reaching her lower back. She stood tall like her mother, a solid five inches above her sister, which allowed more of her physique to show, with her long torso separating the very apparent breast size and perky, rounded backside. The sisters were very blessed in the areas that all women desired to be blessed.

Sealyn had shimmering emerald eyes that would captivate even the wildest beast and a smile that would light up an entire palace. Her warm olive skin tone was kissed with freckles, just like her sister's, but Sealyn had a mind that proved unpredictability could be a blessing and a curse to any parent.

She never went along instantly with what was asked; she would question why and then try to find a better way to accomplish the task, and if not better, merely faster.

Sealyn could be found in all places: the library, the training grounds, the kitchen, the treetops, the waterfalls, the stables, and the forbidden mud holes. Everywhere a princess should and should not be was where Sealyn existed.

She wanted to live vibrantly and experience all she could—to be well-educated in both books and life. She excelled in archery and could handle the sword just fine, but she was already the queen with a bow and arrow. What her parents noticed the most was her charismatic personality; hence, this could lead to wild decisions within the kingdom, so they were unsure whether she would be the best fit for the throne.

Ryker set his gold goblet down and stood. "Both would be great, and the easiest choice is Siany." He paused mid-step, pointing his finger in the air. "But is easy the right solution, or does this role at this time require growing pains?" Ryker rubbed the back of his head as he walked to his writing desk and began making notes with his quill.

Incredulously, the queen remarked, "Are you saying you want to make the transition harder than it needs to be?"

Ryker threw his hands up, ink dripping. "No, no. I am saying that perhaps we need to review who can handle enormous amounts of pressure and complications. Is it the daughter who needs order and structure to thrive, or is it the daughter who meets chaos head-on and laughs about it?"

Graelynd folded her arms across her leafy satin gown and paused. "I didn't think about it that way."

Ryker tapped his head with his finger. "I don't know how to help guide impulsiveness, but I can mold one who understands regulations." Ryker finished writing a final note and placed his green-feathered quill in its stand.

Graelynd dropped her arms and quickly stepped toward Ryker's desk. "Are you saying you've made your decision then?"

Ryker shook sand over the ink. "I believe so, but I have an odd feeling."

"Odd feeling? What does that mean?"

Ryker discarded the sand in the canister. "My love, I feel that we will meet opposition in this decision. I'm unsure where or by whom, but that's how I feel."

The royals exited their bedroom chamber and passed into their vast gray stone hallways. They held hands as they walked along the decorated walls, with generations of monarchs in portraits hung with gold-trimmed frames.

Each hallway corner held a long, slender, emerald banner of the reigning family's crest, and standing beside the banner was a trusted royal guard dressed in his vibrant green and white uniform. Their family crest was a gold phoenix with its wings spread wide, and in front of the phoenix was a small emerald shield outlined in white. Two white crossing lines on the shield created four sections, each with a symbol describing the family's greatest strengths.

On the top left was a white triquetra, representing trust. The top right had a white bow and arrow to represent military tactfulness. The bottom left was a white book representing knowledge, and the bottom right was a white tree to showcase their care for their land. Each symbol was outlined in sparkling gold.

As they slowly walked, the king and queen breathed in the calming scents of eucalyptus and jasmine. The relaxing aromas came from the brooms. The Elysians tied stems of eucalyptus and jasmine to their brooms, and as the floor was swept, they created a magnificent fragrance for all who walked the halls.

Ryker and Graelynd saw her when they rounded the corner near their daughter's room. Both froze because they knew what came next.

"Mother. Father. What are you doing in the hall at this time?" Princess Siany asked with concern.

# Chapter 3

# THE CHOICE

Graelynd answered, "My darling, we need to speak with you about an urgent matter. Please, let's go into your sitting room to discuss."

Siany's room was full of uniquely colored tapestries with all the different creatures across the seven lands. Where there was no tapestry, there was a bookshelf dedicated to her studies. The famous red marble fireplace in the central wall crackled and popped with fresh wood. Everyone always thought a red marble fireplace was strange, but there it was, standing prouder than ever, coughing out heat just like every other fireplace. Above it hung an intricate landscape portrait of the gardens that her mother painted. Faded mint curtains draped across the windows had worn edges and several holes. Siany never would let anyone replace them with new ones. The king and queen sat on one of the red velvet couches while Siany sat on one of the pale olive chairs next to the couch.

As Graelynd gazed around the room and drank in the jungle of orchids, she noticed for the first time how distinctly the tapestries, the drapes, the furniture, and the rugs didn't match; they looked more like organized chaos than decorations. Her train of thought was abruptly interrupted by Sid jumping onto her lap.

"Oh, Sid, you scared me! You silly little cat." She petted the sweet cat while it purred in her lap. Tid, the other gray tabby, was nowhere in sight. He usually took longer to warm up to visitors than Sid.

"Siany," the king started, "we're here to discuss the transferring of thrones." Siany's eyes grew wide in nervousness. "We feel this kingdom deserves law and order and needs strength to grow. I admire how you're educating our people and still keeping up with your studies and training. I believe you would make for an excellent queen. But . . ."

"But," interrupted the queen, "first, we want your thoughts about being queen. We're not trying to pressure you into something your heart does not desire."

Siany paused, mulling over what had just happened in her head. She thought to herself how fantastic it would be to rule the people and be able to instill education as a top priority. She could emphasize new challenges for each age group, build more educational facilities, train more adults to become teachers like her, and erect more libraries for the people.

She smiled to herself, ever so slightly, but then fear struck. She wondered what she would do if a battle emerged. Could she tell fathers, mothers, sons, and daughters to go into battle for her? Could she handle the economic pressures of the whole empire? If she said no, the throne would fall to Sealyn. Her sister wouldn't be a bad choice for the kingdom. An incalculable choice, but not wrong. Sealyn would also support her dreams of furthering the people's knowledge. How could she not? Sealyn loved to read and was a brilliant scholar on most topics.

"I'm so honored you would consider me for queen, but I must respectfully and honorably decline."

"What?" her father exclaimed. He rose to his feet, and Sid's eyes grew large.

Siany raised her hand. "I'm not trying to be difficult, but I don't believe I'm what this kingdom needs for its future. I believe my sister will not only do what is needed but will also challenge the people to greater heights than we can imagine."

"But she's impulsive," Graelynd remarked.

"Irrepressible!" added Ryker.

"And sometimes impetuous."

"Stop saying '*I*' words! She's my sister! She might be all those things, but just because she approaches life differently than you do, doesn't mean she's an incurable monster." Siany placed her hand on her head. "Ugh! Now you're making me say '*I*' words! What I mean is—she will be a queen unlike any we've ever seen. She has a heart for the people and Creator; she'll be amazing."

Siany beamed with her support for her sister. The king and queen exchanged glances, and Graelynd stood, making Sid jump from her lap.

King Ryker walked to his daughter, put his hands on her shoulders, and sighed. "You're a brave and wise princess. We'll respect and honor your decision." The king then kissed her head and nearly tripped when Siany's Nicht, Milola, smashed into the door with a small thud.

The princess cupped her hands around her mouth and yelled, "You pressed the wrong side of the door again, Milola! Your entrance is opposite the doorknob at the very top."

With that reminder, Milola burst from the tiny door into the room, dropping two of the four sweets she was carrying for Princess Siany. Her small, hand-size height and glittering wings always made the royal family smile, especially Siany. Milola seemed more like another sister than a Nicht.

The family always hated that all seven kingdoms called them Nichts, a name to brand them into submission to humans. Lord Branov of Korpam was the one who started an uprising against these creatures when one overheard his secret plans to overthrow the throne. He reversed the accusation by twisting the truth into a lie. He convinced his followers that he wanted them to understand how their words were never concealed—that these creatures lurked around every corner, listening for conversations to use against humans.

Many began to fear these innocent creatures, so Korpam declared that they should all be rounded up and killed for the protection of the kingdom, labeling them no longer by their true names but as Nichts. Korpam sent this decree to the rest of the kingdoms, but when the news reached King Saven Dovinus, he refused. Instead, he issued a decree that all Nichts were welcome in Elysium and were to be treated kindly. He hired several Nicht families to tend to his own family to show his confidence in the Nichts. Because of this, Nichts have forever been grateful to Elysium.

"Your majesties! Please, please forgives me for my intrusion. I hads no idea that you were's in here," Milola begged nervously.

Nichts were also known to make words plural when not necessary. Her speech made her endearing, especially with a head that looked too large for her arms and legs, yet this was the look of all Nichts.

The queen smiled. "Oh, Milola, no need to fear. We are finished with our chat. We'll see you all in the banquet hall this evening."

The king gently put his hand on Graelynd's back, escorting her to the door, and quietly whispered, "I said I had an odd feeling. See. I'm always right." They both chuckled out the door. Siany quickly closed the door behind them and turned to Milola with a derisive smile.

"Oh, I'm's so embarrassed!" Milola squeaked, "Please forgives me! I did brings the chocolates you asked for's."

Princess Siany held out her hand, receiving the candies, and said, "There's no need to be dramatic. You've made many unexpected appearances before." Siany licked her lips. "Now for those chocolates." She quickly bit into the delicious round treat that melted instantly in her mouth. Flavors of caramel, salt, and strawberry burst into a dance covered in creamy chocolate.

"Mmm, my absolute favorite! What does Pastry Nicht call these again?" Siany asked, wiping chocolate from the corner of her mouth.

"I believes this one is Chocolate Jabbles. Pastry Nicht keeps changing it, but she said's this name she likes."

Milola's mouth started watering as she watched Siany eat the second piece. Siany realized she was being watched and picked one of the Chocolate Jabbles out of her hand for Milola. "You know you want it. Here. It's yours."

Milola squealed with joy, taking the candy and hugging it like gold. She realized this was a mistake as chocolate covered her mint and purple dress. However, once she licked the treat, the thought of not being tidy quickly subsided, and the two enjoyed their delicious treats.

As Ryker and Graelynd strolled through the gardens to think over what had just transpired, they heard screams. They looked at each other in terror and started running toward the yells. Panting, they began to hear laughter with the shrieks, and before they could think another thought, an orange pipscot burst all over King Ryker's robes, hitting him right in the center of his chest. A green pipscot zipped by Queen Graelynd's head as she dodged the glittering, powder-filled ball. They both crouched down to see the spectacle before their eyes, and there it was: a pipscot war between Princess Sealyn's Vinurs of the Court.

Seeing a pipscot throwing match was beautiful if you were not the target. All the sparkling colors of the world whizzed past bushes and trees. The garden barely had any green left except for the dusty greens that had been thrown by, of course, Princess Sealyn. She always chose to represent her kingdom when reenacting past wars. Lady Zuri's intense azure eyes lit up when she hurled a massive blue pipscot directly at Lord Sakul's back, making him tumble down to his hands and knees. Laughter erupted again. Sakul tried to regain his composure and dusted off his ebony skin, but quickly had to duck again from one of the yellow dust balls.

With black, frizzy curls springing around her head, Lady Sorcha shot up behind a dusty golden bush, aiming for Lady Zuri, but her terrible throw hit Lady Norella's arm instead. While everyone's eyes were on Norella's glittering purple arm, Lady Pinx popped up right behind Lord Favien, bursting a pink pipscot over his head! Pinx ran from Favien's chase with her two black braids bouncing behind her.

Lord Char hurled a red pipscot, striking Lord Jashun in the ankle and causing him to tumble into a bush, scattering yellow dust all over him. Out from behind the phoenix statue, Lady Madilina burst two balls on top of Lord Char's head, sending Lord Sakul into a fit of laughter. A rainbow explosion of twinkling colors filled the garden from the friends' game.

Poor Lord Tybalt was the last to throw, and the smoke of colors clouded his aim, which did not bode well for the two royals trying to avoid being struck by a pipscot. Regrettably, Tybalt's cobalt pipscot burst in front of the king's bent knees, sending powder up his nose and causing him to sneeze loudly.

Immediately, the powder throwing stopped, and all eyes were on the king and queen as the royals rose to their feet. Each lord and lady sprinted in front of their majesties to apologize.

With his jade eyes sparkling, Sakul leaned close to Char, cousin to Sealyn, and whispered, "Did you see how Lady Sorcha avenged me after Lady Zuri's pipscot?"

Char whispered, "Not now, Sakul! Can you not see we are in deep sh—"

Startling Char's whispers, Adalina bellowed out, "Your Majesties! Please forgive us. We didn't know you were near. If we did, we never would have allowed any color to stain your robes." She had tears in her lime, almond-shaped eyes.

Tybalt's face was crimson, either from embarrassment or from a pipscot. Who could tell, but he held his head down low, hoping his shaggy brown hair would hide his worry-filled eyes.

The king gazed at the pitiful sight in front of him, everyone covered in various colors, with their clothes ruined. He wondered how this pipscot war started in the first place. All stood silent except for a small giggle; then, the giggle grew louder and turned into laughter. Ryker looked behind the deplorable wall of young lords and ladies and saw his daughter with her hand over her mouth, walking with a slight skip toward him. When Sealyn stepped in front of her friends, she laughed so hard that it made the rest of her friends start snickering. Even sweet Tybalt lifted his head with a crooked smile.

Ryker folded his arms. "And what, my young princess, is so funny?" the king demanded.

"I am so sorry, Father, but it's just so hard to take you so 'kingly' with a shimmering blue face!" she replied with more laughter. "You look like the most gorgeous, sparkling blueberry our land has ever seen!" She could barely get the words out while laughing.

More chuckles and snorts came from her friends; some found it almost impossible not to burst. Char had tears streaming down his orange face.

Ryker smiled and tilted his head. He motioned with his hand for his daughter to come to him. As he put his hand on her shoulder, he let out a small chuckle, seeing his daughter covered in an assortment of reds and yellows. How ironic, he thought, that this innocent, young girl would soon be the heir to the most powerful throne in all the lands.

LORD CHAR ARAELIEN

# Chapter 4

# THE MARKET

Fifteen years later…

For the first time in history, kings, queens, lords, and ladies from all lands had been invited to Elysium's Crowning Ceremony. More importantly, the invitation sent by Queen Graelynd hinted that they might choose a suitor from one of the other kingdoms. Elysium was buzzing with the news; the people both feared and excitedly anticipated it. Elysians understood the potential peace a marriage bond could bring if their king and queen could find the right match, but an outsider? The coronation marked the beginning of a week-long celebration, a jovial time regardless of the looming questions.

Avondelle, the capital of Elysium, is situated in the Aelgridon territory, perched at the top of the region, providing lush scenic views of the Blissendelle territory. The capital people loved decorating the city with their green and gold Elysian colors and symbols. Being Elsyium's declared creature symbol, Phoenixes were everywhere, from the painted stone streets to the merchants selling squawking red and yellow phoenixes in the market. Rich aromas of freshly baked pies and sugary cakes wafted through the marketplace, while cheerful music echoed throughout the area for miles.

Avondelle's market was unique because it was renovated from the massive stone ruins of an ancient castle. The royal family dedicated it to the people thousands of years ago. While the main roof had been torn down, the stone floors remained. The sturdy stone chambers, forming the rectangular perimeter, were converted into shops; fortunately, those roofs were intact. Without walls in the center, beautiful wooden booths with tents displayed a variety of intricate trinkets, the latest clothing styles, and fresh, delicious foods during the day.

Lord Jdru Araelien and Lord Char Araelien, sons of Lord Quinten Araelien, the king's youngest brother, ran the market. These two became quite the spectacle whenever one of their notorious arguments erupted, which occurred at least once a day, and having the business named *A Brother's Bond* led to mocking laughter.

Their stone shop offered a variety of the kingdom's building and farming materials and the finest weapons for hunting and fishing. The two esteemed lords managed the rents owed for the stone shops and the fees for the tented booths. It was painted a dark forest green with several palmate palms planted in front, but not blocking their large spying window. *A Brother's Bond* was situated at the market's entry on the left. They chose this location because it allowed them to see everyone who entered and provided a great view of the square.

The square was a large, four-sided wooden platform situated at the center of the market; it was slightly elevated and featured tall wooden pillars at each corner. This square was the favored location of the marketplace's celebrations. Musicians would play music throughout the day, and talented performers would act scenes from history's past, but at night, the square was the center space for the Elysian dances. Every night was filled with the most exhilarating choreography that lasted long into the night during a coronation celebration. When the music started and everyone came together on the floor, the people painted a masterpiece with their bodies moving perfectly together.

The square had been freshly painted with a grand emerald phoenix at the center. Lush garlands adorned with creamy pearlescent flowers hung from pillar to pillar. On top of the posts were tall potted white fire flowers to keep the stage bright all night; the market was filled with fire flowers that would glow for all to see, but one of the most enjoyable establishments of the Market was *Liquid Courage*, the local tavern.

With his neatly trimmed brown hair, Lord Char was guzzling down his third ale when his brother, Lord Jdru, entered with another rant. "I thought I told you to finish the inspections hours ago!" Jdru said with force. "Yet here you are again, drinking, while we have the biggest celebration in history to prepare for." Jdru lifted one of his arms and dropped it in exhaustion while the other scratched at his reddish-blonde beard.

"Oh, brother! Come now. We've been planning this for months," Char said with a hiccup. "I promise nothing will go wrong." His large jade eyes sparkled at the chance to tempt his shorter-than-him brother. He handed Jdru a cup of ale while placing his hand on his brother's shoulder. "Have a drink with me before I go finish the inspections?"

"No! I will drink when everything is finished! You never understand responsibility! You think this world revolves around you. I don't know why I continue to work with you! Drinking ale right next door! You are always . . ." Jdru lost his words when an alluring young barmaid walked by, offering him a drink.

"My lord, would you care for a refreshing ale?" she asked with a sly smile.

"Refreshing? Oh, well, I didn't know the ale was refreshing. In that case, yes. I think, I'll have an ale," Lord Jdru tried to say with loud confidence.

Char rolled his eyes and shook his head. He leaned one elbow against the bar, watching his brother sit down with the blonde barmaid; then with his smuggest grin, he said, "Were you not just saying we need to be responsible and finish our work?"

"You hush!" Jdru shot his brother a glare, motioning for the barmaid to fill his cup.

"Would you like another, my lord?" the bartender asked.

Char chuckled. "No, but thank you. I need to finish the inspections." He paid the bartender and then brushed back loose strands of hair. He started walking out the door but turned and yelled with a slight slur in his brother's direction. "Someone has to be responsible around here!"

The tavern, *Liquid Courage,* erupted in laughter. Jdru threw grapes at the door, and with that, Char danced his way to the next business for examinations.

*Liquid Courage* was to the left of the brothers' shop. Since this was a loud establishment, the engineers of the market felt it was only fair not to carve a shop right next to the tavern, so they left ample space between the tavern and the next shop, which was Sir Clive's men's clothing shop called *His Finest*. The only color of *His Finest* was the small caerulean fire flowers that grew all around the perimeter, giving the shop an icy glow at night. At first, many thought his shop was a ludicrous idea, but Sir Clive was brilliant; his business only allowed men inside, offering lounge seating at the front and advertising free whiskey with any purchase. Clive was intelligent enough to create tunics that would help an ordinary man in his tasks and create a style that made his customers look prodigious.

Lord Char had already picked up his new dress tunics for the coronation the day before, so he felt no need to stop by today, knowing Clive would be extremely busy.

The charming neighbor to *His Finest* was the enchanting apothecary shop operated by Lady Zuri. Most ladies did not have a regular job like this, but Lady Zuri felt that she needed to win the hearts of Elysium since she was from the kingdom of Len Nove. Healing the people of Avondelle seemed like the perfect way to earn everyone's trust.

Char strolled into Zuri's shop with a broad smile. "Good morning to you, Lady Zuri. How are you doing on this fine festive day?" He nodded his head to her, then leaned on the countertop.

Zuri laughed. "Good morning to you, my lord." Giving him a small curtsy, she said, "I'm enjoying the excitement of the market. I already had two mothers pass out this morning from being overly excited."

"Well, I know they were in perfect hands if you attended them," he said as charmingly as possible.

"Don't toss your flirts at me, Lord Char. Remember, my emotions are ice cold," she said, flicking her hand in his direction.

Char put his hand over his heart, saying, "You wound me. I've never felt such pain! Oh, Creator, help me! I believe my heart is breaking in two. My gorgeous, blue-eyed lady, do you have anything in your herbs to heal a broken man?" He gave her a pitiful look on his handsome face, poking his lip out.

"You are such a toad's wart," she giggled, putting her hands on her hips. "If you weren't Princess Sealyn's cousin..."

"You would what?" he interrupted. "Have your Ice Nichts freeze me? Darling, you do know that this heat between us would simply melt that ice away?"

They both laughed until their bellies hurt. Zuri was smart enough to know not to entertain Char's flirts. He was a ladies' man. He had women lining up to marry him, and she couldn't blame them. He had the looks, the charm, the humor, and he was a royal.

Lord Char looked at the sun from her large window with dried flowers hanging all across. He turned back to Lady Zuri. "In all seriousness, Zuri, is everything well? No issues so far?"

Zuri tucked her long, light-brown hair behind her ear. "No issues. Thank you for checking on me."

"Good!" Char smacked the stone counter with his hand. "And knowing that, I will be off to the next inspection." He gazed around her shop, filled with shelves and jars of herbs and elixirs. He pointed toward the glowing indigo herbs, but Lady Zuri shook her head and pointed to the door. Char winked and said, "Oh, and one more thing, my beautiful ice princess..." Zuri rolled her eyes and smiled. "Don't let anyone tell you your emotions are cold because of where you come from. I know people have said this, but there's no truth in it. You have a heart of gold, not ice."

Zuri swallowed against the stones in her throat. "Thank you, Char. Your words speak more than you know," she said with a slight whisper.

Char turned left out of *Avondelle's Apothecary* and walked past the twin sisters' women's clothing shop. Theirs was a small shop with lovely dresses and hats for everyday use. Char thought he better avoid *Look Twice,* or else he would find himself in a conversation lasting for hours, so instead of stopping by, he merely looked through the window. He saw the twins with their flowy, straw-colored hair styling an older lady who had no business wearing a dress that low, and on he walked.

The library was closed today, which was one less place for him to inspect; then the smells hit him. He could already taste the flaky crust of the Jam Pies that he was about to devour. Lavender fire flowers grew naturally like vines near the Nichts' bakery, hanging like grape clusters off the stone roof. Being a corner shop, the bakery was one of the larger shops in the market and was painted a soft lavender with a mild green stripe and gold trimmings. The entire shop was engulfed in smells of sugar and chocolate, allowing these sweet aromas to drift into the market. In the corners were baskets of freshly baked bread with drizzled honey.

Purple wooden shelves on the long stone wall had rows and rows of individual slices of cake: chocolate and strawberry, coffee and caramel, vanilla and raspberry, and more. Next, the pies—the famous Puffin Pies had the most prominent display with their fluffy cinnamon-swirled crust and apple filling. These were no bigger than the size of cupcakes, and the Nichts would drizzle a sweet liquid icing on top that would complete the delicious treat and have everyone's taste buds asking for more.

Jam Pies were also a classic choice. These were individual dough pockets filled with an assortment of jams and baked in a circle so that when everyone sat down to eat one, you could take one tiny section of the Jam Pie and enjoy the flaky crust with a fruit jam of your choice. The larger Jam Pies had three different jams: strawberry, blackberry, and blueberry, while the miniature pies had only two jams: strawberry and blueberry.

A grand selection of neatly lined rows of Chocolate Jabbles and Moon Roons was at the center of the displays, with several customers poring over them, trying to decide which to buy. The bakery was busier than normal, but the crowd parted for him when Char entered.

"Good day to you all!" Char said in his cheerful voice. "Who's ready for the coronation?" He threw his hands up for dramatic effect.

Applause echoed through the stone walls. Char smiled; he loved entertaining.

Char lifted his finger. "But more importantly, who's ready for tonight's dances?" he roared with excitement. Cheers and clapping erupted inside again. Char laughed. "Me too. Please carry on. I only came to ensure our amazingly talented baking Nichts had no trouble."

Bella, the head baker's wife, fluttered in front of Char. "Thank you for coming's to check on us. Everything is fine's. Would you allows me the privilege of giving's you a large Jam Pie?" she said in such a sweet tone. "No charge, my lord." Her dark hair was covered in white flowers with chocolate smudges on her face, and her wings fluttered as she anxiously waited for Char's response.

Char smiled broadly. "I would, of course, oblige but never would accept your 'no charge.'" He handed her payment with an extra tip and grabbed a large Jam Pie, deeply breathing in the delicious aroma, making his mouth water. Char knew what was needed to go with his scrumptious pie—one of Nijeel's hot spiced coffees.

A traditional Avondelle market experience would be to buy yourself a scrumptious Puffin Pie and then walk to *Nijeel's Choice* for a cup of coffee or tea.

Sir Nijeel ran his family's coffee and tea shop for years. Nijeel was a tall, filled-out man with a bushy red beard and glasses. The people complained that his family never named the café, and when the shop was passed down for him to run, he said it was his choice to decide whether to name the shop or not. Growing weary of the arguments, he finally chose *Nijeel's Choice* as the title out of spite. Oddly enough, that name satisfied people. Small wooden tables and chairs were outside the bakery and *Nijeel's Choice,* allowing friends to sit and eat while soaking in lovely afternoons.

"Lord Char!" shouted Lord Favien. "Come join us!" Favien was sitting at one of the large outside tables with Lord Tybalt, Lord Jashun, Lord Drystan, and Lord Doebromir. They had just finished some military training from a morning session.

"Good day, gentlemen!" responded Char. "I will join you as soon as I get one of Nijeel's finest." Char quickly entered *Nijeel's Choice*, placed his order, checked on Nijeel with a handshake, grabbed his drink, and joined his friends.

Char quickly started the conversation with a troubling question. "How prepared is Avondelle to handle the outsiders coming this week?"

"There should be no worry," Drystan said, puffing out his chest. "Our army is the finest in the land." He brushed back his blonde locks while flexing his bicep.

Jashun rolled his sage-infused eyes and sipped his dark coffee. He was never impressed with Drystan's boasts but liked to keep that to himself. Jashun was not the fastest nor the strongest of the group, but he was great with strategy. He hated confrontation but enjoyed a good gossip, especially when the ladies were stirred up. Jashun brushed some dirt off his caramel-brown arm, slicked back a straggling piece of raven hair, and spoke up, hoping to avoid hearing more of Drystan's boasts: "Has the palace expressed any concerns?"

Char shook his head, leaned in, and whispered, "The royals are keeping details very secretive. They did say they would brief all military sections this afternoon."

The sun bounced off Doebromir's shiny bald head. "Yes, we were told to report to the palace grounds to find out which units will be on duty tonight." Doebromir shifted his large body in his chair. "That's also why we're here at Nijeel's and not the tavern." He chuckled with his contagious laugh.

They raised their cups and sipped. Favien fidgeted in his seat, wondering whether he should address the concern that was most likely on everyone's minds. Favien had tanned skin, a dark beard, and hair shaved on the sides like Char. He couldn't believe the royals sent out invitations to Stoltland. Those people couldn't be trusted; every historical battle had them against Elysium.

Favien cleared his throat. "So I know we shouldn't worry, but can we at least discuss Stoltland?" He scratched his dark beard.

Everyone looked at each other with concern, then started nodding their heads.

"I wouldn't be so concerned with Stoltland but with Korpam!" Drystan said with fervor. "They fight with no regard for how many lives are lost. Human lives mean nothing to them. This is why I don't believe picking an outsider for our future queen is right!" There was anger behind his mossy green eyes.

"You stop right there, Drystan," Char growled. "Princess Sealyn is smart and knows what's best for our land." He folded his arms. He would defend his cousin, even if he had no idea what she was doing.

"How does a baby queen know anything yet? She should be picking someone strong and from her land." Drystan slammed his cup down, surprising the group that it didn't shatter.

"And who do you have in mind?" Jashun questioned. "Yourself?"

"I would be better than anyone from Stoltland or Korpam; that's for sure!" Drystan pouted.

At that moment, Lady Zuri, Lady Sorcha, Lady Adalina, and Lady Norella walked up behind Drystan.

"Careful, Lord Drystan. Aren't you already engaged to marry Lady Pyry?" Sorcha said disdainfully.

Drystan slumped down in his chair, hanging his head. Tybalt immediately stood with a passion to greet Norella, but when he smiled, he forgot he hadn't swallowed his coffee yet and drooled the drink all over his training attire. The lords and ladies burst out laughing, but Norella melted for his innocent charm. Tybalt attempted to speak, but he was mesmerized by Norella's perfectly sun-kissed skin, glorious teal eyes, and sunbleached brown hair. Her hair was neatly tied in a braided updo with tiny white flowers in the middle, and she wore a flowy, mint dress.

"Pardon me, Norella. Your beauty overcame me," Tybalt managed to say finally. Zuri and Sorcha giggled.

Favien whispered loudly, "Eloquently done, my lord."

Norella blushed. "We wanted to stop for a quick hello before rushing off to the palace," she said. "Princess Sealyn has already sent her long-distance Nicht, Trit, to tell us that our dresses have arrived, so we can begin getting ready for tonight."

Zuri put her arm through Norella's arm and patted Char's head. "We bid you farewell until tonight." Zuri winked.

Char sighed as he shook his head, watching Zuri walk away. Favien placed his hand on Char's back, trying to hide laughter. "That is a battle not worth fighting, my friend. Her sapphire eyes are for someone else."

"I believe you may be right, but until I know for sure, I'll have fun finding out! Good day to you, fearsome lads. I will see you all tonight."

# Chapter 5

# MAEKEL

Pincess Sealyn sat in her stunning, emerald ball gown, staring into the mirror, trying to remain calm, but all she could feel were her nerves bouncing in her stomach. She wore long, matching satin gloves with a large emerald necklace that felt like it weighed way more than it should. She kept telling herself, "Stay calm. Just breathe. You have nothing to fear. Today is about celebrating, not puking." Sitting on each side of her golden mirror, her potted white fire flowers enhanced the worry in her eyes, making her wish that just once, these flowers wouldn't shine so bright. She wished she could hide in the dark forest so she wouldn't have to face what awaited her downstairs.

Maekel, Sealyn's Nicht, fluttered gently upon the gold vanity where she leaned against Sealyn's perfume bottle. She had long velvety black hair with hints of blue. Her wings were almost translucent except for sparkles of pink, and the edges looked as if they were lined with ice crystals.

"You know's the more you worries, the more grief you lay's upon yourself," Maekel sweetly spoke.

Sealyn let out a dramatically long sigh. "Yes, I know. I just want tonight to go smoothly." She twirled her hair nervously. "I doubled the pressure for this night, and I know I only have myself to blame, but I truly do believe it is for the best."

Maekel stepped forward. "I must to say's though, I'm on's your side. All the kingdoms needs a way to come's together, so perhaps this is the first steps."

Maekel beamed with her words, but still felt worried for Sealyn. Representatives from all seven kingdoms would be at the coronation ball for the first time in history. Sealyn wanted to make a bold statement on her first night as queen, and she most definitely would have her hands full in a palace full of friends and enemies.

Maekel knew what an undertaking this would be for Sealyn, but she also knew that her princess wasn't afraid of a challenge. Sealyn had chosen her, the smallest out of her family, to tend her. Maekel's family told her that she most likely wouldn't be picked for such a vital role, but here she was attending to the future queen. She found that her duties weren't complex either. Sealyn mainly wanted her there for her opinions and company rather than errands. She did help with the dressing, but that included two other Nichts and a few human servants, so again, not that difficult. She did find herself tired after a long day carrying many messages to people throughout the palace. Thank goodness Sealyn enlisted the long-distance Nichts to take notes outside the palace walls, especially since that meant she could catch a glimpse of Trit; he was ever so dreamy.

As Maekel's eyes glazed over, imagining her and Trit's wedding, her elbow slipped off the perfume, and she landed right in Sealyn's face powder. A small cloud of smoke lifted out of the bin, and so did a coughing Maekel. Sealyn let out a chuckle.

"Oh, I needed that laugh, Maekel. Goodness. You are covered in powder. I hope flying about can rid you of it," Sealyn said with a cheeky smile.

Coughing and shaking her dress, Maekel fluttered around Sealyn's changing room, almost bumping into Lady Pinx and Lady Zuri.

"Maekel, this isn't a costume ball! Why are you dressed as a ghost?" Zuri shouted with a sarcastic tone.

Maekel stopped midflight, put her tiny hands on her hips, and glared at Zuri.

Sealyn giggled. "Careful, Zuri, Maekel fell into the face powder. She's afraid her ghostliness will frighten Trit away." Maekel gasped.

Zuri smiled. "Don't act so surprised, Maekel. We all know you want to marry him."

"I do's not!" squeaked Maekel. "I have's never even spoken's to him!"

"Ah, but you dream about marrying him, don't you?" Sealyn's lip curled. "Trit will be gracing us with his presence at the ball. I'm sure he will fall madly in love with your powdery dress."

Maekel shuddered. "What? He's coming's tonight? To tonight's ball? The same's ball I will be attending's?"

"Why, yes. He deserved to have some fun, and I knew my dear sweet Maekel would love nothing more than to dance the night away with her charming Trit."

Maekel hugged herself and twirled. "Your Majesty! You have given's me so much to lives for! Do you mind's if I change my dress and fixes my face, please?"

Sealyn nodded, and Maekel was out of the room before the ladies could laugh.

"I've never seen Maekel fly so fast," Pinx remarked. "I do hope Trit asks her to dance."

"Me too," agreed Zuri. "The little bug deserves love in her life."

Sealyn chuckled and shook her head at Zuri. She knew Zuri didn't mean any harm. She loved Maekel, but Zuri was still adjusting to life in Elysium rather than her homeland, Len Nove.

Len Nove was Elysium's northeastern neighbor. It had dramatic winters in its northern territories and mild summers in the lower regions, but that mysterious kingdom hadn't seen summer weather in hundreds of years. Zuri escaped this land after she could take no more of its slothful decline, and Sealyn graciously chose her to be among her Vinurs of the Court. Sealyn and Zuri spent many long nights discussing what could have happened to the land that once was very prosperous. Len Nove was a profitable kingdom with people everywhere enjoying life; then, the people seemed to fade over time. The lakes seemed to sparkle less. The land went silent. The whispers are that if one travels to Len Nove, one sees no one. Nothing is happening, and no one knows why. This is one of the tasks Sealyn set herself to solve once she became queen.

Sealyn gasped as she gawked at Pinx and Zuri. "You both look so lovely! Zuri, I'm so pleased you chose to represent your country with its colors. The ice-blue velvet matches your eyes perfectly!"

Zuri bowed, allowing her friends to see her brown braids twisted with ivy and tiny white flowers among her long hair. Her caerulean dress was trimmed with white rabbit fur and adorned with shimmers of silver on the bodice.

Sealyn looked at Pinx. "And you, Lady Pinx, I like the bold choice of pink, but I love the green lace that edges the bottom."

Pinx blushed as she always did when someone complimented her. She was one of the prettiest girls in the room, yet she always seemed surprised when someone complimented her beauty. Pinx had long black hair and intriguing almond-shaped jade eyes. Humility was one of her greatest assets.

"I feel like tonight will be magical." Pinx spun in her dress, humming an Elysian tune.

"Speaking of tonight," Zuri interjected, "Princess Sealyn, you're late!"

Sealyn jumped up, knocking over her chair. She raced to her bedroom window to look out. There, she saw the uniquely designed carriages from all the different lands with high banners. She could also hear the music from the marketplace and envisioned the dancing already happening at the square.

Sealyn regarded the fun that was happening in the distance. "I want something to look forward to tonight if things don't go as planned."

Zuri folded her arms. "Being crowned queen isn't enough to look forward to?"

"The crown is a weight, not something fun," Sealyn said, a little too coldly.

"What did you have in mind?" Pinx asked curiously.

Sealyn gave a mischievous smile. "The square."

Pinx gasped. "You're joking! Don't you remember what happened last time we were caught there after hours?"

"We were seven!" Sealyn said with a wave.

"We were locked in the dungeon!" squeaked Pinx.

Sealyn shook her head. "Again, we were seven, and my parents were trying to scare us."

"Well, lesson learned!" huffed Pinx as she glared at Sealyn.

"Tonight will be my last night for an opportunity like this. The guards will be mainly watching the visitors, so I could sneak out, and with the help of our friends in the guard, I'm sure we can achieve this."

"Why not?" Zuri shrugged. "Let's make this a night we'll never forget."

Everyone remembers their Firsts. First kiss. First heartbreak. First death.

However, it's the first meeting that baffles me.

The first meeting of your true love, the first meeting of your forever enemy. What if you knew? What if you knew the First time you met someone—who precisely they would be to you? Would you change anything?

Queen Sealyn Araelien
Diary Entry 197

Madam Bip

# Chapter 6

The throne room was filled with an enchanting and mysterious atmosphere, alive with the presence of royals, lords, ladies, esteemed guests, and lively Nichts—all whispering their theories and gossip about what could happen. It was at last the moment for the grand coronation. The palace glimmered like never before, its splendor enhanced by opulent candle-lit chandeliers and magnificent golden fire flowers blooming in every corner. Verdant ivy vines wove gracefully around the lustrous pearly columns, which were decorated with fresh white gardenias, adding a touch of nature's beauty. The gleaming white marble floors and walls showcased the vibrant greens of Elysium, celebrating the kingdom's unity and proclaiming to the world that Elysium was a land of harmony, not to be trifled with. At the opposite end of the doors, the emerald velvet-cushioned throne chairs, trimmed in gold, welcomed their future queen.

All were marveling at the palace's exquisiteness, except some were eyeing it for its imperfections and looking for weaknesses. Dressed in an inky black gown that shimmered with each movement, Lady Corentine hated where she stood. The bright, cherry redhead thought the palace was an overdone spectacle, trying too hard to impress the outsiders. Her pitch-black eyes narrowed as she studied the crowd, noticing her enemies standing across from her and her family. She pulled her youngest son, Lord Tahbert, close to her, keeping her arm on his shoulders, warning anyone against him.

"This is absolutely ridiculous," huffed Corentine. "I can't believe we came. We shouldn't be celebrating with these people; we should be creating battle plans against them."

"Hold your tongue, woman!" snapped Queen Phyre of Stoltland. "We do have a plan, and we are guests—if you haven't noticed, surrounded and outnumbered by the Elysian Royal Guard. Your words would send us all to the dungeons. Do you want that for your sons?"

Phyre glared at Corentine with a look that would instill fear in battlefield warriors. Phyre's relationship with Corentine had been rocky, but she tried to appease her only for the sake of her son and the deal she had made all those years ago; she now regretted it. The struggles Phyre faced over the years had aged her. Her hair was now gray, and wrinkles had set in, and she hated that she needed a cane to keep her steady as she walked. Though her tenacity had never weakened, this was the main obstacle the people of Stoltland had to face: stubborn pride.

Sometimes pride can be good, but for the people of Stoltland, it was a plague that tormented their land, devouring anything that had the potential to be virtuous. Even with her worthy intentions, Phyre would be snuffed out either by herself or someone close to her.

Music began to play. Powerful streams of notes echoed off the walls as the doors opened. King Ryker and Queen Graelynd walked beside one another, the queen's hand lying elegantly on top of the king's elevated, strong hand. They appeared formidable, a force never to be shaken. Certain lords winced at the sight of Ryker again, having lost bloody battles against him before. Siany followed her parents, still feeling uncomfortable in her dress, but her nerves dissipated when she caught sight of her royal family members in attendance. She smiled at them and stood in front of her chair as her parents did.

The lords and ladies of the Vinurs of the Court entered gracefully, each wearing a different color to represent the kingdoms. The queen believed that the visitors would feel more at ease if their colors were visible on their people. The doors closed, and the final announcement was made that the future Queen of Elysium was about to enter. The musicians' notes turned to a tone mixed with victory and bravery. The doors opened, and out flooded the Nichts of the Palace, throwing white and pink flower petals with gold glitter.

Ryker's mouth gaped at the spectacle of Nichts. "You realize we'll never be rid of that gold glitter?" whispered Ryker. "Did you know she was planning this?"

Graelynd chuckled. "Of course not, but did you expect 'predictable' from Sealyn?"

Princess Sealyn walked down the aisle with her eyes fixed on her parents. Her long, emerald velvet robe trailed many feet behind her. Although the room crackled with excitement, Sealyn felt a cold chill run down her spine. She sensed a tug and glanced slightly to her left, where she spotted the scowling face of Corentine. Sealyn returned the scowl with a confused expression. Why was this woman so irritated with her? She shook her head and refocused on her throne. Corentine gave a sly half-smile, thinking she had won a small victory over the princess.

Everyone watched intently as the crowning ceremony commenced, except for one. Jace, the eldest son of Corentine, leaned against the cool stone with one foot propped against the wall in the back corner, staring at the balconies. He folded his arms, wishing this night would end. Of course, he was glad to come along on this honorable adventure, but he already knew what the night would entail: his parents pushing his stepbrother to the new queen, his family dancing with royals and nobility, and whispers of him traveling around the room like wildfire during a drought. It would only be a matter of time before everyone in this room would know him as the illegitimate, gray-eyed son of Lady Corentine.

He ached for the warmth of someone who would see him as worthy, as more than just a colossal mistake. Jace yearned to merge with the world around him, yet his haunting silver eyes betrayed his uniqueness, starkly contrasting with the dark eyes of his kingdom. No matter how fiercely he labored or how much effort he poured into every task, he always felt the crushing weight of disappointment against his mother's unyielding expectations. This trip was the final abuse he would take. His family harbored a hidden agenda for his presence, yet he, too, possessed a clandestine plan—one that would alter the course of his life in ways unimaginable.

He sighed, watching his stepfather pat his stepbrother's shoulder. The two never got along, despite Jace's numerous attempts to bridge the gap. Prince Haedon and Jace had nothing in common. Haedon enjoyed sword fighting, while Jace preferred archery. Haedon disliked reading, whereas Jace loved learning. Haedon detested being out at sea, while Jace adored everything about the ocean. Haedon enjoyed chasing women; Jace was shy and kept to himself. More importantly, Haedon loathed all silver eyes.

Once the newly crowned queen walked down the aisle, leading everyone to the ballroom, Jace leaned up to look for his family. He smoothed back his chestnut brown hair, tied at the back of his head, and scratched his newly shaved chin. His look and presence were fierce, yet he had a gentle face with a perfect jawline. His mother waved for him to join them, but he shook his head and waited for the crowd to pass through the doors. He felt like an outsider because he knew he was. An outsider in his homeland and an outsider in a foreign land. What was he to do in this situation?

A servant walked by Jace carrying a gold tray filled with tantalizing aromas. His head spun quickly to catch a glimpse of the most delicious-looking desserts he had ever seen. These must be the famous Jam Pies he had heard so much about, so that was now his task: to taste all the savory treats Avondelle had to offer, and why shouldn't he? After all, wasn't this part of his plan?

Queen Sealyn shifted her glance to her ladies, hoping to catch a glimpse of what was happening around the ballroom, only to be interrupted by yet another greeting from another lord with whom she had no interest in conversing. She could see her friends dancing and laughing. Her heart ached for her childhood. She could no longer attend balls for the sake of having an enchanting evening; instead, she had to attend to form alliances and find a suitor. Nausea seemed to set in after another father introduced his son to her while the mother beamed from behind, but suddenly, it was not nausea; it was a cold chill—the same cold chill she had felt earlier. She turned and stood face to face with Queen Phyre. The room stilled—the two historic enemies were now inches apart.

"Your Majesty." Phyre curtsied. "I would like to introduce my grandson to you, Prince Haedon of Stoltland." Haedon took the new queen's hand and kissed the emerald glove. "He is strong, brave, and well-versed in the military arts," continued Phyre. "Prince Haedon would be the best match for you."

Sealyn's eyes twitched slightly, looking down at the tiny queen. What a bold statement, but she expected nothing less from Stoltland. She had to remain calm.

Pushing through the sea of people, Corentine interrupted, "Of course, we only want the perfect counterpart for our glorious Prince Haedon as well. He needs to be equally matched as a king would be over the queen." Corentine tipped her chin in the air, exposing the black streaks running through her crimson hair.

"Forgive me, Lady Corentine, but you're mistaken," Sealyn said flatly. Corentine's family stared intently at Lady Corentine, waiting for what would happen. No one ever dared to correct her.

"I beg your pardon," Corentine snapped.

"Your Majesty..." Sealyn corrected with a slight head tilt.

"I'm not a majesty, Queen Sealyn. No need to address me with such titles."

"Exactly, but I *am*, and I expect you to address me with the same respect that you address your Queen Phyre, so when you say, 'I beg your pardon,' you conclude your shock with 'Your Majesty.'" Sealyn stepped forward, showcasing her power in her palace. She looked down at the pale-faced Corentine, for Sealyn towered over her by nearly seven inches.

"Forgive me, Your Majesty," growled Corentine, bowing her head. Corentine's jaw tightened.

"All is forgotten." Sealyn waved her hand. "But I don't believe you're well-versed in Elysian customs. Regarding your statement 'a king would be over the queen,' the reigning bloodline of the throne, whether male or female, is *the* crown with the most weight."

Corentine cringed at the truth Sealyn posed to her. She had never met someone who would stand up to her and challenge her; only Phyre was willing to do so, but rarely anymore. Age was catching up to her, finally.

"Of course, Your Majesty," intervened Phyre. "Lady Corentine was merely excited about the possibility of our kingdoms uniting." She hoped that would assure the young queen. Corentine smiled a fake smile. The Stoltlanders then escorted themselves to the food tables.

"How could she be that blatantly disrespectful?" Sealyn whispered to her father.

Ryker put his arm around her shoulders. "Easy, Sealyn. We have an entire week to get through with these people. Let's not start another war on the first day."

"Perhaps day two?" Sealyn teased.

Laughing at his daughter's wit, King Ryker held his hand to Sealyn and said, "Shall I have the first dance? I know the Lavendon is your favorite."

Smirking, Sealyn took her father's hand, and he led her to the dance floor. She loved the Lavendon dance. It was the dance made to honor the great victory their warriors had achieved at the city of Lavendon.

After the dance, Sealyn walked to the mystical drink table, her heart set on the legendary elixir known as PurFizz, crafted by the renowned Madam Bip. This mesmerizing drink was concocted from the rare and vibrant azzi berries, flourishing solely in Madam Bip's enchanted garden, where the air held the land's secrets and magic. With a sprinkle of the potent Wildemont flower root powder, the azzi berries were transformed into a sweet, effervescent elixir that promised to elevate one's vitality to extraordinary heights, filling the spirit with a delightful spark of dynamism.

Sealyn desperately needed extra liveliness if she was going to make it through the night and commit to what was to come. From suitors thrown at her to kingdom negotiations and even whispered scandalous proposals, all were overwhelming her. Incredibly, she caught sight of Madam Bip, seated at her peculiar table, where an enigmatic crystal bowl of purple PurFizz glimmered ominously in the center. Madam Bip was a rather large woman with wide, evergreen eyes glinting with secrets, while her curly hair was a chaotic blend of gray and ink-black frizzies. She had an inviting smile and gave the best hugs, especially on hard days. Her ebony skin glowed with the palace lights, and her dark purple dress twinkled with every turn she made.

Grabbing her busty chest, Madam Bip sang, "Oh, Queen Sealyn! You honor me wid' your presence. May I pour you a glass of my finest batch of PurFizz?" She held up a finger. "As I always say, find your purpose wid' PurFizz." Madam Bip beamed at her catchy phrase. Sealyn nodded, and Bip poured her a sparkling glass of the delightful lavender beverage.

"Madam Bip, I must agree with you. This is the finest batch I've ever had. Well done to you!"

"Oh, Majesty! I don't know whether 'dere was ever a time I was more proud in my life."

Sealyn tipped her drink to Bip. "Careful…I wouldn't want you to get too prideful and see you end up in Stoltland." They both chuckled. After her third sip, Sealyn continued, "Now, Madam Bip, I'm about to give you a direct order." Bip's face froze. "I order you to step away from this table and participate in at least one dance this evening; perhaps even find yourself some trouble." Sealyn gave a devilish grin and a wink.

Bip let out a deep belly laugh. "Queen Sealyn, I believe 'dat is one order I'll look forward to." Sealyn nodded. She started to walk toward the throne for a quick rest, but she saw several families waiting with their sons. Sealyn sighed. "I don't have the patience to deal with these people," she said to herself. Instead, she darted behind the drink and food tables and fled through the first door she opened.

# Chapter 7

# JUST JACE

Jace had finally sampled enough dishes to make a well-informed decision on what his full plate would consist of, but then he caught sight of the alluring crystal bowl filled with sparkling purple liquid. His curiosity was piqued.

"Greetings, my lady. May I try some?" Jace asked politely.

Eyeing Jace up and down, Madam Bip quickly flirted, "Oh my! What a delicious dish you are! Callin' me a lady, 'den lookin' like a tasty tart. I just might fall over in a faint."

Jace's eyes grew large. "My apologies if I offended you. I didn't mean any harm."

"Not at all, my dear. I'm Madam Bip, and 'dis is my famous PurFizz. As I always say, find your purpose wid' PurFizz! Let me pour you a glass." She gently lifted the ladle and poured the violet fizzing liquid into a silver goblet.

"Why, thank you, Madam Bip." Jace took the goblet, sipped a large gulp, then let out a burp. "Forgive me! I did not realize the drink would burn my throat."

Madam Bip laughed at the innocent young man. She waved her hand. "No'ting ta' forgive, my dear. Although I would be mindful of a select few who seem ta' be whisperin' about you."

Bip tipped her head in the direction of a few Elysian ladies. Jace could feel the hair on his neck stand up. He instantly felt exposed as if they knew all of his dark secrets. He needed to escape, but where to run?

"Madam Bip, could you be so kind as to tell me whether there is a quiet place one could go to be alone and out of public sight? Not for mischief, but to be free of the prying eyes."

Bip took pity on the boy and felt it was her calling to help him. She knew those silver eyes made him an outcast, but there was something about Jace. She felt a stirring deep inside her; ancient whispers whirled around her. She quickly shot her eyes to a door behind the food and drink tables, forgetting who had just entered that room. Jace nodded with understanding.

"Go quickly as I distract them," Bip whispered. Lifting her skirts and dancing toward the crowd, Bip called out, "Good evening, my ladies! Let me bring you 'de elixir of 'de evenin'. I'm sure it will give your night 'de perfect jolt you've been missin'. As I always say, find your purpose wid' PurFizz!"

Jace dashed around the tables, trying not to spill his PurFizz and filled plate, managing to drop only a few grapes. He paused at the door, ensuring that no one was watching him. Setting his cup down, he turned the knob to enter. Little did he know that this door would lead to a whole new life.

The Garden Library was one of Sealyn's favorite rooms in the palace. Thousands of books adorned the walls of the dark wooden shelves, except for one wall filled with large glass windows that offered a full view of the blooming summer garden. The room was cozy, featuring jade couches and soft blankets; thick gray pillows rested atop Elysian-patterned rugs near the fireplace. The dark wooden fireplace displayed intricately carved figures of a phoenix on one side and a horse-like creature on the other. A grand family portrait of the current royal family gathered around a table was placed on the mantel, with lovely fresh-cut flowers in blue and white vases on each side. The room was so tall that a walkway ran along the perimeter of the bookshelves, and the only way to reach it was by climbing the black iron spiral staircase in the corner. Both sizable and small plants filled the library spaces, providing a perfect accent of fresh smells to the books' aroma.

Sealyn felt relief as she entered the Garden Library, escaping from all her guests. In her haste, she had forgotten that the library had a door leading to the ballroom. Usually, she entered through the secret passageway she wasn't supposed to know about. In this room, she knew she could regain her composure in peace. She sat down on the comfortable couch just for a moment when, all of a sudden, the ballroom door burst open and in walked a very tall, handsome young man.

"What's the meaning of this?" Sealyn asked, jumping up from her seat.

Jace's head jerked up. He felt the life drain from his face. He was in a private room with the queen! How was this possible? Why was she not out there with the rest of the guests? How was he supposed to talk to her? *Was* he supposed to speak to her? Jace kept pondering numerous thoughts and realized he had been staring at the queen for minutes without saying a word.

"Uh, uh. I mean, er, um." Jace stumbled with words and hated himself for ever being born.

"Your name, please." Sealyn smiled sweetly.

Jace could barely look at her. Her beauty aroused feelings that he knew he wasn't supposed to have. He had never seen a face or a body like the queen's. He felt captivated—lost in a sea of temptation, and whether it was the PurFizz or being entranced, Jace finally spoke.

"J-J-Jace, my queen. Or not *my* queen. I mean, you are queen, but not *the* queen. I mean, yes, the queen, but not of my land queen, but yes, my queen here. I mean." Shaking his head, Jace stuttered his words, then sighed. "I'm just Jace, Your Majesty."

Sealyn enjoyed watching Jace squirm. "Well, Just Jace, welcome to my quiet Garden Library. You may sit with me if you're trying to escape the pressures of the court." She motioned for him to join her in the chair adjacent to the couch where she was standing. Jace had to command his body to take each step. He was still in shock at his present circumstance. "So, Just Jace, why are you trying to hide?" She couldn't help but flirt with the dashing and dangerous-looking young man.

"I'm truly sorry for disturbing you, Your Majesty. I just wanted to avoid all the stares and gossip."

Sealyn raised her eyebrows. "Stares and gossip? Why would people stare and gossip about you?" She could understand why people would stare. How could they not? Jace was so handsome and had a hairstyle that was nothing like what her people had, but she found herself liking it—really liking it.

"Because I'm the outcast of my family. I bring only shame wherever I go. When people see me, the stories of my past start." Jace dropped his head.

As he finally neared her, Sealyn saw his shining silver eyes and fully understood. Even here in Elysium, gray-eyes were tall tales, but never seen. Of course, her people would gawk at his uncommon heritage. "I believe you may be right and wrong," remarked Sealyn. She didn't like it when people felt uncomfortable. Jace's head popped up, looking confused. "I trust you are an outsider to your family as you did not announce yourself as prince or lord, not even sir, but rather Just Jace; however, you're wrong that you bring shame wherever you go. If that were the case, your family would not want to bring you to such an event."

Jace smiled and felt the queen trying to comfort him. Little did she know why his family brought him with them—it wasn't love. "Thank you, Your Majesty, but unfortunately, for this situation, it's more complicated than that. My mother wears my birth like a medal of honor, and one would think that would be considered sweet, but her agenda is sympathy. She succeeded when my stepfather fell for her games because of her circumstances. She wanted to rise in her status, and my stepfather, being the son of Queen Phyre, would provide that for her. Regardless of her status at court, I'm still the outcast of Stoltland. Besides, she's not the mother I would've chosen."

Jace clapped his hand over his mouth, shocked he would speak so boldly and openly about his mother to a stranger, the enemy to his kingdom. Oddly enough, Jace looked deep into Sealyn's eyes and felt for the first time in his life that someone was listening to him, actually seeing him as his own person.

Sealyn stared into Jace's silver eyes and felt the pain in his voice when he said outcast. That eye color echoed his history. "Jace, my heart breaks to hear you say those words. I can only offer you the truth as I know it. From the moment we're created by Creator, we have a purpose; so, Jace, you have a purpose. Whether or not someone has an agenda, they can't stop your destiny."

Jace felt his wrists burn. He tugged his black shirt sleeves to keep his scars covered.

Sealyn studied his movements; there was something off about them. Yet, sitting next to him felt like a magnetic force was pulling them together, as if a power greater than the two of them wanted them united. What was this?

She brushed a loose strand from her face and leaned closer to him. "In my kingdom, you'll never be known as a mistake; you'll be known as a friend to the crown."

Jace fought back tears and swallowed the lump in his throat. How could a queen say this to him? Jace shook his head in awe. "No one has ever spoken to me like this before. Your Majesty, I don't know how to express my thanks to you."

"Well, I do," Sealyn spoke with a sly smile. "How about we give this party something to really talk about?" Jace's face went pale. "Ask me to dance, Jace."

He blushed. Jace had never asked a girl, a lady, and most definitely not a queen, to dance before. His heart raced, and his palms began to sweat. Jace cleared his throat. "Your Majesty, will you do me the great honor of sharing a dance with me?"

"Excellent idea, Jace. I would love to, and as my friend, you can be a little less formal and call me Queen Sealyn."

She extended her hand for Jace to take, and although his hand may have been shaking, he reached out, and as soon as his fingers brushed Sealyn's, electricity rippled through their skin. Sealyn's eyes glowed. She felt something awakening deep within her. She wasn't sure what this meant, but the new queen was determined to find out.

All heads snapped up like meerkats to see Queen Sealyn escorted by the outcast of Stoltland to the dance floor. The gasps and whispers swept through the crowd, but Sealyn paid no attention. Her eyes were locked on Jace, but Jace glanced around, seeing people leaning into one another, judging what they were seeing. His heart pounded, preventing him from hearing the music start.

"Jace, take my waist and hand, and keep your eyes focused on mine," Sealyn commanded.

Within seconds, Sealyn and Jace found themselves twirling gracefully on the dance floor, their eyes locked in a gripping gaze that seemed to stretch into eternity. Jace longed for this moment to last forever. He yearned to draw her even closer, embracing her in a tender warmth that would never fade. Her emerald eyes sparkled, tantalizing his desire within him for everything this moment could be, a promise of a new future to unfold. How was he ever supposed to go back to ordinary life?

And just like that, the song was over. He felt a pit in his stomach. Growing up, he never asked for anything, but now, he would give his right arm if it meant he could stay here; maybe even be part of her world. He shut his eyes, remembering his place in society. Jace prepared to walk away and return to hiding in the corner, but instead, Sealyn locked arms with him, allowing him to escort her. He found himself greeting guests with her as if they were old friends. What was happening?

Corentine glowered at the new queen. What was she doing with her son? Why did she dance with a silver-eyed? Was she trying to gain intel about Stoltland? What game was the little bird queen up to? She quickly stomped over to the couple, who were chatting with Char, Pinx, and Favien. "Your Majesty, I believe you've uncovered a hidden talent of my son," Corentine said sarcastically. "I didn't know he was such a good dancer." Jace looked down immediately.

"That's odd that a mother wouldn't know her son could dance." Sealyn watched Corentine's nostrils flare. Sealyn turned her attention to Jace and smiled. "I'm sure he only needed the right dance partner for him to shine." Sealyn winked at Jace.

Anger blazed from behind Corentine's dark eyes. "Perhaps. Jace, why don't you leave the queen to tend to her guests? She's much too busy for you to slow her down." She motioned for Jace to join her, but Sealyn pulled at Jace's arm.

"No need for that. I need a strong escort this evening, and Jace seems extremely fit for the job. He's my chosen companion for tonight."

Jace's mouth gaped, and his ears burned. He didn't know how to process this type of attention. He was used to ridicule and disgust, but kindness? How do normal people handle genuine compassion?

Leaving Corentine stewing in her obsidian feathered gown, the group walked away to greet Lord Sakul and Lady Sorcha, who were laughing with Adalina, Norella, and

Tybalt. Jace looked back only once to see his mother still in the same spot, shaking her head with folded arms. He could only imagine the punishment she was plotting for him.

"Lord Sakul, you outdid yourself with the ball. I've quite enjoyed myself." Sealyn put her hand on Sakul's shoulder.

Sakul beamed and stood a little straighter. His coffee-colored skin was glistening since he and Sorcha had just finished dancing. Sakul was not the most in-shape man, but he ensured he could outdance anyone in the land. He and Char liked to compete with the ladies to see who was the better dancer.

Sakul rubbed his neatly trimmed black beard and smiled. "Thank you, Sealyn. I mean, Queen Sealyn."

Sealyn snickered at her dear friend. "When it's just our crew..." she looked side to side. "Call me Sealyn."

Sorcha's ivy-shaded eyes sparkled with mischief. "Well, Sealyn, we heard about the market adventure."

"Honestly, there are no secrets among any of you," Sealyn huffed playfully. "Has anyone seen Lady Zuri?" Everyone shook their heads. Sealyn lifted her gaze toward the ceiling to find her special Nicht.

Maekel sat beside her childhood crush, enjoying every minute of the ball. She kept surveying the room for any questionable actions or conversations, of which she had witnessed many. She had so much to tell the queen. Many rude stares came from the visiting families, so most Nichts kept to themselves for the evening. Maekel noticed Sealyn looking directly at her, so she immediately flew down to greet her.

"Good evenings, My Queen. Is there's something you needs?"

"Yes, I need to know where Lady Zuri is," Sealyn whispered.

"She has been speakings with Sir Rav, the architect from Korpam, for quites some length of time," Maekel scandalously observed. "They danced two dances this evenings, and he fixed her severals PurFizz drinks."

"Wow. Someone has kept her eye on the party." Char gave a cheeky grin to Sakul, who couldn't help but take the bait.

"Char, I've told you this isn't a party four times! This is a ball! Don't make me tell you again!" exclaimed Sakul. Everyone giggled, and Char bowed to Sakul.

"Maekel, I need you to tell Lady Zuri it's time. And tell her she can bring her new friend as I will do the same." Sealyn gave a glance at Jace to make sure he was still enjoying himself. "There are some changes, though. We must go through the Garden Library since guards are positioned at the kitchen door. Please make sure to tell the others. Maekel, we need the distraction. Is everyone informed and ready?"

"Yes, Your Majesty. We're exciteds!" Maekel fluttered off with her orders.

"Wait, what's going on? And why would you need a distraction?" Jace panicked.

"Well, Jace of Stoltland, are you ready for our first Elysian adventure together?" Queen Sealyn flirted.

An adventure with the Elysian Vinurs of the Court? Whose life was he living? "Together?" questioned Jace. "Absolutely!"

Lord Drystan

# Chapter 8

As soon as the familiar music roared, the Nichts released gold and white rose petals from the ceiling. The guests began to run to the dance floor; they all wanted to take part in this dance and be among the falling rose petals. With all eyes on the petals and the dancing, the queen and her Vinurs fled into the Garden Library.

Char quickly shut the door, making sure no one saw them enter. Everyone looked around the room, accounting for each other.

"Where's Lady Madilina?" Sealyn asked.

"You know where she is," remarked Brenna. "She's preparing for her month-long honeymoon with Lord Max."

Madilina was a favorite of the royal family. Her heart was pure, always wanting to help the less fortunate. She and Lord Max had just been wed a few weeks before the coronation and wanted to ensure they were both present for Sealyn's crowning. Sealyn had significant plans for Max once he returned, but had yet to discuss them.

"My biggest question is, how will we get out of here?" Sakul asked with fear.

"We can't go through the gardens. They posted guards every seven strides," informed Char.

"So we're stuck in here?" Jashun questioned.

"Not even a day completed, and you've already lost faith in your queen?" sneered Sealyn. "Perhaps the staircase can lead us to our path."

She walked over to the bookshelf behind the spiral staircase and tilted back a worn-out book with faded letters on the spine. Instantly, the floor in front of the iron staircase opened. They gathered around the hole and could see stairs leading down.

"Now this is an adventure," Jace whispered to himself.

"Char, hold this book the way I am. I must go down first to hold the other lever to keep the door open for the last person."

They followed Sealyn slowly down the dark stairs. Sealyn held the stone lever at the base while Char joined them. Once she released the lever, the floor resealed itself, and darkness was everywhere.

"How are we to see?" squeaked Pinx

"Stomp your feet," Sealyn instructed while pounding her feet on the stone floor.

They did as Sealyn commanded, and slowly, dim white lights started appearing down the stone tunnel. The white fire flowers revealed themselves and grew brighter the louder they stomped.

Sealyn wrapped her arm around Char's shoulders. "Did you know that fire flowers shine light when they feel vibrations?"

Char rolled his eyes and, like the dramatic actor he was, dropped Sealyn's arm and pointed his finger at her. "How dare you keep this secret passage a secret from me!"

Sealyn ignored Char and shoved her cousin aside. She intertwined her fingers with Jace's, feeling the same tingling again. She took a deep breath and began to run. Everyone followed her lead. Hearts pounding and laughter echoing through the walls, the Elysian queen and the Vinurs of the Court were off on their escapade.

Sealyn jetted around corners, navigating the maze of tunnels with ease. Finally, she stopped abruptly before a bulky stone with a rusted handle. Seven dark olive hooded capes hung on the wall beside the cold stone door. Sealyn grabbed the capes and handed them to the ladies, hoping these would help conceal their identities. She pulled open the door, and the mouth-watering aroma of the Nichts' bakery came spilling in.

"Are you kidding me, Sealyn?!" roared Char. "This passage leads right to these Puffin Pies, and you didn't tell me?"

"Char, I don't think right now is the time to discuss who may or may not have known about secret passages that may or may not lead to treats."

"Well, I feel hurt and betrayed. I want that stated for the record." Char tapped his palm with his finger for emphasis, only to be met with laughs.

Crowds gathered around the square to watch the dancing and listen to the vibrant music. The queen and her ladies quickly pulled their hoods over their heads, slipping through the massive crowd. The music ended, and everyone erupted with cheers and applause. Then, the musicians started playing the song "Night of the Rising Phoenix." It was a top favorite. Sealyn took Jace's hand and pulled him to the dance floor. While the rest of the space swirled around him, Jace knew he had found the only queen he ever wanted to serve. The Vinurs of the Court joined the other market people, twirling across the square and enjoying every minute of their adventure.

After four dances and two ales, Jace felt that he finally belonged somewhere. Here, the people accepted his differences, while back home, he knew no one would genuinely see him as an equal; his haunting and abusive past proved that. Jace sat at a small wooden table, sipping on a smooth-tasting ale and eating honey popcorn, watching the square. He observed Sealyn dancing with her friends, smiling and laughing. How could he leave her? His heart physically hurt with the idea of parting from her and this place. Could he pull off his plan? He could hide somewhere, but his mother would send out a search party, and he didn't want to cause any problems for Sealyn.

He hadn't thought his plan through, but there must be a way for an outsider to relocate, but Elysium had closed its borders to accepting new citizens from Stoltland hundreds of years ago. Sealyn's coronation marked the first time in over five hundred years that Stoltlanders crossed the Elysian border peacefully.

Char noticed Jace sitting alone and joined him. Char patted Jace's shoulder twice and smiled. "Well, Jace, are you having a good time?" Jace smiled and nodded. "See, our quest wasn't so terrible."

"No. It was definitely worth every risk." Jace stared at Sealyn.

Char saw where Jace's gaze was. "I can't help but notice a connection between you and my cousin, Sealyn." Char placed his hands behind his head. Jace blushed. "Oh, I didn't mean to embarrass you, Jace, but Sealyn doesn't take notice of just anyone. She's had many suitors, but none were her equal."

"I'm no one's equal. I'm an outsider, the misfit."

"I believe those gray eyes may have you blind." Char chuckled. "Have you not seen how Sealyn looks at you?"

Jace's head lifted. "What do you mean?"

"Jace, let me fill you in on some secrets about Sealyn. She never does anything she doesn't want to do. She's completely unpredictable and untrustworthy since she chose not to tell me about the secret tunnels to the bakery, but she has a special gift. She can see a person's potential when no one else can, which is why she's the perfect leader for us. She has a predictive vision that is truly quite scary." Char sipped his tasty ale.

"She sounds perfect." Jace paused. "Well, aside from her obvious betrayal to you, but let's be realistic, Char; being with Queen Sealyn is a dream. One that I'm sure almost every man here wishes he could be a part of, so how does a silver-eyed, illegitimate child from an enemy country with no title, no land, no wealth, and no rights to anything stand a chance against princes and lords?" Jace looked toward Sealyn, who happened to lock eyes with him. Her smile vexed him, and she motioned for him to join her.

Char lifted his hand to Sealyn. "I don't know, Jace. You tell me. You're the only man she's allowed to dance with her tonight besides her father."

Jace contemplated his whole life. All the torture he had endured. All the mocking. All the abuse. Then, he imagined what a future with Sealyn could look like. Was this real, or was this a charity project for the new queen? Could she really have romantic thoughts about him? What could he offer her?

His thoughts were instantly interrupted when he saw Drystan approaching Sealyn aggressively while Lady Pyry trailed him with a concerned look. He watched in horror as Drystan ripped back Sealyn's hood, revealing her identity. The music stopped. People gasped and lowered themselves. Jace saw her face, shock and terror in her eyes.

Drystan lifted his hands, and with a slurring speech, he announced, "Good peoples of the market! I give you your queen! Queen Sealyn Arrrraelian of Avondellllllllllle!"

The crowd cheered and applauded, but Sealyn was on high alert. This put her in a dangerous and vulnerable position. She did not have her palace guard with her, and it was clear that the guards on duty in the market had been partaking in ale, as evidenced by Drystan's outburst. She would deal with him later. Now what? She was obviously in the spotlight and needed to say something to her people.

"Good evening to you all! I heard the most glorious music, food, ale, and dancing were here in the market, so I felt the need to see for myself, and do you know what I have found?" Sealyn jeered.

The crowd roared, "What?!"

"I believe this party is much livelier than the palace!"

The people erupted in laughter and clapping.

"Now, esteemed musicians, would you be so kind as to play one of your favorite tunes so that I may have one final dance with these fantastic people?"

She then took off her cape and threw it into the crowd, where two ladies scrambled to claim it. She looked toward where Jace had been but couldn't see him since the number of people surrounding the square had increased.

Drystan pushed his way back to the queen, knocking down Pinx. Seeing Pinx crash to the floor sent Favien into a rage. Drystan yelled, "I want the final dance," but Favien kicked Drystan in the back of his right knee. Drystan collapsed to his knee while Favien quickly wrapped his arms around Drystan's neck, kicking his left ankle out from under him. The giant Drystan fell face forward, but before impacting the floor, he braced himself with his extended right arm, grabbing Favien's arms with his strong left hand, prying himself loose.

Everyone knew Drystan didn't stand a chance against Favien. Once anyone was on the ground with Favien, even a man twice his size, Favien always won, which is why he was Head Groundler, meaning Drystan would lose in the next few seconds.

Sealyn gave her father the idea of having groundlers as a part of their military strategy. Swordsmen and shieldsmen walked in rows with enough space to have a short man crawling on the ground behind the shields they were carrying. The groundlers hid behind the long shields, so once the swordsmen and shieldsmen reached the enemy, they would grab the ankles of the enemy, pulling them to the ground for hand-to-hand combat. While the groundlers held their victims, the swordsmen would finish off the enemy with their weapons. This tactic won great victories that no one ever believed the Elysian armies could win, so for Favien to be head of the groundlers was an esteemed honor.

Once Drystan pulled apart Favien's tight grip around his neck, Favien spun around like lightning onto Drystan's extended right arm, pulling Drystan on top of himself, almost knocking the wind out of his lungs. The crowd cheered and chanted for Favien. The other swordsmen cheered on Drystan, advising advances, but the ladies screamed in terror, protesting the fight. Other squabbles between groundlers and swordsmen started escalating. These noises did nothing to distract Favien, though. His focus was entirely on avenging the love of his life, Pinx. Favien latched his legs around

Drystan's neck, finally making him pass out. When the crowd saw the limp body of Drystan, they chanted, "Favien! Favien! Favien!" Pinx rushed to Favien's side, helping him to his feet. His head was spinning, and he was short of breath.

Pinx smacked his arm. "What were you thinking? Why would you rush such a man?"

Barely able to speak, Favien replied, "Because I love you, Pinx!" She jumped slightly, and both hands pressed against her chest. This was the first time she had heard his declaration of love for her. Her heart raced, and her face blushed. Favien continued, "I've always loved you and will always protect and honor you and, in this case, fight for you."

The crowd cheered even louder when the head of the groundlers pronounced his love for Pinx. Elysians loved a good romance story.

Pinx leaped into Favien's arms, embracing him and drawing his face close to hers. "I love you, too! I've been waiting for this moment for so long!" She had tears of joy running down her face, and surprisingly, so did Favien.

The scuffle captured too much attention for Sealyn to feel comfortable anymore. More people were pouring onto the square floor to congratulate Pinx and Favien and to speak to her. The arguments between the groundlers and the swordsmen were turning more into pushing, and she felt a panic coming over her body, but then, a calming sensation went through her skin; she felt *his* hand on her waist. How could she already recognize his touch? His other hand cupped the side of her face with his stormy gray eyes, looking intensely angry and scared. Sealyn suddenly felt safe, as if she were a ship on the high seas, spotting a lighthouse in the distance, calling her home. His thumb caressed her chin, igniting a longing within her. She pressed her hand against his, captivated by the moment.

"Please, Queen Sealyn, let us leave this place. Where can we go?" Jace frantically asked.

She nodded. "Follow me. We'll go to *Mimby's Morsels* at the corner of the market. She's always open." She gestured to her companions, and away they went from the square.

*Mimby's Morsels* was empty. Everyone preferred to enjoy the festival foods outside rather than come inside Mimby's food house. Most people found Mimby to be a little odd. Her black hair was pulled back tightly and stayed in a bun daily. She had copper skin with a slightly wide nose. What was most fascinating about Mimby was that her only true friends were the Fire and Ice Nichts, which shocked people because those two classes of Nichts didn't always get along well, but they united under Mimby's friendship. Together, they made a wonderful food house of unique blends of dishes. Since they agreed their companionships were odd, they decided their cuisine should be equally bizarre.

Jace read the scribbles on the menu parchment: "*Mimby's Morsels*: Make It Odd." His eyes widened when he read the first category of food: "Frozen Creams and Crisp Potatoes." This is clearly what Mimby meant by "make it odd." He had never had frozen cream before but had heard of it from his brother's many travels. His country did not serve such spectacular foods; usually, just roasted chicken with vegetables and rice. The Ice Nichts did not exist in his land. Those who survived the mass extermination of the Nichts fled to Elysium or were enslaved in other kingdoms.

Mimby briskly walked to the corner where everyone was seated. "Your Majesty." She curtsied. "I'm so honored for you to be here. Please let me know what I can fetch for you."

"I believe I can see Jace's mouth watering over your frozen creams and crisp potatoes. I'm sure he wouldn't mind trying the chocolate and crisp strips with the pink salt." Sealyn smirked at Jace.

Mimby served four flavors of frozen creams, all made from coconut milk: chocolate, vanilla, chocolate-vanilla mix, and peanut butter. The Ice Nichts were the famous creators of the frozen creams. They spent years working on the perfect blend of ingredients and practiced using the exact amount of ice power to keep the mixture from becoming a frozen block. Jace felt giddy like a child about to taste his first dessert. He thought his emotions were going to burst from him. How did these Elysians seem so calm?

Mimby also had different selections of how the frozen creams were served on the potatoes. This is where the Fire Nichts were able to show off their control, especially when most people feared the Fire Nichts. One could order half a potato, long strips, or small chunks of their delicious fire-roasted potatoes. Elysium only produced three of the four types of salts: pink, purple, and blue. From pink to blue, the amount of saltiness grew. The yellow salt was imported from the Shunal kingdom, Elysium's western neighbor. This salt was unique because it not only had a salty taste like the pink salt but also had a sweet flavor, which was very valuable. Of course, the Shunalians would have this salt—greedy little snakes.

Mimby's establishment had large wooden beams in each vertical corner that ran perpendicular along the ceiling, and dark green chandeliers hung from each one.

"Would anyone else like the chocolate and crisp strips?" Six other hands sprang up. "Oh my, what a hungry group you are. Not to worry. We'll prepare these right away."

"May we also have the fruit-and-fish pink salt block starter?" Queen Sealyn gazed across the table at her hungry friends. "Actually, make that four of the starters and the largest fish and cheese scavenger bread you have."

"What is fish and cheese scavenger bread?" Jace asked.

Sakul loved educating people on Elysium customs. "It's delicious. Just wait! Mimby wraps fish and cheese inside the dough, rolls it into balls, and bakes it to perfection. She has a special stone bowl from her grandmother, who bought it at the Glatania Port Festival many years ago. The Glatanians brought hundreds of their favorite cooking tools, among many other items. I think people are still shocked that Glatanians even showed up. Wasn't that the first time in hundreds of years Elysians had ever seen purple eyes?"

Sealyn nodded, impressed with Sakul's information.

"I can hardly wait to try it. We don't have such food pairings in our land." Jace looked down, wishing they could forget where he was from. How could anyone forget, though? His eyes were a constant reminder. Gray meant mixed—a contaminated bloodline. His parents were not from the same kingdom: Corentine, obviously a major enemy of Elysium, but his father's origin remained a mystery. Jace had no idea whether his father came from another enemy or perhaps an ally. He didn't even know his name.

Mimby brought the four salt blocks along with fresh fruits—watermelon, strawberries, and apples—plus servings of cucumber, dates, and olives. Jace's eyes narrowed when he saw raw fish sitting beside the cucumber. This must surely be a mistake. The Fire Nichts probably forgot to cook the fish, but that theory was quickly dismissed when he saw Favien grab a piece of raw fish, add it to a slice of cucumber, and then eat it without hesitation. He thought he felt a bit sick, but he copied Favien, and what an unusual, tasty sensation exploded on his tongue. Cool refreshing sensations swashed around with hints of salt flaring up as he chewed, which he concluded came from the pink salt block. How clever to put the food on the salt block for flavoring.

The queen could see everyone's mood lighten as the rest of the mouthwatering plates were served. She thought this would be the perfect time to share her plans for the future with them, and after a few more mouthfuls of the sweet and salty foods, she began to confide in her Vinurs.

"My lords and ladies, and our new acquaintances, I wish to share my vision for this great kingdom and our world. As you know, the neighboring kingdoms were invited to attend the coronation celebrations to demonstrate good faith and hopefully serve as the first step toward future peace talks, but you didn't know that each visiting person had been monitored and vetted for a different purpose. I hope to ask one person from each new land to stay in Avondelle. If those chosen prove themselves worthy of the stay, they shall form a new council called the Council of Lands and advise on the peacemaking efforts that will come."

The faces around the table were amazed by the bold challenge the new queen would undertake in her first week. This would no doubt cause the kingdom to question her leadership, but it could also pave the way for peace.

Leaders throughout history have attempted, and failed miserably, to achieve peace, outwitted by the curses. Sealyn wanted younger lords and ladies because their youth would most likely protect them from irreversible corruption. All kingdoms except for Stoltland were accounted for, at least until she met Jace. She knew there was a reason for her hesitancy with Stoltland. Sealyn took a sip of her wine and nudged Zuri. Rolling back her shoulders, Sealyn turned to the deep orange eyes of Sir Rav, the architect from Korpam.

"Sir Rav, I've heard many great things about you and your skills. We've actually been investigating you for months." Sealyn felt a tinge of joy at the way Sir Rav's jaw dropped. "You mentioned to your carriage driver that you thought you were invited by mistake, but I assure you, sir, your invitation was extremely intentional. I want you to be the first lord to join my Council of Lands."

"Lord?" Sir Rav questioned.

"Yes. Lord. By accepting this new task, you will be granted a new title and a house with a small piece of land. Do you accept?" Already knowing his answer, Sealyn popped a crispy potato smothered in chocolate into her mouth.

This news overjoyed Rav. "My queen, why ye—"

The doors flew open, and the Royal Guard rushed inside. King Ryker stormed in, his face a mask of worry and anger. Everyone quickly stood and bowed, except for Sealyn, who remained seated, irritated by the interruption.

"Queen Sealyn, my daughter, we have been looking for you. You shouldn't be out in the market during your coronation celebration."

Sealyn glared. "Father, I believe these conversations are best left for private rooms and not public food houses."

The king hesitated. "Of course, allow us to escort you and your guests back to the palace."

Sealyn turned back to the table, digging into the pocket of her dress for coins. She placed several gold coins beside her plate, then pinched a finger full of the filled scavenger bread while eyeing her friends to do the same if they wanted. They all grabbed one more quick bite before they left. Queen Sealyn felt her heart hang heavy. She was quite embarrassed to have been caught. She knew her adventure would be deemed careless, but her desire to be among her people couldn't be seen as impure. She would stand up for tearing down the barriers between royalty and commoners.

# Chapter 9

Early the next day, the sun rose with a glorious sunrise of vibrant pinks and oranges. The morning weather brought a cool breeze that tickled the trees as they swayed back and forth. Ryker had been up early in Sealyn's sitting chamber, engaged in a heated discussion. Graelynd tried her best to calm both sides, but neither wanted to concede.

Ryker paced heatedly. "I don't know how else to explain that your ridiculous adventure was careless!"

"You say careless, and I say bold."

Ryker stopped pacing. "Ha! How can you see it that way?"

"The people loved me being there. It showed them I want to participate in what they love, too."

Ryker shook his head. "I speak of the dangers. Someone could have kidnapped you and held you for ransom or worse!"

"Really, you two. Can you please find a way to resolve this?" Graelynd pleaded, placing a hand on Ryker's shoulder.

Sealyn waved her hand. "All right, the resolution is this. I recognize that my sneaking off without the guard and without notifying the palace of my whereabouts was inconsiderate of the physical dangers we could have faced." The king lifted his eyebrows in surprise. "But you must admit that it's time the palace participates more with the people so they feel a genuine connection to us."

"I believe that's an excellent resolution. Well done, Sealyn," Graelynd cheered.

Sealyn stood, nerves flooding her. "Let's also be clear that I am queen now, and as such, I can no longer be scolded in public by my parents. If you disagree with something I say or do, those conversations must take place in here or another private chamber." She looked only at her father.

"Agreed," they both said, though one was more reluctant than the other.

Sealyn nodded. "Good. Now, can we please go to the breakfast room? I have much more to discuss, but I'd rather do it over Baker Nicht's cinnamon rolls and coffee."

The breakfast chamber was the only oval room in the palace, featuring two fireplaces that faced each other. Both were a beautiful aqua blue, and each season brought a change to the shades of blue. They were amusing that way because the stone was made from the rock of the Ever-Changing Mountain. Legend has it that the mountain was cast with a seasonal blessing spell hundreds of years ago, causing the rock to change shades of blue depending on the season. The reasons behind the casting of this spell remain somewhat of a mystery.

Needless to say, the breakfast room fireplaces were a favorite of the guests. The walls were painted a pale yellow with gold trimmings, and on the wall opposite the doors were large windows on both sides of the fireplace, stretching from floor to ceiling. In the center of the room was the giant oval oak table, and today, large juicy green and purple grape clusters and ripe plums lined the center of the table. Breakfast was meant as a lighthearted social time for the royals and their guests, so stationed around the room against the walls were tables filled with silver platters of flavorsome foods: steaming goose eggs, spiced sausages, crispy turkey strips, fresh melons, and baked cinnamon rounds.

Jace couldn't believe his eyes at the display of food and drinks. He quickly walked to the coffee table, poured a cup, added some oat milk, and enjoyed the soft, creamy drink. Unfortunately, his joys came to a halt when he caught sight of his mother blazing toward him with a stern face.

"Jace, you're alive. I wasn't sure what happened to you trust you, considering we saw nothing more of you after the queen took you from us." She stood beside Jace, surveying the room.

"Sorry, Mother." He hesitated, but for once, just once, he wanted to share a meaningful memory with his mother, and for it not to be used against him. "I, um. I made some new friends and ended up having a wonderful time."

"From what I've gathered, you and your new little friends had quite the scandalous evening."

Jace tightened his jaw. "You had spies at the square, didn't you?"

Corentine jerked her head to face Jace with all of her red hair flipping behind her. "You watch your tone with me, son, and I didn't mention the square. You did." She smiled and walked away, leaving him feeling defeated.

Corentine grabbed a pastry and dropped it intentionally in front of Drystan. Drystan bent down and handed it back to Corentine.

"My, my. Thank you, Lord..." She gave a questioning pause.

"Lord Drystan, my lady."

"Wonderful. Thank you, Lord Drystan."

Drystan took her hand as she curtsied to him. Once she walked away, Drystan realized she had left a note in his hand. Curious, he discreetly opened it, and it read, "Volunteer." He was completely confused by this vague message, so he kept his eyes on her.

Jace was unaccustomed to sitting at a family breakfast, so he stood in the corner, savoring a scrumptious cinnamon roll with his coffee. Finally, the butler announced the arrival of the royals, and Jace's heart skipped a beat. He felt like hiding, but he also wanted to scoop Sealyn up in his arms once again. He had to keep his emotions in check and avoid embarrassing himself.

Sealyn entered, followed by her parents and sister. The queen's grandparents preferred to have their breakfast in the conservatory and then take pleasant walks in the gardens. Sealyn always snuck down to enjoy a cup of coffee with them; she cherished their conversations and tried to spoil her grandparents as much as possible.

Sealyn lifted her cup. "Cheers and a good morning. I hope you all had an entertaining evening and a pleasant sleep. Enjoy your breakfast."

Everyone raised their cups to appreciate the queen's statement and began eating.

"Your Majesty," Corentine started, "I have heard of the beauty of your gardens and waters, so I am quite looking forward to taking a tour later, but I was hoping one of your guards would aid in escorting me so I don't get lost."

Jace stilled. Something wasn't right. His mother never admitted to having weaknesses, so why would she speculate about getting lost? Corentine was a calculated person, so she would have a reason for this request. Should he take the risk to find out?

Sealyn's eyes narrowed, but before she could object, Drystan spoke up. "Your Majesty, I would like to volunteer for this task."

"I'm sure you would." Sealyn scowled at Drystan, still irritated that he pushed Pinx down and fought with Favien. Why would he volunteer? Drystan was very clear about his feelings toward Stoltland. Perhaps he was trying to make up for last night. "It's settled then. Lord Drystan will accompany you on the tour of our fine gardens." Sealyn still needed to sort out her feelings about Drystan revealing her to the crowd and the ridiculous fight, but right now, she felt eyes watching her.

Sealyn looked around the table at her guests gobbling up their food and laughing about various stories being told, but she couldn't find Jace. She glanced at the far corner, and her heart ached. Jace was pressed against the wall, staring out the window, sipping coffee. Her mind raced. Why wouldn't he join the table? All too quickly, she realized that Jace must have never felt welcomed at a royal table. Anger stirred deep within, urging her to throw Corentine into the dungeons for making Jace feel this way.

Jace turned his head and caught Sealyn staring at him. He blushed and offered a half-smile, unable to hold the tempting gaze as he looked down.

Sealyn's heart skipped a beat. The way he looked at her... the way he made her feel... how was this happening so fast? It scared her, but there was something about him. She needed answers, but first, she wanted to change Stoltland's branding of him as an outcast.

Drystan found himself deep in the gardens with Corentine, listening to her drone on and on about how wonderful Stoltland was compared to Elysium. He tried to ignore the apparent bragging, but he felt an odd pulling from somewhere deep inside him, wanting to know more.

"Our most esteemed military leaders have grand estate homes and lands, so you can imagine their wealth beyond what they earn from their palace wages," Corentine bragged, watching Drystan's eyes closely. "We always make sure they have first pick over the newly imported horses from shires to stallions." She paused and turned to face Drystan. "You could have your pick."

Drystan paused. "My pick? What do you mean by my pick?"

Corentine waved her hand in the air. "Oh, I just meant if you lived there, which, of course, you don't, so it was innocent speculation." She laid her hand on his forearm gently. "No harm in speculating, right?"

Drystan glared at her, then shrugged his large shoulders and started walking again, brushing off her touch.

Corentine flashed a predatory smile. "Military leaders have several servants, too."

"Servants? Really?" Drystan was shocked by such wealth and power. He thought about his small, modest home, knowing it wasn't enough for Lady Pyry.

"Ah, yes, many servants, not these Nichts but actual humans who can do the job properly. Depending on the size of the estate and rank, some leaders have hundreds of servants."

"Hundreds? Wow, that seems a bit extreme."

Corentine shook her head and scrunched her face. "Nonsense. Military leaders are too important and busy to bother with such matters that a servant should be doing. Don't you agree?" She was hoping he would take the bait.

Drystan shrugged, trying not to sound too interested. This was a dangerous conversation for an Elysian. He had to fight against envy or else he would end up on Reformation Rock. "I mean, it can be difficult to balance training and keeping up my house, but it's small, so it doesn't take much tending."

"Small? I do pity you," she spoke with a sympathetic voice and patted his shoulder.

Drystan jerked his arm from Corentine. "Pity? I don't want or need your pity, so stop wasting my time. Why did you want me to volunteer?"

Corentine crossed her arms over her deep V-neck, onyx feathered dress. "To tell you just that—I pity you, but also, I could give you everything we talked about. You could have the grand house with the large lands, be a high-ranking military leader with your own troops, and have all the servants you need. Why would you not want that?"

Drystan froze, feeling the effects of the curse. His mind felt fuzzy, and the air around him thickened with a light green haze. "I guess I really haven't thought about it. We don't let ourselves think about such things."

Corentine already knew this. Elysians and their jealousy—such weaklings. Drystan was too easy a target, and her plan was working. "Then start thinking about it. Do you want to stay here or move forward and have wealth beyond what Elysium can offer?"

She stepped closer, just inches from his face, breathing in his scent of sweat and pine needles. The stinging sensation in her nose nearly made her vomit. She hated Elysians and wished she could stab Drystan's envious eyes, but she needed a scapegoat. She slipped a coin pouch into his hand and gave a sly wink. Then, leaving him speechless, she walked away, proud of her simple victory.

Drystan stood, dazed and confused. He felt strange; a burning desire to possess what the Stoltland military leaders had flooded his veins. Why did her offer have to sound so enticing? He had never needed fancy privileges before, so why was he feeling small and incomplete compared to the Stoltlanders?

Later, when he peered inside the doorway of his home, he suddenly felt embarrassed and started imagining what a large estate would look like as his own. Why should he not have that? He glowered at a painting of his grandfather on the wall. "I work harder than anyone else," he said to the faded colors. "I do deserve servants and all the stallions I want." With those echoed words, envy quickly took root and began to fester in the cavernous depths of his heart.

At the end of the coronation week, Avondelle's citizens were exhausted from the endless festivities. Today, the sky was dark, and clouds rolled in quickly, with lightning streaking across the horizon. The rain fell like waves, preventing anyone from traveling. Sealyn curled up in her nook in her bedroom, gazing out her window with her head propped against the sill. She felt sick, truly heartsick, because she wanted Jace to stay. The time they had spent together these past few days had stirred feelings she never thought she would have for someone, especially a silver-eyed Stoltlander. She needed to decide on the Stoltland representative for the Council of Lands.

Maekel fluttered to the window and stood on the cushion, worrying about Sealyn. "Your Majesty, what can I do's to helps?

"Nothing, Maekel. There is no tonic for what ails me."

Maekel dropped her head and tried to fight back her tears. She hated seeing Sealyn this way. She loved her like her own sister. Sister! Excellent idea. She immediately flew as fast as she could to retrieve Siany.

Siany entered Sealyn's bedroom with a gold tray filled with two Puffin Pies and fresh, creamy coffee. She set it on the wooden table near the nook and sat opposite Sealyn.

"You do realize the guests have been extremely worried about you since this morning." Siany studied Sealyn's blank expression, but when she noticed the tear stains on her cheeks, she worried. "Sealyn, it's not my place to tell you what to do, but you are queen now. The country follows you. You've already made some pretty incredible decisions. I keep hearing the people praising you for them, too, so what keeps you this sad?"

"Stoltland will remain an enemy," Sealyn responded flatly.

"Stoltland? You're upset that you didn't strike a peace deal with the one kingdom that has been at odds with us since

Creator began this world?" Siany was baffled by her sister's illogical goals. Stoltland would never want peace. They only wanted power.

"Yes. And, well, no. Not that extreme. I just can't bear Jace and I being on opposing sides."

Tears flowed down Sealyn's face. Siany knew her sister enjoyed Jace's company and that they had become fast friends, but what could be done? He couldn't stay here. What reason would Sealyn give? Elysium's borders were closed to Stoltlanders. With his station, there was no justification for Jace to remain in the kingdom. Not only was he from their number one enemy, but he was also the gray-eyed, illegitimate son of Corentine, which meant he had no title or land. What could he offer for breaking their laws?

"Look at it this way—our two lands may not have war in our lifetime," Siany said, trying to comfort Sealyn.

Sealyn jerked her head toward her sister. "But if we did, and it was my arrow that killed Jace... I couldn't live with myself." She shook her head and muttered, "I hate these rules we live under."

Siany smiled, eyes twinkling with playful intent. "From what I remember, you weren't much for following the rules—more like breaking, justifying, and amending them."

Sealyn sat up. "You're right! Burn the rules! Jace will stay, and he will become one with this land. He will become bone of my bone, breath of my breath, and we will have one heartbeat."

Siany's mouth fell open. She was at a loss of words. Did she hear her sister correctly? Surely, Sealyn wasn't saying…no, of course not. Sealyn wouldn't marry a silver-eyed Stoltlander—would she? She raised her hand. "Wait? You're choosing Jace as a husband prospect?" She saw the excitement in Sealyn's eyes. "No, Sealyn. I thought you might choose him for a new horse trainer or maybe the Council of Lands position. And that's a big maybe, but this?"

"You seriously thought this was about politics? No, my sister. This has always been a matter of the heart." Sealyn smiled and wiped her cheeks.

Siany looked around the room, frantically trying to gain inspiration from the white and gold walls of Sealyn's bedroom. Nothing. She had to prevent her sister from making a huge mistake.

She glanced at the vast, dark green bookshelves, hoping to see a book she could recount with wisdom, but her mind went blank. She looked above the fireplace and noticed Sealyn had redecorated. On the left side hung portraits of Grand Queen Karis, mother of Queen Mother Graelynd, and of Lady Ebbalee Araelin, mother of King Ryker. On the other side were portraits of herself and her mother. In the painting, Queen Karis wore a long pale-green dress and stood next to the garden fountain with three amaryllis flowers in her hand. Siany thought, "What would Grand Queen Karis tell Sealyn?" She knew what her grandmother, Lady Ebbalee would say: "Jace is a very good-looking man. Marry him yesterday." Siany smiled at her grandmother's portrait of her painting a red and blue parrot.

Siany remembered standing for such long hours in her uncomfortable green and white dress. The bodice had been so tight she could barely breathe. She chuckled to herself, seeing Sid and Tid captured in the background, and was glad the painter had her carrying a book instead of her sword.

Siany turned her observation to what her mother was holding in her hand: a basket full of food and flowers. This was the symbol of a giver to the less fortunate, which described her mother exactly. She wore a green dress with dark lace overlaying the bodice, draped over her shoulders slightly, with a high neckline.

Siany fixated on the covered portrait over the mantel. "Sealyn, have you not seen your portrait?"

"I actually forgot about that. I'm not sure I want to see it."

"Why?"

"Well, to be honest, I had a little wine when telling the artist what I wanted. I blame Char. He encouraged me with the wine and asked me to do something different."

"Oh, Sealyn, what did you do?"

Sealyn walked over to the portraits and pointed. "You see how you all have side views." Siany nodded. "Well, I wanted a straight portrait."

Siany shrugged. "That doesn't seem that bad."

"It gets better. I also wanted to hold not just one object. I wanted something in both hands while standing in darkness and light."

"How does a painter paint that?"

Sealyn laughed. "No idea, but when a wine-infused queen requests it, then I guess you get what you asked for. I'm eager to see how he captured the dress, though."

Siany stood beside her sister in anticipation as Sealyn pulled the gold cord. The sheet fell, revealing a stunning masterpiece. Both mouths gaped. Sealyn stood in the center of the painting in an emerald-green gown with green embroidered crystals that made intricate designs around the shape of the bodice, extending down the arms and the mid-torso.

The dress was fitted in the bodice and flared at the top of the hips, cascading down past the floor in layers of feathers. The silk material stopped midway at the knees. The edges of the fabric were not only embroidered with green diamonds but also cut in a star pattern, creating a high-low design around the dress. Attached to each hem were gold-dipped phoenix feathers that reached all the way to the floor.

The background was exactly as she asked. One side showed a storm, while the other side beamed with sunshine. Resting on her right arm, with the sunlight, was a young green phoenix with a long emerald and mint green tail. In her left hand on the dark side, she held a golden bow and arrow. Her expression was fierce but also beautiful at the same time. The royal crown fit her perfectly, with her hair in long waves on each side.

"What would this queen tell you to do, Sealyn?"

Sealyn paused. She could tell her sister didn't want her to see Jace as a husband prospect, and maybe she shouldn't. Something tugged at her heart, a yearning to know more about him. What future could a silver-eyed outcast and an emerald queen have? Never in the history of the world had a gray-eyed person held a position of power. Should this sway her decision? Did she want to continue with how history had always been, or…could she be the one to break the chains that history had bound them in?

Sealyn straightened her back. "That queen would ask: What will you do with the unexpected? Will you create more darkness, or will you be the light?"

Sealyn felt she would face much darkness during her reign, but when she looked into the mythical green phoenix's yellow eyes, she saw who she was going to be—and it scared her.

The royals jumped at the entrance of Maekel. Her face had a look of fright.

"What is it, sweet Maekel?" Siany asked.

"Majesty, I overheards Lady Corentine speakings to her lady's maid, Maid KeKet, as they were walkings in the hallway. I heards something that was most odds."

Sealyn raised her arms. "Well, don't keep us waiting in suspense, Maekel."

"My apologies! Lady Corentine whispereds to Maid Keket, 'I've convinceds him. Now, all he has to dos is finds the Heart of Elysium.' Maid KeKet replieds, 'My lady, do's you really thinks he will be able to finds it?' Then Lady Corentine saids quite forcefully to KeKet, 'You dares question me? He's highly motivateds. His Elysian weakness wills become our strength.'"

Sealyn and Siany looked at each other blankly. What was the Heart of Elysium, and who was the "he" they were talking about?

"Thank you, Maekel. I really don't know how you're able to find out all these details without being seen, but I'm very appreciative of you. I must find out from our father what exactly the Heart of Elysium is." Queen Sealyn remembered, though, that her father was at the Crystal Fort for the day and would not return until morning. She looked up at the portraits by the fireplace. "In the meantime, I will go see Grand Queen Karis. I have a feeling she may hold more answers than we realize."

Siany nodded. "Wise to seek the wise."

The calling is strong. I feel it every day pulling and whispering. I was tempted today, but I resisted. How hard it is not to desire what someone else has. I believe the infection is among us, though.

I'm afraid. For the first time, I'm afraid.

Lord Char Araelien

LORD FINN
LORD JASHUN

# Chapter 10

The rain continued to fall as thunder rumbled in the distance. The roads were thoroughly soaked, thwarting all attempts to keep one's shoes clean. Char shook his long gray coat as he entered *Liquid Courage*. He took a seat on a tall wooden chair. The barman cheerfully walked over to Char, stopping to fill a cup of ale and then placing it in front of him, small streams of amber liquid and foam gliding down the wooden tankard.

"Good day to yo', me lord. Fresh ale. Just opened."

"Thanks, Barm. I really could use it." Char raised his cup to Barm.

Barm's real name was Sir Csdar, but no one knew how to pronounce it, not even Barm. His mother was blind and mute, so she wrote the only letters she knew on the birth parchment. During his childhood, most playmates called him Ceadar, but when he became a bartender, everyone called him Barm, short for barman. He was a sweet, plump man with a bald head and scraggly beard.

"Me lord, I have a concern for you." Barm leaned over the counter.

"Lay it on me, Barm. I don't know that it could be worse than this storm outside."

"Well, it's Lord Drystan." Barm wiped the counter with a dirty cloth.

"Drystan? What'd he do now?"

"Oh nothin', nothin'. It's just that he came in here very early and has been drinkin' all day." Barm pointed toward the far corner, and in the shadows sat Drystan with his head face down on top of his arm while his other hand still grasped a cup of ale. "I don't like to make trouble with the military gents, but he's puked three times already. Ax won't clean up the last one because she's too mad." Ax was the nickname of the barmaid—the blonde Lord Jdru swooned over. She was as beautiful as a flower but had a tongue as sharp as an ax, hence the nickname.

Char stretched his neck to see the vomit on Drystan's boots and table. He gagged. If there was anything Char hated, it was vomit. "Let me see what I can do. Bring me bread and coffee. Lots of coffee."

The stench of the vomit pierced Char's nostrils, making him dry heave. Char was confused why Drystan would do this. He knew Drystan was days away from marrying Pyry, but that arrangement had been made seven years ago, so why would Drystan be upset now? Perhaps that wasn't it. Was he still embarrassed about the fight with Favien? He thought

Favien and Drystan put aside that evening after Drystan apologized. Did Sealyn say anything to him? He knew how harsh Sealyn's words could sound when she spoke the truth, especially if it had anything to do with a man's pride.

"Drystan. Drystan." Char poked Drystan's shoulder. "Drystan, wake up." Char shook him and yelled louder, "Drystan! Stand your ground! We're under attack!"

Drystan floppily stood at attention, spilling the ale over his boot, and projectile vomited on Char's pants, which prompted Char to vomit on the floor, too. Barm looked to Ax with a pitiful look, but Ax huffed and kept cleaning the windows.

Char was furious. He grabbed Drystan and dragged him into the middle of the street, pushing him down to the wet stone ground. Drystan rolled onto his back, letting the rain pelt his face. Char stood in the pouring rain, washing away the vomit and hurling insults at Drystan. Finally, both of them walked and settled into the chairs under the overhang of Liquid Courage.

Drystan hung his head, water beads dripped from his chin to his wet pants. "I'm sorry, Char. I . . . I drank too much."

"Well, that's obvious, but why? Why embarrass yourself this way? You're usually way more collected than that."

"I'm avoid..." Drystan trailed off. "I don't want to talk about it."

"Avoid? Who are you avoiding?"

"Char, leave it alone. I *really* don't want to talk about it."

"Are you avoiding Lady Pyry?" Char wiped his face and blinked his jade eyes.

Drystan's jaw tightened. "Yes. Yes, I'm avoiding Pyry."

"But why? The storm will subside. There's no need to worry. I heard she mentioned to Lady Zuri that she was upset the wedding would be held at the old Crystal Fort Ruins instead of the palace gardens. Not sure why. The ruins are spectacular, and Sakul has worked tirelessly with Lord Hueweyn to restore them and change them into a beautiful event."

Drystan knew he couldn't reveal his true reasons for drowning himself in ale, so he took the opportunity Char handed to him. "Lady Pyry had her heart set on the gardens. She wants an elaborate wedding. She and her parents are spending an outrageous amount on this wedding. The pressure is becoming too much."

"The pressure of the wedding plans or the pressure of the lifestyle after the wedding?"

Drystan sighed. "Both. I want to give Pyry the life she's accustomed to living, but my rank won't allow that."

"Wait, aren't you going to move into the main house on the estate, and her parents are moving to the guest house?"

"Well, yes."

"Sounds like the exact same lavish lifestyle to me."

"I would agree, but it won't be me providing it." Drystan shook his head, trying to dry his golden curls. "Char, if you had an opportunity to provide all that and more... the more being more than you can fathom, you would take it, right? Especially if this could happen overnight?"

"Overnight? No such thing...unless you plan on marrying my cousin, which I'm fairly certain she's made abundantly clear won't happen. Where's this coming from? Has someone said something to you that's making you..." Char hesitated and swallowed down the vile in his throat. "Jealous?"

"No, no, no! I'm not jealous of anything! I was just playing a game, I always do when I've drunk too much—a hypothetical game. Perhaps it's more fun when the other person is also intoxicated. Forget I mentioned it." Drystan leaned his head on the stone wall and closed his eyes.

But Char could do no such thing; in fact, Drystan's hypothetical game was all he thought about for the rest of the day.

Piercing through the air, an arrow glided precisely, finding its target easily. The arrow sank deep into the red-painted circle on the round hay bale. Jace grinned confidently as he lowered his bow.

"Nice shot, Jace." Lord Finn patted Jace's back.

"Thanks, Finn. I believe it's your turn."

Finn stepped onto the small wooden platform, which began to wobble. The platform had a round bottom to create instability, simulating an "in-battle scenario." Sealyn had implemented this type of additional training when she was only sixteen. She protested that not every arrow shot would have a firm foundation, so why should archers only train on stable ground? Since adopting this new style of training, the archery team was a deadly force.

Finn was struggling to find his balance, but finally, he felt a confident medium between his core and legs. He pulled back the bow and released the arrow. He missed the red circle by only a few inches.

"Excellent improvement, Finn!"

Finn's face broke into a good-humored smile. "Yes. Let's not mention the other four that went over the target." Finn was from Len Nove and, as such, had bright blue eyes. He didn't like to speak about his home kingdom; it was too painful. He had ivory skin with light freckles across his nose. Finn was easy to get along with; nothing much bothered him, which Jace appreciated.

Jashun opened the door to the archery training room and joined Jace and Finn. He had been outside, evident by his onyx hair dripping wet, yet he still wore a smile on his face. "I thought I heard voices in here. Mind if I join? I've yet to master this device."

Jace handed Jashun his bow and an arrow. Jashun was used to sword fighting, not the wobble blocks, as he liked to call them. He stepped onto the block, and his legs began shaking uncontrollably. He thought he could still fire the arrow but didn't anticipate the weight shift when he drew the bow back. This caused him to fall backward, releasing the arrow straight up. All three men scrambled to dodge the falling arrow, but when it didn't return, they looked up, seeing it lodged in the wooden ceiling.

Jashun giggled nervously. "I just wanted to leave my mark, is all." Jashun pushed himself up from the ground and dusted off his knees. "So, Lord Finn, I hear that you've been invited to stay and join the Council of Lands for Len Nove. Is this true?"

"You heard correctly," Finn responded eagerly. He was relieved. Elysium felt like home, and he wanted nothing more than to stay as far away from Len Nove as possible.

Jace's heart dropped. He felt a tinge of jealousy but was happy for his new friend. Friend—the word was foreign to him, but he had actually managed to make friends.

"Does this mean you will accept?" Jashun asked inquisitively.

"I believe I will. Queen Sealyn already has a task for me, and since I've been here, I've never felt more alive. That might sound odd to say, but it's as if I woke up from a deep sleep when I entered the palace on the coronation night. It was the most fun I've had in over a decade."

Shock plastered across Jashun's cinnamon-colored face. "Seriously? You don't have big parties like that in Len Nove?"

"Oh no. Len Nove is nothing like Elysium. Apparently, it used to be, but now..." Finn seemed to trail off into a lost thought. His eyes glazed over as though he were in a trance.

Jace cleared his throat. "Finn?"

Finn scratched his light brown hair and shook his head, embarrassed. "Sorry, sorry, I got lost in my thoughts of home. Regardless, I'm looking forward to staying here and starting fresh."

Jace hung his head. "I completely understand. I'm happy for you." Jace wondered if Finn could help him escape his return to Stoltland, or would that put Finn's life at risk? He didn't want to be responsible for the death of another person who had been kind to him.

Jashun patted Finn's back, excited for a new pal. "Yes. It'll be great having you join us." Jashun cut his mischievous eyes to Jace. "I heard the travel for everyone is postponed, though, for a few more days. Lady Pyry has even asked to extend the visitors' stay until after her wedding. Looks like you both will experience your first Elysian wedding, and apparently, this wedding will be one for the records. Pyry's parents are spending a fortune! I heard the amount so far is ninety thousand gold coins and growing!"

"Ninety thousand gold coins for a wedding?" Jace questioned incredulously.

Jashun lifted one hand. "I promise! I overheard the girls talking about it. Brenna, Adalina, and Lulana were discussing it after breakfast. I choked on my coffee."

"Seems like a big waste to me. Couldn't that money be used for something better? How can a family have so much wealth to spend on a party?" Finn folded his arms.

"Pyry's father owns several trading ships, so he does business with the palace and other kingdoms. Not to mention, he has miles and miles of land that he makes a fortune from, too. Rumor has it that the pressure of managing his estates is overwhelming Drystan, so much so that he's been drowning himself in ale at *Liquid Courage* for the past three days! Char even tried to help, but Drystan just went right back to drinking. Finally, Ax had had enough and chased him out with a broom." Jashun reenacted the chasing with an invisible broom. The warriors chuckled.

Finn shrugged. "I don't envy Drystan at all. Taking on that much responsibility sounds awful."

"I don't know. I wouldn't mind a challenge, but I definitely wouldn't want to marry Lady Pyry." Jace covered his mouth with his hand. "I didn't mean any disrespect toward Lady Pyry. She's just not what or who I would want."

"No need to get worked up, Jace." Jashun laughed. "We all know who you'd marry tomorrow if you could." Jashun made a crown with his hands on his head and skipped around. Jashun smirked. "C'mon, let's go. Food should be on the training tables by now. You two are welcome to join, but we don't want to get there late!"

Queen Sealyn was still mulling over her conversation with her grandmothers when the king walked into the war room.

"Why in the name of all seven kingdoms are you in here?" Ryker asked.

"When you're at war, you plan in the war room. Honestly, Father, I thought you were a king once?" A crooked smile formed on her lips. She loved teasing her father. Most found him extremely serious, but when it came to her, she somehow managed to pull the kid out of him.

"Ah, I see someone's in a better mood, and whom may I ask are you at war with?"

"Myself."

Ryker nodded and clasped his hands behind his back. The room was a perfect square with a tall ceiling depicting a battle scene from the 2000s. Those were said to be the most gruesome battles fought until the Great War of 4010, which lasted for a thousand years.

Long emerald banners hung in front of the perimeter walkway. The walkway connected on all four sides with multiple corridors. Pearly marble columns braced the walkway with carved weapons in each. Ryker stopped pacing in front of the banner of King Saven, Graelynd's father.

"Your grandfather was such a brave man. You know he went against his advisors' vote on the Nichts' extermination?"

"What? They voted to exterminate them? I thought the Elysian council was in favor of saving them."

Ryker shook his head and began to pace. "After he made his proclamation, he wanted to make sure the Nichts felt no threats, so he published the voting as unanimous in support of the Nichts' freedom and protection. The council later thanked him for his selfless act because they saw what a benefit the Nichts were." He paused his pacing and looked directly at Sealyn. "This must remain a royal secret."

Sealyn leaned back. "Naturally. Wow. I had no idea. Ol' Saven up to his old tricks."

Saven was known to be fierce, but everyone knew about his pranks as well. One of his great friends left a frog in his goblet, so for revenge, Saven had a wagon full of sand dumped in front of his friend's door that reached the roof! His friend and his family had to dig their way out while the king sat in the front yard eating grilled frog legs.

"Yes. You see, Sealyn, sometimes being a king or queen requires sacrificing your pride. Humility is one of a person's greatest assets. As a ruler, you must look beyond the council's advice and envision how this will shape our kingdom." Ryker took the seat next to his daughter.

"I understand. I think I'm about to unnerve several people, maybe everyone, but I believe it's best."

"Know that I'm here for you. Whenever you need advice or simply to still be my little girl. A ruler is still human, so you will have grace with me."

Sealyn tried to ignore the emotional lump in her throat. "Thank you, Father. I really needed that. I believe it's time for my final decision on who will join the Council of Lands from Stoltland."

"And who might that be?"

Sealyn gazed up at her father's banner before returning her focus to the man who raised her. This decision would forever change history. "Jace."

Favien, Tybalt, and Jashun clinked their cups together as they received their third refill of ale. Doebromir finished his fifth plate of food while Jace and Finn sat with their dessert plates. The training food tables were under the shaded walkway, and thankfully, the rain had finally stopped. Rav, Hueweyn, and Sakul entered the walkway from the side entrance, stomachs growling.

"Mind if we join you, gentlemen? I'm afraid we missed lunch in the palace." Skaul said. He wore a cream, sweat-soaked shirt, and beads of water were pouring from his bald, ebony head.

"Of course!" Favien shouted. "Let me get another pitcher for the table. Sit here."

Jashun chewed his chicken and swallowed. "You gents better eat up before Doebromir devours everything, even the plates!"

Doebromir patted his chest. "You know, big boys have to grow."

"Tell us how the wedding preparations are going?" inquired Tybalt.

Sakul shook his head. "Oh, sweet Creator, the requests they are demanding are hurting my head."

"I agree," Hueweyn moaned. "We're trying to reconstruct the old Crystal Fort, but now they want the missing walls strung with white fire flowers."

"How would that even work?" Jace licked his spoon.

With his brown skin and inky hair, Rav raised his hands, drawing an archway in the air. "If there's a missing section, they want us to tie strings to connect the space and then weave white fire flowers to those strings. So far, our attempts have failed."

"After being cut, how long do fire flowers stay lit?" Finn asked.

"Great question. We don't always know. Some last for hours; some last for days. We think the white flowers last five days, so we're running tests now." Sakul chugged his ale.

Everyone's heads jerked toward the Nichts' doors as several of the long-distance Nichts came flying through. The Nichts placed small scrolls tied with emerald ribbons in front of Finn and Rav.

"Our official invitations to join the Council of Lands!" Finn exclaimed. He carefully opened the scroll, marveling at the golden letters. His new life was finally here.

"Are you accepting?" the orange-eyed Rav asked Finn.

"Yes, absolutely. Are you?"

"Me too. I can't see myself anywhere else."

Jace lowered his eyes and swirled the chocolate on his plate with his wooden spoon. He didn't want to feel envious of Finn and Rav. They were great men and would do well, but he wished, just for a second, that he could be one of them. In the history of all seven kingdoms, no gray-eyed child had ever held a title or high position anywhere. He researched for years for just one person, but all his efforts showed that the world was cruel toward those like him. The kingdoms considered silver eyes the worst of humankind.

A winded Maekel fluttered through the Nichts' door holding a scroll with the queen's golden seal and an emerald velvet ribbon. She went through the crowded table and handed the scroll to Jace. Jace's face went pale.

Maekel panted. "My Queen asked me to personally gives this to you. I'm sorrys it tooks me so long. I'm not's as fast as the long-distance Nichts."

Jace's mouth was dry. He could barely speak. "Not to worry. Thank you for your trouble."

Jace couldn't stop staring at the queen's seal. "Personally give to me," he repeated in his head. Sealyn wanted her personal Nicht to hand this directly to him. What could this mean? Maybe she found work for him on the training grounds. He was willing to clean the stables or plow fields; he just wanted to stay. He knew it would be painful one day to watch Sealyn marry another, but until then, if he was here, he could be her friend.

He unrolled the paper and read,

*Just Jace,*

*Do you trust me?*

*Noon tomorrow, the banquet hall.*

*Respectfully,*

*Queen Sealyn Araelin*

Jace had no idea what to make of her letter. He felt nervous because the last time Sealyn asked whether he trusted her, they ended up at a forbidden party with a brawl over her and Pinx. What could she be up to now? He could see all eyes on him, wondering what the scroll entailed. Should he tell them? Perhaps he could leave out the parts that were "just" between him and her.

"Ah, c'mon, Jace! You're killing us with suspense!" Favien hiccupped.

"The queen requests my presence at the banquet hall tomorrow. She doesn't say why."

"She didn't mention an invitation to stay?" Jashun asked.

"No. I'm sorry to say she didn't." He felt his hope drop. Surely, if she was hiring him for a lowly position, she could've stated that in the letter, so why the mystery?

Finn patted Jace's back. "Well, just because ours did say that doesn't mean it won't happen."

No one noticed Drystan had walked up behind them. "True, but inviting a gray-eyed kid to join a council seems a far stretch to me."

"Perhaps no one asked you, Drystan!" Favien snarled.

"Jace, regardless of what anyone's opinion is." Doebromir grinned at Drystan, then back to Jace. "Receiving an invitation from the queen is potentially a good thing, so chin up! Maybe your life is about to change—for the better." Doebromir raised his cup. "A toast to new possibilities. For we never know what form they may take, but may we not be afraid to embrace them."

They followed the traditional pounding of their cups twice and chugged the remaining contents of their drinks. They started exiting the walkway, but Jace noticed Drystan leaving in the opposite direction. Drystan turned his head and glared at Jace before disappearing around the corner. Jace knew he had made an enemy, but he could not say why.

# Chapter 11

The banquet hall was a glorious room, adorned with jade fabric walls featuring gold phoenixes embroidered in repeated patterns. At the center of the room stood a long rectangular table that could accommodate up to forty people. The chairs had cushions that matched the green walls, complemented by golden frames. Today, only ten seats displayed the Elysium gold place settings.

One by one, each invited guest found his or her name on a place card and sat down. Jace had thrown up twice this morning, which made him slightly behind schedule. He hoped no one could tell and quickly took his seat. He was glad Sealyn had not arrived yet, but wished he could have spoken to her privately before. He hadn't realized others would be joining their meeting.

Sealyn entered, escorted by her father. She took her seat at the head, and he took the seat to her right, while Lady Pyry sat to her left. Jace was happy to be seated next to Finn but felt out of place since no one was sitting across from him like everyone else. He wondered whether this was a bad omen.

"Good day to you all." Sealyn greeted them. "I'm so happy you all accepted my invitation for lunch. As you know, my goal is to create peace among the kingdoms, which has failed over the last four thousand years."

An odd feeling fell over Jace. Where was the representative from Stoltland? Where were his brothers? Had Haedon turned down the queen? Maybe he was running late; it was a big castle, so he might have gotten lost. Jace's thoughts ran wild; that's who was supposed to be sitting across from him—his stepbrother, Haedon.

Sealyn continued. "I don't believe everyone has met yet, so I will start with introductions. I'm sure I don't need to introduce my father, King Ryker, so I will continue down the line. To his right, Lady Runihura from Shunal. To her right, Lord Rav from Korpam."

Zuri blushed and thought Rav was dressed rather nicely in his gray tunic and orange sash that matched his eyes.

"And to his right, Lady Adma from Glatania. Starting from my left is our representative for Elysium, Lady Pyry. To her left, Lord Jem from Havas." The ladies ogled Jem with his blonde hair and handsome face. His red eyes didn't deter them. "To his left, we have two representatives from Len Nove: Lady Zuri and, to her left, Lord Finn. I will explain that reasoning later. And finally…"

Jace's heart skipped a beat. Sealyn must have seen his brother come in. He started looking behind himself and the doors, but saw no one. Sealyn grinned widely. "From Stoltland, we have Lord Jace."

Jace's face turned red as a tomato. Did he hear her correctly? Lord? Did she say, Lord Jace? How? His thoughts were spiraling out of control so rapidly that he thought he was going to pass out. He braced himself with his hands on the table and looked down. What was she doing? A silver-eyed person couldn't hold a position of power. How was this possible? He tried to focus, but his hearing was muffled. Did someone actually choose him? And not just any someone: a queen! A cloud came over him. Did he hear her wrong? Maybe she hadn't picked him. He looked around the room. No other Stoltlander was there, and this was the Council of Lands. His heart pounded. Was Elysium now his home? Did he not have to return to a land full of hate and torture? Was he free? Jace sucked in a breath and tried to swallow the rocks in his throat.

"That's why we have both Lady Zuri and Lord Finn for Len Nove. If you have further questions, please wait to discuss them afterward. I believe we are going to make something magnificent." Sealyn looked at Pyry, who had her light brown hair in a tight bun, and the two smiled at each other while Pyry winked. Pyry became a fast friend to Sealyn years ago, and it seemed as if they were inseparable. Sealyn had her concerns about their friendship, considering Drystan's character flaws but was hopeful everything would be better after their wedding.

Sealyn nodded to the butler, and the staff served the first course of savory foods that began a long day of negotiations. Everyone but Adma seemed to be enjoying the first course. Adma was used to the sugary diet of the royal court in Glatania. She barely fit on the green chair, and the buttons of her purple dress looked as if they were about to burst. Something dark lay hidden behind her violet eyes as she adjusted her spectacles while studying Lord Jem.

After the first course, the palace Nichts handed each delegate a scroll outlining the purpose of the Council of Lands along with the delegate's intent. The scroll also included the properties and lands they would receive once the document was signed. Many had questions, especially Jem, who appeared extremely worried about revealing the secrets of his homeland, not out of loyalty but out of embarrassment. His red eyes widened as he spoke with Sealyn, but she seemed to calm his worries.

After the second course, those who had already signed the documents received another scroll from the Nichts, which held their official new titles. Runihura brushed back her shiny blonde waves and continued trying to negotiate more land and a higher position, but Sealyn didn't budge and insisted all would start equal. Runihura's cheeks flushed, and her bright yellow eyes darkened. No one knew whether she would accept the terms. Rav whispered to Runihura, which made her sit very still. She smoothed her satin yellow dress, took another sip of cucumber water, and nodded at Sealyn.

Finally, the main course arrived, consisting of juicy smoked chicken with herbs and spices, cooked vegetables, and baked purple potatoes with coconut oil and yellow salt. Jace drooled over his plate. He felt like the luckiest person in the kingdom.

Finn whispered to Jace, "How great is this?"

"I don't believe the words have been invented for how happy I am. This is the best day of my life."

Runihura and Jem finished signing their intent scrolls, then received their titles. The servers placed warm Puffin Pies in front of everyone and handed each person a tiny syrup saucer that contained the sweet icing topping. The steam elevated from the Puffin Pies, intoxicating each nose.

Sealyn set her coffee down. "I want to thank everyone again for your cooperation and willingness to join me on this journey. The road won't be easy, but the destination is worth it. You will find a schedule in your new residence with our meeting times. Remember, the next time we meet, I want your notes about your kingdoms as we discussed." She noticed Adma fumble with her fork, eyes darting around the room. Something felt off about her. She might need to keep a watchful eye on that one. "Please feel free to enjoy your coffees, but I must adjourn now. Lord Jace, will you escort me?"

Jace scrambled to break free of his chair and rushed to her side. He couldn't help but notice her form-fitted, mint gown, dark green lace covering the bodice and her arms. He liked the dark lace against her skin. Heat rose inside him.

Sealyn caught him staring. "Am I amusing to you, Lord Jace?"

"Oh no, my queen. I'm sorry. Forgive me. I didn't mean to…"

"If you don't think I'm amusing, why didn't you sign the scroll? Do you not want the position?"

Jace smacked his head with his hand. "I forgot! I was so caught up in excitement that I completely forgot to sign. I'll sign once you dismiss me."

"See that you do." She gave him a flirtatious smile. "Um, Queen Sealyn, may I ask why you chose me? Why not one of my brothers?"

Sealyn stepped closer to Jace with their bodies almost touching. She could see his heart beating in his throat. Their eyes locked intensely. "Because you first chose me."

"What do you mean?"

"Everyone else chooses my title or what my title can do for them, but you—you chose just me. I want to know why a Stoltlander would do such a thing."

He held up his arms. "For starters, I'm no Stoltlander, and secondly…" He paused, scared to continue, but swallowed his fear. "I will always choose you for as long as you allow me to." He hoped his intention was clear. He was completely without any doubt enraptured by this woman.

Looking up at his new manor, Jace stood in shock. He was excited to have fields next to Finn. They had already discussed a system that would profit both of them. He knew Finn would make a great business partner. Business partner. Those were two words he never thought would be uttered about himself. He kept pinching his arm, making sure he wasn't dreaming.

He walked into the red brick manor and was greeted by his butler and his manor's Nichts. He felt extremely uncomfortable having servants, considering the way his family treated servants in Stoltland. He vowed to be different—to treat them with kindness and fairness. The butler gave him several scrolls: the appointments, a map of Avondelle, a map of Elysium, a map of the market, and a current inventory of his new assets. Jace was overwhelmed.

"My lord, allow me to introduce myself. I am your butler, Zedvornair, but if it pleases, you can refer to me as Zed." He bowed graciously. "Pardon me for noticing, but you seem disturbed. Is the manor not up to your satisfaction?"

Jace shook his head wildly. "No! Not at all! This is all very new to me. The manor is perfect. Well done, and thank you all for your hard work."

Zed and the Nichts beamed at this compliment. Zed was an older man with a sweet face. He presented Jace with a silver tray holding a goblet of cucumber water and biscuits.

"Thank you. I believe I do need this."

"Perhaps, my lord, if you tell me what helps you in your times of stress, I can help recommend solutions."

Jace thought for a minute. "Well, I usually like to swim to clear my head."

A wide, toothy grin streamed across Zed's face. The Nichts fluttered past the three-tier white marble fountain in the spacious entryway and opened the two glass-pane doors to reveal a long rectangular pool. Jace's mouth gaped. He could see that part of the pool was under the upstairs portion of the manor, and the rest was in the open air. He had never seen architecture like this before. This was his. This life was really his.

Zed guided his hand toward the pool. "My lord, why don't you have a swim now, and in a few minutes, we will bring you ale and refreshments."

Jace didn't know how to respond. He wasn't used to this. Yes, his residence might have been the Stoltland palace, but he lived in a tiny room above the kitchen. It was a poor excuse for a bedroom, meant for storage. Such grandeur would take some getting used to. Jace blinked away his shock.

"Thank you, Zed. That sounds like perfection to me."

Jace was finishing his seventh lap when he noticed a blurred image at the end of the pool. He popped his head up to see Char twirling a dagger.

"Well, if it isn't the famous Lord Jace." Char squatted, knees slightly cracking. "I thought we could have a chat."

"Sure. Yes. Of course, let me just find a towel."

"Oh, Zed laid out a few towels for you and some brandy and food."

"Brandy? It's one of those talks?" Jace quivered.

Char huffed dramatically. "Yes. You have your title now and have both eyes on my cousin."

Under the overhang, the two lords sat in chairs beside the pool, peering out over Jace's lush grounds. Jace was enjoying the sights of the palms and grazing creatures. He realized he didn't actually know the name of the creatures he was seeing. How was he supposed to manage creatures he knew nothing about?

Char thumped a glowing blue beetle. "So, let's be clear and direct. Queen Sealyn has to marry and marry soon." Char sipped his brandy, watching Jace's every move.

Jace's brow furrowed. "What does that have to do with me? Doesn't she have to marry a royal and one with Elysian eyes?"

"No, you rat-tart! Sealyn can marry any title she wants, whoever she wants. No offense, but there's only one reason she would pick *you* to represent Stoltland for the Council of Lands." Char stretched his legs and crossed his feet.

"And what reason would that be?"

"She's attracted to you, Jace. You know nothing of Stoltland's strategies or the future plans they hope to employ. You're not privy to drawings of your capital; nor have you been present at any palace meetings, so you tell me what you can bring to the Council of Lands?"

"I know more than you think," Jace mumbled.

"Jace, I'm not trying to belittle. I'm trying to give you confidence."

"Confidence?" Jace questioned incredulously. "How is pointing out that I'm ineffective for the job I've been handed supposed to give me confidence? Don't you think I've had these same thoughts? These same doubts?"

Char folded his hands behind his head. "What I'm trying to communicate, but obviously failing at, is that if I know all these things and you know all these things, then Sealyn knows them too, and she chose you regardless. We have the worst relationship with Stoltland, so we needed a representative who could join us together. The world will not see you as the one to do that, but Sealyn's vote is the one that counts. She chose you not for title, not for peace; she chose you out of love. The only way the people would be willing to accept a marriage with you two is if you had a title, and now you do."

"Love? What's this nonsense? That's never been said! How could she love someone like me? How could anyone? Have you not seen my eye color?"

"Jace, one thing you'll learn about me: I expose as it shows. I can read Sealyn like one of her many books. She's drawn to you, so what will you do?" Char dropped his hands and leaned forward, deepening his tone to a serious tone. "You have no excuse now. She gave you the title to win her with."

Sealyn read her invitation from Jace to Pinx and Sorcha as they walked through the gardens. This would mark the beginning of a forbidden romance. Silver eyes had no place in society, but she didn't care. There was a mystery beneath him, and she wanted to uncover it. For him to have survived this long, he must have a greater purpose than anyone realized. From his chiseled jawline to his tanned skin, she desired him. She needed those silver eyes to peer into her very soul and find refuge. Just as he had protected her in the square, she wished to protect him.

"Wow, what a smile that scroll brought to your face," Pinx teased.

"Why, Queen Sealyn, you're blushing! I don't know whether I've ever seen you blush like this." Sorcha stroked Sealyn's cheek.

"I can't believe I'm feeling this way. He's completely not what one would expect for me?" As soon as the words escaped her mouth, she felt bad for saying them out loud, but they were true. How would the kingdom accept an illegitimate Stoltlander who only had a title because she gave it to him? And gray eyes! Most of the world viewed silver eyes as abominations, but oh, those silver swirls of temptation made her weak, weak for him. What was this pull he had over her?

Sorcha folded her coffee-colored arms. "And just what do you mean by that?"

"My apologies. I didn't mean to offend, honestly. There just has never been a position of power held by a gray-eyed person anywhere in history, and he's much younger than me."

"That could be fun!" Pinx jeered.

"Pinx!" squeaked Sorcha. "Sealyn, it's your choice how to proceed. Jace seems very respectable and kind. He does come with mystery, but that could prove in your favor."

Sealyn folded her arms, closed her eyes, and embraced the sunshine. "Who he is, or rather who his family is, *does* concern me. Lady Corentine is oddly suspicious. Do you think she would conduct a scheme on Elysian soil?"

Pinx shivered. "She frightens me. Everything about her screams dangerous, so I wouldn't put it past her to conjure up some elaborate scheme."

Sealyn opened her eyes and paused. "Have either of you heard of the Heart of Elysium?" Both shook their heads. "I asked my grandparents, who were reluctant to give me much information. There's something that's not being said."

"Do you have any suspicions?" Sorcha's jade eyes flashed. She loved a good scandal.

"No, but to me, nothing is just a coincidence. Why would Drystan volunteer to escort a high-ranking lady from a kingdom he hates? Maekel also overheard Lady Corentine whisper to her maid Keket something about 'convincing him and finding the Heart of Elysium.'"

Sorcha gasped. "You don't think Drystan would betray Elysium, do you?"

"I must think of all plausible possibilities, and unfortunately, one of those is that Drystan is a traitor. If he is, then that would explain his excessive bender."

Pinx lifted her hand. "Well, before we accuse, let's try to stay optimistic. After all, this is Drystan we're talking about. We all know him; we grew up with him! He's been loyal throughout many battles. Sealyn, you're even helping his wife with his wedding. Drystan could be nervous about the marriage, which *is* what he told Char. If this is true, someone else is out there betraying you."

"You're right." Sealyn glanced at the trees' shadows. "My guard is signaling that it's time for my meeting. I will charge you both with this task: question as many Nichts as possible on Drystan's comings and goings in the past week. Find out who he's talked to, where he goes at odd hours, his body language when talking to people—everything. Don't say anything to anyone else, though. I can't risk rumors flying around that there may be a traitor among us."

Sealyn left Pinx and Sorcha in the gardens. Everything seemed rather quiet for a moment. Only birds singing and the fountain water could be heard. Both ladies looked at each other with worried expressions. A traitor's exposure weighed on their shoulders.

Over the next couple of days, the sun beamed down, feeding the rich Elysian lands and drying the muddy roads. Jace's heart pounded as he and his Nichts placed blankets before the phoenix fountain. He felt that this was a more private area of the garden with a clear view of the palace pools. He had arranged for Sealyn's favorite foods and drinks, along with plenty of pillows for comfort.

"Good afternoon, Lord Jace," Sealyn greeted.

"Good afternoon, Your Majesty."

"Your picnic spread looks divine." Sealyn tucked loose strands behind her ear from the wind. "Shall we sit?"

"Yes, please." Jace gestured to the pillows.

Once Sealyn was seated, the wind blew even harder, making them shout to hear one another. Finally, Sealyn had had enough when the spray from the fountain splashed on her face. Before she could finish wiping the water off her cheeks, sand and leaves attacked them in a whirlwind.

Sealyn stood. "Jace, I know you don't know me very well, but this just isn't enjoyable. Please note itis isn't against your company; it has everything to do with the intrusive winds." Another gust of wind splashed water across the picnic. "May I make a suggestion?" Jace nodded. "Thank you. I suggest we have our picnic in the Garden Library."

He saw the way Sealyn was looking at him. It was as if they had a secret that only they knew about. The Garden Library was their library, where they first met. It was sacred. Jace quickly signaled for the Nichts to help pack everything up and carry it to their beginning room.

Thankfully, the wind didn't ruin their picnic, and now they could finally share another private moment. "I'm noticing my favorite foods. Are you a seer?" Sealyn asked sarcastically. "Or perhaps you're a fantastic gambler?" She paused, then put her finger on her cheek, teasing him. "No, I'm thinking you recruited help."

"I may have polled some of your most trustworthy citizens."

Jace and Sealyn conversed over their love of the Elysian foods, the people, and the dances, but in Sealyn's mind, all she could think about was getting to know who Jace actually was. What was his story? How could he have gone through such a tragic life and be so pleasant? She wanted to unlock all his secrets.

"Jace, I want to know more about you. I want to know what made you *you*."

Jace stiffened, not wanting to recall his past. That needed to stay tucked away forever. "I'm afraid there's not much to tell. I'm not a very interesting person. I might have scandals attached to me like a barnacle, but I, myself, am no extraordinary person."

Sealyn's eyes narrowed. "Do you think I'm a foolish queen?"

"By no means, Your Majesty!"

"Then why would you question me? If I say you're interesting, then you must be." Sealyn's lip curled.

"Well, when you put it like that, I guess I will try to tell my story with intrigue."

"Let's sit on the couch if you don't mind. My legs are going numb."

They made themselves comfortable on the couch facing the fireplace lit by candles. This was the way during the summer days.

How odd, though. Two people who were supposed to be the greatest enemies were seated right next to each other, enjoying their conversation, while the carved creatures in the fireplace stared back: the phoenix and the horse. An odd pair indeed.

"Tell me what you feel comfortable sharing, perhaps starting with your birth parents?"

Jace's shoulders slumped. "Honestly, I don't have all the facts. I have what some family members have told me, and then there are the rumors. I don't know who my father is." He hung his head.

"Perhaps your mother, then. What can you tell me about her?" Sealyn hoped he wouldn't sense her pushing. Something was off about Corentine. She was her enemy, and now she had potential inside information. She felt bad using Jace for this information, but before romance, came her kingdom, and Corentine was on her soil, plotting against them.

Jace squirmed. He wasn't going to reveal his past, just his mother's. "She's the youngest of many, many siblings. My grandfather had many wives."

"Many wives?"

"Yes, in Stoltland, there's a law allowing a man to have multiple wives as long as they don't live in the same territory, so he had five wives—or it honestly could be more." Sealyn mouthed the word five and blinked multiple times. "This didn't include the other women he would frequent in the taverns. The wives weren't close, which kept the siblings apart to a degree. My mother's mother was not kind to her, nor did she care to instruct her three daughters how to be ladies. She cared more about being seen in town, trying to gain sympathy to receive party invitations."

"Sympathy? How?"

"She was wife number five, and yet it was known all over that grandfather still showed up at pubs looking for women. My mother rebelled against being a society lady, so she chose a life in one of the large coastal cities called Navlind."

"Navlind? I've heard of this city. It's a big trading port city and military ship hub, right?"

"Correct. You know your geography."

"I enjoy reading. It's lifesaving."

"The only part I know about my birth father is that he and my mother met in Navlind during one of its big military festivals. I've always wanted to go, but my mother won't allow it. They met on the first night, and after a week or two of too much ale and dancing, well, here I am." He threw his hands in the air.

"And no clues as to who he might be?"

Jace shrugged. "No one will talk about him. I would love to know who he is and find out whether he and I are alike. Rumors and tales circulate, suggesting everything from him not being allowed to marry her to him boarding a ship and leaving, not wanting anything to do with a gray-eyed child."

"What does your mother say?"

"The last time I asked, she said that she tried to have him involved, but he was too distracted and preferred the sea." The truth was something he couldn't reveal to her, not yet. He wasn't sure if he ever could. His mother was much more sinister than Sealyn could imagine, but Jace didn't want to scare Sealyn away, so she would have to receive the fairytale version of his story.

"The sea? Is he a fisherman or perhaps a military man?"

He was growing tired of dodging the truth. He needed to end this. A heavy sigh escaped his lips. "The only true evidence everyone has to agree with is that he was not born of Stoltland; otherwise, my eyes would be black, not gray." He blinked twice.

Sealyn sensed his uneasiness, but his lack of eye contact during their conversation didn't sit well with her. Could she blame him, though? Somehow, Corentine had managed to keep a silver-eyed child alive—that came with strings attached or was due to the father's bloodline. What if it was both? Either way, she had to decide whether she could trust Jace. She wasn't innocent; she had been prying for knowledge to protect her kingdom, and Sealyn had secrets in her past that she wasn't keen on sharing either.

"Jace, I want to thank you for sharing with me. I really do appreciate it and know that it's never easy to open up about the pains we have in our past."

A stillness caped the library as Sealyn gazed into Jace's eyes—those silver, intoxicating, should-be-staying-away-from eyes. The way he looked at her felt like they were the only two in the entire kingdom. How could she feel a loss of breath yet, at the same time, feel like she wanted to dance among the clouds?

Jace slid closer to Sealyn and placed his hand on top of hers, daring to be the outcast to affectionately touch the most powerful woman in this foreign land. Like a moth to a flame, he was drawn to her. He felt like a fish out of water, and she was his ocean.

Sealyn's stomach fluttered, and her heart beat rapidly. Her toes tingled at his touch, his presence. A silver-eyed enemy crossed the forbidden line. He was off-limits. He was dangerous. He was bold, so bold, and she liked it.

Jace leaned close to her ear and whispered, "I want to thank you for listening. No one ever does."

Sealyn gently laid her other hand on his and turned her head, inches away from his lips. Jace blushed. His mouth went dry, and his hands started to sweat. His heart was racing. Should he? Should he lean in to those lips, her plump pink lips? Did she want that? Was this her way of signaling to him? Char said she was attracted to him, so why not? Blame Char if she gets upset.

Jace moved his head forward, their lips connecting. Excitement and fear coursed through Jace's body like a bolt of lightning. Her lips were tender and moist, even better than he had imagined. Jace cupped the back of her neck and gently held her cheek with his other hand. His fears subsided; he felt her lips welcoming his, matching his passion with hers. He wanted her and would forever long for her body from that kiss on.

The guard knocked twice, sending a shockwave between them. They both stood looking at the door. The Queen Mother entered with her mother. The two appeared very pleased with themselves.

"Pardon us, Queen Sealyn, but you're needed for your market meeting with Lord Jdru and Lord Char. My apologies, Lord Jace." Graelynd nodded.

Loathing her two cousins for finally being on time for a meeting, Sealyn shook her head. "I completely forgot about that meeting." She turned to Jace. "Forgive me, but I must go. I've put them off far too long."

"Don't worry about anything. We'll make sure Lord Jace is taken care of," said Grand Queen Karis.

Watching Sealyn exit, Jace's head spun with thoughts of what had just transpired. He had crossed into risky territory. Sealyn was the queen! What was he doing? She was looking for a king, not a nobody from her enemy kingdom. But he wasn't her enemy anymore. He was now part of Elysian society—a lord even. Would she choose him to be king? If he became King of Elysium, did that mean he would be an enemy to his family? Could he fight against his mother? These questions plagued Jace, but all fears melted when his lips remembered that kiss.

I had the same dream again.
Feathers. Always feathers.
What could feathers possibly mean?
When the feathers part, I'm standing in
a pool of blood, a place I'm unfamiliar
with, whose blood I cannot tell.
Bodies lay scattered. My heart aches.
Rage builds up inside me.
He's stolen. But who? And who
stole this person who could make my heart
feel ripped out? I awoke from a
screeching sound. Why feathers?


Queen Sealyn Araelien
Diary Entry 249

# Chapter 12

# THE MORNING AFTER

Drystan paced aggressively outside the palace stairs. Today's sunshine felt like a poison eating at his flesh.

"Oh, Lord Drystan, how kind of you to be so patient waiting on us," Corentine said.

Drystan snarled. "I was not expecting so many of you."

Corentine descended the stairs with her entire family, except Jace, whose new manor they were touring today. Corentine requested Drystan for their escort. He helped load the family into the royal guest carriages and climbed into the carriage with Corentine, Prince Svagon, and the young Prince Tahbert. In the lead carriage were Queen Phyre, Lord Prince Haedon, and Lady Anabeth—Corentine's older sister, whose twin did not attend, accompanied by one of Stoltland's royal guards.

"Tell me, Lord Drystan, have you been to Cerise Manor before?" Corentine narrowed her dark eyes like a spider observing a bug caught in its web.

"Yes, but not for visiting. I helped with the harvesting of the fields. The previous owner passed away a few years back. His unmarried daughter was going to sell the estate to Lady Pyry's father, but unfortunately, she died in a caelidon riding accident before the documents could be signed. She was quite the daring girl. She mastered riding the auraeon and the nomosev, but the caelidons are a different beast."

"What's the difference?" Svagon asked.

"All the flying horses have wide wings, but the caelidons are special because their manes and tails are feathers, not hair. The auraeons have feathered manes but not tails, while the nomoseves possess the opposite: tails of feathers and manes of hair. With the most feathers and the largest wings, the caelidons are the most dangerous of the winged horses to ride because they can fly at exceptional speeds, and their turns are extremely sharp."

Seeing an opening, Corentine said, "Well, that sounds exciting, so your future father-in-law did not receive the land?"

"No, the land fell into the palace's possession. This only happened a few months ago. The palace hired more help for those who needed more earnings."

Corentine tilted her head. "Are you in need of more earnings?"

"I want to provide for my wife the lifestyle she's accustomed to enjoying. Cerise Manor and the lands would have ensured that." Drystan clinched his jaw and tightened his fist. He was tired of Corentine's games.

The manor guards opened the tall, dark iron gates for the carriages. The royal family peered out of the windows, taking in the sights of Cerise Manor. The entry road was made of square ashen stones forming a round circle. Inside the stone circle stood an enchanting alabaster statue of two caelidons on their hind legs, engaged in a fight with their wings spread wide. Perfectly trimmed verdant grass surrounded the powerful statue, yet nothing could overshadow the breathtaking red brick manor. It rose three stories high, with glorious chimneys towering at each corner. At each end, protruding octagonal villa towers featured dark green roofing.

The Stoltlanders walked through the white limestone door frame, but before they entered, Corentine turned to face Drystan. She made him stop. "How do you feel now, Lord Drystan?"

"What do you mean?"

"I mean, how do you feel about this property being handed to your enemy, and not just any enemy—an unfit, silver-eyed child?" She looked at him from head to toe, then snapped back around.

Envy and anger surged within Drystan. He despised Stoltlanders, particularly Corentine, but now Jace had ascended to the top of that list.

"Greetings, family, and welcome to Cerise Manor," Jace said nervously. "How was your ride over?" This was the moment he had been waiting for his entire life: the moment his family could finally see him as a valuable member, maybe even an equal.

"Splendid, darling, just splendid." Phyre embraced Jace, an oddity that hadn't happened in his lifetime.

Jace's eagerness flooded his heart. It was working. He looked at Corentine. "What do you think of the manor, Mother?"

"It's nice, son." Corentine looked around the room, squinting. "Our palace, though, is probably three times this size. Wouldn't you agree, Svagon?"

"I'm sure you're right, my love."

Anger and sadness welled up inside Jace. Three times this size? Did she really need to point that out? Jace finally had something of his own; he was finally employed and given a title! How could she dismiss how much this manor truly meant to him? Her pride blinded her to where she could no longer see his feelings, and his heart broke.

Plowing through the disappointment, Jace placed his hand on Zed's shoulder. "Allow me to introduce the butler, Zed. He's been a terrific help. I would be lost without him." Zed blushed.

"Well, of course, Jace—what do you expect slaves, I mean, servants to do? They help. He's doing what he's paid to do." Corentine huffed and shook her head. "Butler, we need some refreshments." She waved her hand, expecting complete control.

Zed looked at Jace for confirmation, and Corentine screeched, "How dare you, peasant! How dare you not take my word! You look to a child for your orders?!" She stomped toward Zed and grabbed his uniform. "I commanded; therefore, you fetch what I desire. That is how royals and servants work!" Zed's sage eyes filled with tears, and he fled the room toward the kitchen.

"Mother!" Jace yelled. "Why would you do such a thing? He meant no disrespect."

Corentine gasped. "I can't believe you're going to take that tone with me after we cleared our schedule to come see your fancy new home. Who do you think you are now?" She pointed her short, skinny finger at Jace, nails beginning to blacken.

"I'm sorry, mother. I'm not meaning to be disrespectful, but speaking that way to Zed or any other staff member can't happen."

Banging her cane, Phyre shouted, "Stop this nonsense at once. Corentine, you need to shut your trap. We're still on Elysian land. Don't invite trouble to our door."

"Perhaps a walk about the gardens would help clear the air?" Anabeth suggested dreamily, as her hands floated through the air, trying to catch invisible pixies. She had obviously sniffed more mushroom powder, her glassy eyes looking far away.

Drystan listened from across the room, trying to contain his emotions. This wasn't right. How could Sealyn hand Jace this property? The manor should be his. It should be him hosting guests, not some gray-eyed outsider. He could see the family discord. He almost felt vindicated that Jace was a misfit among his own flesh and blood.

After staying up all night, Drystan formulated a plan, ensuring he would play his part perfectly; tonight had to be successful. He had plotted and practiced over and over each scene he would encounter. Today's visit to Cerise Manor made him all the more motivated. No mistakes could be made, and once done, turning back would not be an option.

Elegant tables were arranged in front of the old Crystal Fort, and Sakul had several fires lit in large copper cauldrons around the rehearsal party. Musicians strummed some Elysian favorites, providing a special treat for all guests.

Drystan felt sick, but he couldn't appear suspicious. He had to be hospitable and present, not dwelling on his other challenge. Drystan needed to ensure he was seen by every guest at the party and that they overindulged in ale. He instructed the serving Nichts never to let a glass go empty. His horse was saddled in the old stable, nibbling on a small amount of hay to keep him quiet. Everything was in place.

The guests enjoyed their dinner and drinks. Red and orange sparks from the fires danced in the air. Drystan slithered his way to each group of guests, patting backs, shaking hands, clanging ales with friends, hugging the ladies, and complimsanting the royals as much as he could. He knew that King Father Ryker and Queen Mother Graelynd would not be easily fooled, so he had to do the only thing he could to distract Ryker.

"My king, please, *please* tell us all again of your battle at Calenburg!" Drystan begged loudly. The crowd near him cheered.

Ryker gestured to silence the cheers. He loved telling this story. "Okay, okay." He paused for dramatic effect. "We were outnumbered by at least five hundred," he said with an exhilarating tone.

"Five hundred? I thought last time you said three hundred?" Favien jeered, spilling some of his ale.

"You weren't there, young pup, and tonight it's five hundred!" They all laughed and clapped their goblets together. "There we were, seven hundred short to theirs, and we crawled on our bellies like snakes through mud and briars…"

Drystan slowly backed away until he was near the food tables. He told the Nichts three different stories that would provide him with plenty of time to race to the palace and back. If someone tried to question him about one, he had the other white lies to rely on. Being a childhood playmate of Sealyn, Drystan knew the palace well, so entering and finding the room he needed wouldn't be any trouble. He saw his moment. No one was watching, so why did he feel like there was still a set of eyes on him? Maybe he was just being paranoid. This was it, now or never.

Drystan took off sprinting at adrenaline-charged speeds. He jumped onto his trusty horse and sped toward the palace. Without looking back, he dared to change his circumstances and was doing it on his own terms. He didn't need to abide by Elysium's rules. He discovered another avenue, a quicker path to the life he desired. Tonight, he would make that abomination, that silver-eyed dog, regret ever having come to his kingdom.

The morning-after breakfast was always an awkward affair for everyone attending. Elysium's custom for weddings involved a day of recovery between the rehearsal dinner and the actual wedding day. This day was particularly important for the bride and groom to reflect on their decision one last time; meanwhile, the guests were to recount the dinner events of the previous evening.

The morning-after breakfast became a tradition when Princess Vree was set to marry Lord Marrun in 3182. The wedding party woke the next day only to find Lord Marrun in bed with Princess Vree's sister; the kingdom still doesn't speak her name. Turns out, Lord Marrun was having an affair not only with the sister princess but also with three maids, the barmaid, the palace seamstress, the gardener, and the butler. It was a debacle for the ages. Truths came out over many poured ales, and apparently, the herbal healer had suspicions about the seamstress since he saw the lord going into the shop several times throughout the week, so he took it upon himself to put a few drops of truth elixir in the rehearsal dinner wines.

When the aftereffects wore off, everyone gathered for breakfast, recounting the rumors they had all heard. A screeching, jealous maid ran into the breakfast hall, closely followed by the princess sister, who wore only sheets, and was pursued by the naked lord, who managed to grab only small pillows to conceal his bulging areas. Every secret was exposed that night, some so serious that battles broke out. The king immediately banned the production of truth elixir; even though he was grateful to the healer for revealing the scandal, it also brought shame to his house.

This is why the Elysian people call it "the morning-after breakfast." Many people actually looked forward to it just for the drama. Drystan, however, had planned a father-son outing of hunting and fishing. He would avoid that breakfast like the plague. Normally, a cart wouldn't be taken on such an outing, but Drystan hired a year-one swordsman to accompany them while he had his horse haul the cart. He had already fabricated the cart's wheel, so he could easily pull one pin loose. Then the wheel would come apart, leaving them stranded for hours; thus, avoiding the scandalous chatter.

The first round of Tomato Fury was over, and the tart tomato and refreshing celery juice combo had done its job of alleviating everyone's hangovers. As the second course of Hircus Delight and Puffin Pies was served, the guests at Pyry's house began to share their tales of the evening. Pyry appeared on edge, swiftly moving to each group, ensuring she did not uncover anything scandalous. She reminded Sealyn of a tree frog hopping from leaf to leaf.

"Lady Brenna. Lady Lulana. Lady Adalina. Good morning to you all," Pyry greeted. "Tell me, how was your evening?"

Fitting snugly in her pale blueish-green gown, Lulana said, "I had a delightful time. One of the best nights I've had in a while, to be honest." Her light brown hair was neatly combed and trimmed just below her chin, a style she was attempting to make fashionable but was failing miserably.

"I must agree with Lulana," Brenna said quietly. "The music was my favorite." Brenna fidgeted with the short sleeves of her dark green dress. She always preferred darker colors, even though they made her look extremely pale. She wore her snowy blonde hair in two braids, cascading over her shoulders.

Adalina batted her almond-shaped, jade eyes. "You already know I had a good time, but I'm concerned. You look so worried, Pyry. Did you hear something?"

This piqued all three ladies' interests, the major gossipers of the group.

"Oh, Creation, no. I've only heard good stories. Drystan was so amazing last night. He even surprised me with this matching necklace and bracelet. Look at how they sparkle!"

Pyry held out her wrist adorned with a dazzling diamond bracelet and glided her fingers down the length of the necklace. They noticed something peculiar about the jewelry. The necklace was studded with numerous diamonds, but nestled between them were tiny dark gems that appeared black. No jeweler in all of Elysium made or sold black gems. The neighboring exporters would not even attempt to sell jewelry featuring those stones to Elysium. Black was Stoltland's color, and no one wanted to wear the colors of Stoltland.

"Is that a black gem?" Adalina asked fearfully. She tucked a small piece of her raven-black hair behind her ear, trying not to panic. She knew about jewelry, and that was, without a doubt, an onyx stone.

"Of course not, silly. Drystan said it's a dark green stone. One of the rarest in the lands," Pyry bragged with a twirl.

Pyry left the ladies and approached the next group, but her friends exchanged glances, their Elysian eyes filled with disagreement. They knew there was no dark green gem that appeared that dark; Drystan had lied, but why? And how did Drystan acquire jewelry with black gemstones?

Pinx and Sorcha happened to overhear what Pyry conveyed. They both looked at each other with fear. Could this be a sign that Drystan had dealings with Stoltland to afford such lavish jewelry with blackened gemstones? They needed to tell Sealyn.

Jace and Finn gulped down their second Hircus Delight with mixed feelings.

"Do you know what's in this drink?" Finn asked Jace.

"I don't."

From behind Jace, Sakul answered, "It's made from hircus milk, corn starch, purple salt, and cinnamon."

Jace looked confused. "What's a hircus?"

A smile bloomed on Sakul's ebony face. "Sometimes I forget we have creatures here that Stoltland doesn't. A hircus is similar to a goat, but instead of one set of horns, a hircus has two. One set grows at the top of the head, facing behind him." Sakul gestured with his hands on top of his head. "And the other set grows below its ears, curving below the jawline. Almost all are solid black with one thick purple stripe down their back and purple hair to cover the black hooves. They say that the milk from the hircus has healing powers, which is why the milk is used to cure hangovers."

"I've seen those over at Tybalt's farm, correct?" Finn gulped down more Hircus Delight, feeling the healing effects on his headache.

"Yes." Sakul wiped a milk mustache with the back of his hand. "His family has been raising them for hundreds of years. They also herd the capras, but make sure you never drink the capra's milk," Sakul warned.

"Why?" Jace asked.

"Their milk is poisonous to humans, but can heal every other creature in all seven kingdoms! No one knows why. I hate looking at them. They look possessed. They have solid white fur with icy eyes and spikes running down their spines with horns protruding forward." Sakul took a bite of Puffin Pie and swallowed, eager to change the subject. "How did you two enjoy your first Elysian rehearsal dinner?"

Lord Finn shrugged. "It was okay, I guess. I was expecting more theatrics since we grew up hearing the stories of Princess Vree."

Jace folded his arms, not wanting to tell them this was the first wedding festivities he attended as a guest. We had snuck under tables, plenty, and watched, but never as a proper invite. "I found it fun. Although I did hear something odd." He lowered his voice. "One of the long-distance Nichts told King Ryker that he saw Lord Drystan heading to the palace in a fury, not sure why. Is that strange?"

"Perhaps he had to check in with the guards?" Finn suggested.

Sakul loved a good murder mystery. When he wasn't planning a party, he tucked himself into a cozy nook at Mimby's Morsels and read thrilling novels. If he were about to live out a real-life mystery, he wanted in, so he couldn't help but offer wood to the fire. "Or perhaps he stole something."

Sakul didn't think Drystan stole from the palace, but he was too busy creating a story worth telling. He looked around, hoping to lure others into the scandal. He gestured to Sorcha, who was briskly walking with Pinx.

Lady Sorcha's dark, tight curls seemed to bounce extra as she hurried over. "Lord Sakul, I don't mean to be rude, but can this wait?"

"No, woman! Anything I have to say is always important." Sakul grinned, enjoying his teasing. "We just need a moment."

Sorcha rolled her jade eyes and folded her smooth brown arms, which Sakul found himself staring at. "Fine. Speak."

Sakul rubbed his hands together. "We heard that Drystan was riding at high speeds to the palace last night." Pinx and

Sorcha looked at each other. "Jace heard it from one of the guards telling King Ryker. Have you ladies heard anything odd about Drystan? Was anything stolen from the palace?"

Pinx stuttered. "Well, we overheard Pyry telling others that Drystan gave her jewelry."

"Jewelry? So what? That's the least interesting thing a future spouse could give to a bride." Sakul folded his arms, irritated that his amazing story was about to fizzle.

Sorcha put her hands on her hips. "This jewelry has black stones. Drystan lied and said the stones were dark green, but we all know there's no such thing. They're black gems, Sakul. Black."

Sakul's stomach dropped. All his fantasizing about solving mysteries halted. This wasn't a book; this was happening right in front of them. Drystan gave forbidden jewelry to his future wife. His possession of black stones meant only one thing—bribery.

The next course of sausages, fish, and fruits, served with freshly squeezed orange and pineapple juice, arrived with extreme yearning. Pyry's breakfast hall was a large square room with two windows facing outside, and on the opposite wall stood a white brick fireplace. A simple painting of pale green, white, and gray brush strokes hung above the mantel. The walls were covered in light-yellow fabric featuring tiny green leaves embroidered in a neat pattern of rows. There were no chairs in the room, just the large table displaying food for people to help themselves.

Sealyn was engaged in a comedic rendition of her father's famous story from Favien when they spotted Drystan finally entering the room, covered in sweat and mud. He motioned for Pyry to step outside with him. Favien scratched his neatly trimmed beard nervously. Something was wrong.

Sakul, Sorcha, and Pinx rushed to Sealyn. Pinx put her hand on Sealyn's arm. "Queen Sealyn, we need to speak with you urgently."

"Please, tell me. It's okay to talk in front of Favien."

Sorcha whispered, "Sealyn, we heard that Drystan gave Pyry jewelry with black stones."

"And he was seen riding like the wind toward the palace last night, too," added Sakul.

"What do you think this means?" Pinx asked.

Pyry entered the breakfast room without Drystan. She looked flushed and frustrated, not like a gushing bride.

"I have a hunch, but I think we are close to finding out," Sealyn said.

Pyry clapped her hands. "May I have everyone's attention, please?" "My beloved fiancé faced a tragic wheel-breaking accident while out hunting with his father. He asked for your forgiveness for not being here for breakfast, and thanks you all for coming. Sadly, I ask that this breakfast come to an end, though."

Sealyn wasn't convinced of this show and slowly walked toward the door.

Lady Pyry's father raised his glass and asked, "What say you, Bride?" Everyone raised their glasses with him.

"I say yes to the groom!" Pyry giggled with excitement.

The room echoed with cheering. While everyone was congratulating her, Sealyn slipped out the door and hurried down the hall to the outdoor hunting shed, where she knew Drystan must have gone to drop his boots and gear. Jace saw and quickly followed.

"A cart on a hunting expedition. My, my. This day is full of surprises," Sealyn said incredulously.

Sitting on the mudroom bench, Drystan finished untying his muddy boot and pulled it off. He looked up and glared. "Your Majesty, you shouldn't be out here." He continued untying the other boot.

"Why? Is there a plot of land in my kingdom that's out of bounds for the queen?"

Drystan rolled his eyes and tossed his other boot, wiping his hands on his trousers. "My apologies. I wasn't suggesting anything of the sort."

"I'm sure not." Sealyn folded her arms, angry that her childhood friend was acting so distant. "Now, tell me why you would take a cart on a hunting expedition the same day as your morning-after breakfast?"

Jace hung in the shadows, listening to the conversation. He hoped Sealyn knew what she was doing.

Drystan stood, hands on his hips. "I'm sure you're not implying anything scandalous occurred on a hunting trip. I packed meals as a surprise for my father. Honestly, Sealyn. What is this?"

She ignored his question. "You couldn't have packed that in your saddlebags, especially with the extra rider? I'm sure all the excess food could have fit in Sir Oren's saddlebags." She tilted her head.

"How did you know Sir Oren was with us?"

"Drystan, I know the movements of all my men, especially the young and impressionable ones."

"Listen, Sealyn, or should I say, Your Majesty? I didn't do anything wrong. We just broke a wheel and had to fix it. I tried pushing the cart for a bit, which is why I'm covered in mud, but luckily, Oren is a fast rider and could make it back in good time to bring us another pin."

Sealyn processed his words quickly. "Those pins are almost melted to the wheels. I'm surprised it just…fell out."

Drystan stepped forward, closing the space between him and Sealyn, but Jace came out of the shadows and stood behind the queen. "Ah, I see. Hired a new guard dog, did you?"

"How dare you!" Sealyn snapped, pointing her finger at Drystan. "You realize I can throw you in prison for such insults."

"Insults that weren't aimed at you, My Queen."

"It's fine, Queen Sealyn. Perhaps we should leave the groom to clean himself. No bride wants to marry something that dirty," Jace baited.

Drystan reared back his fist, ready to punch Jace, but he saw Sealyn's face daring him to try. If he started another fight, then she would have the ground to throw him in the dungeons for months, which would completely ruin all his plans. He lowered his arm and bowed to the queen.

"Your Majesty, I ask you to grant me leave from your presence so I may prepare for the signing of the marriage scrolls."

Sealyn nodded, and Drystan walked past them, slightly knocking Jace's left shoulder.

"Are you okay, Queen Sealyn?" Jace asked anxiously, placing his hand on her lower back.

Sealyn tried not to think about the touch of Jace's hand. She wanted to wrap herself in his arms, but her duties begged her to stay focused. "Of course, but something is telling me Drystan isn't in his right frame of mind. I sense a bad spirit around him." Was it the curse?

"Perhaps the others may know more. Your Vinurs are gathering at *Nijeel's Choice* for more talks. Why don't we go?"

Sealyn turned around and faced him. "A great plan, but, Jace…" She grabbed his hands. "They're your friends now, too, not just mine."

# Chapter 13

# THE SECRET MEETING

The queen's Vinurs of the Court gathered at the tables outside Nijeel's Choice. They clustered the round tables together so they could chat privately. Sealyn felt relieved to join her companions.

Sorcha spoke with concern, "Queen Sealyn, did you happen to leave the breakfast to speak with Drystan?"

Sealyn hesitated. "I did, but as suspected, he dodged questions and aimed to insult Lord Jace."

Once Nijeel noticed the queen seated at his tables, he hurried to serve her. He brushed his curly red beard and swept off his apron, which had plenty of old coffee stains. "My Queen, how may I serve you? I had no idea your magnanimous presence would be with us today."

Sealyn smiled. "Oh, Nijeel. No need to make such a fuss, but I would love a fresh cup of coffee if you don't mind. Thank you."

"Right away, Your Majesty. Right away!"

Char raised his cup. "Uh, Nijeel. Might I trouble you for a fresh cup too?"

"My apologies, Lord Char. I'm much too busy."

Char's mouth gaped. "But you just asked Sealyn!"

"I asked the *queen*, Lord Char. You can place your order inside!"

Char huffed. "But you're coming right back here with Queen Sealyn's order!"

Nijeel pointed to his shop and hurried away. Char's mouth hung open as he looked at his friends for validation, only to be met with laughter.

"Guess you have to be the queen to get good service around here," grumbled Char.

Sealyn laughed. "It has its perks." She winked.

They discussed the strange coincidences of Drystan's movements throughout the week and during the rehearsal dinner. Sealyn even recounted her misgivings about his morning hunt with the cart and how she approached him afterward. Everyone agreed that none of Drystan's actions seemed normal. They were the actions of a man with a secret, not the Drystan they had grown up with.

Sealyn kept the conversation she had with Maekel about what Corentine said to herself for fear of Jace. She was extremely concerned that somehow Corentine and Drystan were involved in a scheme, so sharing this news could potentially cause a problem between her and Jace. She wasn't ready to face that kind of trial yet.

After Nijeel finished serving Sealyn, she decided she needed to calm her friends' fears. After all, her friends were still her subjects and deserved respect.

"My dear friends. I want to assure you that your concerns have been heard and understood. I will address Drystan again with all the evidence once the wedding is over. I don't think it would be fair to Lady Pyry for me to accuse her groom of treason the day before the wedding, especially if the rumors aren't true."

"I agree," said Brenna.

"So do I." Jashun eyed Brenna with a flirtatious grin.

"Is it wrong, though, that he would then be linked to Lady Pyry's fortune and be a potential traitor?" Adalina inquired.

Norella brushed back her long hair. "Would it not be in Lady Pyry's best interest to contractually prevent him from being able to steal away her fortune if he is a traitor?"

Sealyn nodded. "There's the traitor's clause. It's written at the bottom of every marriage and business contract. The clause has been there for hundreds of years. If you're found guilty of treason, all assets will fall to a family member chosen by the current crown, and if the crown can find no innocent blood ties available, then the crown will decide either to keep the assets or give them to another bloodline that has earned it."

Doebromir set his cup down. "Queen Sealyn, does that mean you could decide not to give the assets back to Pyry if Drystan were found guilty?"

"It does." She observed the realization in her friends' eyes of just how powerful their childhood playmate had become. She sighed. "The crown may have perks…" She elbowed Char. "But the responsibility is substantial. Let's remind ourselves that this is hypothetical and still be happy for both of them tomorrow. And if you could, please don't remind Drystan of the traitor's clause or anyone close to him."

The wedding day of Pyry and Drystan finally arrived. The weather was perfect, even though it was slightly warmer than Pyry had wished. Hueweyn and Sakul were putting the final touches on the white fire flowers, while Adalina was busy directing Nichts on where to place the candles. In the center courtyard, round tables covered with white cloth were adorned with bright pink, teal, and yellow flowers, featuring a large white candle in the middle. At each place setting, Pyry chose to use her family's china. Each plate was stamped with a silver merchant ship flying three sails, with the middle sail imprinted with the family K.

The old Crystal Fort was not made of crystal. It was named for its first mission: protecting Princess Crystal. During the Battle of the Red Stars, Stoltland broke through the second line of the capital's defenses, which triggered the escape plan of the king and queen along with their children, except for the next in line—Princess Crystal. They devised a plan for all royal members to escape to Briar Mountain Fort, while Princess Crystal would flee with her chambermaids to Broad Stone Fort.

The royal family was ambushed along the journey to Briar Mountain Fort, and the Stoltlanders slaughtered each one, including the children. They left one guard alive to inform the city of what had happened. Stoltland believed the royal family was finished, so they returned to their ships to celebrate and take over the Elysian palace in the morning. When Princess Crystal heard the news, she rallied the remaining troops to avenge her family's deaths by setting the ships on fire while the Stoltlanders were too drunk to save themselves. Those who escaped the ships were captured and held for ransom.

Stoltland did not want to pay the high ransom, but their pride compelled them to do so. This ransom provided Queen Crystal with a new army and facilitated the reconstruction of the capital, hence the appropriate name change from the Broad Stone Fort to the Crystal Fort.

Lady Corentine could hear the musicians practicing their cheery tunes, irritating slugs. These ridiculous sounds annoyed her. Corentine gulped down her second glass of wine, trying to drown out the Elysium zeal. She was so close to achieving her goal. Frustrated, she crumpled the invitation from the young queen and threw it in the fire. She didn't want to attend another brunch with that entitled brat. Corentine wanted to solve the clue and be done; however, Drystan had ensured that wouldn't happen until after his wedding—selfish pig.

He had ripped the clue in half. She didn't think the troll was that smart, but what do frantic, insecure people do? They surprise you with desperate attempts to secure their future. Drystan did the only thing he could do to safeguard the Stoltlanders, not to leave without paying him. She read again the thick parchment:

"Never the Same.

Forever Still.

F"

What did these words mean? How was she supposed to know these answers? Rage bubbled from below. As a scream of frustration came out, her husband came rushing in.

"My dear, are you well?"

"No! I've been reading these stupid words for two days, and we're no closer to solving it." She slammed the wine bottle down after refilling her glass. "What have you been doing to solve it?"

Svagon stuttered. "Well, I've been talking it through with Haedon."

"Haedon? Seriously? And what did the great Lord Prince Haedon have to say?" she mocked.

"Haedon has good ideas, Corentine. He suggested the rivers."

Corentine straightened, her head dizzy slightly. "Rivers?"

"Yes, because rivers are never the same."

"But rivers are not still."

"Correct, but perhaps there's a still river in Elysium. They have many mystical landmarks here. They wouldn't believe we have a waterfall of fire, but I have the burns to prove it."

Corentine's eyes twitched. "Perhaps you're right. We should investigate as many of their water resources as potential possibilities. We don't have much time. I will send out Keket, Haedon, and Anabeth to discuss the water resources in the market. I'm sure someone will slip up with the details." She strummed her fingers against the goblet. "And regardless, Drystan will give us the rest of the clue. The curse is taking over him." Corentine let out a wicked laugh. She had waited years for Elysium's undoing. It was almost here.

"His envy will be the beginning of Elysium's collapse," snickered Haedon.

"When did you walk in?" his father asked.

"Long enough to know my part in the market. I'll be off now." Haedon snatched the bottle of wine.

Jace was overwhelmed by the food buffet, wondering how Sakul was so creative. The foods were made into sculptures of creatures and landscapes. His mouth salivated at the juicy pineapples, but he refrained from taking a piece since the display perfectly portrayed three upright galloping horses. Pineapples made the bodies, and strips of long carrots created the manes and tails, while the hooves were massive strawberries. Several blackberries created fierce-looking eyes to the point where Jace felt like they were actually looking at him.

"My son," cooed Corentine.

"Hello, Mother. Are you enjoying yourself?"

"Sure. I just wish there was some normalcy to this place. Foods don't have to be so dramatic." She took a toothpick and stabbed one of the horse's blackberry eyes. "Look, my darling boy, we are leaving in the morning, and I wanted to get some time with you tonight to discuss a few things."

She was being kind. She wanted something. "Tonight? Mother, we're at a wedding. I don't think this is the time or place to have discussions."

A scowl crinkled her face. "You will do as I ask, or do you not care about your family anymore? Have you forgotten who clothed you and fed you all these years? Who is the only person who loves you?"

"You, Mother. I just don't want to be rude and wanted to..." Jace paused and looked over at Sealyn's table.

"Ah, I see. You think you could have some precious time with the queen tonight, didn't you? She will be much too busy tonight for someone like you, so put aside your boyish ganders and act like my son. I will send Keket to you when we are ready."

Corentine stomped off, and with each step, her words echoed in Jace's ears. "Someone like you." Why did his mother think so little of him? He had to remind himself that she didn't know about the intoxicating kiss he and Sealyn had already shared. That kiss would serve as his constant reminder that perhaps one person in this world valued him. He dreaded what the family discussion might entail.

Sealyn and Pyry twirled around each other on the dance floor, laughing and singing along to the songs. The Vinurs glided smoothly across the polished marble, perfectly bouncing to the song's rhythms. Norella and Pinx excelled at dancing, which naturally challenged Char and Sakul, who viewed themselves as elite dancers.

Seeing Drystan and Pyry happily dancing together, Sealyn looked for Jace but couldn't find him. Her heart ached to dance with him again. Where could he be? She sat alone at her table, watching the crowd of guests enjoy themselves.

Taking the chair beside the queen, the faith commissioner, Herb said softly, "Fear not, My Queen. For it will be your turn soon."

Queen Sealyn gave a half smile. "Herb, do you really believe that?"

"I do. I can see how much you desire what they possess, but I believe you will attain something greater. There's a feeling about you, Queen Sealyn. One that instills fear in me, but also excitement and peace. To endure those emotions simultaneously, you need a partner who is weak where you are strong but strong where you are weak."

"Weak? You think your queen is weak?" Sealyn teased.

A toothy grin flashed across his ebony face. "My Queen, royalty cannot intimidate the truth from being spoken." He winked. "Perhaps we have not yet discovered your weakness. We all know an Elysian's weakness, of course, but we do not know your personal one. Here's the beauty: your future king will not only be the anchor during your storms, but he will also be your fight when your hope is lost."

Tears welled up in Sealyn's eyes. All she could do was hold Herb's hand and nod. She adored him; he had been a mentor to her since she was a young child. He bowed his shiny bald head and moved toward the dance floor. He always knew how to make her feel special. She laughed at his toothy smile, which shone extra bright tonight against his dark brown skin. She was surprised by how great a dancer he still was, even after the horrible wagon accident that damaged his hip.

Movement caught Sealyn's attention. She watched Drystan heading down the long, unlit arcade opposite the wedding festivities. Well, if that wasn't suspicious, then she apparently didn't understand the word. She motioned for Maekel to join her.

"Yes, Your Majesty?" Maekel said as she bowed.

"Maekel, I need you to follow Drystan. He just went down the arcade over there." Sealyn pointed her finger toward the darkness.

"Right aways, Your Majesty."

Drystan approached the dark ruins of the ancient Crystal Fort with hesitation. He hated agreeing to meet Corentine during his wedding reception. He knew it was a power play by her. He was surprised to see Jace among the Stoltlanders. Why would she include the son she obviously resents? Could Jace be part of some scheme? Of course! Corentine wanted Jace to win Sealyn's affections; to keep her attention while they steal the Heart of Elysium. Jace was a trickster— unworthy of Sealyn's flirtations, unworthy of that giant manor. He vowed to kill Jace before he died. For now, he would remain silent about the agreement between him and Corentine in front of Jace.

"Well, if it isn't the man of the hour," snarked Haedon.

Drystan glared and raised his arms. "What's this meeting all about? If you haven't noticed, I have my wedding to attend."

A wicked curve formed across Corentine's red lips. "Why, Lord Drystan. There's no need for crudeness. You know we are leaving in the morning, and we merely wanted to offer you a job."

"Job? What job?"

"The job of looking out for our sweet Jace." "We only want his protection in this foreign land. A land that is still considered his enemy." She cupped Jace's cheek.

Jace and Drystan scowled at each other. Neither of them wanted help from the other. Jace knew this was a lie. His mother didn't care to protect; she cared to control. Was Drystan to spy on him? His mother must want to know his advances with Queen Sealyn. This wasn't good.

"What an honor it would be to protect your young son, Corentine," Drystan smugly said.

"I don't need a watchdog," grumbled Jace.

"I am no dog! You silver-eyed freak!"

"Easy, boys." Corentine intervened. "Allow me to offer some sweetness to the pie. I'm prepared to offer Lord Drystan a handsome sum to protect my son from harm since he is choosing to stay in this place. In exchange for this agreement, I will ensure my thousand ships off the east coast of Elysium don't attack. They will return from their posts once they receive word we've left."

"What?! Mother, you have ships on Elysium's coast?" Jace panicked. He searched through his mother's words. Thousand ships? That calculation seemed off. He had never read any reports declaring such a large fleet.

"That's a declaration of war!" shouted Drystan, pointing his finger at Corentine.

"No, that's called proactive thinking. You foolish children," snorted Corentine. "Did you really think I would step foot on Elysium soil without assurances?" She flicked her crimson hair.

"Fine. I'll watch your pathetic child for you."

Jace's heart pounded. If war broke out, whose side was he supposed to fight on—his mother's or Sealyn's? He needed to de-escalate the situation. "Mother, you must send these ships away immediately."

Corentine squeezed Jace's shoulder. "Don't worry, my child. Trust me, no harm will come to your new little friends with Drystan as your guardian. Now, why don't you run along? I need to discuss the procedures of protection with *Lord* Drystan."

Jace hesitated to leave. He feared there was another plan kept secret from him, or was this truly his mother showing that she actually cared about him? After all, he was the one who chose to stay in a land considered his people's enemy. He was the one willing to live far away from her, so why wouldn't she want to find a way to ensure he stayed safe? His heart warmed at the thought. Could she finally see him as part of the family? Jace didn't return to the wedding party. Instead, he walked back to his manor to contemplate his decision: to stay or to return with his mother.

"How could you blindside me like that?!" Drystan hissed.

"Pipe down, you fool! Can't you see that I need a reason for sending you money in case you're caught with extra financials that you can't explain?" Corentine threw her hands up. "Such stupidity. Here's the truth. My son has betrayed me, choosing your self-righteous people over his own family. I will break him eventually, so in the meantime, I need that final piece of the clue from you."

"You're not getting it until I see full payment."

"We figured you would say that, so here's how this will go. Since we've learned this clue will potentially lead to a landmark, you will be the one to find the location and extract what we need. We can't do this without you, so money will be your motivation." Corentine nodded to Haedon.

Haedon tossed a sack in front of Drystan. With the loud clanging, there was no mistaking what was inside the bag: betrayal.

"Consider this the payment for the first and second halves of the clue. With each message you send us that has value, we'll send payment in return."

Drystan was cornered, like wolves encircling their prey. He pondered over her plan. He was protected at every angle. No one would know.

"Agreed." Drystan shook hands with Svagon.

Fireworks began to explode, covering the night sky in sparkles of greens and blues. This signaled the end of the wedding, and he needed to get back.

"I must return. I'm needed for the final dance."

"Not until you give us what we came for," snarled Haedon. He cracked his knuckles, ready for a fight.

"Pay up, Drystan. You either want a better life or not," Corentine ordered.

Drystan hung his head low and spoke the treasonous words, "Fall into Blue. Four will tell."

Have you ever been betrayed by a friend? I feel it now. I feel the pain and rejection. A friend choosing envy over your offer of pure friendship. How does this happen? How can jealousy be this powerful? It infects. It takes root and festers. It's a poison you willingly swallow. You can choose a different path, but if you choose envy, your path will be empty and bitter. Fight against this curse. Fight against the darkness of old.

Queen Sealyn Araelien
Diary Entry 325

Grand Queen
Karis Dovinus

# Chapter 14

When Maekel returned, the guards prevented Maekel from entering Sealyn's bedchamber, stating that the queen had ordered not to be disturbed until morning. Maekel was uncertain about what to do with the information she possessed. She blamed her slow flying for not arriving before Sealyn left.

Treason, betrayal, war, and corruption were all part of the Stoltlanders' conversation with Drystan and Jace. If the queen was not to be disturbed, then she needed to speak to the next best person: the king.

In his bedchamber, King Ryker sat comfortably in his favorite brown leather chair, reading *The Spies of King Saven Dovinus*. The fire was dying in the limestone fireplace but still provided enough warmth that he didn't need his blanket yet. The Queen Mother was busy in her dressing room, changing into her nightsleeps with the help of her Nicht,

Rayn. The king's skinny, brown-headed Nicht, Trey, was tidying up the king's personal desk when he heard the knock at the Nicht's door.

"Maekel, what are's you doing here's? Is the queen well?"

"Nothing is wrong's with the queen, but I needs to speaks with the king."

"The king? Can this waits till morning?" he huffed.

"I wishes, but it's too importants, and the guards won't lets me see the queen."

"Fine. Follows me, but if he asks you to leaves, then you leaves fast."

Maekel nodded and flew close behind Trey, fearing to deliver such terrible news. How would the king react? Would war be caused by her words?

"My king, Maekel needs to speaks to you," Trey announced.

"Maekel? Is my daughter safe?" Ryker slammed his book shut.

"The queen is safes and guarded, but they won't lest me tell her what I needs to, so I cames here," she sniffed, feeling the pressure of the secret she held.

"Well then, do tell me this time-sensitive news."

"The Stoltlanders have's thousands of ships on the east coast. Lady Corentine is paying's for secret clues from Lord Drystan, but she's coverings it up by paying Lord Drystan to protects Lord Jace." She paused, making sure she remembered everything. "Oh, and Drystan doesn't likes being called a dog."

Ryker felt a cold chill go down his spine. He couldn't waste another second; betrayal and treachery were at his doorstep. "First, Trey, call in Prince Adomin, Lord Favien, and Lord Doebromir to my chambers, immediately." The king pulled the steward's fabric cord to summon Lord Steward Briar. "Next, I will need you, Maekel, to ensure the Queen Mother stays in her private quarters tonight. She will need her rest."

The Queen Mother's private quarters were separate from the king and queen's bedchamber. Between the two chambers was a large sitting room designated for informal private meetings. The king and queen had their own private quarters for times of sickness or when they needed space. Graelynd's quarter was beautifully decorated with peacock-themed decor. Large white vases filled with bright purple and blue feathers stood on either side of her large dark mahogany bed. Massive tapestries hung on the walls, showcasing the purple and blue peacock, the white peacock, and the green and orange peacock. Her fireplace was made of deep plum marble imported from Glatania. A beautiful family portrait hung above her fireplace. She even had a pet purple and blue peacock named Peppy; Princess Siany named her when she was young.

The king continued, "Make sure the Queen Mother does not feel scared. I do not want her to feel there is a need for panic."

"My king!" Lord Steward Briar came barging through the door. "What can I do for you?" Trey saw his cue and flew to give the orders to the guards.

"Lord Steward, I have several needs for this night. I will organize a meeting with several military staff in here. Please also bring Lady Stewardess Pame to me."

"Right away, my king. Right away!" Lord Steward ran out of the room.

Favien crunched on some almonds and bagels while Doebromir sipped his Hircus Delight, needing the wedding ale to leave his spinning head alone. It was not often they received a late-night summons to the king's bed chambers.

Prince Adomin, eldest brother to Queen Mother Graelynd, lifted his hand. "Well, King Ryker, we're all here. Explain why I'm not in bed with my wife right now."

"Easy, Adomin. We've heard that Stoltland has a thousand ships on our east coast," Ryker informed.

"What?!" exclaimed Doebromir..

"Aw, that's a giant needlebob's turd if I've ever heard one," said Favien. "How do we know this isn't a trick?"

"You're smarter than you look, Favien. We should question this news. From our last scouts' count, Stoltland only processed one hundred ships. That's a far leap to a thousand. Wouldn't you agree, Adomin?"

Adomin adjusted his spectacles and poured himself a cup of coffee. "Quite. We've been prepared for an attack from Stoltland for months. Our scouts and lookouts would've told us." He sipped the steaming liquid, confusion plastered against his face. "What would they gain from lying?"

Ryker nodded. "Excellent question. That's what I want to know. Drystan is involved, and I believe Jace might be as well—maybe not directly."

Favien lifted his hands in protest. "There's no way Jace is involved."

"I agree with Lord Favien. Jace and his mother have a strained relationship. He may be strange, but Jace is a good man. I would vouch for him," Doebromir proudly stated.

Ryker cleared his throat, unsure of Jace's allegiance. "Regardless of your friendships, we must be realistic. Jace is from Stoltland, and his mother is incredibly tenacious with her schemes against Elysium. We must make sure her claims are false. Doebromir, send out your fastest riders to the east. One thousand ships would be hard to miss. Favien, I want twenty of your best men stationed along the route the Stoltlanders will take tomorrow." Ryker slid his finger across the map from Avondelle to the middle coastline of Clarien, Elysium's southwestern territory. "Here is where their ships are docked. Once they are out of sight, set the signal fires."

Lord Steward Briar cleared his throat. "My king, Lady Stewardess Pame is here."

Lady Stewardess bowed. "My king, how can I help?"

"Lady Stewardess, I need you to assist Queen Sealyn tomorrow morning. She will need to be in the war room at sunrise. Please arrange for her breakfast to be set in that room. I will also need urgent notes sent to the captain of her archery unit to meet her in the war room. Please specify in the note that we must ready her top thirty archers for tactical treetop monitoring.”

“Absolutely, Your Majesty. Consider everything done.” The muscular woman dashed out of the room.

Prince Adomin swallowed his coffee. “I believe the last piece of business is to discuss what to do about Lord Drystan.”

Ryker resisted giving orders; he sometimes forgot that the reigning crown was not his to bear. “The queen will decide his fate. For now, we mention to no one what we know. The Nichts are sworn to secrecy as well as the stewards.” Lord Steward nodded his head to the king. “As king, I will say that allowing your enemy to think he has the upper hand is the greatest positioning for the most stunning victory.”

Queen Sealyn sat in her dark green leather military uniform at the round war table, making notes. The giant map of Elysium was pieced together on the surface with figurines representing Doebromir's stallions, Favien's groundlers, Max's archers, and the Stoltland caravans. Lord Max was still new to leading the archers, but Sealyn was pleased with her choice of him. The military lords sat in the other chairs alongside King Ryker and Prince Adomin, each wearing intense expressions.

Doebromir burst through the door. "My queen! My scouts report that there are no ships on the east coast. Not even one."

Sealyn paused. His riders must have ridden through the entire night. She jotted a note to give them a special reward. "So Lady Corentine fed this false data to Drystan and Jace. Why? Does she want us distracted?"

Sealyn was losing patience. Jace's credibility was on the line. She knew his loyalties would be in question, and why shouldn't they be? Why didn't Jace come to her about this plot? Had Jace been a spy this entire time? She shook her head; she had to stay focused on the current task.

Sealyn looked at her bearded friend. "Lord Favien, your groundlers are assembled in the back courtyard, correct?"

"Yes, Your Majesty."

"Good. Lord Max, take ten archers to follow the caravan with the groundlers. Split up into equal groups on either side. Do *not* be seen. The archers will hit the treetop checkpoints and join the monitoring with you all. Again, remain unseen for the entire journey. Once every Stoltlander is on board and ships are sailing, each one of you will walk forward to reveal our numbers. This will be the final declaration that their empty threats do not fall on deaf ears. They will then question whose loyalty wavered: Drystan or Jace."

Her heart fluttered at the mention of his name. Guilt plagued her mind. She despised using his name in the same sentence as Drystan, Drystan the traitor. She had no choice; her people must see that she was loyal to Elysium first. Corentine played her moves well, but Sealyn was already thinking several moves ahead.

"Lord Favien and Lord Max, you have your orders. Please proceed." They bowed and left. "Lord Doebromir, I want fifty more men at the capitol's perimeter. Lord Prince Tilmond, I want twenty of your javelin stallion riders stationed at least three hundred horse lengths between each rider down the Stoltland caravan road. Lord Natildor, send the distance Nichts to inform your ship captains to anchor three ships on either side of the exiting Stoltlander ships." Sealyn peered at the map, eyes darting from city to city. "Gentlemen, do not let your kingdom down. Make sure this mission runs perfectly. Dismissed." She crossed her right fist over her left shoulder, and the others did the same.

The doors closed, echoing in the silence of the war room. Sealyn felt an odd sensation about Drystan and Jace. Something was missing. "The meeting doesn't add up. Are you sure you told me every detail Maekel said?"

Ryker shook his head. "Actually, no. I needed privacy for this next piece. What I'm about to tell you belongs only in the family, and even then, not every member of this family needs to know."

"You believe Uncle Adomin is worthy of such a secret?" Sealyn snidely remarked while grinning.

"Even during trouble, you find your sense of humor," Adomin chuckled.

Ryker leaned over the stone table. "Listen. Maekel whispered to me about the conversation without Jace. Drystand and the Stoltlanders spoke of a clue. She only knows part of the clue, though. Apparently, Drystan gave them the first half before his wedding and held onto the second half as insurance."

"Clue? Clue for what?" Sealyn asked. She was relieved this part had nothing to do with Jace.

Adomin ignored Sealyn's question. "What did she hear?"

"Fall into blue. Four will tell."

"What? What does that mean? And a clue for what?" Sealyn asked again. She quickly scribbled down the words before she forgot them.

"Better yet, what is this clue for?" Adomin winked at Sealyn.

Sealyn cut her eyes to her uncle. "Seriously?" He smiled.

Rising to his feet, Ryker hung his head and placed his hands on his hips. "This has everything to do with the Heart of Elysium."

Ryker slammed shut the empty secret drawer of his private desk. Sealyn knew whatever information her father was about to reveal would change everything.

"It's been stolen!" yelled Ryker. "But how did he know?"

"What was stolen, Father?"

"The first cryptic veil for the Heart of Elysium's location."

Sealyn reminded herself not to react. "Will someone in this room please explain to me what exactly the Heart of Elysium is, and why would clues be involved?"

Ryker hung his head. "My apologies, Sealyn. This is the part of the crown I thought I wouldn't need to discuss with you, especially so soon. The Heart of Elysium is essentially the driving power of the kingdom. Every kingdom has one. The heart must remain here. Elysium will kneel to whoever possesses it."

"Wait!" Sealyn threw up her hand. "Are you saying that the Stoltlanders have a way to find the location of the one thing that could give them total control over Elysium?"

"Yes."

"Then we should stop them at the border! There's still time!" Adomin exclaimed.

"No," Ryker protested. "There's more to this." He looked at Sealyn with apologetic eyes. "Several clues are arranged all over Elysium. No one even knows what the heart of Elysium looks like, or what it is for that matter. The first cryptic veil was passed down to each ruler with the same instructions: keep this envelope hidden to secure Elysium's hope." Ryker sank back in his chair. "I failed. I don't even know what the clue says." He dropped his head into his hands.

"Well, that's not entirely true now, is it?" Sealyn smirked. "We know what the last part of the phrase is." She looked at the blank expressions on her parents' faces and continued. "Fall into blue. Four will tell. I'm also betting I know one person still alive who might know how to help us because she just so happened to have sneaked a peek at that letter."

"What?!" Ryker said.

"Sealyn, please tell us who," Graelynd spoke urgently.

Sealyn chuckled. "Why our nosey ol' birdie: Grand Queen Karis."

"My mother?" Graelynd was shocked.

"Of course, your mother. Grand Queen Karis is the nosiest woman out there." Sealyn paused. "Actually, that's wrong. Father's mother is, but Grand Queen Karis is right behind her. Either way, when I questioned her about the Heart of Elysium, she told me that she had sneaked a peek at a hidden letter when she was newly queen. I didn't understand the meaning of her words because no one had explained to me the veils of concealment." She eyed her father. "During her reign, the battles were getting closer to Avondelle's borders, so she thought the safest action would be to memorize whatever was written and then burn it. However, as we all know, King Saven won the remaining battles of that war. She didn't burn it, but she did see it."

"In that case, I believe we need to visit our dear sweet mother." Adomin nodded to his sister.

Grand Queen Karis and Princess Siany were enjoying the last of the summer fruits when Sealyn, Ryker, Graelynd, and Adomin entered the music hall. The room was long and slightly narrower than the other rooms. On the same wall were three evenly spaced fireplaces. Instruments from across the lands were scattered throughout the room, accompanied by shelves of music books and pages of compositions not yet bound. During this time of day, the palace harpist strummed softly in her favorite corner of the room. Upon seeing the royal family's entrance, the harpist excused herself.

Karis whispered to Siany, "Well, this can't be good with that pack together."

Graelynd took the seat next to Karis on the sapphire velvet couch. "Mother, we need your help with an urgent matter."

The king and the prince sat on the matching couch, seated opposite them, while Sealyn stood.

"By all means, please, tell me how I can assist," Karis encouraged.

"Grand-Ris, can you please share with us the words you read on the parchment hidden in Grandfather's desk?"

Fear scattered across Karis's face as she paled. "Oh, I see. It's come to that. I fear that I don't remember all of it. Only pieces. It wasn't long. Four small phrases." Karis closed her eyes, remembering that terrifying night.

"Grand-Ris, the words we know are 'fall into blue' like the color, or perhaps it is blew like 'the wind blew.' We're not sure, and the last part is 'four will tell.' Again, unsure of the exact word spelling. Could be the number four or f-o-r, for."

Karis drifted back into the memory and winced at the sounds of her people screaming. "It's blue like the color. I specifically remember that part because I thought it strange. Also, the number four. There was something about never staying the same and remaining still." She opened her watery mint eyes.

Siany squeezed her grandmother's hand. "I believe that's enough for one day."

"My apologies," Ryker said with regret. "We didn't mean for you to relive that pain."

"I would rather relive that pain today if it means preventing more pain for our people tomorrow."

Sealyn knelt before Karis, hugging and kissing her with mixed emotions. She hated putting her through that turmoil, but she knew how brave her Grand-Ris was. "Siany, I need you to come with us. It's time to bring in the scholars."
They had to act quickly. The Stoltlanders had the same task of solving the riddle. They were now in a race. Avondelle possessed some of the most brilliant minds in all the kingdoms, so she felt confident they could solve it swiftly.

Prince
Adomin
Dovinus
Prince
Royce
Dovinus

# Chapter 15

# THE BREAKFAST FIREPLACE

The time was mid-morning, and the breakfast room was filled with members of the Council of the Wise and the Council of the Scholars. The queen had given no indication as to why they were there, but they steadily conversed about the possibilities. A lavish brunch was laid out across the table, begging to be eaten.

From the Council of the Wise, Queen Sealyn chose not to invite her mother and grandparents; they needed a break from the distress. Her father would attend this meeting regardless, even though he was considered a member of the Council of the Wise. Three of her uncles were present: Prince Adomin, Prince Royce, and Lord Ryland. The other unrelated members included Lord Stevonten and his wife, Lady Song, along with the faith commissioner, Herb.

Siany was seated opposite her sister. She was in charge of the Council of the Scholars. She organized the seven members, including herself. Pinx focused on education with her teammate Lord Micdoeclaven, or Mic, who made it his life's passion to read every book in the library at least once. Centering her efforts on law, Norella found herself working well with Tilmond since he was in charge of the Stallion Military Unit. The final team was the most brilliant in medicine: Sorcha and Lord Prince Brandle. Siany was confident that with such brainpower in one room, they could solve her sister's task.

Sealyn greeted her guests: "My wise and brilliant friends, thank you for coming on such short notice. I can't give you all the details for what I'm about to share, but everything discussed here must remain here. No one else will be privy to this information. Is this clear and acceptable?" Everyone nodded. "Here's your task: solve the riddle, 'Something that never stays the same but remains still. Fall into blue. Four will tell.' We know the last phrasing, 'fall into blue' and 'four will tell' are the exact words. The first part is paraphrased as accurately as possible, and we have confirmed that 'blue' refers to the color blue and 'four' refers to the number four. I need this solved with haste."

Everyone began writing down the phrases. Some asked for it to be repeated numerous times. Others began to pace the room, murmuring to themselves. Sealyn sat back in her chair to observe. Her mind started drifting. She couldn't help thinking about the letter she sent to Jace.

She had sent Maekel with a letter requesting his presence for a late lunch with a note at the very bottom stating, "Be prepared to discuss your involvement with your private Stoltland meeting at the wedding. Burn this letter."

If he were guilty, Jace would escape, and she would never see him again; however, if he showed up, that would be the hard part: determining whether he was a really good spy or truly innocent.

She longed to kiss him again, and the fire he ignited within her only motivated Sealyn further to uncover the truth. She wanted to either be glued to him or have her heart completely shattered. The unknown was the worst romantic torture she could imagine.

"Water!" shouted Stevonten. "It has to do with water."

"Explain your theory." Tilmond folded his arms, towering at least a foot above everyone in the room.

"Well, with rivers, the water is never the same, and most of our waters are aqua blue," explained Stevonten.

"That wouldn't account for being still," Ryland said, adjusting his glasses. Ryland was the eldest brother of Ryker and wicked smart.

"What about the rivers that flow into our lakes?" asked Mic, who had thick black locks of hair and brown skin. "The water is still once it reaches them, yes?"

Second eldest brother to Graelynd, Royce tilted his head. "Excellent, but how does that solve the 'four will tell' portion?"

While the brilliant ones chatted about different theories, Sealyn took the faith commissioner away from the table for a more private conversation.

Herb looked worried. "My Queen, how can I help?"

"How fast did they just solve that riddle?"

"In my opinion, they solved it with blazing speed," said Herb. "That was quite impressive."

"Exactly. If this Heart of Elysium is so important, why make it that easy to solve? Wouldn't you want it protected even from the brilliant?"

Herb grinned. "I believe you may have just answered your own question."

Sealyn returned to her seat. "Allow me to interrupt. I applaud you for your efforts thus far, but let's think past easement. Water was too easy a guess. It can't be this. Elysium is unlike any other kingdom out there. We have resources that other lands can only dream about, so perhaps think of something native only to Elysium. This would hinder our enemies in a plot against us."

After another hour of arguments, theories, and one cup thrown by the white-haired Stevonten, Sealyn thought it best for them to take a break. She arranged a pleasant garden walk with refreshments. It was evident from everyone's quick exit that the break was much needed. This was also the time Jace would arrive for their lunch. Of course, Jace arrived early, so the Nichts didn't finish clearing everything from the breakfast table before he entered.

"My apologies, Queen Sealyn. I didn't know I would be interrupting a meeting in here." Jace stood awkwardly at the doorway.

"No apology needed for being punctual. Please join me." Sealyn's tone was sharp and more formal than usual.

Jace slowly took a chair in front of Sealyn. "Forgive me for saying so, but you seem frustrated. Is it me or the meeting before?"

Sealyn bit her bottom lip, wondering how honest she needed to be. She was running out of time. "Both. I don't have the patience to dance around the point of today's conversation." She folded her hands on the table. "You were seen at a private meeting with the Stoltland guests, along with Lord Drystan, at his wedding. There is no crime for private meetings, but the contents of the meeting are what alarm me. I must know whether I can fully trust you."

Jace interrupted. "You can!"

Sealyn pursed her lips. She loathed being cut off. "Please don't interrupt me, Jace. This is extremely important." Jace nodded apologetically. "Lady Corentine threatened to have a thousand ships off our east coast. Yes or no?"

"Yes, she did." He felt the color drain from his face.

"Since hearing that, you made no efforts to report this news to any military advisor, guard, or me—correct or incorrect?"

Jace feared his answer. "Correct, Your Majesty."

"Why? Why, Jace? Why could you not come to me about this?" Her voice caught in her throat. She had wanted all this information to be wrong.

Jace could see how much his actions resembled disloyalty. He had no choice but to reveal the truth to her. He just despised how this admission would lead to more of the same—exposing and betraying Stoltland.

"Your Majesty, I didn't come to you because I believed this information to be false. You see, I know Stoltland doesn't have a fleet that large, so there couldn't be a thousand ships waiting off your east coast. In fact, the existence of any ships on your east coast is likely a lie. I didn't want to create more tensions between our two countries if it wasn't necessary."

"Shouldn't that decision be up to the queen?"

Jace lowered his head. "Of course, Queen Sealyn."

Sealyn sat up straighter and cleared her throat. "What I see, Jace, is that you know more than what your family believes you to know."

"Why would you say that?" He crumpled his face.

"Because if they had any idea you knew this much about their military, they wouldn't have allowed you to stay." Sealyn stood and walked to the other side of the table and took the seat next to Jace. She placed her hand on his. "Jace, there's a reason she wanted Drystan to feel threatened. Do you know what that reason is?"

Jace searched his memories of that night and any conversations he had with his family since their arrival. There was nothing tangible to assist in this mystery. The loyalties to Stoltland versus Elysium would eventually pose a major problem, but until then, he needed to focus on the present.

Jace shook his head with disappointment. "I wish I could remember something that would help."

"I understand." Sealyn found herself disappointed. She hoped that Jace would reveal the plan, demonstrating his loyalty to Elysium.

"Perhaps everything will be revealed with time and patience." He nodded toward the fireplace. "Just like the Ever-Changing Mountain, we must wait to see its blue color change through the seasons."

"What did you say?"

"I. I only meant to imply to see the good in waiting like the—"

"Ever-Changing Mountain!" Sealyn exploded with excitement. She stood quickly. "Jace, Stoltland doesn't have a color-changing mountain, does it?"

"No, Your Majesty. We really don't have many fascinating landscapes like Elysium. Unless you consider a waterfall of fire fascinating."

"Perfect. Jace, I really hate to conclude our lunch, but a matter of utmost importance has arisen, and I need to take care of it now. I would very much like to make this up to you."

"Oh, yes! Of course, it's perfectly fine to end early. I have to help Lord Finn anyway. We have a new breed of elephants arriving this afternoon. I believe these are the special breed you ordered from Shunal."

Sealyn's eyes sparkled. "I completely forgot! I'll come by tomorrow once you have them settled. I can't wait to see the exiguums. I purchased as many as the Shunalians would allow because they mainly breed them for their tinted tusks."

"That's horrible!"

"I agree, which is why I will continue buying them and protecting them here. They're incredibly adorable."

"I've yet to see one of these tiny, furry elephants, but I heard once you see one, your heart melts." Jace smiled at the queen.

"Yes, your heart will melt." She stared into his silver, intoxicating eyes, feeling herself melt. "I'm planning on keeping two here on the palace grounds. One purple and one blue, which is another reason why I'll come by tomorrow, but I really must be going now. Thank you again, Jace." She squeezed his hand.

Jace stood, taking her hand and kissing it. "The pleasure is all mine, My Queen."

Sealyn's insides squirmed. His lips felt so soft on her skin. Her breathing sped. She wanted his lips on hers, but she wasn't certain if she could trust him. Where did his loyalties lie? Jace stepped closer, their fabrics grazing against one another. A breath caught in Sealyn's chest. She didn't care. She didn't care that falling for him was dangerous. Her chest rose heavily up and down.

She threw caution aside and lunged, capturing his face and drawing it closer to hers. Jace wrapped his strong arms around her, his hands sinking into her back. Her lips hungrily tasted his, her body aching for more. A flash of her nightmare shattered her passion. Would Jace be the cause of the death and destruction in her dreams?

Sealyn pulled back, breathing heavily. She braced her hand against his chest, feeling the pounding of his heart. Her brows furrowed—an expression she couldn't shake. She started to speak but instead turned and walked away.

Jace stood torn. What had just happened? His mind spun. Did this mean she trusted him or not? He thought about his mother. Sealyn knew Corentine was scheming, yet he almost felt compelled to warn them, but warn them of what? Would Drystan be someone to consult about this? No! He could never imagine him and Drystan finding common ground, so he needed to discover what the Stoltlanders were searching for before anyone else. When he did find out, whom would he tell first?

After their hours of break, the Council of Wisdom and the Council of Scholars gathered in the Breakfast Room, eager to understand Sealyn's exhilaration.

"I have brilliant news for you—the Ever-Changing Mountain." She pointed to the fireplace, still lit with lovely candles. Everyone's eyes grew large, and they started nodding their heads.

"Excellent, Your Majesty!" said Stevonten.

"With the 'fall into blue' phrase, my theory is that our fall season is only a couple of months away, and the mountain's fall blue color will reveal the last part of this clue somehow. What do you advise?"

Brandle scratched his chin. "I believe your theory is correct, and if you're right, then we have the advantage of two months to research everything we can about this mountain."

Norella nodded. "Yes, we can secure all copies of books and scrolls about the Ever-Changing Mountain. This way, if anyone working with Stoltland figures out the clue, then he or she would be crippled by a lack of knowledge."

Tilmond raised his elongated hand. "Given that our adversary may not identify the Ever-Changing Mountain but might notice the lakes as we initially did, scouting the lakes could uncover potential spies. We ought to dispatch scouts to the lakes near Avondelle." Tilmond suspected Drystan was part of this issue since he heard scandalous rumors around the training grounds. Drystan wouldn't want to leave his new bride, so searching nearby lakes would make more sense. Tilmond sensed that his cousin, Sealyn, didn't want this information about Drystan to be public, so he kept his thoughts to himself.

"My son is wise," Adomin said proudly. "I believe we should send the scouts to the lakes, but also the mountain. This may reveal that our enemy knows what we know."

Sealyn agreed and sent word to Commander Elmond to complete the tasks. Sealyn felt extremely confident that the clue was pointing to the Ever-Changing Mountain. She needed to make sure that Drystan and any other revolting little spy of Stoltland didn't suspect that the palace knew the letter was missing. How can you convince your enemy that you're not poring over their plots night and day? By throwing the grandest-scale fall festival Avondelle has ever seen, just as Perdonair is set to arrive in two months.

220

How can you fight Love? Why would anyone want to fight against it? What if the Love you choose is that Love that destroys you? An all-consuming passion of love, the love that blinds you into submission. The love that deafens you into hearing the darkness. A love that feeds you to the very creatures you swore you would never bow to. A love whose aroma intoxicates you into a spell-bound puppet. But a love that, at the touch, electricity pulses through your veins, screaming out for more. Do you fight that? Or do you dive into the dark waters, accepting every consequence?

Queen Sealyn Araelien
Diary Entry 341

Lady Sorcha

# Chapter 16

The air had turned crisp, with a light fog gliding over the hills. The market was filled with aromas of freshly baked apple pies, pumpkin bread, and, of course, the famous Puffin Pies. Rows of cinnamon sticks lined several table booths near *Nijeel's Choice*. Since the coffee shop served hot apple cider only a few months out of the year, this led to tables selling cinnamon sticks for people to add to their steaming, fresh cup of cider. Autumn held a special magic that accompanied the season. People appeared to smile more, dance more, and connect on deeper levels. It was a time of peace and harmony.

As Queen Sealyn stirred a freshly poured cider with her cinnamon stick, she savored the memories that the past couple of months had brought her. Her kingdom was flourishing and had even added two new trading lanes with Shunal, focusing on new livestock that Elysium had never raised. The second Avondelle school was already filled with children. The raids on the southern border from Korpam had finally stopped, yet the mystery of Len Nove still hovered in her mind. She felt warmed by how the palace's munificence brought several families out of crushing debt and revived countless villages throughout the kingdom.

Her relationships with many people had also changed. She had set aside her desire to abase Drystan and instead tolerated him. She maintained a particularly close friendship with him and Pyry. She enjoyed her time with Pyry, but she felt quite uncomfortable with Drystan's grandiloquence around Jace. She could tell he was testing his limits with how far he could taunt Jace.

With the thought of Jace, her body heated, and her cheeks flushed. A quiet smile tugged at the corners of her lips. Every conversation they had, every touch they seized, and every kiss they shared confirmed that the silver-eyed mystery was her soulmate. She hadn't divulged this revelation to him yet, but she was planning on telling him at the end of the holiday celebration.

The Perdonair holiday is a jubilant celebration that begins with exhilarating days brimming with vibrant parades, electrifying dances, thrilling contests, and sumptuous feasts. At the heart of the festivities lies the beloved game of Feydom, a tradition among the Elysians that translates to 'fated to be cursed.' Over three grueling days, teams engage in fierce but friendly competition in Feydom. The final day, pulsating with energy and anticipation, arrives just before the grand celebration of Perdonair, ensuring that all teams have ample time to revel and create unforgettable memories with friends and family on the magnificent holiday itself.

Feydom's first day of competition starts with seven teams from across Elysium, all with one goal in mind: to collect all fourteen flags and win. This first round, called Clod, consists of eight roamers and nine tacklers, each with a specific job. The roamers journey through the terrain to collect their team's flags and return to their campsite, while the tacklers block the opposing roamers from capturing the flags. Once a team accumulates all fourteen flags at their campsite, the game is over; however, if no team has managed to collect all fourteen flags within twenty-four hours, the team with the lowest number of flags is eliminated from the game.

The second day of Feydom begins even though the Clod phase is not complete. Clod continues for the roamers and tacklers, but a new phase also commences: Vision. The game introduces horses in this phase. The two types of players are six horsemen and seven shields. The objective is for the horsemen to use their bows and arrows to shoot the extra-large pipscots that are prehung in massive nets from tree branches. The first team to shoot all ten of their colored pipscots wins.

This adventure is a crowd favorite, as spectators enjoy watching the pipscots explode into beautiful colors throughout the territory. If, by the end of the second day, no team has gathered fourteen flags or burst ten pipscots, the game continues to the final round. Once again, the team with the lowest points does not advance.

Wings is the final and third phase of Feydom. This phase is the hardest to train for because players must not only ride flying horses, but no one knows how the construction of the contest will be arranged. These terms are revealed just before contestants begin the game. Flying horsemen aim to throw painted rocks onto a target without breaking them while avoiding flying blockers who can shatter the rocks with exploding arrows. The first team to secure seven rocks wins. If no team gathers fourteen flags, explodes ten pipscots, or secures seven rocks by the end of day three, the team with the most completed tasks wins Feydom.

Queen Sealyn inhaled another deep breath of the crisp air. "I'm so excited for this year's Feydom game." She smiled at Pyry.

"I quite agree. I heard such good remarks about the teams this year, especially for the Yellow Phoenixes."

"The Yellow Phoenixes?" Sealyn scrunched her nose, defending her favorite team: the Green Phoenixes. "Oh, yes, that reminds me. Doesn't Lady Adalina have a former fiancé on that team?"

"You're correct. She does, but she has many of those," snuffed Pyry, waving her hand.

Sealyn tilted her head, not understanding why a friend would be so condescending. "I meant that this could be awkward for her, perhaps painful."

"Oh yes, I'm sure it could pose a potentially uncomfortable experience for her." Pyry stumbled over her words, embarrassed at being called out.

Sealyn quickly changed the subject. "I heard several of our Avondelle military lords will be on the Green Phoenix team, along with my sister, of course. Siany's an excellent roamer." Sealyn beamed with pride. Her sister was not only a terrific athlete but also a strategic one.

"I agree." Pyry nodded. "I'm not sure why my Drystan traded teams this year. He's playing for the Black Phoenixes." Sealyn choked on her cider. Pyry ignored the queen and continued, "Can you believe that? He hasn't even practiced with them! They moved him from a roamer to a tackler! No wonder they always lose, can't figure out where to put their best players."

Queen Sealyn tilted her head. "The Black Phoenixes? Really? I can't imagine why he would trade his green colors for black." Sealyn felt as though she had swallowed dirt. It was another sign that Drystan was a traitor, and she had to sit before his wife, acting like everything was perfect. She stared hard at the cinnamon swirling in her half-empty teacup.

"Do you think Jace will be a contender? Do they even play Feydom in Stoltland?" Pyry asked with a pompous tone.

"Of course, they play Feydom there." Sealyn snapped, losing interest in pretending to enjoy herself. "Every kingdom loves this game, but the rumors I've heard are that each kingdom has its own version, so I'm not sure it would be wise for *Lord* Jace to participate this year."

Sakul dripped with sweat as he ran through the market. He headed straight for *A Brother's Bond*, knowing that only Char could help him untangle the mess he was in. Holding onto the door frame before entering, Sakul gasped for air. Those extra Puffin Pies would surely revisit him if he didn't catch his breath. Suddenly, he felt a swift smack on his back and nearly plummeted to his knees.

Sakul wavered slightly as he noticed Char standing in front of him, grinning. He shouted, "Char! Why'd you hit me so hard? Can your foolish eyes not see I'm a man dying before you!"

Char chuckled. "Dying?" He folded his arms, pleased with himself. "All I see is an out-of-shape man who ate one too many Puffin Pies for breakfast and is now spitting up on my doorstep."

"Char! I need your help!"

"Gladly. Would you like your coffin dark or light wood?" Char propped himself against the doorway, waiting for Sakul's reaction.

"You'll be the death of me one day, Char, but today is not the day for such things. Listen, I can't get these crazy flying horses under control!"

Char pushed himself off the doorframe and dropped his hands. "The nomosevs? They're here?"

"Yes, those vile creatures have arrived!" snarled Sakul. "I must have everything organized before the game starts tomorrow, but tonight is also the banquet for the contestants. You must help me."

Char almost laughed. He had no idea how to help. He hated going near those savage, winged creatures, but they were majestic to watch. Madilina quickly came to mind. She was the one who whispered to wild animals and calmed them to sleep. She would be Sakul's best chance.

"Lady Madilina would be your hope, Sakul. I've seen her talk a possessed needlebob into a deep sleep. If she can do that, she just may be able to quiet down the nomosevs."

Lord Sakul shivered as he remembered his first encounter with a needlebob as a child. The tiny golden creature rolled right across his bare foot, leaving hundreds of needles embedded deep. The more he moved, the further the needles pressed into his dark skin.

The worst part about a needlebob's needle was the hallucinogenic poison. Like clockwork, the poison released thirty seconds after detaching, sending young Sakul into a five-hour hallucination until finally, young Sealyn came across him on one of her horse rides. She and her guard scooped him up and rushed him to the palace doctor, saving his life. Since then, they have remained as close as brother and sister.

"Thanks, Char," Sakul finally managed to say. "I'll find her and ask for her assistance." Sakul hesitated before leaving. "On a serious note, did you hear that Drystan has changed to the Black Phoenix team?"

"I did hear that, but I wasn't sure whether it was true. It's been confirmed, then?"

"Yes. I had my morning coffee with Lord Favien and Lord Doebromir, who were talking strategies about Feydom when I sat down. I asked them for any new news about the games, and Drystan trading teams was one of the two pieces of information they shared."

"Traded sounds right," Char huffed. "One of two? What was the other piece of news?"

"Favien made captain this year!"

"Wow! That is great news *for him*." Char folded his arms, pouting. "Curse it! Now, I owe my brother five silvers. I thought for sure Doebromir would have it again."

"Everyone thought that too, but apparently at the final team meeting, Favien presented new strategies that showed he should be the rightful captain."

"Speaking of strategies, have you figured out why Lady Sorcha keeps going to Queen Sealyn's Butterfly Natatorium with Lord Prince Brandle?"

Sakul sighed, wiping sweat from his brow. "Char, I'm not sure. Part of me feels torn, almost as if she's a new person since Sealyn commissioned her to the palace those months ago. She is now leading a clandestine life. Brandle is married and very committed to his family, so I don't believe he would conduct himself in such a way."

"Seems as though you have nothing to worry about then? Why are you questioning your potential relationship?"

Sakul shrugged and kicked a loose pebble. "What if she sees something in him that I could never be? I'm not of royal blood. I'm not a doctor. I can't compete with a man like that."

Char smacked Sakul's arm. "Sakul! Pull yourself together! You're walking dangerously close to being…" Char paused and looked around, then whispered, "Envious!"

Sakul gasped and shoved Char. "I'm no such thing! I don't wish to be him, nor do I want to change who I am. I just don't know whether who I am is enough for a woman like Sorcha."

"I see. Well, find a way to communicate this to her. Otherwise, you'll overthink, which could lead to crossing lines. We can't have that, Sakul."

Char spoke from a place of friendship, not rudeness. If Sakul kept heading down the path he was on, he might end up on the side of envy and then be sent to Reformation Rock. Some people spent months or years there, while others were banished from Reformation Rock to live out their days on the remote island of Elysium's Fall. This island belonged to Elysium, but it was not considered part of the kingdom. Sakul wanted no part of that life; he had to talk to Sorcha.

Yellow butterflies fluttered their wings gracefully through the columns of the Butterfly Natatorium. On a royal's sixteenth birthday, he is granted permission to construct any structure his heart desires. The Butterfly Natatorium, crafted by Sealyn, featured a magnificent pointed glass roof that reflected sunlight, making the blue waters of the pool shimmer like jewels. Gray stone walls tower around the space, embellished with grand bookshelves that stretch from floor to ceiling. At one end, three evergreen couches invited relaxation, while at the opposite end, two wooden tables draped with papers and books awaited curious minds, surrounded by cozy green chairs.

Sorcha folded her arms over the book she had been reading for the past two hours and rested her head on them. She was exhausted, but so were all the appointed members of the queen's secret mission. The banquet was tonight, and she needed to change, but her eyes were too heavy.

"Lady Sorcha, are you feeling well?" Norella asked with concern.

Sorcha slowly sat up and stretched her arms. "I am. I'm just exhausted. We really should change into our banquet gowns."

"I agree. Let's organize our notes and then walk to the palace."

"I'm grateful Sealyn had the books moved here from the dusty historical records," admitted Sorcha. "This place provides so much more ability to think and concentrate."

Norella chuckled. "You know it is the plants in here that help stimulate your mind?"

"Really? How?"

"From what I gathered, Sealyn researched which plants gave off aromas of brain stimulation. She imported plants from all seven kingdoms to create a masterpiece of enhanced brilliance for this one room. Some plants even emit sounds that resonate with your mind's vibrations to accelerate thought processes."

Sorcha placed her hand on top of her head. "Wow, maybe that's why I feel dizzy. Seriously, though, this is all quite impressive. It must have taken her years to complete."

"Seven," Lord Prince Brandle piped in.

"Of course, seven." Sorcha smiled at the lord prince. "Did you have a nice nap?"

"Nap? You saw me sleeping?" Brandle blushed.

"We did." Norella giggled. "But we didn't want to wake you. You said earlier how the baby didn't sleep through the night, so we let you sleep."

"Thank you. That was very kind of you both. Are we off now to celebrate the beginning of the great Feydom games?"

"Yes. We're about to walk to the palace now. Our dresses are with Queen Sealyn's seamstress." Sorcha nodded.

"Excellent. I'll escort you ladies to the palace. Let us all enjoy the favorite holiday of our beloved King Perdon. May he find peace in rest."

Sorcha suddenly felt dizzy again, but it seemed more like knowledge unlocking itself within her mind. Could all the scents and vibrations be on the verge of unveiling something that had been in plain sight? Why did King Perdon's name feel like a key that had been absent for the past three hundred years since his declaration of the holiday Perdonair?

"Lord Prince Brandle, you said Perdonair was King Perdon's favorite holiday, correct?" Sorcha tried not to give away the hope she had.

"Correct. Why?"

"Didn't we read that it was King Perdon who changed the clues during his reign after the Stoltland raid stole the first clue letter?"

"That's also true." Norella nodded, rolling up another scroll.

Sorcha closed her eyes and absorbed the sweet scents of the flowers along with the gentle hum of butterfly wings. She allowed the plants' music to reveal all the secrets of King Pardon to her. Suddenly, her eyes opened, and she smacked the table with her hand, nearly spilling the last of Madam Bip's purple PurFizz onto the books.

"I have it!" exclaimed Sorcha. "King Perdon's favorite holiday is Perdonair. Named because he needed forgiveness from the people for allowing the Stoltland raid to happen. Since then, we take time to forgive on this day if we've been withholding forgiveness from anyone."

"Yes, Sorcha, but I don't think..." interrupted Norella.

"Wait! I'm not finished! His intentions were exceptionally good to proclaim this holiday and its purpose, but he hoped that the extravagance of the celebrations would hide its true purpose: the timing for when the second clue could reveal itself!" Sorcha clapped her hands together and started bouncing up and down like a child.

Brandle scratched his chin, trying to follow Sorcha. "So this means that the exact shade of blue the Ever-Changing Mountain needs to be to show us what 'four will tell' means will happen on the day of Perdonair?"

"Yes!" shouted Sorcha. "Don't you see? It's perfect. Everyone is too tired from the celebrations, and plus, the tradition is to be in your homes meditating on forgiveness and concluding the day with a family meal. No one goes to the Ever-Changing Mountain on Perdonair!"

"We must tell the queen!" screeched Norella.

"Quickly, ladies. There's no time to spare." Brandle stacked books and shoved papers together.

All three flew out the door, almost knocking over Sakul. Everyone stood for a moment in shock, wondering why Sakul would be near the natatorium.

"Lord Sakul," Sorcha gasped. "Why are you here?"

"My pardon to you all. I merely wanted an opportunity to speak with Lady Sorcha—privately."

Sorcha's heart skipped a beat. She adored Sakul and hoped one day he would finally see her for who she desired to be: his wife.

"Lord Sakul, I would love nothing more than to fulfill your request, but you see, we have urgent news to carry to the queen." She looked at Norella. "We simply can't delay this information. Let us speak later at the banquet?"

Lord Sakul nodded and bid them farewell, his heart slightly broken because there wouldn't be much time tonight to speak at the banquet. Too many distractions lay ahead this evening, and the players always ended the banquet in a scuffle or with something broken. Tonight would not be suitable for discussing matters of the heart. Instead, he would focus on ensuring Sorcha had a delightful and safe evening away from any princes or dangerous Feydom players.

Lady Norella
Lady Rnx
Lady Zuri

# Chapter 17

Norella immediately sat up in her guest bed when she heard a loud crash. She panicked, looking around Sealyn's bedroom, only to find that Pinx had rolled off the guest bed and onto the floor. Pinx landed on her breakfast tray and was covered in coffee and smashed oatmeal.

"Lady Norella," Sealyn hoarsely spoke. "Please tell me enemy forces are not attacking us and that noise was only a clumsy, hungover lady?" Sealyn grabbed her extra pillow and laid it over her face.

Norella groaned. "Yes, just Pinx feeding oatmeal to her nightsleeps."

"Did you tell her that we're not supposed to do that in the early mornings?" Sealyn chuckled.

"Of course, but she seemed quite determined, and who am I to stand in the way of someone's dreams, Your Majesty?" This sent the girls into painful laughter.

"I can hear you all," Pinx squeaked. "Can someone call Maekel for another nightsleep? I can't be seen at breakfast like this!"

"At breakfast?" questioned Sorcha. "I thought we were having breakfast in the queen's chambers today?"

"Yes, it's tradition. The day before feydom begins, the Vinur ladies of the court always stay the night with their royal. We've been doing this for years!" Breanna flipped her blonde hair.

"She knows," snapped Zuri. "She hasn't been in Avondelle as long as you, Brenna."

"Ladies!" exclaimed Sealyn. "Loud noises are not welcome until after lunch hours."

The ladies groaned at the loud knocking on the door, but they needed the coffee and the healing from the Tomato Fury and Hircus Delight. They also knew that on the other side of the door was the entire breakfast staff waiting to serve them the traditional Feydom breakfast.

The staff entered with golden carts, one for each lady. Sealyn's mouth watered as soon as she saw the immaculate display of bagels with tree-nut cream cheese and smoked salmon, accompanied by a baked egg inside an avocado half. Sipping her first taste of the Hircus delight warmed all her senses. She needed her wits about her today.

"Did anyone see that dark and dreamy player for the Blue Phoenixes?" Adalina fantasized.

"Blue Phoenixes? I thought I saw you talking to the tall blonde blocker for the Red Phoenixes," questioned Brenna.

Adalina giggled. "Well, maybe I was talking to a few."

"I knew there would be a fight between Green and Black," growled Sorcha. "I mean, how could Drystan expect his teammates to be fine with him trading teams last minute and then sit down and try to have a civil conversation?"

"I saw Doebromir throw the first piece of food, though," added Norella. "I feel like he started the fight because of that."

Zuri shook her head. "I disagree. Drystan didn't have to react. He could have walked away."

"I almost wished for a dull evening for Sakul, but instead, he had to deal with that fight, knocking over tables and destroying all his hard work." Sorcha sadly sipped her coffee.

"Tell the truth, Sorcha," remarked Norella. "You're more disappointed that you and Sakul didn't get to have that special talk he wanted."

Gasps echoed around the room. Sorcha couldn't help the large smile forming on her face. She desperately wanted a chance to speak more with Sakul, but that uncalled-for fight broke out, preventing a private moment. Another reason she wanted Drystan gone. Somehow, she felt Drystan would create more ways for her and Sakul not to be together.

"Yes, Norella. You're correct. I regret missing the opportunity to speak with him. I know how busy he is during Feydom, so it'll be gravely difficult to have a moment alone."

Sealyn smirked. "It's a good thing you're connected to the queen, who can organize whatever private meetings she wants." Sealyn winked at her best friend. "Anything for you,

Sorcha. You know that." Sealyn set down her plate. "Speaking of Drystan, where are Lady Pyry and Lady Lulana?"

"Apparently, Pyry sent a note saying that since she is now married, she will no longer participate in our tradition," informed Brenna.

"And Lulana?" Sealyn asked blankly.

"She wanted to stay with Pyry," said Brenna. "I'm sure to help her being a young bride."

"How kind of Lulana," Sealyn said flatly and looked out the window.

Sealyn had to be careful about what she said regarding anyone getting close to Pyry. She must remain neutral to avoid giving any hint about what she suspected. Pyry had already started distancing herself from Sealyn, and this move was yet another attempt to create space between them. Sealyn wondered whether Pyry was aware of the betrayal. Surely, Pyry wasn't capable of committing such a heinous crime. Pyry had a kind heart, but others too easily influenced her. She disliked the effect Drystan had on her. He made her feel insecure, almost as if she couldn't find a better match than him.

Pinx clapped her hands. "Alright, ladies. It's time to place our bets! Which team do you think will win this year? I'm supporting our Green Phoenixes!"

"Of course, you are," Adalina jeered. She tapped her finger against her cheek. "I think I'll be placing a bet for the Yellow Phoenixes! This might make that dreamy blue player jealous."

"Sakul's favorite color, besides our green, is red, so I'll bet on the Red Phoenixes. I always choose a losing team, though." Sorcha huffed.

"I choose our Green Phoenixes as well," Norella cooed. "Tybalt is in charge of Clod this year. I know he'll be the best roamer on their team!"

Before Zuri could announce her bet, the door flung open, and Char entered. He jumped and landed beside Sealyn, stretching his arms behind his head and crossing his legs with a large smile.

"Char!" screeched the ladies.

"Good morning, ladies! May I say that you all have never looked more beautiful than you do in this very moment? Did I happen to interrupt the placing of the bets?"

"Char! That's not for you!" hissed Zuri. "This is just for us ladies."

"Let me guess, my beautiful ice queen," Char flirted. "You will be cheering for the Blue Phoenixes? You know they lose in the first round almost every year?"

"I don't care, Char. And yes, I *will* bet on the Blue Phoenixes."

"I hear the Orange Phoenixes have a trick up their sleeves," bragged Char. "They've been recruiting players and practicing throughout the year as a whole unit. I even heard one of their riders flew a caelidon."

Sealyn choked, coffee dripped from her nose. "A caelidon? I heard no such news."

Char laughed and nudged Sealyn's arm. "I knew that would get my feisty cousin's attention. I'm assuming you're betting on your gallant Green Phoenixes?"

"Do you even have to ask?"

"Of course not!" Char tossed a strawberry in his mouth. "You ladies had best get ready for the opening ceremony. I definitely don't want to miss what Sakul has planned!"

"We're not changing with you in here, Char!" Norella demanded.

"Why not? I'll be as quiet as a mouse."

"Get out!" screeched the ladies.

Char threw his hands up in defeat and ran out of the room, dodging the pillows thrown at him. He enjoyed teasing the girls. He hoped one day he would find his match, and they both could tease each other till their last day.

Adrenaline flowed through the veins of the Feydom competitors. The intensity in their eyes was hard to miss. Each player was envisioning the game-winning move. Favien had thrown up twice that morning. He felt the pressure of leading the Green Phoenixes. Last year, the Green Phoenixes suffered their first loss in eleven years. It was the biggest shock in Feydom's history.

The Yellow Phoenixes made a bold move by using all their players to shoot the pipscots. The Green Phoenixes were in the lead for the final day for wings, but once the horn sounded, all the yellow flying horsemen and flying blockers dove into the trees. They created easier pathways for their horsemen to shoot the pipscots; even the roamers and tacklers would spring out of nowhere, scaring the other teams' horses and preventing them from making precise shots.

Yellow dust spread across the territory. After the victory medals were awarded to the Yellow Phoenixes, the other teams contested the results, alleging that the Yellow Phoenixes had violated Feydom rules. However, the royals ruled in favor of the Yellow Phoenixes, declaring that no rules existed to prevent such a tactic. This shifted how everyone perceived Feydom.

Doebromir patted Favien's back. "Favien, I don't envy you at all, for your task is heavy these next few days."

"Thanks, Doebromir, but I wish that helped my stomach."

"No worries, Favien. This game has a thousand different outcomes. We only expect you to anticipate 999 of them, not all." Jdru jeered. Jdru, Char's brother, loved Feydom and looked forward to this tournament all year.

Each player wore a painted white phoenix outlined in gold on the back of the long-sleeve emerald pullover. The Queen Mother and her mother-in-law loved painting the Green Phoenixes' jerseys each year.

"Don't listen to them, Favien," Siany encouraged. "You have a good plan, and we all have it memorized. We'll do well."

"Thanks, Princess Siany." Favien sighed. "I really am glad you decided to play again this year, and you recruited some amazing players, especially your cousins. We really lucked out with those two."

"I agree. Their sheer size will put the fear of Creator in the other teams!"

Jashun fiddled with his uniform, nervously watching the Orange Phoenixes dance in their traditional chant. "I don't wish to cast doubt, but has anyone seen that new player over there? I don't believe I saw him at the banquet, or perhaps he was sitting down, so I didn't realize how tall he actually is." Jashun pointed to the orange team. "See. Look at player S5. He's huge!"

"Why would they choose such a tall player for a shield?" asked Finn.

The extremely tall Tilmond strolled over to the conversation. "If you ask me, it's quite brilliant. A tall rider makes for an easier block against the horsemen. Is it not obvious why I'm a shield?" Tilmond puffed out his chest to highlight his S1 on his chest.

Jashun nodded with his dark hair falling over his jade eyes. He still felt uneasy about possibly facing that large, muscular, orange opponent, but decided it would be best not to mention that. He was a roamer anyway, so their meeting on the territory was highly unlikely. Patting his painted R3 in the middle of his chest, he laced up his brown boots.

"Perhaps a real green phoenix will help us win if we find ourselves in a bad way?!" chanted Max. Max was always an overly enthusiastic person and the one with the most questions.

"A real green phoenix?" taunted Doebromir. "Max, you know those birds don't exist, right?"

"They don't?" asked Finn.

"No," barked Doebromir. "They're just a childhood story. Nothing more."

"Now wait a minute, Doebromir," retorted Tybalt. I read that they weren't merely made up but rather a legend from the old years. The curse caused their extinction.

"Look, Tybalt. I know you normally know all these unusual facts, but on this topic, you're wrong. For something to be extinct, it had to have lived at some point, but the big parrot never existed; therefore, it's not extinct."

"You didn't live during the days the green phoenix did exist, Doebromir," objected Tybalt. "Legend says that the green phoenix only rises from fire, not ash, which is how its wings are fire resistant. It only answers the call of one not infected with the curse."

Doebromir held up his hand. "So you're telling me that I have to be on fire and squeaky clean of any envy in order for the green phoenix to appear?"

Tybalt scratched his head. "Technically, yes."

"Well, let's hope for my sake that the fate of the world doesn't depend on me being on fire to save it. I mean, this face is too pretty to burn." Doebromir patted his cheeks, making the group laugh.

Favien clapped his hands, gaining his comrades' attention. "Today, my fellow teammates, we *are* the Green Phoenixes, so let's go make legends of us all!"

The team erupted in cheers! Favien inspired his teammates to become the best players they could be. He felt as though he could fight a bear in that moment, but suddenly, his knees went weak, and his mouth went dry like the desert plains in Glatania. Gliding like a mystical creature, Pinx slowly walked past the Green Phoenixes until she stopped in front of Favien. Her pink silk gown twinkled from her shoulders to her toes. Pinx handed Favien a sparkling frosted-pink rose. These roses grew during the cold months, producing white tips with tiny crystals on the ends of deep pink petals, Lady Pinx's favorite.

Favien tried to speak, but no words came out. He felt as if she could read his soul and didn't want to interrupt the connection they both felt. He wished they would stay in each other's eyes forever.

"Lord Favien, I'll be cheering for you today. May fortune be on your side," whispered Pinx.

All Favien could do was stand there, holding the majestic flower, entranced by Pinx's almond-shaped green eyes. He grinned and nodded.

As Pinx walked away, Favien finally found his voice. "Lady Pinx!" he shouted. "I *will* win Feydom for you!" He pointed at the white-painted *Captain* on his shirt, then slid to his R1. Pinx blushed and joined her friends.

"I think we should light Favien on fire right now. I'm almost convinced the green phoenix would rise," teased Doebromir.

Rav and Hueweyn had worked tirelessly to construct the large rectangular stadium seats. They even had to beg Lord Prince William, or Will, the eldest son of Prince Royce, to return for some final help in fitting the anthem seats together. Lord Prince Will was possibly the most dashing of all the royal men, with his raven curls, deep green eyes, and smoldering smile, but what made him truly amazing was his brilliance with inventions. He took after his father in his desire to modernize the kingdom and achieved great successes. His expertise created the perfect puzzle-fitting stadium the kingdom had ever seen.

The elevated, rectangular stadium extended around the perimeter of the Feydom territory. The pillars raised the seats four feet high, which gave the first few rows the best view of the roamers and tacklers. Towering at 250 feet, the stadium's top seats were for those who loved to watch the flying horses and wanted the best glimpse of the fireworks from the flags and exploding pipscots.

The stadium had painted sections with the team colors, encouraging loud team spirit. The Royal Box, however, was painted gold and was situated at the opposite end of the green section, which typically had the most supporters. The Royal

Box was filled with members of the monarch's family and Vinurs of the Court. This year, Lord Prince Will installed an elevator system featuring pulleys and donkeys, a clever addition.

Queen Sealyn opted for her hunter-green battle pants, complemented by a gold belt and a matching green and gold overskirt that split in front. She appeared battle-ready, yet the skirt provided an elegant touch. Her hairstylist even added three dyed green phoenix feathers to the left side of her half-up hairdo. She wanted Drystan to fear her; she needed him to fear her.

With everyone finally seated in the box and the parade led by Sakul concluding around the sand crystals that separated the stadium from the Feydom territory, Queen Sealyn stepped up to the large seashell cone constructed by Hueweyen to amplify the queen's voice.

"My fellow Elysians," she began. "I want to welcome you all to the start of our wonderful celebrations of our beloved Perdonair holiday. This means, of course, our sacred Feydom!" The crowd cheered! "Let us remember the symbolism of this game, for we face this each day we choose to rise. Our ancestors faced a treacherous battle against our enemy. Three hundred years ago, King Perdon faced an uprising of traitors, who were possessed by the curse and plotted to overthrow the crown." Children's gasps were heard. "For three days and nights, the faithful Elysians protected our lands and eventually won the war against the enemy traitors!"

She left out the part about the Heart of Elysium.

"Before the victory, though, hope seemed lost," she continued. "The obstacles became harder, and the enemy outnumbered us. This is why our brave Feydom players face more defenders because sometimes life sends more obstacles in your way to keep you from your goal, but my friends, I'm here to tell you, no matter the numbers, no matter the opposition you face, you can achieve victory. It just takes teamwork and loyal companions. This is who we are: brave and loyal. Let us raise our glasses and cheer for our comrades. Let Feydom's fate begin!"

The crowd rose to their feet, cheering and clinking drinks. The drums resounded, signaling the entrance of the teams. The games used to be dull since the trees and rocks blocked most of the viewing, but the invention of Prince Royce's Lux Masks changed the game for fans.

The masks featured team colors on the front and soft, thick velvet on the back for comfort. Prince Royce collaborated with the Fire Nichts in the mines of the Lux crystals to create this invention. Royce discovered that by applying pressure, the crystals could distort images, making them appear either farther away or closer than they truly were. The Fire Nichts assisted in cutting the crystals to the precise shape needed for the masks, while Royce designed a small wheel crank on the mask, positioned at a person's temples, not touching the ears.

Once a person turned the wheel, the gears inside shifted the shaft attached to the crystal, applying pressure and allowing the spectator to adjust their viewpoint of the game. These masks were mass-produced by the Fire Nicht families, enabling them to amass great wealth. Most spent their fortunes attempting to buy Fire Nichts' freedom from Stoltland, but that was kept secret from the throne.

As the teams walked around the sand crystals carrying their banners, each team stopped in front of the colored seats representing their own. Fans threw flowers while shouting encouraging words. Once the queen struck the gong, the roamers and tacklers sprinted into the territory, dodging trees and jumping over rocks. Feydom had officially begun. The remaining teammates walked to their campsites inside the designated territory.

Sealyn surveyed the room and saw Jace standing at the back of the royal box, looking confused. She was glad he accepted her invitation, but now she needed to resolve whatever was troubling him. "Lord Jace," she spoke with a friendly tone. "You seem troubled or confused. Could I be of assistance?"

Jace smiled. "My apologies, My Queen. I didn't mean to cause you worry. I'm just used to a different kind of Feydom game." Jace's expression grimaced. "Stoltland plays it very differently from Elysium."

"Really? What is different?"

Jace swallowed. He didn't want to describe what Stoltland did; it was barbaric. "Well, first, the teams are from the prisons; usually, the ones who've been in prison the longest. It's a brutal game, but they at least have the chance to win their freedom. It's the same timeframe of three days, but they basically torture the prisoners." He folded his arms and gazed out the window, not wanting to meet Sealyn's eyes.

"Oh, Jace. I'm sorry. This must be difficult for you."

"They set the territory on the edge of one of our sea cliffs. In case anyone wants to escape, they jump to their death." Tears formed in his silver eyes, remembering how many times he had been threatened with being tossed into the arena. "During the nights, they release fire creatures from the firetail tigers to the red-horned dragons. Needlebobs are dropped from the sky during the day raids. It's incredibly painful to watch. Most don't survive past day two, but those who do usually take their lives by day three. The horrors they endure shouldn't be experienced by any human. I'm glad to see that Elysium has found a way to make this game worth playing.

Sealyn tilted her head. "I am surprised Stoltland even knows of this game since it was our King Perdon who invented it."

"You know Stoltland; if Elysium has something, then Stoltland must outdo them."

Sealyn felt uneasy knowing that Elysium had influenced another kingdom and possibly others to commit such horrible actions. She made a mental note to investigate whether more kingdoms were engaging in inhumane games and, if so, to determine how to put an end to them all.

*My Dearest Queen Sealyn,*

*Remember, sweet girl, there is no secret to a happy marriage. With your grandfather and me, I put his happiness above mine, and he puts my happiness above his. When you have a selfless partnership, you can have the most fun!*

*Love for Always,*
*Grandma, Lady Ebbalee Araelien*

# Chapter 18

Heart pounding, Tybalt jumped and slipped over another rock, hoping his pants wouldn't rip. He could see the number five flag in front of him, but the Blue Phoenixes had it surrounded by a few of the Black Phoenixes. He needed to outflank them to truly capture their attention so the treetop roamers could do their job. He felt hands grabbing him from behind; his legs flipped over his head, and dirt filled his mouth.

Coughing and spitting, Tybalt blinked to see his adversary. One of the Orange Phoenixes, T7, had flipped him to the ground. Tybalt quickly swung his leg around, tripping the orange T7 backward. Orange T7 knocked his head hard on the ground, letting out a loud yelp.

His hiding place was no longer secret. Tybalt had to dash for another cover spot. He saw the Black Phoenixes heading straight for him. Gathering dirt in his hand, he threw it in

Orange T7's face, hoping that it would distract him long enough to make a getaway. He needed to get closer before revealing himself. The Black Phoenixes helped Orange T7 up, asking him which way the Green Phoenix had gone. Orange T7 looked disoriented and pointed in the wrong direction. "How fortunate," thought Tybalt.

Now was the best time for him to step into the light, allowing the blue tacklers to chase him away. He looked up and nodded his head to the treetops. Tybalt sprinted straight toward flag five. Blue T2 and T9 blocked Tybalt's path. Blue T9 wrapped his arms around Tybalt's feet while Blue T2 landed on top of Tybalt.

Tybalt hit the ground with a hard thud that knocked the breath out of him. He lay there, hoping the plan worked and that he wouldn't die. Seconds later, emerald fireworks exploded in the air, signaling that the Green Phoenixes had captured another flag.

Buried fireworks were attached to the flags, so when a player snatched a flag, the fireworks were pulled above ground, igniting and releasing them.

Tybalt saw Favien's hand in front of him. He grabbed it and was helped to his feet by Favien and Jdru.

Jdru patted Tybalt's back. "Excellent job, Tybalt. We dropped from the trees like panthers!"

"Tybalt, why don't you take the flag back to the camp?" said Favien. "This way you can have a minute to catch your breath."

Tybalt shook his head. "I'm fine, Favien."

"I'm not asking, Tybalt. We can't afford to lose the flag in another siege. Jdru and I are supposed to meet up with Siany and Lizz at flag eight. You can take the flag back, then head to flag four. I heard Jashun is really struggling, so Dinyelle will need your help."

Darkness was closing in, so arguing was only wasting time. Tybalt wouldn't mind hearing how the tacklers were doing anyway. He trotted off toward the campsite, scoping out the terrain for possible attackers.

At flag eight, Lady Aellizzabelle, normally referred to as Lizz, and Siany were outnumbered. Lizz was much faster than Siany, allowing her to outflank at least three of them, but seven tacklers stood around the flag. Lizz tightened her strawberry-blonde hair and signaled to Siany that she counted seven. Siany nodded. They heard a gentle rustle behind them, and both girls almost squealed when Favien and Jdru emerged from around the trees. Their confidence grew. They could handle capturing this flag with all four of them.

Lizz and Jdru were the fastest, which meant Siany and Favien would serve as distractions. Spreading themselves evenly around the flag, Siany made the first dash toward it. Purple T6 leapt at her, missing by inches and face-planted. Yellow T4 and T6 sprang toward her. Siany fell backward, bracing her fall with the palms of her hands. She felt pain surge through her left arm, annoyed that it was most likely sprained.

Three tacklers were down, so Favien seized his moment. He sprang forward from behind a rock. Purple T9 lunged, but Favien ducked lower, flipping the purple T9 over his right shoulder. Then, smack! Red T4 speared Favien, knocking him backward. Favien couldn't regain his footing because the purple T9 was behind him, which caused Favien to fall as well.

This was the moment Lizz and Jdru needed. One tackler remained from the yellow team. They ran toward the flag. Lizz jumped high over the short yellow T3, hoping she could turn in midair to grab the flag. Seeing Lizz's great acrobatic skills, Jdru took a different approach; he slid right between Yellow T3's legs.

Jdru's hands grabbed the flag, but it wasn't enough to yank it from the ground. Yellow T3 bent his knees, and in an instant, he was sitting on the back of Jdru's head. Jdru tossed the flag as hard as he could, hoping Lizz was still midair. She caught the flag and ran safely away from the flag zone. The emerald fireworks shot high into the sky, bursting with sparkling green colors. Jdru shoved Yellow T3 as he rose, angry that he had dirt in his mouth and eyes.

The Green Phoenixes huddled together, clapping for another victory, but their celebration quickly ended when they saw blue and red fireworks shooting up simultaneously. The game wasn't over. They could celebrate later.

Siany volunteered to take the flag back, knowing she had to wrap her wrist for support. She felt that her team was doing a great job. They managed to capture five flags before sunset. The plan was for all roamers to return to the campsite once the sun had completely set, but the tacklers would not return. They needed to stay out and guard all night. Roamers were to take food and water to every tackler before returning to the game.

Favien remembered the Feydom game when the Orange Phoenixes decided to keep their tacklers and roamers out all night without food or water. The poor team ultimately collapsed in the middle of Vision. He wasn't going to let that happen to his teammates. They all had a long night ahead of them, so he wanted them nourished. When the roamers returned to the campsite, the horsemen, shields, flying horsemen, and flying blockers had a warm fire going with freshly seared meat and boiled potatoes. Each team was given the same rations to start. They had to be wise about how much they would eat and drink each day since no more was provided during the game.

"Here are the totals so far: blue has two, red has one, yellow three, black two, and green *five*." Max emphasized the green score, while patting Favien on the back.

"I thought I didn't see any orange or purple fireworks," Finn observed. "I had heard from Char that both of those teams had a weak Clod offense because they recruited for Vision."

"Not to worry," assured Tilmond. "We'll be able to defend the pipscots. Our team is strong."

Favien gathered the remaining roamers to head toward the next flag. He wanted to gain as much of an advantage as he could during the night. Many teams chose to sleep and regain strength for the next portion. Others opted to play only half the night. Favien's plan was to have no sleep. He concluded that the Orange and Purple Phoenixes would be playing at least half the night, if not the whole night. Yellow would most likely sleep since they had three flags, which meant the Black and Blue Phoenixes would also play for half the night. No one would expect the Green Phoenixes to play the entire night due to their significant lead. This was Favien's plan, though: to be most aggressive on the flags. Few Feydom games were ever won with flags. They won the majority of their Feydom championships through their Vision team, but this would be the Clod year.

As he ran through the darkness, his thoughts drifted to Pinx—Pinx and her beauty. He thought about the beautiful rose she had given him and how foolish he had been. He should've been the one giving her a rose before leaving for the game. He made up his mind. If the Green Phoenixes won Feydom by clod, then he would declare his intentions to Pinx when he received his medal. She would be his ultimate prize.

With the festival and games, local and distant vendors set up small tables and tents near the fairgrounds to sell their goods and food. Sealyn walked side by side with Jace through the Feydom marketplace, while the rest of the royal family followed behind, sampling different treats. Jace stopped in front of a booth filled with small wooden ships. He picked one up and studied it intently.

"See something you like, Lord Jace?" Sealyn spoke flirtatiously.

Startled, Jace set the boat back. "No. No. It just reminded me of something."

Sealyn's eyes narrowed. "And what did the little boat remind you of, Jace?"

Jace gazed into Sealyn's emerald eyes and almost thought he saw sparkles floating within them. He felt lost in the sea of those eyes, but more than that, he felt he could trust her with his darkest secrets. Did that make Sealyn dangerous, or did it mean what he felt was love? Jace had never been in love, so how would he know?

"There was a rumor about my past in Stoltland," Jace explained. "A few of the bartenders would tell me stories. Some said that my father was a seaman. Others speculated that he was a traitor to his country. I have a love for the sea that I can't explain. I would sometimes venture to the coastline, lying in the sand, imagining my father on a great sea voyage, and one day, his travels would bring him to where I was. We would then sail all the seas, fighting sea monsters and swimming with whales."

"The world is full of possibilities, Jace. You never know. You might get that grand sea adventure with your father just yet." She tossed the small boat to Jace.

He caught it with a laugh. "What's this for?"

"For you to never forget your dreams." Sealyn loved encouraging people to follow their deepest desires, their hopes, their longings, but oddly enough, her dreams haunted her. She had the same nightmare three nights in a row, each one more intense than the last. Why green feathers? Why so much blood? She feared one day she would know.

Sealyn left payment on the boat table and winked at the local wood carver. She knew Maekel would want to see the exiguums, so they strolled in that direction. Char ran to catch up with Sealyn and Jace. He handed Sealyn their favorite coastal fair food: chicken kabobs. Luckily, he brought one for Jace, too. When more green fireworks exploded in the night sky, they cheered and toasted their kabobs to one another.

Sealyn knew happiness but thought perhaps this was something more. She felt a jolt of lightning make its way up her arm to her heart. She looked at her hand dangling beside her overskirt, and there was Jace's fingertip lightly holding onto her small finger. She understood love to a degree, and she knew what it was to be passionate about someone, but this—this was something else entirely, and she wanted more—much, much more.

Drystan sat cold at the Green Phoenix's flag. He wanted desperately to tackle Favien. He wouldn't mind sending that loudmouth Doebromir to the infirmary, too. If the queen had any indication about his plot, then those two idiots were a part of it. Many injuries occurred during Feydom, but deaths were quite rare. Doebromir's estate was large, not larger than Drystan's new estate, but if Doebromir lost his life, then Drystan could claim his property. He could even frame Doebromir for his actions!

Surely, a dead man could take away a living man's sins? Drystan pondered how to plant the evidence in Doebromir's house. He could even tell the queen that Corentine, Jace, and Doebromir had plotted against Elysium, so he decided to kill Doebromir during Feydom. He would be a hero! People would write songs about him. History would record his name with valor. His thoughts were interrupted when he saw an orange jersey running toward him.

"What do you want?" Drystan reprimanded.

"Oh, relax, Drystan," Orange T8 exhaled. "We must work together on this one. We all saw Green get another one a while back."

"I'm not worried about this flag."

"And why not? Just because your very presence is here?"

"Not my presence but my brilliance."

"Brilliance? Drystan, I'm not here to stroke your ego. I'm just trying to play a clean game of Clod, then enjoy the festival."

"No wonder your team will lose. I already set a trap for this flag."

"Trap? What do you mean by 'trap,' Drystan?"

"Well, while you cowards were off doing whatever orange birds do, I recruited players from the Blue Phoenixes and more of my fellow Black Phoenixes to dig a trench around the flag, then cover it with brush." Drystan smugly pointed around the flag.

"Drystan! You're not allowed to bring in tools, and besides, that's barbaric!"

"We didn't bring shovels, but any military man knows how to find rocks and dig."

"I can't be a part of this." Orange T8 held up his hands.

Drystan's survival instincts kicked in. He grabbed the orange T8 and hurled him against the nearby wall of rock. Orange T8 felt his head crack on the stone, and pain shot down his back, making him cry out. He fell face down, limp. He tried to push himself up, then fell into stillness. Drystan felt sick. Did he just kill him? He panicked instead of helping and ran toward another flag.

Running through the trees, Drystan ran smack into another orange tackler. What a stroke of luck. He quickly helped the orange T3 up and patted his back.

"Did you hear that scream?" Orange T3 wheezed.

"I did. I thought I heard it coming from that direction." He pointed behind the orange tackler.

"No, I just came from there. It sounded pretty bad. Let's go this way and check."

Orange T3 sprinted toward the evidence of Drystan's violence. Drystan jogged behind the competitor and planned to mimic Orange T3's reactions. Once they arrived, two other purple tacklers were kneeling beside the still body. Orange T3 gasped and ran to his teammate's side.

"This looks bad," Drystan said. "We must signal for help. He needs more attention than we can give. We need to save him!" He felt the urgency in his voice would soothe any suspicions.

Each player was given a medic-firework signal. The medic-firework first exploded into a white 'M'; then another firework of his team's color burst into his jersey number. The tube from which the fireworks were shot glowed bright so that the medic Nichts could first locate the injured player; then the human medics arrived to carry the player to the infirmary. Since the game had begun, they had already seen five medic signals. The game was intense.

Drystan held his breath as the medics carried off the orange player. He didn't choose the life of a murderer, but murder seemed to offer opportunities. If he could take Doebromir's lands, then he wouldn't need Stoltland; he could free himself from being a traitor. Doebromir liked to charge headfirst into a situation, so Drystan's trap would devour him. Drystan had placed logs in front of the dug-out portion, concealed by brush—that way, Doebromir would have to leap, landing directly in his trap. His leg or legs would snap instantly; blood loss would cost him his life.

Even though night blanketed the world, Drystan sensed an even deeper darkness surrounding him, wrapping him like a suffocating shroud. Instead of warmth, a chilling dread seeped into his bones. The wind howled ominously, carrying haunting whispers that slithered through the rustling leaves. "You did this, Drystan. There's no escape now," hissed the sinister breeze, twisting his thoughts until he could no longer tell where his mind ended and the malevolence began.

lady lizz

# Chapter 19

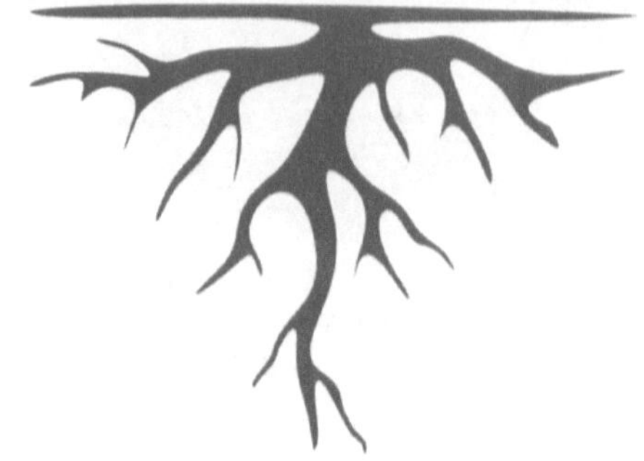

# SNAKES IN THE HOLE

Siany felt her eyes growing weak. She could barely stand. They had been running all night, and her joints ached, not to mention her wrist still throbbed. She and Lizz were assigned to stake out flag twelve. They knew the number of tacklers would start to dwindle toward the end of the night, presenting the perfect opportunity to make their move. Shivering, she felt a chill in the air and wished she had made a small burrow in the ground like Lizz had.

She pulled her green hood over her head and tried to wrap her arms tightly around herself. She grumbled at the lack of light, which prevented her from seeing how many were left guarding the flag. The medic lights always helped the most, but that was a terrible thought to have—wishing for more medic fireworks. She was glad her team only had one player hurt. Poor Jashun twisted his ankle near the beginning of the game; a nasty goose egg swelled around it. Jashun usually didn't play Feydom, but Drystan's abrupt change made Favien move Lord Saeth from R8 to T6. Siany remembered Jashun's reluctance when Favien asked him to join the team. She felt sorry for him now.

Tiny glimpses of daylight crept over the horizon, reminding Siany of what was at stake. They only had the morning hours left before the game would stop for the counting. She looked to Lizz for her headcount. Lizz held up four fingers. Siany nodded. She counted four as well, but her mind started playing tricks. Were they counting the same four, or did Lizz see another player that she couldn't, and vice versa? She tried to signal to Lizz, asking whether she was sure, but Lizz was confused by her hand gestures. She didn't have her sister's connection with Lizz. Sealyn and Lizz were excellent teammates at Feydom. They grew up together as infants, so it was as if they shared one mind. Siany needed those connections right now.

She tried to remember the correct hand signals, but she recalled that Lizz and Sealyn would create their own version and even speak in a language so no one could intercept their conversations. Why did her sister have to be so difficult? She felt a tap on her shoulder and nearly jumped out of her skin, only to recognize the green jersey with R5 painted on the chest. It was Dinyelle! Siany was so relieved.

"I'm so glad you're here," whispered Siany.

"I couldn't let you and Lizz have all the fun." She grinned with a wide smile that lit up her face.

The morning sunlight beamed through the trees, highlighting Dinyelle's light freckles on her nose. Her hair was in several black, frizzy braids; some even had green feathers woven into them. She crouched low and peered between the leaves. A purple and orange caterpillar inched its way across her light brown hand, but she didn't move. She could make no sudden movements. She held up four fingers to Lizz.

"I'll sneak around to the other side to double-check the number," Dinyelle whispered. "We need to do this quickly. Send me a sign when you're ready."

"Sign? What sign?" asked Siany, but Dinyelle was already gone.

Siany huffed. How was she supposed to signal? How would they confirm the number? She needed a final headcount before charging forward. She paused before listing more questions in her head; Sealyn wouldn't hesitate. Sealyn would charge forward, screaming at the tacklers, creating her own aura of chaos and fear. Siany wasn't like that, though. She needed her lists and needed them checked multiple times before taking action.

As she pondered what signal to send Dinyelle, Siany looked over at Lizz, who was scrambling to get out of her hole. To Siany's horror, she saw snakes slithering out of the same burrow. When Lizz looked back to see how many snakes were emerging, she let out a blistering scream and sprinted toward the flag. She resembled a runaway tiger, dodging trees at high speed.

Dinyelle thought this was Siany's signal; she popped up from across the clearing, running for the flag as well. Siany knew to wait a few seconds after all the tacklers were preoccupied with the other girls; then she would make her move.

Lizz sailed past Purple T1, who looked half asleep, then juked past Purple T2. She thought she was going to get the flag, but Orange T4 grabbed her ankle, making her crash. Dinyelle shot past Purple T9 with ease, but Purple T6 had been hiding in the brush and tackled her from the side. She went down with a hard thud, back aching. Siany saw her chance moments before Dinyelle was tackled. She grabbed the flag fast, pausing to watch the green fireworks dance in the radiant morning sky. The dirt-stained girls leaped in celebration, embracing each other. They felt like nothing could stop them from winning.

Before the royals announced the points, each team gathered in front of their team-colored sections of the stadium. They smelled horribly, and the Clod members were covered in dirt and sweat. The fans had gathered again in the stands, cheering for their favorite players. Some called out praises to the members who had grabbed the flags, while others chanted their colors.

Sealyn walked gracefully to her speaking post. She looked over all the teams, remembering what it was like standing there waiting for the tally. The nervousness had made her want to vomit each time. She would make the counting quick to spare them.

"Greetings to you all, and thank you for joining us," Sealyn began. "I emphasize how each player feels right now: tired, hungry, hurt, and exhausted. Because of this, I will make the counting quick." The teams clapped. They all remembered the year King Ryker told a long Feydom story that kept them there for an hour. "To ease your exhaustion and pain, I decided I would read the one hundred nineteenth diary entry from our beloved King Daevedon to renew your strength and courage." The crowds moaned, and the players' mouths gaped.

Two hundred years ago, King Daevedon ascended the throne and considered himself a poet. He wrote countless diary entries each day, but the 119th entry turned out to be the most famous because it was his longest. One evening, he read for two hours to his military troops. The military has never forgotten this night.

Sealyn giggled. "Of course, I'm only joking. I could never be so cruel to my former teammates and fellow Elysian citizens." The crowd roared with laughter and cheers. "Let's get started, shall we? The counting is as follows: black seven, blue six, green ten, orange four, red six, purple three, and"— she paused for dramatic effect—"yellow nine." Green pipscot powder was thrown from the green seats, covering every spectator and the players. The other teams, still in the game, decided to throw their team-colored pipscot powder as well.

"Thank you, Purple Phoenixes," Sealyn said with kindness. "We acknowledge your efforts, but now take your leave to recover and join the festival. To the rest of you, they are the ones getting off easy. Your two-hour break begins now. Hurry to your campsites."

The players ran through the trees back to their campsites, where the medical Nichts awaited them. These two hours were crucial for mending wounds, catching up on sleep, and strategizing. The Green Phoenixes believed they could win the game during Vision; they just needed to defeat the Yellow Phoenixes. Everyone was shocked by the number of flags they collected, as double digits were not typical for Clod. Proudly, they stood ready to face their next challenge.

# Chapter 20

Stoltland was a dark kingdom, full of ancient secrets and lies. Shadows whispered of the prophecies, words no one wanted to acknowledge. Darkness seeped into the very soul of the kingdom, devouring anyone willing to accept its deception. Corentine's hatred overwhelmed her, a haunting reality that she needed to make bold moves if she was to defeat Elsyium. She stood beside the dark river that flowed behind the palace, a cold, bitter wind blowing through her bright ruby hair.

The water flowed swiftly across the obsidian rocks of the river. Purple and black moss grew over the shallow stones near the bank, emitting wet, earthy smells. Corentine stared at the river, watching the trapped night creatures. She wished she could push Sealyn into its deadly waters; perhaps one day she would get that chance. A smile tugged at her lips at the thought.

The river suddenly reminded her of *him*. Now, why would *he* come to mind? Surely enough time had passed that his sea palms did not need to grasp her thoughts. She still blamed him, though. Everything would have been different. She could have become a proper lady, married without hidden agendas, and maintained her freedom longer, but *he* stole that from her. One day, she would make him pay, too.

Her black eyes looked across the river and saw dark mist coming toward her. She started to panic as it hovered above the water.

"What do you want?"

Silence.

"Are you mine to command?"

Silence.

This wasn't the first time she encountered the mist. She rummaged her mind for a plan. Last time, the mist obeyed her commands with just her thoughts and body movements. Perhaps, she should try again, and this time really give it a test.

She thought to herself, "I wish to cross the river. Be my bridge." As she pointed to the water, she watched the mist flatten itself across the water, forming a slight arch. Evil amusement swept across her face. Corentine lifted her onyx skirt and took a step onto the mist, which felt hard as wood. She took another step, and the same thing happened. Heart pounding with excitement, she ran across the misty black bridge to the other side. She let out a small cackle, but when she looked back, the mist was gone. Why did the mist sometimes show itself and other times not? She needed to figure this out. If she could find the source for summoning the mist, then she could potentially use this as her greatest weapon.

"My lady?" Keket inquired. "How'd you get across without getting wet?"

"Never mind that. What do you want?"

"Pardon me, but you have an urgent letter from Drystan. Apparently, the letter arrived days ago but was dropped behind a table."

"Why are servants so empty-headed? Take the letter back to my study."

"Do you need assistance crossing the river?"

"No. Do as I say, Keket." Corentine glared toward her. Keket turned and ran back toward the house, although her run ended quickly. She took several breaks to catch her breath. Keket was a very plump woman with vibrant purple hair. Corentine was surprised she made it up the hill without collapsing. Once she saw Keket was out of sight, she tried to focus on calling the mist, but nothing happened.

"Where are you?"

Again, silence.

"I command you to appear."

Silence.

What was she to do? If the mist obeyed her thoughts, then perhaps she needed to have the same thoughts or emotions she had when the mist arrived. She closed her eyes to review what she had been thinking about: her past, annoying sounds, *him*, and that pompous child-queen. She opened her eyes to the dark mist, as if fog could stare back at her.

This would be a painful game to play with herself and the mist. She didn't want to think about her past and *him* to summon the mist, but she could think about that green bird girl.

"Carry me across the river."

The mist divided into two sections, both forming what looked like giant hands. Each dark hand cradled one of Corentine's arms and then lifted her through the air, setting her gently on the other side. Her inky eyes sparkled with torturous ideas. She could feel her love for dark magic growing, and she knew how she wanted to use it.

Keket poured red wine into the silver goblet and placed the bottle at the center of Corentine's dark mahogany table. She made sure the silver plate with the small sandwiches was perfectly arranged along with the letter. She gazed around the room and gave a tiny shudder at the sight of the stuffed alligator. She hated alligators. Corentine entered the room with a smug grin on her face and petted her dogs as they greeted her.

"My lady, I have your refreshments and wine ready for your letter reading."

"Excellent, Keket. Now, leave me so I may read alone."

Keket bowed oddly and left the room. Corentine took a sip of her wine, then opened the letter.

*Dearest Lady Corentine,*

*Your son is fairing Nicely. He's fitting in sO well That you would hardly know he was from Stoltland. He's Taking a liking to raising tHe nEw exiguums; even the queen bought two fRom hIm. He's making many new friends as well, but the most notable is the Queen herself. They have been seen on seVeral outings in a courting fashion. Yes, I bElieve the Queen is couRting your son. What a great day fOr youR Ladyship this must be to LeArn this joyous news. I hope this letter finds you in Kind hEalth.*

*Respectly,*

*Lord Drystan.*

Corentine blinked in disbelief. Did her son actually have a chance to become a queen's spouse? She never thought Jace would rise to any high social position, especially a royal one. Pride festered within her. She loathed that bird queen. If she married him, her son, the outcast of society, would outrank her. She would have no control over him. Panic surged through her body as she gulped down more wine. "I must disrupt this new courtship. Somehow, I must convince the queen he's unsuitable for her," she said to no one in the empty room.

Tapping the letter on the table, she remembered the secret code Drystan had to include in the letter. She quickly scanned the words and saw large letters that shouldn't be capitalized. She wrote them on the side of the letter.

*N-O-T-T-H-E-R-I-V-E-R-O-R-L-A-K-E.*

Knowing what they were investigating, she recognized immediately what the secret message was: not the river or lake.

She threw her quill across the room. "Curse that wretched kingdom! Now what? I have to figure out where this Heart of Elysium is!" She slammed her hand on the table and rang for Keket.

"Yes, my lady."

"I need to speak to my husband immediately. I will also need to have an audience with the queen."

"Yes, my lady. I will get these messages out right away." Keket scurried out the door, bumping into Prince Svagon. "Pardon me, my prince, but your wife would like to speak with you." She bowed graciously.

Prince Svagon entered Lady Corentine's study to find her pouring another glass of wine. "My lady, Keket said you wanted to speak with me?"

"Drystan wrote telling us that the heart of Elysium is not in the rivers or the lakes, so we'll have to figure out where the clue leads, and we'll do so by spending the winter months in Elysium."

"What do you mean by months?"

"Exactly what I said. We will spend the winter months in Avondelle. Why? Well, I will tell you why!" she spoke loudly, answering her own question. "Because the queen is courting my son! My son! I will end their courtship."

"She does seem quite old for him."

"Old? She's ancient compared to him!"

"Well, I think ancient is a bit excessive. They are six or eight years apart, yes?"

"I don't care whether they are one or one thousand years apart! I don't want him with her. We will travel by sea with our entire family. I will send word to Jace today."

"I believe our queen needs to approve such a massive travel request."

"I know," she snapped. "I've already arranged a meeting with the queen. You see how inconvenient it is for me not to be queen? She needs to name you the crown's heir; then I can finally drop this lady title nonsense, and Tahbert can become Prince Tahbert as he should be."

"If she grants this winter expedition, then we will have all the time in the world to approach her on the subject while we travel to Elysium."

"Excellent, then I will be a better and more powerful queen than little Sealyn could ever imagine."

Corentine wondered whether the mist would follow her to Elysium. Did the mist only exist on Stoltland's land? She would test her theories on their ships and in Avondelle. Once she had the Stoltland crown and the Heart of Elysium, she would be the most powerful person in history, especially as she embraced her new darkness.

Queen Sealyn,

My beautiful granddaughter, I beg you to remember these virtues: gratefulness, thankfulness, gratitude, kindness, humility, and mercy. Allow these to be your heartbeat. The curse may be strong, but you are stronger with these virtues.

Always with love,
Grand Queen Karis Dovinus

Lord Prince
Tilmond
Araelien

# Chapter 21

Two arrows fired from Lord Max's bow struck one of the huge green pipscots, sending massive clouds of sparkling emerald powder over the territory. The exploding pipscots were captivating for the spectators to watch, but for the players, the clouds of smoke obstructed visibility. Players' jerseys began changing colors to the point that players sometimes couldn't correctly identify each other.

Tilmond galloped fiercely on his white horse, now covered in green, orange, and black powder. He saw the Black Phoenix horseman lining up his shot. Too far away to make a standard shield block, he threw his throwing shield, praying it would follow the perfect trajectory. Smash! The shield collided with the arrow. Before the horseman could line up his next shot, Tilmond positioned himself in front of the black pipscot, ready for proper shielding. Black H3 realized he wouldn't be able to make his shot, so he guided his chestnut horse toward another path.

Lord Max, Lord Aerrik, and Lady Rivers trotted up behind Tilmond. Each one was covered in green powder.

"Excellent block on that shield throw, Lord Prince Tilmond!" exclaimed Max. Tilmond nodded.

"We were hoping you would block those arrows. We really didn't want to wear black powder." Aerrik chuckled.

"How did you all become so green?" questioned Tilmond with a big grin.

"Max shot the pipscot, and we were riding right behind him, so there was no way to avoid a mouth full of the greenness." Rivers smiled big, showing her tinted teeth.

"Does anyone know the counts?" Tilmond asked.

"I lost count a while back," Max admitted.

"If I'm remembering correctly, the Clod team only has two more flags left, and we cleared at least three pipscots so far," Aerrik said.

Tilmond sighed. "Well, with darkness closing in, we need to get one more pipscot to feel comfortable; then we can reconvene at the campsite."

Max nodded. "I agree. Rivers. Aerrik. Let's go. May the arrows fly to your shield, Tilmond!" The three Green Phoenix horsemen raced toward their next target with green dust flying from their backs.

Kolt, the green T4, swung his leg around Orange R5's waist, trying to keep him pinned to the ground. Orange R5 slipped from Kolt's grip and kicked dirt into his face. Kolt coughed and jumped to his feet. He called out to his tackling partner, Cian, for help. Cian, the largest tackler the Green Phoenixes had ever seen, moved swiftly over the rocky ground. Despite his size, Cian moved like a cheetah. He barreled into Orange R5, wrapping his arms around him. Both crashed to the ground with a loud thud, and dust floated around them.

Kolt jogged over to the human pile and stared down at the orange player with a cheeky grin. "Well, Cian, I think you flattened him even more than he already was!"

Waddling his way to an upright position, Cian dusted himself off. These were the two fierce cousins of Siany and Sealyn, although not by blood but by marriage. "I expect he won't be able to breathe normally for a few hours, but at least this flag won't be going anywhere tonight."

Doebromir and Jem ran to the scene of Cian, Kolt, and the flattened orange R5. "We heard the commotion, so we thought we would come help out," Jem said while panting.

"No need to worry. We handled the young one quite nicely." Cian chuckled.

"Jem, how are you liking Feydom?" asked Kolt. "They don't play this game in your kingdom, correct?"

Jem lowered his crimson eyes. "Apparently, they used to. Feydom is well known across the seven kingdoms, but it hasn't been played in my kingdom for years. I was ecstatic to play." He brushed back his blonde hair, hoping those would be the last questions about his homeland. His kingdom of Havas had too many dark secrets; some he would never reveal to the queen.

"Great to hear, Jem," responded Kolt.

"By the time we make it to the campsite, it'll be dark," remarked Doebromir. "Favien wants to go over a new strategy based on the counts for tonight. Let's head back now. We can tackle a few on the way back, too." He rubbed his hands together with intensity.

"What a sight this is," Drystan mocked. "The outcasts of the Green Phoenixes."

"Ignore him," growled Doebromir.

"Come now, Doebromir. After all, you were the one who failed to be captain again, and I find you with two sirs with no land to their names and a red-eyed fox. Tell me how you're not the outcast crew?"

"Too far, Drystan! Now shut your face, or I'll shut it for you," Doebromir growled.

"How about a deal instead?" Drystan smiled slyly. "If you can catch me before I reach your team's flag just behind that tree thicket, then I'll pull my men from guarding it, and your roamers can take the flag freely."

"And what's in it for you?" questioned Doebromir.

"When you lose, you have to muck out my horse stalls for a month." Drystan laughed loudly. He wanted Doebromir to take the bait.

Doebromir considered the deal. His team only needed two more flags to win, which would provide them with the ultimate advantage going into the night with one flag left. However, something seemed off about Drystan. They had raced many times, and he almost always won, not Drystan. If possible, he appeared even more smug than usual. Could this be a trap?

Finn jogged into the circle of men, looking bewildered with his caerulean eyes. He surveyed the scene, wondering why all these tacklers were standing around, merely talking to each other.

"What's happening?" asked Finn.

"We're about to see who's better, me or Doebromir, but looks to me like Doebro-baby is too scared to find out!"

"That's it! You conniving backstabber!" yelled Doebromir. "I'll race you, and Finn here can take the flag back to the campsite once I win!"

"Wait, Doebromir," said Finn. "We haven't scanned this site yet. We don't know the terrain."

Drystan pointed at Finn and laughed. "Seriously? You need to vet a flag site before charging? Such scared little ladies I have surrounding me."

"Enough, Drystan. Let's get this race over with," commanded Doebromir.

They stepped side by side, and Drystan pointed straight ahead. Kolt, Cian, and Jem ran ahead. Finn stood behind the two racers and yelled, "Go!" Drystan and Doebromir took off like the wind. They dodged branches, jumped over rocks, and darted around boulders. The two barreled toward the flag with victory in sight. Drystan began to breathe heavily and slowed down. Doebromir knew he was going to win. He kept his eye on the flag, his heart pounding.

He spotted an easy jump over a few logs to claim the flag, and his team would be one step closer to winning Feydom. Doebromir didn't slow down; instead, he picked up speed. He leaped over the small logs, expecting to land on solid brush, only to find himself sinking into a deep hole. He heard a snap and hoped it was branches breaking, but the most agonizing pain shot up his leg. Something was broken. Doebromir screamed for help in rapid breaths. He glanced down at his leg and saw his bone protruding through the skin, blood pouring out. He felt nauseous and vomited.

Finn sprinted from behind, urgency coursing through his veins as he reached for the medic flare. The response team arrived in a blur, moving with frantic determination. After the medic team hastily whisked Doebromir away, Finn's heart raced as he scanned the chaotic scene where Doebromir had fallen. He shoved aside the brush in a desperate panic and stumbled upon the horrifying truth of what had happened. The more he moved the brush, the more he realized he was uncovering a dug-out trench. Blood boiling, he motioned for his teammates to see what he had discovered.

"Do you see what I see?" asked Finn. "This was intentionally made."

Jem cleared his throat. "You don't think Drystan did this, do you? Would he be that devious to dig a trench and trick Doebromir into that race?"

"I think Drystan is capable of anything at this point," whispered Kolt. "He doesn't care for anyone except himself."

The four men needed to get back to their campsite. They were already late for the meetup, but vengeance surged through them. They saw that only four tacklers remained, all Black Phoenixes. They devised a plan that was completely outlandish, but they wanted to try.

The three green tacklers charged at the flag, with Finn hiding behind them, throwing the Black Phoenixes off guard. The four Black Phoenixes turned to face the emerald force approaching them. Finn stayed low, ready to make his move when the collision occurred. Cian stretched out his arms and grabbed the two end tacklers, Black T6 and T3. Once Jem saw that Cian had the two end tacklers, he knew he could take down Drystan solo. Kolt slightly curved to his right, tackling Black T9. They fell forward, pinning both Drystan and Jem to the ground.

Finn spotted his break. He darted around the scrambling piles of men and dove for the flag, sliding several feet—just enough to set off the fireworks. Finn rolled onto his back to watch the glistening jade light dance across the night sky. He could hear the echoes of the distant crowd cheering. Finn looked at the flag and felt truly part of Elysium. This was home.

Jace watched from the royal box, hoping to see green fireworks. He felt incredibly proud of his friends. It almost made him forget the letter he had received from his mother earlier that day. He was on edge, wondering why she wanted to spend part of the winter season in Avondelle. The ships would take weeks to arrive, but that didn't settle his nerves. Everything was going so smoothly here, and he didn't want her to disrupt the peace.

He knew he needed to tell Sealyn how he felt before his family arrived; he wanted no distractions. It was time to be brave.

"Am I interrupting your celebrations?" asked Sealyn flirtatiously.

Jace jumped to his feet. "No, not at all, my Majesty. I mean. Your Majesty. My apologies."

Sealyn giggled. "No need to apologize. If I weren't the queen, I might have enjoyed your possessive comment."

Jace swore to himself that if he was going to be with her, he would need to hire someone to remind him to breathe in her presence. How could he forget the basic norms of being human when he was around her? Jace coached himself: "Breathe, you stupid fool. Good. Now, blink. Blink, man, blink! You look like a frozen idiot."

"Jace, are you alright? You haven't spoken in almost five minutes, and you look worried."

"Yes, Your Majesty. I'm quite alright. How…How are you?"

"Excellent. I'm enjoying the counts for the Green Phoenixes immensely."

"Of course. I'm very happy for them as well," Jace agreed.

"You seem deep in thought, Jace. Is there a situation you wish to discuss?"

Jace cleared his throat and rubbed his chiseled jawline. "I had a letter from my mother this afternoon. She says that she and the family are coming to spend part of the winter season here."

"Really? I've heard of no request from Stoltland." Sealyn narrowed her eyes. "They'll have to petition for entrance. Either way, if you want me to deny them entry, then I will." She hoped he wouldn't want to see them. This move by Stoltland put her in a bad position.

Jace raised a hand. "No. Please don't deny them entry. I don't want to cause any issues between our kingdoms. I just worry about how they'll act once they're here. I don't mean to cast a shadow over your happy time."

"Seeing you happy makes me happy, Jace. I thought you would have figured that out by now." She nudged his shoulder with hers.

Jace watched the queen walk to the window and look out toward the Feydom territory. He chuckled to himself when he saw her face crinkle at the sight of an orange pipscot bursting over the trees. Could this future be in his grasp? Could he really have moments like this for the rest of his life? Laughing with Sealyn and having deep conversations with her was all he could think about—well, that and a few other things, but he tried to keep those thoughts at bay. Should this be his moment to reveal his feelings to her? They were alone. Jace's heart pounded as he walked to stand beside her.

Jace gently took Sealyn's hand and held it near his heart. "Queen Sealyn, I need to speak what's in my heart before my courage disappears. I feel as if I've somehow walked into one of my dreams; only this dream is better than any normal dream I've ever had. I wake up excited to start my day. I almost don't want to sleep at night, afraid I'm missing time with you. My reality is better than any dream I can dream, and I don't want that to end. Every reason for this is because of you. I know I'm nothing, but I must ask if you feel the same."

Heat burned Sealyn's cheeks, and a smile broke over her face. "Of course, Jace. I was going to wait until after the celebrations to share the same feelings with you."

Jace laughed and hugged her instantly. He leaned back and passionately cupped her face, kissing her with all the hunger his heart would allow. Their lips felt as if they were gliding through a perfect dance. They were giving in to each other's desires, tasting every sensation that sent tingling feelings to their toes. Jace pressed her body against the glass window; every inch of his body groaned for more.

Through the window, a bright white light illuminated the room. They both recoiled to see what had occurred. Stomachs dropping, they read the medic call for Lord Doebromir: Green T1. Queen Sealyn gasped. It must be a terrible injury for Doebromir to ever request a medic. She grasped Jace's chin and pulled him in for one last kiss.

"As much as I don't want to leave this room, I need to see to Lord Doebromir's condition," Sealyn said with conviction.

Jace smirked and slid his thumb over her bottom lip. "I would never want to keep a queen from her duties."

How in all creation was she supposed to leave him after that? She felt flushed. Her cheeks were red, and her chest rose up and down quickly. She must leave now, or else she would find herself back in his strong embrace. "Doebromir. Yes, focus on Doebromir!" she thought to herself. She nodded her head to Jace, and with mischievous smiles, they both exited the room.

Siany held out bowls of warm soup to Lizz and Dinyelle as they took their seats near the fire. Siany always enjoyed the campsite part of Feydom. The campfire made her feel protected and free from responsibilities. The sounds of the crackling fire seemed to wash away her exhaustion, providing a welcome sensation. She looked around the large circle of her teammates and felt sad for all those missing due to injuries.

Favien took another sip of his warm tea, wrapping his worn and dirty fingers around the tincup. "I just want to say that you all have done a great job so far. We've taken some hard losses, but I'm proud of the way we've still managed to have high counts. I want this to be a team effort, so I have a couple of options for everyone to decide how we approach these next hours. Tybalt, why don't you share the first option?"

Tybalt chewed fast to finish his big bite of bread. "Of course, Favien. Well, it's simple, really. Clod will attack full force on the last flag. Large opposition will be there, but I'm sure we can handle it." He smacked his knee and nodded toward his teammates.

Once Favien pointed in his direction, Max cleared his throat. "As far as Vision goes, we know how dangerous it is for the horses to speed through the forest at night, so Vision players will sit out the night hours."

"Sit out?" questioned Finn. "Why can't you all just join us to capture the last flag?"

"That's against the rules," Siany instructed. "A horse player must remain mounted."

"My apologies. I'm still learning." Finn dropped his head.

"Don't hang your head, Finn!" the giantlike Cian roared. "You captured our thirteenth flag! You're doing great."

"I propose that our roamers and tacklers stay on defending the flags rather than capturing the last one," Jdru proclaimed. "Sorry, Favien. I wasn't sure whether it was my turn to speak yet or not."

Dinyelle stood. "I agree with Jdru. It makes more sense that our competition will be heavily guarding our last flag, and the other teams who are behind usually use the night to gain counts."

"Dinyelle speaks wisely," said Kolt. "Also, we don't have any idea what the surroundings are with the last flag. With what we experienced at the last one, we need daylight to make sure Drystan and his gang didn't set any more traps."

"Drystan did that?!" Favien asked aggressively.

Finn looked around and decided to speak when no one else did. "That seems to be the closest explanation. Why else taunt Doebromir into a race during Feydom? He would only do that if he had prior knowledge of something looming in the future for Doebromir's demise. Besides, the trench we uncovered was clearly dug."

"Let's quickly take this to a vote so we can get to it," commanded Favien. He tried not to sound angry, but he was livid with Drystan. Aside from Feydom, they were military brothers. What could make one brother harm another? Could Drystan be infected with the curse? His heart skipped a beat. He would set that fear aside and finish the game; then he could deal with Drystan.

"All in favor of Tybalt's plan, raise your hand," Lizz said. "All in favor of Jdru's plan, raise your hand." With a confused expression, she looked at Tybalt, who was raising his hand for Jdru's plan. "Tybalt, what are you doing?"

"What? It's a good plan," Tybalt said.

Chuckling, Favien spoke, "Before we depart, let us raise our cups to our injured teammates. To the roamers: Lord Jashun and Princess Siany, even though she's playing through her injury. To the tacklers: Lady Devan, Lord Mervin, Lord Saeth, and Lord Doebromir. To the horsemen: Lord Stawyer. And to the shields: Lady Nellvian and Lord Jecko. We salute your sacrifices."

Once they drank to their teammates, the Clod team prepared itself and ventured into the darkness. Max watched his teammates leave, wishing he could join them, but he felt something different stirring inside. Something was telling him that a bigger battle was coming, and not a Feydom battle either. He felt it when Finn spoke about Drystan's betrayal.

He knew that betrayal would lead to even worse consequences, and he would be prepared. He felt confident in his comrades, but also in the secret weapon he had yet to reveal to the queen.

# Chapter 22

Aerrik stretched his arms and gave a giant yawn at the morning light. He felt stiff on the hard ground and could smell the smoke from the fire that had died down during the night. He opened his eyes and blinked, trying to figure out what he was actually seeing. Squinting, he saw glass clouds. Surely not. He sat up quickly and smacked Temm and Tilmond.

"Hey! Watch it, Aerrik!" shouted Temm. The short, bearded Temm was not a morning person and made sure to let everyone know once he was disturbed. "We still have another hour before we have to wake."

"Look!" Aerrik pointed to the sky.

"What is that?" Tilmond asked.

"It looks like glass clouds to me," remarked Aerrik.

"Glass clouds don't exist," snapped Temm.

Aerrik folded his arms, frustrated. "I know that, but this is Elysium. I've seen stranger things than that before."

Tilmond stood up and shaded his eyes with his hand for a better look at the strange object in the sky. "Wait, it looks to have rounded edges."

With the sounds of pounding hooves and snorting nostrils, Max and Rav returned on their horses and saw everyone looking at the sky with dazed expressions.

Max laughed. "Should we tell them what these objects are, Rav?"

"Objects?" questioned Aerrik. "You mean there's more than one?"

Max held up three fingers. "There are three."

"It's for wings, isn't it?" asked Tilmond excitedly.

Max nodded, then dismounted his white-spotted horse, boots crunching on the ground. "Correct. They're thick ice bowls. We've concluded that this is what the Wings players will face. The stones are heavy, so possibly, the heavier rocks you toss onto the ice, the greater the chances of the ice breaking."

"If the Wings players don't figure out how to toss the rocks gently, then the bowl will surely break," said Rav.

"How does a person gently toss a twenty-pound rock onto ice while riding a crazy nomosev?" asked Temm incredulously.

"I guess we'd better go break the news to our flying teammates," Tilmond said while laughing.

Before the Vision teammates could make their way to the Wings' cots, they saw Jem and Tybalt jogging back to the campsite.

"Jem! Tybalt! Is everything alright?" asked Aerrik.

Panting, Jem spoke up first. "Yes, we volunteered to bring water and some breakfast back to everyone."

"You mean they're not coming back for a break?" Max didn't like hearing that his teammates weren't stopping. "Jem. Tybalt. Sit here and rest. Eat and rehydrate while we fix the food and water to carry back. Tell us what happened through the night."

"Thanks, Max," Tybalt said gratefully. "It was madness. You could tell everyone was expecting us to charge our last flag, so it was the right move not to go for it. Blue must still be at the bottom of the counts because their entire team stayed throughout the night." He wiped sweat dripping from his nose and forehead, smearing dirt on his face. "We mainly focused our efforts on purple, orange, and black, but it was clear the Yellow Phoenixes decided to rest the night."

"They also sustained the most injuries so far as well," added Jem.

Max thought deeply about what his next move should be. He needed to step up and lead his teammates to something large. He felt the pressure because he was filling the queen's shoes. "Sealyn. Yes, Sealyn. What would Queen Sealyn do if she were here?" he asked himself. She would come up with the unexpected.

"Team, what is expected of us right now?" asked Max.

Tybalt looked confused by the question. "We're supposed to return with food and water, and Vision is supposed to head back to the territory for a couple of hours before the count."

Max asked one more question, "What is expected of Vision?"

Jem looked at Tybalt and squinted his face, then looked back at Max. "To burst some pipscots, Max. Isn't that the job of the horsemen?"

"Exactly!" Max jumped to his feet. "We're going to do what isn't expected!"

"Now, wait a minute, Max." Tybalt started standing.

"Just hear me out. If everyone expects us to do that, then so does the competition. Let's honor our unconventional queen and do what she would do: the unexpected, the unpredictable."

"And what would that be?" asked Temm smugly.

"We all attack our flag! We could end this right now, before the counting even begins! Come on, team! I personally don't feel like constantly looking up, wondering whether shattered ice and heavy rocks are going to fall on my head today."

Max crouched low to the ground, and using sticks and rocks, he devised an attack strategy on the ground. "This could work. The horse shields could go first, followed by tacklers, then horsemen, and lastly, our remaining roamers."

"I'm in!" Aerrik raised his fist high in the air. "Let's do this!"

The men quickly rose, packing the horses with food and water for their teammates. Once everyone had saddled their horses, they galloped off to find their teammates, dust flying behind them. The scents of the forest soon filled their nostrils, heralding the impending scent of victory.

The Green Phoenixes waited for their scouts to return from their last flag position. This was it. They could feel adrenaline flowing through their veins. The roamers and tacklers were still gulping down water when Brooke, Temm, and Aerrik arrived at their hidden position.

"There aren't as many as we figured, but there's enough for everyone to have a job," Aerrik spoke quickly.

Max gathered the team around his drawing on the ground, again using sticks and rocks for visual coaching. He advised each player on how to defend, and Favien instructed them on how to be offensive. They had a limited amount of time to complete this final mission. It had to be now. The Vision players mounted their horses, while the Clod members positioned themselves at the correct distance from the horses.

Favien's heart pounded. He remembered his promise to himself. If this plan were to work, he would have to be brave twice today. "Green Phoenixes! Together, we win!" yelled Favien. "Now!"

The ground trembled with the pounding of the horses' hooves. Their nostrils flared as they plunged toward the final flag. Fear shot through the opponents as they saw the entire force of the Green Phoenixes heading straight for them. They charged forward, trying to instill chaos in the horses. Black T5 and T8 threw handfuls of dirt at the horses' eyes. Receiving the dirt, Tilmond and Rav's horses reared up, almost bucking them off. With his raven hair blowing in the wind, Rav's horse continued to buck its head and blink, trying to clear the dirt from its eyes. Tilmond attempted to manage his horse, which began spinning in circles, so Tilmond used this to his advantage. He pulled the reins to the left, guiding the horse toward Black T5.

With a loud smack, Tilmond's horse collided with Black T5's head, a horse vengeance if he ever saw one. The first wave of horse shields created enough panic that when the green tacklers rushed in with such force, almost none of the opponents saw them coming.

Jem wrapped his muscular arms around Orange T2 and landed on the ground with him. Yellow T7 juked past the massive Cian but painfully met the backside of the still-spinning horse of Tilmond. This horse was two for two. Cian took the opportunity and jumped on top of the Yellow Phoenix, making sure he didn't rise. Kolt managed to grab one ankle of the fast Red T9, so Corter dodged the horses and came to Kolt's aid. Corter slammed himself right into Red T9's side, and down they both went. Kolt dove away from the bucking horse that Rav was no longer on.

The green horsemen had to use excellent precision to cut clear paths through the pandemonium for the roamers, and they had to avoid stepping on their teammates in the process. Max steered his horse hard right, evading Jem, who was now in a wrestling match with Orange T2. Seeing Max coming more toward his side, Temm kicked his black horse harder to avoid crashing into Max. His horse then had to jump over a small boulder he hadn't expected. Max did suggest doing the unexpected. Yellow T6 leaped from another boulder next to the one Temm was currently jumping over and seized Temm from his horse. The two crashed down violently, rolling away from each other—each was injured. Temm felt his elbow crack, and pain shot up his arm. He knew he was out of the game.

Aerrik swiftly jumped his horse over the scrambling pile of Corter and Kolt with Red T9. He charged his horse toward Yellow T5 and T8. Yellow T5 dove right, dodging the horse, but Yellow T8's shoulder absorbed the impact of the horse and spun to the ground.

Brooke and Beth rode side by side with their horses in the same stride. They chased after Black T1 and Blue T7. Both opponents ran into the forest, not wanting to participate with any horse hooves. The roamers came pouring into the clearing, seeing most of their opponents had been taken out. Siany, Tybalt, and Dinyelle were the decoys for the roamers. They sprinted hard toward the flag, only to have the massive Red T7 and T1 take out all three. Red T7 grabbed Siany's shirt, causing her to fall backward, landing again on her injured wrist. It was officially broken at that point. Red T7 gained his footing and tackled Dinyelle to the ground, knocking the breath out of her. Tybalt tried to juke past Red T1, but Red T1 was too agile and wrapped his arms around Tybalt's knees. He was stuck.

The fastest of the Green Phoenixes were left. They heard the five-minute drums start to play. Hearts pounding in their ears, Favien, Jdru, Lizz, and Finn raced toward the flag. They were no longer just in competition with the opponents; now they were racing against time. Yellow T5 recovered his footing after evading Aerrik's horse and tackled Finn. The remaining Green Phoenixes remained focused on their target. Lizz leaped onto a boulder, preparing to jump, but lost her footing and slipped off. Favien and Jdru held steady but spotted two remaining tacklers: Blue T2 and Orange T3. Out of the corner of their eyes, they noticed the other opposing tacklers escaping from their green counterparts. Fear struck Favien. How was he and Jdru supposed to face off against the two tacklers in front of the flag while being pursued by the other tacklers from behind?

Seeing the issue, Max led his horsemen and shields into a single-file line, creating a protective circle that enclosed their roamers. The opposing players couldn't cross the continuously circling horses. This was the moment they had to win. Favien started to veer left while Jdru went right, but the tacklers met them head-on.

Lizz managed to tuck and roll out of her stumble and gained fast momentum behind Jdru and Favien. She darted to Favien's side and slid into Orange T3's legs. Lizz's move scared Favien, as he hadn't realized she was still in play. The adrenaline sent him jumping over Lizz and Orange T3. He looked to his right and saw Jdru was trying to stiff-arm Blue T2, but the Blue Phoenix was preventing Jdru from gaining access to the flag. Jdru's bald head and reddish beard were covered in dirt and grime; he was doing whatever it took to win.

The only hope the Green Phoenixes had was Favien, and there was no one in his way. The forest stilled, and for just a second, everything was silent. No crowds cheering. No birds chirping or grunts from teammates—just peace. A blurry image of Pinx stood next to the last green flag, his sign to finish the game and claim his true prize. With all his remaining energy, Favien sprinted and snatched the flag with force, sending up massive celebratory fireworks.

All of Avondelle could see that the Green Phoenixes had won Feydom with emerald fireworks bursting in the morning sky. Favien looked up and smiled at the dazzling greens and golds displayed above him. They had done it. They had won Feydom with Clod! His teammates joined him in cheering, hugging, and patting each other on the back. The horsemen dismounted and joined in the revelry. Now, it was time to truly celebrate.

King Ryker threw his napkin onto the table, knocking over his orange slices. He stood and paced around the room impatiently. Queen Mother Graelynd glanced at Grand Queen Karis and then at Queen Sealyn. She shook her head at Sealyn, hoping to quell the conversation, but once Sealyn set a goal, she was determined to accomplish it.

"Father, I'm tired of frustration constantly having a seat at our table," Sealyn exhaled. "We must face the fact that tomorrow night, we'll have no idea what we're looking for."

"I don't believe in sending troops blindly into a fight," Ryker snapped.

Sealyn threw her hands in the air. "Fight? How many times must I say this? We don't know if there will be a fight. I understand being prepared, but we must have brains as well as bronze surrounding that mountain."

"And you think you're going to be there?" Ryker demanded.

"Oh, absolutely."

"No! I forbid it!"

Lady Ebbalee, mother to King Ryker, leaned into Karis. "Oh, that's not good."

"Forbid?" Sealyn glared at her father. "May I remind you, Father, that I am the queen, the reigning, heaviest crown, so if I choose to be there, then I will, and I do *not* need your consent."

Ryker sighed. "Sealyn, I know you're queen, and I would not like to challenge you there, but I will remind you that since you are the reigning queen, you must protect that crown at all costs. Sometimes that cost is your pride."

Graelynd clapped her hands. "Alright, that's enough, you two," she calmly scolded. "I'm sure there's a perfectly reasonable plan that can satisfy both of you, but barking at one another will not help." She tossed a few pieces of bread to her peacock, who followed her around like a colorful shadow.

"Beg your pardon, Your Majesties," Lord Steward Briar said, entering the breakfast room. "I need to announce that the Green Phoenixes just won Feydom by Clod."

The royals clapped their hands and let out cheers. Ryker walked to Lord Steward Briar and shook his hand. "Thank you for letting us know. This is great news."

"It's fantastic news," Lady Ebbalee said. "Lord Char owes me twenty gold coins."

"Lord Steward, we must cancel the traditional counting preparations and prepare immediately for the winner celebrations and awards ceremony," instructed Sealyn. "This does give us more time to prepare for tomorrow, and I'm sure we can come up with a proper plan, as Mother said." Lord Steward nodded and left the room to the royals.

"Here's what I advise," started Ryker. "You stay here; then we send out four divisions of the smartest military units we have. That way we can cover the entire mountain."

"I agree with your plan, but I will add that the younger of the Council of Wisdom will join." Sealyn looked around the room at her parents and grandparents. "Are you all willing to concede to this plan?"

Lady Ebbalee's eyes widened. "Why would you think we get a vote?"

"I've learned that this family doesn't make decisions without the entire unit agreeing," Sealyn smirked at her grandmother.

"Well, Ryker, it seems that our little bird just might be a queen someday," Lord Marin joked.

"Gramps, what do you mean someday? I'm already queen, you silly goose."

Marin smiled. "My darling, just because you have a title, doesn't mean you are a queen yet. One day, you will know without a doubt that you are truly *the* Emerald Queen."

Favien was relieved to have a few extra hours to prepare for the award ceremony. His team bathed and dressed in their clean Green Phoenix uniforms, ready to receive their rewards. Favien nervously held onto the game-winning flag, eagerly anticipating presenting it to Pinx. His heart raced with excitement and hope.

He led his team up the outdoor steps of the palace and stood at the end of the line. Sealyn started speaking, but Favien could barely hear anything. His mind was so loud, repeating the words he wanted to say. He watched as each of his teammates received a shiny gold medal draped around their necks with emerald satin. The crowd jumped and cheered for each player. Finally, it was Favien's turn to receive his medal. He walked slowly but proudly. Sealyn hugged him after placing his medal around his neck and smiled. He turned to the crowd, watching them erupt in celebration. This was it; it was time for him to be brave again.

Favien walked to the edge of the large stone entryway and waved his arms to silence the crowd. "If I could have everyone's attention. I would first like to say that I'm incredibly proud and grateful to be standing here because of my amazing teammates." The crowd erupted again, throwing gold sparkles in the air. "I made myself a promise before Feydom started, though, and I intend on keeping it. Lady Pinx, will you come up here, please?"

Gasps echoed through the people. Pinx blushed and smiled. With her pink lace dress, she made her way through the crowd until she was face-to-face with Favien. He took her hand and kissed it.

"Lady Pinx, you're my sunshine on a stormy day, my rose in a desert. You keep me grounded yet also make me feel as if I could fly among the clouds." Tears began to slide down Pinx's cheeks. Favien choked over his words. "Pinx, I'm trying to say that I love you. I mean, that's not why I called you up here. I mean, I do love you. Ugh! Pinx, I promised myself, so here it is. Marry me!"

Pinx leaped into Favien's arms, kissing him as if tomorrow weren't promised. The crowd loved what they saw. They cheered and threw gold sparkles alongside green pipscot powder.

"Pinx, I almost forgot!" exclaimed Favien. "I have this for you. I know I'm supposed to present something of priceless value to you along with a ring, so I want you to have the game-winning flag." He handed Pinx the flag, and as she ran her fingers over the fabric, she noticed a gold ring tied at the tip. She gasped at the intricate craftsmanship. The band was smooth, adorned with gold phoenix wings stretching outward, and at the center of the wings was a beautiful pink diamond shaped like a rose. She loved it!

In his wheeled cart, Doebromir stretched out his arm to Favien, and Favien clasped Doebromir's forearm.

"I believe it's time to celebrate, my friend," Doebromir hooted. "Allow me to be the first to buy you a drink tonight."

"You're too late, Doebromir," Sealyn patted his shoulder. "I already have a celebratory table prepared at *Mimby's Morsels*. You can get the second round." She winked at him.

"Don't tempt me with a good time, Your Majesty." Doebromir laughed, wincing slightly at his leg.

Favien looked at Pinx. "This has got to be the best day of my life. I mean, I'm sure my birth was pretty amazing, but this day definitely tops all my previous days."

"I suppose this is my future," Pinx cooed dreamily. "And I can't wait to see where this life will take us."

"To Mimby's!" yelled Jdru.

As the team started walking toward the market, Max stayed behind. He was nervous to tell Sealyn the discovery he had made. "Your Majesty, may I have a few moments?"

"Of course. By the way, how is your wife, Lady Madilina? I heard she was a little upset that the nomoseves didn't get their chance to fly. The stable keepers said she did a fine job keeping them calm."

"I'm sure she will be grateful to hear such a high compliment, Your Majesty. She's well, though. Thank you for asking."

"What would you like to discuss?"

"You see, I discovered something. Something during my honeymoon."

"Max, I don't think discussing your honeymoon discoveries with me is quite appropriate." Sealyn raised an eyebrow.

"No, no, Sealyn. I mean, Queen Sealyn. What I'm trying to say is that I discovered a secret weapon."

"Weapon? What kind of weapon?"

"Oh, this weapon is one for the skies." He smirked.

Lady Stewardess Pame approached Sealyn and Max. "Your Majesty, you're needed most urgently in the war room."

"Thank you, Lady Stewardess. Lord Max, we'll need to continue this conversation another time, but soon, Max. Soon."

To know someone is to know
their shadow, not the exposed.
It's the hidden pieces
that make you who you are.
What lurks in your shadows?

Queen Sealyn Araelien
Diary Entry 386

# Chapter 23

The sea crashed against the wooden boats as they sped forward, the horned whales guiding them at the front while the slaves rowed below. Stoltland decided thousands of years ago that they wanted to dominate the sea, which, for them, meant capturing and controlling sea creatures. They started with baby horned whales, aiming for each generation to be increasingly compliant. The whale trainers tied ropes to each horn, guiding the whales around the blocked-off sea pens. Stoltland spent years designing these sea pens before their endeavors. They dropped large boulders from ships to create underwater fences. The underwater fence was a whole ship wide and twice the length of the horned whale above water. Stretching for miles, the entire enclosure was wide and deep enough for three ships to conduct practice runs simultaneously. At one end, there was a massive gate to allow the trained horned whales to exit the pen.

Stoltland refused to disclose their high seas strategies to ensure that their enslavement of sea creatures remained concealed. They also declined to sign the End Slavery Treaty that Elysium and Len Nove had signed. Stoltlanders experienced a euphoric sensation when they realized they owned someone else's life. The curse ran deep in their blood regarding that issue.

Corentine walked along the boat's bow, breathing in the salty air. She loved how the sea made her feel, but it also reminded her of *him*. The past didn't matter, though; her future lay ahead of her. She assessed how far they were from their land, and once she confirmed they were halfway between Stoltland and Elysium, she decided to begin her task of dethroning queens. Her first target was Queen Phyre.

She walked into the queen's chambers. "Good day, Your Majesty." Corentine bowed to her mother-in-law. "I wanted to speak with you if that pleases you."

Queen Phyre hesitated. She didn't want to be left alone with anyone, especially Corentine; her intentions were never pure.

"Of course, but keep it brief. My guards will remain."

"As you wish." Corentine nodded. Queen Phyre, I wanted to discuss the future of Stoltland with you."

Queen Phyre sat back in her chair. She knew where this conversation was going, but how much did Corentine want the throne? Would she kill her in her sleep or throw her overboard?

"And just what about Stoltland's future would you like to discuss?"

Corentine's black eyes narrowed. "The dethronement of you."

The five guards drew their swords and stepped closer to Phyre. Phyre stood up. "How dare you!"

"How dare I? How dare you, you old hag! You selfish crow. You stay seated on the throne, old and fragile, while your son is fit and healthy to be the king."

"No doubt you are ready to be queen."

"Being queen would give me the title I deserve."

Phyre mocked, "Deserve? You're joking! You've been trying to overthrow my crown since I met you, tramp. You tore my son from me! You manipulated him with your witchcraft."

"There was no witchcraft needed to secure his loyalty. Besides, I want Tahbert to have the title he deserves. Stoltland kept Haedon's title as prince but decided not to give my son what should be rightfully his."

"Rightfully his?" questioned Phyre. "Corentine, what you're asking is not of Stoltland law. The code you speak of is Elysian law. Perhaps, like your other son, you too would prefer a change in scenery?"

Corentine glared at Phyre. She hated her. For years, Phyre had suppressed her, belittled her, and ignored her, but no more. She would be respected by fear!

"Queen Phyre, I'll give you one chance for diplomacy. Announce my husband as your heir and rescind the throne today."

"Today? Corentine, even if I were to consider your request, we're in the middle of the sea. I can't just denounce the crown and hand it over."

"Yes, you can. While Your Majesty was paying no attention to the inventory and staffing of the ships, I made sure to include my personal guard and our Nicht slaves, so you can send word of your denouncing to the kingdom. We can have a crowning on the deck."

Phyre's eyes twitched. Something else was fueling Corentine. "What drives you to need this much control?"

Corentine pointed to Phyre. "What are you without control? You are a slave. You either enslave or become the slave. I will never allow someone else to think he has power over me. I will be the one who gives the commands."

Phyre stood. "I refuse to bow to you. You're a wretched creature with filth stirring in your bones. You and your half-breed were a plague to us since the beginning."

Corentine closed her eyes, feeling the sensation of passion and pride pour over her skin. The dark mist rose from her feet, like a slow geyser. A cold chill ran down Phyre's spine as she watched in horror. The mist formed a sharp knife against her throat. She gasped and tried not to move.

The dark mist formed three more knives and plunged the black blades into the guards' stomachs. Phyre panicked as each guard dropped to his knees, covered in blood. The crimson rivers beneath the guards reminded her of what she had done in her past; she was no innocent queen. Perhaps, fate had finally found her.

Corentine's powers were undeniable—she had given herself to the darkness, to the curse of Stoltland. Phyre was beaten. If she wanted to remain alive, she would have to cower to this beast before her.

Phyre gritted her teeth. "Fine. You win, witch. Use the powers of old, but be warned—they *will* consume and destroy you."

Phyre opened the black velvet-lined chest with the king's crown inside. She carefully picked up the gold crown, and as she moved it in front of her son, she caught a glimpse of herself in the large black diamond. This would be the last time she saw herself wearing the reigning queen's crown. She loved the sculpted gold roses and the beautiful vines that formed the crown. She shook off the memory of her crowning day and placed the king's crown on Svagon's black hair, looking away from her reflection.

She felt as if she and her crown were connected. What would she be without this? Would the kingdom just forget about her? Would she still hold value? She gracefully lifted the crown from her head and turned it to see the front one more time. Slowly, she raised her head to lock eyes with the murderous Corentine, who looked more eager than a snake trapping a mouse. With bitterness, she managed to lay the crown on Corentine's red head. She wished she could press it through her skull and watch her blood spill to the deck.

"Captain," King Svagon bellowed loudly.

"Yes, my king."

"Have the Queen Mother's belongings removed from the reigning crown's chambers and placed in Haedon's chambers. Move Haedon's belongings to our former chambers and make sure he knows about the change. We wouldn't want any embarrassing mix-ups."

Phyre fought back tears. She knew what he was doing; he would stash her away until she was forgotten. She would become an afterthought for the rest of her life. She promised that with her last breath, she would find a way to destroy Corentine.

Before descending the stairs below deck, she looked back to glance at her family with their new crowns. She knew that Stoltland would be more infected by the curse under Corentine's rule—unless someone was brave enough to face the darkness plaguing their world.

Corentine swirled her wine in her onyx goblet and propped her crossed feet on her chaise. "Darling, don't you want to thank me for your crown?"

"Thank? You want me to thank you for giving me this title? The title that comes from my birthright, not yours?" Svagon said incredulously.

"Absolutely. There's more to this story that you don't know, nor need to know. Besides, I have a master plan."

"What master plan?"

"To be queen of all seven kingdoms." Her eyes flickered.

"All seven kingdoms? Are you mad?"

"No. I'm ambitious, and you should be too." She slammed her goblet down on the table, scaring her dogs.

"Corentine, how do you expect us to conquer all seven? There are too many unknowns with these other worlds."

Corentine chuckled. "You're so blind. Elysium is about to be the weakest it's ever been. Their little queen has her heart set on my son, and my son is loyal to me and only me! When the time comes, Jace will be our secret weapon with or without the Heart of Elysium."

"You think Sealyn will hand over the throne because you're Jace's mommy?"

"No! I think Jace will join me in overthrowing their kingdom. I think a wedding will happen, and if it does, then we'll ask Jace to find a way to give us Elysium. If he refuses, then we'll make him kill her," Corentine growled. She filled her goblet with more red wine.

"I'm not trying to argue with you, love, but I don't know whether I see Jace as the kind of boy who goes along with a plot to murder the woman he loves."

"Leave this to me. Now, I don't want to talk about this anymore. Let us celebrate. Where is Haedon? Still with that blonde whore?"

"Yes," Svagon whimpered.

"Leave them be. We can celebrate our crowns by ourselves." Corentine leaned into her husband and kissed him passionately. She imagined him as another, as the one she left behind in their palace. Svagon wasn't capable of much; he was so weak and pathetic. His crowning was the beginning of a slow and painful death.

With each kiss, each touch, she forced her mind to plot her revenge instead of being present with her husband. She would win over the childish bird queen with charm and grace, then blindside her. The two plans for overtaking Elysium were in motion, and no one could stop them. Drystan would find the Heart of Elysium since the curse was infecting him. He was now a slave to envy. Jace would be the tricky plan, but she didn't doubt that his mind could be molded to her agenda, as it always had in the past.

# Chapter 24

The morning of Perdonair came quickly, too quickly. Sealyn could feel the regret from the late-night celebrations. Today, though, she felt braver than before. She knew what she needed to do to ensure that Jace never questioned her feelings for him. She leaned up, slightly propping herself on her elbows, and noticed Maekel organizing her breakfast tray. Sealyn realized that Maekel had made herself scarce over the past few months.

"Good morning, Maekel. I love your new dress," Sealyn complimented. "Is there a special occasion?"

Maekel blushed. "Good morning, Your Majesty. No. I just thoughts I would wears something nice, and if it happens to catch someone's eyes then so be's it." She flipped her dark brown hair and turned back to organizing the tray.

Sealyn chuckled. "Wise words. I have something special on the agenda for today. I need a private table prepared in the middle of our vineyards."

Maekel fluttered around. "Vineyards, Your Majesty? Why's in the middle of the vineyards?"

"I believe a romantic gesture needs a romantic setting. Please make sure that you send Lord Jace an invite and specify the location." Sealyn rose from her bed and slipped on her emerald wool slippers, then walked to her breakfast table. "Have Commander Elmond escort Jace to the table. The usual royal guard can form the normal perimeter while we eat. Please also inform the housekeeper and kitchen staff that we will be taste-testing the new wine infusions."

Maekel fluttered near the breakfast table, nervously pulling at her dress. She didn't want to disappoint her queen, but the more she was around Jace, the more uncomfortable she felt. She wanted to tell her queen everything, but she had been sworn to secrecy. Yet surely the Nichts could trust this royal family. Was it time for Elysium to finally learn what had been happening in the shadows?

Sealyn noticed how odd Maekel was acting. "Maekel, would you care to share anything?" Sealyn saw the struggle Maekel was having, so she thought perhaps now would be the perfect opportunity to present Maekel her gift. Sealyn slid her hand under her mattress and pulled out a small wooden box. She placed it in front of Maekel on the tray.

"What's this, Your Majesty?"

"It's a gift for you, commemorating when you first came here."

Maekel's pink wings fluttered excitedly. She opened the gold hinge, revealing a miniature porcelain tea set, exactly like Sealyn's personal set, except that Sealyn had Maekel's name painted on the teapot with pink flowers surrounding the letters. Maekel glided her tiny fingers around the gold rim of one of the teacups. She was amazed by such a lavish gift.

"I had it custom-made for you. This way we can have coffee and tea together." Sealyn set the tiny teapot beside her large one, then filled it with coffee. She did the same for the cream saucer. "Now, let's have coffee and Puffin Pie together this morning. Cheers to Perdonair." They clinked their teacups and sipped the marvelous liquid.

Maekel finally felt courageous. "Your Majesty, I can't thanks you enough for this." She swallowed the nerves down. "I thinks you needs to hears something."

As Maekel spoke, Sealyn felt her anger grow within her. She had no idea how severe Nicht slavery was in Stoltland, not just the Nicht slavery but also many others from all the kingdoms sold into their bondage. She had to find a way to end this horrendous crime against life.

"I hope's you can sees now why I feels slightly uncomfortables around Lord Jace," Maekel sobbed. "I knows he's a good man, but he's still a Stoltlander."

"Maekel, you don't need to justify your fears of Stoltland. I completely understand your viewpoint, but I hope you know that I would never put our kingdom in jeopardy. Nichts and all forms of life will be protected from slavery here in Elysium."

Maekel's chocolate eyes flooded with appreciation. She knew she and her family would be protected. "There's more, Your Majesty," Maekel sputtered. "My family and I have been runnings a secret escape project for manys years now."

Sealyn lifted her hand quickly. "Stop. Maekel, don't tell me anymore."

Maekel's heart froze. Had she crossed the line that would surely ruin their hard work? Her father had started the movement ten years ago, and they had already rescued over seven hundred Nichts. They carefully placed them across Elysium with families who would protect them and help them find work. She didn't want to give up their freedom mission.

"I hope I didn't sound rude, Maekel. I want it to be understood that I stand with your family in this mission. You have my full support. Not only will I help fund the escape project, but I will do everything in my power to abolish slavery across all kingdoms. I'll call for a council meeting when Perdonair is over, and your family will present to the Councils of Wisdom and Lands to help advise on these efforts."

"Oh, thank you, Your Majesty! Thank you! Thank you! Thank you! I don't wants to lose more times, so I will arranges your day now." Maekel bowed and sped out her tiny door, leaving Sealyn deep in thought.

Sealyn's thoughts brought fear to her veins. If Stoltland bought human slaves from other kingdoms, this meant that the path to ending slavery would involve cutting them off at the source. She needed to end slavery in all other kingdoms and force Stoltland into submission. The only hope for this to become a possibility would be for her to rule all seven kingdoms. She stood from the table and started pacing the room.

Rule all seven kingdoms? The question plagued her. Throughout history, many monarchs had attempted to be the first to rule the seven kingdoms, but all had failed. Only one had come close, which caused the Second Chance to happen.

A feeling crept over her, whispering thoughts and ideas. Break the curses. Could she do that? Would that be the requirement for freedom?

She ran to her secret stash of ancient scrolls hidden under a loose floorboard. She knelt down and pulled out the familiar scroll. Her mouth suddenly went dry as she read the words from the Old Law, "One land will have one ruler, for two masters cannot coexist. With such knowledge, mankind will suffer and serve the hand of the curse into which he was born. Yet if one can break the hand of the curse, that person will become the ruler of the curses; the curse breaker. But be warned, the price of breaking all seven curses is death."

Jace felt the ground crunch under his shoes from the first frost of the season. His footsteps followed close behind Commander Elmond as they made their way through the weaving palace vineyards. The smell of Elysium's frosty pathways made him feel oddly warm inside. He wished he could have grown up in this kingdom. His entire life would've been better. Jace peered over Commander Elmond's broad shoulders and could see Sealyn seated at a well-decorated wooden farm table.

"You're in for a treat, Lord Jace," Commander Elmond reassured. "Our queen has prepared a tasting of her special palace infusions. My wife and I have already tasted several of them, and I will say, my lord, they are delicious."

Jace noticed the man's bushy eyebrows as he licked his lips in remembrance of the delightful drinks. Jace felt there was a familiarity to Elmond that he wouldn't quite put his finger on, like a lost memory from his past. Commander Elmond removed his military hat, revealing a thick head of curly red hair. He bowed graciously to Sealyn.

"My Queen, I was just telling your special guest how much my wife and I enjoyed your infusions. We thank you again for your kind gift."

"You're quite welcome, and I hope Lord Jace will enjoy them as much as you both did." Sealyn smiled at Jace. "Please, join me." She motioned for him to take the seat in front of her.

"Good morning, Queen Sealyn. I was excited to receive your invitation, but I will say, this is not what I expected." Jace stared into Sealyn's eyes with a longing desire.

Sealyn blushed. "Did you think I would send Maekel with an improper invite to the vineyards, Lord Jace?"

"Maybe I was hoping for an improper invitation."

Commander Elmond cleared his throat. "Your Majesty, on these uncomfortable remarks, may I resume a position of distance for more privacy?"

Sealyn laughed. "Absolutely, Commander Elmond. Thank you."

"I had forgotten he was standing there," whispered Jace.

"Me too. Commander Elmond has been a treasure to me since taking the crown. He served my grandfather in his final years after Commander Wanden passed away, and then Elmond served my father for the entirety of his reign. I thought it was fitting to keep him in command."

"I think you chose well, Your Majesty. He doesn't look his age, though."

"Not at all, but I'm pretty sure I did see a few gray hairs starting to form. Anyway, he did speak the truth; I would love for you to taste my infusions." Sealyn held out her hand toward the jars filled with flowers, herbs, and spices. "I've been working on these for some time now, and I would like to present them at the Trundatta Ball this winter."

Jace's brow wrinkled. "First, what is the Trundatta Ball, and second, what are infusions?" He asked while holding up a jar.

"Well, the Trundatta Ball is our annual winter ball. Every village and city has its own version, but all follow the same guidelines: everyone must adhere to the palace's choice of theme, and everyone must wear a green accessory with their outfit." Sealyn uncorked the first jar and poured Jace a glass of dazzling pink liquid. "This is my white wine infused with hibiscus and elderflower petals with hints of lime juice. I call it Trust Love."

Jace lifted his gold goblet. "Here's to trusting love."

"Quite a toast, Lord Jace. Do you trust love?"

"I think it depends on the person. Sometimes, someone can love the wrong things or the wrong people, which can lead them to make some poor decisions. I've only ever known conditional love. My family expected me to love them because they provided me with food and clothes. I expected love from them when I met their expectations, so to be honest with you, Queen Sealyn, I believe my outlook on love may be twisted."

Sealyn nodded, considering what he meant. "I truly understand, Jace. I'm not here to convince you with words that unconditional love exists, but I'll promise you that I'll prove to you with actions that unconditional love is no myth." Sealyn took Jace's hand. "I choose to love you with trust and respect. I choose to love you regardless of your past and regardless of who the world tells you you are. I choose to love the man you are now and the man you will become."

Jace blinked, and tears slid from his silver eyes. He had never heard such a proclamation before—such elegant words spoken for him. Yet, everything in him trusted what he heard from Sealyn. Jace wanted her; more than that, his essence needed her.

"My Queen, I believe you. My heart desires to be with you forever. I don't know whether that would even be allowed, but Sealyn, I love you. I'm entangled with love for you."

Sealyn released his hand, grabbed the jar filled with sparkling gold liquid, and poured them both a glass. She looked deep into Jace's eyes. "This muscadine wine is infused with primrose and small traces of lavender with an addition of Lady Raquel's Cane of the Valley sugar sparkles."

"What do you call this drink?"

"Have Hope."

"Do you have hope, Queen Sealyn?" Jace asked while reaching his hand across the lace table runner, slipping his fingers through Sealyn's.

"I do, *Lord* Jace. I have hope for Elysium's future, and I have hope in us—in what we can achieve together. Will you give me something to hope for?"

Jace paused in confusion. Was she hinting at a proposal? His mind felt fuzzy. Was it the strong infusions or his emotions clouding his thoughts? "What are you asking of me, Your Majesty?"

"Marriage, Jace. I want the promise and hope of our union."

Jace's mouth fell open, and Sealyn laughed. Jace tried to compose himself, but he felt torn. Torn from hearing his mother's words that a horse and a phoenix could never work. Torn with wanting to experience unconditional love for the first time. Torn with wanting to give her the world. Yet she owned it, so what could he do for her? Would he ever be good enough for the Queen of Elysium?

Jace took a deep breath. "Sealyn, if I'm allowed to say informally." She nodded. "I would like to give you all the hope the world could offer. I want to give you the hope of marriage because all I've been holding onto is hope. I wake up hoping to hear from you, hoping to see you, hoping to kiss you and hold you. If I could have the opportunity to wake up next to you and do all that freely, then yes, Sealyn. Yes, a thousand times over, I want to marry you. I want to be your husband and you to be my wife, my forever bride."

Sealyn smiled and took the last jar she had on display, which was filled with a light blue liquid that had vibrant blue flowers covering the bottom of the jar. He noticed that tiny bubbles were rising from these flowers to the top.

"This again is a white wine infused with Len Nove's blue butterfly pea flower along with the powder of Lady Raquel's Cane of the Valley plant, which makes it bubble."

"This is amazing! I think this is my favorite drink so far. It's not too sweet and not too dry."

"I call it Faith." Sealyn took another sip, eyeing him suspiciously.

"Only Faith? Nothing else?"

Sealyn smirked. "Nothing else. Because faith stands alone. You must be brave to have faith because sometimes you'll find yourself facing opposition that will make you question yourself, and only your faith will remind you why you must stand firm and persevere." Sealyn's mind traveled to the battles she knew she would face in the future; the scroll's prediction of death. If Jace became her husband, she knew his life would be at risk. Could she do that to him?

"I have faith in you, Sealyn. I have faith in us."

"I'm glad you do because I promise you that I'll be faithful to you and to Creator's laws. I believe that by having trust in our love and hope in us, we can have faith that our future together will change the path of history."

"I agree. I vow to be faithful to you, to love only you, and to trust you unconditionally. Sealyn, I would marry you yesterday, but I don't believe our families would react well to us marrying. I feel the kingdom will think I pressured you into a union with a hidden agenda."

"I agree. I want the kingdom to love you, not question you, so let us make a pledge from the Old Law to each other. This will bind us and quiet any doubts you or I may encounter till an actual wedding day."

Jace couldn't believe this was real. Sealyn truly wanted to marry him; of all men on this earth, she was choosing him. Was this even legal? He guessed so; otherwise, she wouldn't proceed with the arrangement of the Old Laws.

Sealyn coached Jace on the ritual and watched as he made a small fire from twigs and brush. He cut a small strip of clothing from his shirt, and Sealyn handed him her lace glove. He tied the strip of clothing around it, binding them together. They tossed their items into the tiny flames and spoke the words, "I have given freely of myself to the one I pledge my mind, body, and heart to. From this day forth, we are bound as one partnership dedicated to each other for eternity. If one of us fails the sanctity of this oath, may what was done to our burnt sacrifices be done to the guilty person."

Sealyn held Jace's body tightly. She felt safe with his arms securely wrapped around her. Her body never wanted to release him. Sealyn leaned back from Jace. "I hate to leave you, especially now, but we have the feast for Perdonair tonight. You're still attending, correct?"

"Absolutely. I wouldn't miss it. Lord Finn is picking me up along with Lord Max and Lady Madilina." Jace tucked Sealyn's hair wisps behind her ear. He felt her skin—it was so soft and smooth. "Nothing will keep me from coming to you, my wife." Jace cupped Sealyn's face, giving her the passionate kiss he had been waiting for all morning. His body hungered for more, and he felt her pulling him closer. His fingers tangled in her long, dark hair. He sensed her body arch as his fingers glided down her back.

"Your Majesty, you have an urgent message," Commander Elmond interrupted.

Sealyn's breathing was fast. "Yes, Commander Elmond. What's the message?"

"A message from King Ryker: the war room is prepped."

Sealyn grumbled. "Tell him I'll be there presently."

"War room is prepped? Why do you need the war room prepped on Perdonair?" questioned Jace.

Fear crept over Sealyn. She couldn't tell him the truth, at least not yet. Could she truly lie to him right after they made their pledges? Would this lead to more lies?

"Precautions, my love." Sealyn kissed Jace farewell and began her walk back to the palace.

Jace watched as twenty guards appeared from nowhere, escorting the queen. Something felt off. Did she just lie to him? Why would she do that? Did her status as queen require her to tell lies and partial truths for the sake of the kingdom? He had just committed himself to a queen who could never be fully devoted to him alone, one whose role involved keeping secrets. Was this a mistake? If so, could he walk away?

I have only one life here, and
I refuse any part of that time
to be a slave to anything or
Anyone.
I choose life. I choose freedom.
I choose to fight.


Queen Sealyn Araelien
Diary Entry 401

# Chapter 25

Char breathed in the eucalyptus and jasmine of the palace hallways as he strolled breezily along the stones. He could hear yelling as he approached the war room. Why would there be a war meeting on Perdonair? He could hear footsteps nearing the door, and out rushed Sealyn. She looked intensely angry.

"Greetings, my dear cousin," Char jabbered sarcastically.

"Hush, Char." She looked around frantically. "Follow me." She grabbed his arm and quickly ran down the hallway toward the servants' entrance. She stopped in front of a large cream-colored vase embellished with painted ivy vines and a sparkling gold feather on the front. "Be the lookout," commanded Sealyn.

Char looked around the corners and opened the door to the servants' staircase to see no one climbing the stairs. He nodded to Sealyn. Sealyn reached her hand behind the vase and pressed a small stone into the wall. The base of the vase dropped a few inches; Sealyn pushed the vase forward, revealing a hidden passage. Char stood in awe as a small doorway appeared for them to walk through. Sealyn grabbed Char's arm and yanked him inside.

Once the door closed behind them, Char asked, "Where in all creation are we right now?"

"One of the many secret rooms of this castle."

"Again?! You hid another secret room from me? Sealyn!"

"Not now, you whimpering whombil! I need your solid focus. Follow me."

Sealyn stomped her feet, and the fire flowers lit the darkened hallway. She led Char down a few more turns and then opened a black iron door covered in cobwebs. They walked into an old stone room. The walls were covered in half-burned Elysian flags and scorch marks. In the center of the room was a round stone table that was broken in half by a large part of the ceiling falling on top of it. Burned bookshelves, chairs, and weapons were scattered around the room.

Char gazed around in disbelief. "Sealyn, what is this place?"

"From what I've gathered, this was the original war room from the old kings, dating to before the Second Chance."

"What? Seriously? I thought everything was destroyed after that?"

"Apparently, someone tried and failed. Many things were destroyed, but not all. I come here when I feel chaos taking over me. I've also been coming here to find old documents for explanations."

"Explanations? Explanations for what?"

"Char, I believe we've been lied to all our lives. Well, perhaps lied to is a harsh way of describing it, but I believe we weren't told the entire truth of what our past history has been, and what's actually going on in the other kingdoms. I keep finding out more and more horrific secrets."

"Now, you're scaring me, Sealyn. What happened? Does it have something to do with the yelling I heard in the war room?"

"Yes and no. Char, I'm trusting you with way more than anyone is supposed to know, but you're my trusted ally, and I need someone else to help me."

"Sealyn, you know I always have your back, and I'm loyal to your crown."

Sealyn paced around the broken table and ran her fingers across the jagged edge. "Char, we expect Drystan is a traitor and is working with the Stoltlanders to locate the Heart of Elysium, which controls the power of Elysium. We have no clue what the Heart of Elysium looks like or where it is because King Perdonair hid the location in clues. We know Drystan has the first clue, and we were able to solve it with the aid of Grand Queen Karis, but tonight we'll hunt for the next clue and, hopefully, locate it before Drystan does. I've also learned that there's a Nicht smuggling project happening right under our noses here in Elysium. My personal Nicht, Maekel, is involved in securing safe passage for slave Nichts from Stoltland and Korpam so they can live freely here in

Elysium. I want to end all slavery of any kind, but to do this, I must free each kingdom from its curse."

Char stood in silence, trying to absorb the amount of information Sealyn just unloaded on him. "That's a lot to process in seven seconds." Char pondered it all. Treachery. Curses. Power. Mystery. Slavery. Smuggling. How was he supposed to respond to the queen choosing to share this with him? More importantly, how did Sealyn need him to respond?

"Char, I need you to say something."

"What do you need me to do? You said you needed my help."

"My father doesn't want me to go with tonight's unit, which will be scouting the Ever-Changing Mountainside."

Char laughed. "Well, we all know that's not going to happen, so how do you plan on attending this escapade?"

"For starters, I'm not going alone. You're going with me."

"Seriously, Sealyn? You think I want to go on some crazy, dangerous, secret mission to uncover a scandalous secret clue before a rotten traitor retrieves it?" Char dropped his head, then jerked it up with a large smile. "When do we leave?"

Sealyn folded her arms with confidence. "Right after the feast concludes. I'll fake a headache, and you'll kindly offer to escort me to my chambers."

"Of course, since I'm such a gentleman."

"Don't make me laugh." Sealyn snorted. "We'll casually cut through the Garden Library, where we'll use the secret passage to the marketplace. The baker Nichts will be closed since they're celebrating at *Mimby's Morsels*."

"Are you planning on running all the way from the market to the mountain?"

"No, of course not. We're going to sneak to Lord Finn's stables and borrow his new mirrons."

"Mirrons? You expect me to ride one of those horse wannabes? They're rock solid!"

"Their outside skin was just polished today, so their mirror hairs will keep them hidden. I made sure Lord Finn purchased the comfort saddles, so we should ride fine."

"Your idea is sounding worse by the minute, which is why I love it! This Perdonair is going to be one for the records. Now, how do we get out of this burnt, musty place?"

Sealyn pointed to the door behind them. "That door leads to another corridor that goes to the old throne room."

"The original throne room is here?"

"It is, and it's in really good shape, surprisingly. We just have to climb up a hidden staircase that takes us into the current throne room."

"Unbelievable. When all this is over, you're taking me on the secret passage tour."

"Deal."

Sakul stood with his back against the wall, taking in the entire ballroom, which he transformed into a grand, seated banquet. The tables were arranged in a giant rectangle, with seating only on the outside. Sakul ensured there was ample space for guests to walk in the center of the rectangle and serve themselves the delicious treats displayed on three round tables. He made the focal point of the tables the impressive two-tier chocolate fountain.

Each table was decorated in the season's orange, red, yellow, and purple leaves. Small, colorful branches adorned the tables with the fruits of the season, alongside grass baskets filled with jars of honey, spices, and jams as gifts for the guests. The palace selected gold chargers paired with matching goblets and utensils for each person's seat.

Guests poured into the ballroom in awe of the alluring seasonal decorations. Sealyn sat among her family, while the rest of the seats were filled by Vinurs of the Court, along with her sister's. They invited several of her parents' friends as well as members of the Council of Wisdom and the Council of Lands, which made for a very large group. Sealyn needed a big crowd to help with the concealment and distractions. She watched Drystan intently as much as she could without making it obvious. She was quite surprised that he and Lady Pyry accepted the invitation but figured it was part of his ruse. Perhaps he had, by now, recruited others to join his secret quest? That possibility could make this mission more dangerous than she had thought.

Char rearranged his honey and jam jars in his basket, hoping this would catch Sealyn's attention. This was their signal whenever they needed to discuss something during the evening. He stood up and casually walked to the center tables. Char scrunched his nose at the sweet treats. He hated most sweets, except for the delicious Puffin Pies and Jam Pies. He preferred anything sour, so he reached for the green apple slices.

"You needed to speak," said Sealyn.

"Correct. I noticed Drystan isn't drinking any kind of alcohol tonight. He's only had water, and I just saw him ask for a glass of the PurFizz."

"PurFizz? He must be getting ready to make his leave."

"Why do you think that?" Char asked.

"Because the PurFizz's effects only last so long. Sounds to me as though someone needs some courage, and this time it's a different liquid courage."

Char tapped his nose and pointed at Sealyn. "I see what you did there."

"And just what are you two whispering about over here?" interjected Lord Sakul. He grabbed a few purple grapes.

"Lord Sakul," Sealyn started. "You did a fantastic job on this banquet. I'm sure everyone will be talking about it for months. How will you top this at the winter ball?"

"Why, thank you, Your Majesty. I have a couple of thoughts on the Trundatta ball, actually. I'd love to run them by you soon."

"Shut up, Sakul, and get out of here!" snapped Char with a hint of jest. "We're discussing something important that doesn't include you!"

"Did I mention that I poisoned those yummy green apples? Eat up, you unworthy needlebob dung!"

Char laughed. "Speaking of needlebobs, one asked how your foot was doing."

"Char, I…"

"Gentlemen." Sealyn quickly interrupted. "As much as I love to hear the banter between you two, I'm not in the mood for distractions."

"Distractions? Then there must be a game afoot!" exclaimed Sakul.

"Keep your voice down, or you'll find a whole nest of needlebobs in your bed tonight," Char whispered loudly.

"Good evening, Your Majesty. Good evening, Lord Char and Lord Sakul," Jace greeted politely.

Sealyn needed a way to break Char free of this social gathering to find out more details about Drystan. She didn't want to leave Jace alone, but needed to act fast. She quickly threw her drink in Char's face, and it splattered on his dinner coat.

"Oh, Char! I'm so sorry. I was startled by Lord Jace," Sealyn tried to say without laughing at Char's red-stained face.

Char glared and mouthed, "Seriously?" to show his disapproval. Then he spoke, "No need to worry, Your Majesty. I'm sure every woman throws her drink in surprise at the handsome Lord Jace."

"Lord Sakul, let's take Char to the kitchens to help clean him up." Sakul looked confused at Sealyn's suggestion. A queen would never suggest participating in such a lowly task, but this was Sealyn and Char, and something was definitely amiss, so he wanted to find out.

"What a great idea, my queen."

"Lord Jace, I would love to stay and talk, but in my absence, why don't you take a special bottle to Lord Finn and his date, and you three have some fun until I return." Sealyn motioned to the wine Nichts. She then slowly bit a chocolate-covered strawberry, allowing her lips to purse against the fruit and dripping chocolate. While she chewed, she gave Jace a wicked smile.

Jace could barely find words to say after watching the strawberry lip action. "Uh, um, yes, my chocolate. I mean, your strawberry. Curses. I mean, my queen."

Sealyn and the lords laughed and parted ways. Jace grabbed the open bottle in need of its calming effects. Not realizing it was port, he began drinking large gulps. He joined Finn and his skinny blonde date and shared the port with them, still unaware of the mystery happening around him.

Drystan saw his opportunity as Sealyn exited into the kitchens with Char and Sakul. He had to leave. He decided to pretend he had a stomachache. This would provide him with an excuse to stay in the stables anyway.

He and Pyry thanked the remaining royals and made their way toward the exit, but Drystan glanced back to see whether he would notice anything different as he left. He saw several military members crowding around King Ryker and whispering.

They knew. Drystan's heart sank. What was he to do now? He had no choice but to finish the task before him, though Drystan was clever when it came to being cunning.

He quickly dashed away from his wife and her parents, heading straight for the lookout tower on the west end. The new recruits would be working the late-night shift on Perdonair, which would make convincing the military brats to join him easier. Once he reached the top, he saw five recruits. He recognized three of them from the new recruit unit he had trained two weeks ago. One was stoking the fire in a massive black cauldron in the center, while the other four had spread evenly around the perimeter.

"My lord!" screeched the one stoking the fire. They all stood at attention quickly.

"At ease, recruits. Men, I have no time to explain the details, but I've been sent here on a secret quest commissioned by the queen." The men gaped.

"Us, my lord?" questioned the tallest.

"Yes, recruit—uh"

"It's Recruit Quenton, my lord."

"Of course, Recruit Quenton. The queen has many military units assigned to different locations, but we're short a unit to cover the grounds of the Ever-Changing Mountain. We received special intelligence that spies from Stoltland are possibly hiding there. We must move quickly."

"All of us are required to go? No one will remain behind?" asked the fire-stoker.

"No. We need every able-bodied person to participate in this endeavor. Now, quickly, follow me to the stables."

The five recruits charged after Drystan down to the stables. Each man saddled his horse and raced toward the Ever-Changing Mountain. Drystan's heart pounded. He couldn't tell whether it was the wind currents blowing through his blonde hair or currents of fear, but he knew they were blazing toward trouble.

His mind kept seeing Pyry's face with a look of pain. Heat lightning flashed across the sky ahead. He thought he saw the image of large wings, but he figured his mind was playing tricks on him. He was riding to glory, to finish his mission.

He saw the Ever-Changing Mountain slowly getting closer. He pulled on the reins of his black-and-white horse and came to an abrupt stop.

"Recruits, ride ahead and scout the area for anyone. If you see anyone, immediately make the Green Bird Call signal," ordered Drystan.

The Green Bird Call signal was a bird call that King Ryker added to the military regime. It was a very specific bird call only known to the Elysian military. The military had several call signals, so it was essential for each recruit to practice these sounds to avoid potential harm.

"If you see no one, signal with the Blue Bird Call. Go now!" Drystan urged them away. He sat on his horse, waiting for the call signals. He wasn't going into a trap.

He heard the first Blue Bird Call and felt a sigh of relief, but he still didn't budge. He could hear the crickets in the forest beginning to sing their night songs. A few of the fire flowers were still lit on the pathways of the recruits, so Drystan tried to use their light to see any movements. The second Blue Bird Call sounded, following another right behind it. Drystan tried to remain calm and avoid getting excited.

Arriving first would put him at a huge advantage. He heard the fourth Blue Bird Call and waited for the fifth. He needed that last one. His horse started to become impatient and pawed at the ground with frustration. Finally, the last Blue Bird Call sounded.

Drystan kicked his horse, and they took off like a fox with its tail on fire. He loved that the palace probably didn't know he was aware of coming to the Ever-Changing Mountain. Drystan had overheard Lulana and Brenna talking to Pyry when they visited her after the wedding.

"I'm so tired of Lady Norella and Lady Sorcha canceling plans," snuffed Lulana. "We all have busy lives, but somehow they think their lives are way more interesting than ours are."

"Why do you think they keep canceling?" asked Pyry.

"Something about a special project for Her Majesty," taunted Lulana. Brenna rolled her eyes at the mention of "Her Majesty."

Pyry questioned her, "Why, Brenna, have you found disappointment in our queen?"

"She just spends all her free time with that gray-eyed Jace now, and she seems so preoccupied lately," Brenna said.

Pyry nodded. "I agree. Sealyn and I used to be so close, but then Jace showed up. He ruined the friendship triangle between me, Drystan, and her. We were all fine before his silver disgrace came along. I wish he would go back to where he belongs." She paused for a quick moment and then asked, "Lulana, what is this special project those girls are working on for the queen?"

Lulana brushed back her blonde hair behind her ear. "I'm not sure, but it has to do with the Ever-Changing Mountain."

"Why do you think that?"

"Because a scroll fell out of one of their baskets. The scroll had scribbles on it about the Ever-Changing Mountain and King Perdon. I just figured it was Sealyn being Sealyn. You know how she gets with digging into Elysium's history," Lulana said.

Pyry's face looked curious. "Where's the scroll now?"

"Oh, I gave it back. They looked worried that I had read it and made me promise not to tell a soul." Lulana laughed. "So that means you ladies can't tell anyone." They laughed at the irony.

Once Drystan heard this, he quickly put the puzzle pieces together and understood what the clue meant. He found it somewhat laughable that Elysium could be handed over to Stoltland all because a few bitter ladies needed to gossip. He considered the saying from the Old Laws, "A loose tongue will have a kingdom hung."

Lord Sakul

# Chapter 26

Sorcha burst through the kitchen door. She shook her head at the sight of Sakul and Char. "Honestly, you two are the literal worst. Queen Sealyn, how could you recruit the two clumsiest human beings in recorded history to help with your little secret quest?"

"Wait, what?" questioned Sealyn.

"Sealyn, come on. You really don't think you had me fooled, do you? I knew you were going to find a way to sneak out and be there tonight." Sorcha looked both stunning and intimidating in her deep purple gown.

Char huffed. "Number one, I'm offended by your outlandish statement, Sorcha. Number two, Sealyn, are you kidding me?! Sorcha knew about all this before me? Who else knows? Don't you dare tell me my brother knows!"

"No, he doesn't. Now, hush up, Char," scolded Sealyn. Char gaped his mouth and gasped in an overdramatic theater performance. "Sorcha, since you're not here to stop me, we have a short amount of time. Shouldn't you be on the way there now?"

"Yes, I'm heading to the side gate now. The first two military units have already left. We're to be escorted by the remaining units."

"Weeeeeee?" Char questioned.

Sealyn waved her hand dismissively. "Just ignore the imp. We're taking the path through the Garden Library, then borrowing the mirrons Lord Finn has in his stables."

Sorcha cleared her throat. "That may be a problem. Lord Finn and Lord Jace are completely drunk. Lord Jem volunteered to drive Finn's carriage home and drop Jace at his manor."

"That's no problem. We're only borrowing the mirrons for the night."

"You mean stealing?" corrected Sorcha.

Sealyn tilted her head. "No, I mean borrowing without permission and returning without a need to know."

"So stealing." Sorcha laughed. "I must go. They may wonder what's holding me up." She smiled at Sakul and left the kitchen in haste.

"Oh, I saw all that," jarred Char.

"Leave it alone, Char," growled Sakul.

"Sakul, are you coming with us?" asked Sealyn.

"No offense, my queen, but I have no desire to ride a mirron."

Char laughed. "Even if it's to watch over your precious Sorcha?"

"Fine. Count me in." Sakul glared at the cheeky grin on Char's face.

"Listen, you two, we need a distraction that can get us out of here without being noticed."

Char opened the door. "That's easy. Follow me."

Sakul looked concerned. "Is this wise to follow Char without knowing the plan?"

"It's never wise to follow Char even if you do have a plan."

Char scanned the room and saw it was still filled with guests. Some had left, but plenty of little gossips still remained. He looked to his left and noticed a pitcher of water was still there. He figured he could make their escape both a success and fun. He quickly grabbed the pitcher and poured it over the floor near one of the extra food tables. With his hand, he gestured for Sakul to come closer. Sakul was utterly perplexed by Char's actions. Unaware of the trap, Sakul felt the tug and shove along with Char's foot sticking out, causing him to trip and tumble right into the food table.

A loud clash echoed throughout the ballroom, and all heads turned towards the scene of the crime. Servants rushed to Sakul, trying to help him to his feet. He was covered in sauces and bits of food. His blood boiled. He reached his breaking point when Char dipped his finger in one of the sauces on his shirt and tasted it, saying, "I don't know, Lord Sakul. I believe you could use a little more salt." The crowd laughed, and Sakul lunged at Char.

Char dove out of the way, barely escaping Sakul's hands. He darted from the scene with Sakul hot on his heels. Char nodded and winked at Sealyn. Sealyn dashed through the Garden Library door and waited for her foolish companions.

With heavy breathing, Sakul stopped chasing Char once they were both in front of the Garden Library door.

Sakul gasped for air. "I'll deal with you later, Char. I'm going in here to catch my breath."

"Come now, my friend. Let me help. I'll bring you some water," remarked Char.

Sakul made his way into the Garden Library, immediately followed by Char holding a goblet of water. Sakul snatched the goblet and downed the cool liquid.

"Char, I'm going to kill you!" yelled Sakul with water dripping from his mouth.

Char pointed at Sakul. "Your Majesty, you heard it, loud and clear, who will be the future murderer of me. Make sure he pays dearly."

"Uh, thank you, Char, for making my life easier knowing who will be your futuristic murderer, but can we please focus? Right now, the priority is saving Elysium, not who plans on murdering you."

Char gasped. "Are you saying that Elysium is more important than my life?"

Sealyn and Sakul simultaneously said, "Yes!"

Char pressed both hands to his heart. "Hurt. Utterly hurt."

Sealyn sighed heavily. "Why am I stuck with the two court jesters on a top-secret mission tonight?"

"Probably because we're the only two in the entire kingdom who would be willing to escort the queen into dangerous territory without military assistance against the king's orders." Char lifted his hands.

Sealyn nodded. "Good point."

The cool night air filled their lungs as they walked down the road toward Lord Finn's stables. Char thought everyone in Avondelle could hear Sakul's wheezing, but he noticed that Sealyn wasn't put off by it. He spotted blue fire flowers glowing at the entrance of the stables and wondered why they were still lit. What or who had passed by to create the vibrations? The old stable door creaked as they slowly pushed it open. They could hear the animals shifting inside, and the smell of hay and manure stung their nostrils.

"How are we supposed to know which stalls are housing these creatures?" whispered Sakul.

Sealyn pointed to the far corner stalls. "Watch as we move slowly. Do you see how the scenery that you're seeing looks like it's following us?" Sakul nodded. "Those are the mirrons reflecting the surrounding scenery."

Char stopped. "Quiet. Do you hear that?"

Sakul and Sealyn both looked around, trying to locate the sounds that Char was hearing. Sealyn pointed to a large mound of hay that stood against the wall between two stalls. "Was that grunting, or was that a slurping sound, or perhaps both?" Char thought to himself. As the haystack came into view, they immediately recognized who was making the sounds and unraveled the fire flower mystery. Finn and his blonde date were locked in a heated embrace.

Char gestured for Sealyn and Sakul to take cover behind some nearby barrels. Sealyn's heart raced. They couldn't afford to get caught. Finn was too close to Jace, and he was still new to their kingdom.

Char cleared his throat. "Why, good evening, Lord Finn and his mysterious lady."

Finn jumped up, grabbing a handful of hay for coverage. "Char! What are you doing here at this hour?"

Char bent down and handed the young lady her corset. "I heard Lord Jem had to take you home, so I just wanted to make sure you were safe, but then I saw the blue fire flowers lit at your stables. I thought it was odd, so I investigated. I'm mighty happy I did."

Sealyn was grateful the young girl had massive amounts of hair. The blonde stayed silent, trying to hide more in the hay.

"I was feeling better, so I was going to escort Miss Melaina to her cottage. We came to saddle the horses since it's a long walk." Finn blushed, feeling the hay becoming scratchy. "Please, Char, you won't tell anyone about this, will you?"

Char grinned. "Of course not. We've all had our passionate moments. I would suggest waking up your butler and having him, along with one of the female servants, escort Miss Melaina to her cottage. Where is the home located?"

"Just past the old stone oak tree, near Turtle Lake, my lord," Melaina spoke nervously.

Char realized the road they would normally travel would take them right past the Ever-Changing Mountain. "Make sure you take the road going past Lord Aerrik's home. I know it's a little longer, but there have been rumors of dangerous creatures feeding at the Ever-Changing Mountain during the night."

Once the lovers departed, Char signaled for Sealyn and Sakul to dash to the back stalls.

"We must act fast. They'll come back for the carriage and horses. Hurry. Saddle the mirrons," hastened Char.

As they rode away from the barn, one thing was undeniably clear: the saddles were not comfortable at all.

# Chapter 27

Drystan's scouts had searched the mountainside thoroughly but found nothing. He approached two recruits near the base of the mountain, hoping for good news.

"My lord, we've looked around the mountain for anything strange, as you instructed, but we're still unclear about what we should be looking for. Can you tell us more about the mission?" questioned Recruit Redone. He stood with his ebony arms crossed, his expectant jade eyes scanning the surroundings.

Drystan could hear movement in the distance. He knew his time was running out. "Here it is. There's a spy among the queen's military. There was a rumor that he was having a meeting here to recruit others in his plot. We must protect her at all costs. If other military units show up, repeat what I've said to you. This will protect you."

The recruits looked at each other, puzzled as to why they would need protection.

"Should we fan out and watch for enemy activity?" asked Recruit Redone.

Drystan nodded and then found a hiding place among the trees where he could observe the sea-blue mountainside. He heard the soldiers' footsteps and finally saw them emerge into the moonlight near the base of the mountain. He saw Commander Elmond and Favien leading two units, consisting of thirty soldiers in total. Should he run now, or should he wait to see whether they had found the clue's answer? Drystan was about to sneak away when he saw Norella, Pinx, Sorcha, Lord Prince Brandle, and Mic walking side by side with Lord Prince Tilmond and Tybalt. This was odd. Why would these non-military individuals be escorted among the soldiers? This must relate to the secret project the ladies were gossiping about.

He watched the soldiers do exactly what they had already done: dig in the ground, climb nearby trees, and press against the rock. Nothing was found. Just as he was about to give up hope, he overheard the ladies talking.

Pinx stared at the sparkling sea-blue mountain. "Why here?"

"What do you mean?" Sorcha rubbed her hands together to stay warm.

"The clue could have led anywhere, so why would King Perdon choose to lead someone here? How does this mountain keep the secret of the Heart of Elysium?"

Norella nodded. "Excellent questions, Pinx. We know that the mountain changes colors of blue throughout the year, but does it do anything else unique?"

The ladies peered at the mountain together, squinting and pondering. Pinx pointed. "Did you see that?"

"See what?" Sorcha opened her eyes wider and jutted her neck forward.

"Right there on the mountainside, the diagonal lines of moonlight. I'm pretty sure that's not normal." Pinx propped her hands on her hips, squinting at the lines.

"Yes, I see what you mean. Wait, they change." Norella traced the lines with her finger, indicating the differences.

Mic noticed her painting in the air, so he and Brandle walked over to join the ladies.

"What are you discovering over here, ladies?" Mic asked.

"It's the moonlight lines on the mountainside. They change. Watch." Norella positioned Mic's head so he would see exactly what they were watching.

After staring at the light beams, Brandle exclaimed, "It's a number sequence!"

Drystan tried to lean in as close as possible without making a sound. The broken tree branches scraped against his skin, making it difficult to stay quiet.

"Look. Each group of light beams lasts seven seconds. Then the next group appears within three seconds, but the 'start-over' lasts five seconds. Did you see?" Brandle kept pointing his finger at the lights.

"Yes! Yes! I see what you're seeing," shouted Sorcha.

"With that pattern, are you noticing the sequence of two, four, seven, and one?" Pinx asked.

Mic nodded. "Yes, I agree."

Norella stepped closer to the mountain when the single light beam shone across the mountain. "Does anyone else notice that there's a section on the single light beam that shows up darker than the rest? Why would that happen?"

"Perhaps we should send someone up there to investigate?" Mic suggested. They approached the military group and shared their findings and suggestions. Favien volunteered to climb the steep mountainside. If there was a chance for another clue, he figured he should be the one to find it.

Favien slipped on the climbing harness invented by Prince Royce and Lord Prince Will. It resembled a saddle, but without the horn. Instead, three rings were placed on each side, along with shoulder straps that connected to the torso belt. Individual ropes were threaded through the harness rings, with the ends then passed through one large ring attached to a horse on the left side of the climber and another horse on the right side. Six soldiers were stationed at the ends of the ropes to assist. The idea was that if the climber fell, the horsemen would tie the ropes to the saddle's horn and make the horses run in the opposite direction of the climber. Hopefully, the ropes would suspend the climber in the air before they hit the ground. It was an untested prototype, with sacks of potatoes being the only testing subjects so far. Pinx was not happy.

As Favien was halfway up the rock, he realized he had forgotten to kiss Pinx. His foot slipped at this thought. Tiny rocks tumbled down the mountain, but he regained his footing. He could feel his heart pounding. Sweat dripped down his forehead as he tried to stay focused. His legs quivered, but he pressed on.

The climb felt like it lasted hours, yet Favien completed it in mere minutes. He was skilled at climbing everything. As the single light beam shone over the darkened spot, he saw a loose rock. He carefully jiggled the rock loose, letting it drop to the ground far beneath him, and looked inside. In the dark hole lay an old, sealed scroll. He recognized the seal of King Perdon. Quickly, he stuffed the scroll into his pocket and began his descent.

The spectators grew anxious as they watched their fearless leader descend the mountain. The horses kept shifting their stances, as if they could sense trouble. Tybalt noticed Max constantly gazing at the sky.

"Something bothering you, Lord Max?" questioned Tybalt.

Max shifted his eyes to Favien. "Not at all, Lord Tybalt. I just like watching the stars."

"Odd. I didn't know we were stargazing tonight, Max. I thought we were here watching out for spies and Favien's climb?" interjected Tilmond.

"My apologies, Lord Prince Tilmond. It won't happen again." Max adjusted his feet and tried to keep his eyes off the sky, but his heart was filled with fear about what lay beyond the clouds. This wasn't the place or the time to reveal his secret. He needed time with Sealyn.

Sweat beads rolled down Favien's face, dripping onto his hood. He could feel the strength in his legs fading. The moon butterflies began to appear. They were a rare sight, as most people were asleep when they emerged. They only displayed color after being exposed to moonlight for hours. Attracted to the warmth, vibrant, glowing red moon butterflies landed on Favien. They were stunning. Favien watched the glowing creatures with amusement, but then his foot slipped once more.

This time, the sweat on his palms made his hands slide off the rocks. He was falling. Glowing red butterflies fluttered quickly away from his rapidly descending body. The soldiers reacted with remarkable speed. The horses bolted in opposite directions as if they were being pursued by a swarm of bees.

Pinx felt her heart stop. The love of her life was falling to his death, and she had to watch every second of it. She was powerless. She felt as if she were made of stone; her mind urged her to run to him, but her body remained frozen in time.

Tybalt watched his best friend flying through the air. He tried to stay calm, but when he considered the distance to the ground compared to the horses' speed, despair settled over him. Suddenly, one of the knots in the ropes came undone. Now, there was no way to catch him. Favien was going to die. Tybalt heard the screams of the ladies and other soldiers, but he couldn't make a sound. Then he heard an odd command from Max: "Madilina! Madilina! Save Favien!" Why would Max call out to his wife to save Favien? How could the tiniest person, who wasn't even there, help his friend?

Giant gusts of wind swept down from the skies above, sending the red and purple butterflies into a swirling chaos. No one could believe their eyes. Madilina was riding a caelidon! In the blink of an eye, she and the caelidon flew beneath Favien. The brilliant caelidon bit the rope, pulling Favien upward. It then tossed the rope and flew backward, catching him.

Madilina and the caelidon landed gracefully, leaving everyone in awe; everyone except Pinx. She dashed to Favien and jumped into his arms just as he dismounted the feathered horse. The recruits from Drystan's scheme came running out of their hiding spots to witness the miracle that had just occurred. The soldiers drew their swords and advanced toward the recruits. The recruits raised their arms in surrender, shouting the words Drystan instructed them to repeat.

Commander Elmond stood in disbelief at the recruits' story. How did the news of the traitor leak? They said Drystan was among them, trying to help the queen find the traitor. Was Drystan telling the truth? Could this be a tactic to throw them off the trail? He removed his helmet, and the moonlight illuminated the light freckles on his cheeks. One thing was for sure: three illegal actions occurred tonight, and all would need to be addressed immediately.

Drystan appeared from the forest, interrupting Commander Elmond's thoughts. The soldiers looked to their commander for guidance on their next movements.

"Commander," Drystan said while breathing heavily, trying to convince them he had been running. "I came as fast as I could once I heard the screams. Is everyone alright?"

Elmond cocked his head. "All thanks to Lady Madilina."

"Thank the Creator! Why was the rescue needed?" asked Drystan.

"Lord Favien's quest is above your clearance." Elmond stepped in front of Drystan. "Your recruits tell me that you requested their presence here tonight for a special mission to catch spies at the queen's request. How is this so?"

"Commander, your question is confusing, but I'll elaborate. I heard rumors from talk in the stables. I can't be sure of who was doing the talking, but the topic was of a traitor among the queen's military. They spoke of finding him tonight by the Ever-Changing Mountain, so I took it upon myself to gather as many as I could to help our queen."

"What an overachiever you are." Elmond paced. "However, you chose to say that the queen herself gave you this special mission when in fact that's not true. You lied. You had no such permission. This is a high military offense." He turned to face the recruits. "You." He pointed to Recruit Redone. "Were you not trained to know that a command directly from the queen required a royal seal?" The scared recruit nodded. The commander turned his head to the young black-haired recruit who was shivering. "Were you not also trained to ask to see that seal before accepting a secret mission of the queen?" The young recruit nodded. "Lord Favien and Lord Tybalt, have your soldiers escort these six men to the dungeons to await their fate."

The recruits hung their heads, but Drystan nodded. This way, he still had a chance to appear innocent.

"Unfortunately, there is still another who broke the law tonight." He turned to Madilina, who was petting the caelidon's nose. "Lady Madilina, as noble and needed as your rescue was tonight, riding a caelidon is illegal. You must have special permission from the queen, and from the looks of you, secretly riding at night, you don't have that. Do you?" Tears formed in Madilina's bright mint eyes.

Max walked in front of his wife. "Now, hold on, Commander. Madil . . ."

Sealyn emerged from her hiding spot. The night had drained her emotions too much. "Commander Elmond." The crowd gasped and bowed. "Lady Madilina did have special permission from me to practice riding the caelidon. Her husband came to me after they returned from their honeymoon and told me the good news that Madilina can actually ride these fascinating creatures. She was under strict instructions not to tell anyone and was only allowed to fly at night. We needed to protect this knowledge from our enemies. I hope to replicate what Madilina can do with others." She nodded to Max and Madilina, who stood in shock, knowing that no such conversations had taken place. "As far as Lord Drystan and these recruits, I will decide their fate tomorrow evening." She locked eyes with Drystan. "It seems as though everyone was on a well-intentioned mission tonight, so I'll be gracious."

"Well, on that cheery note, I do believe we should all head back to our warm beds before we freeze to death." Char clapped his hands and motioned for people to leave. "Favien, thanks for the show. It was highly entertaining, although you could have at least done some backflips in the air. Can you work that in next time?"

Favien chuckled and squeezed Pinx's shoulders. "Next time, Char, I'll make sure you're the one falling off the mountain."

Char scrunched his face. "Strange. That's twice tonight that someone has threatened my life. Commander Elmond, what say you to being my personal bodyguard?" Char patted Commander Elmond's back.

"Char, stop touching me. Let's not make it a third threat on your life tonight."

"Understood! Now, can someone take these mirrons back? I'd much rather ride in the comforts of a carriage." Everyone shook their heads and laughed. "No? Seriously? Queen Sealyn, are you really leaving Sakul and me to take these rock-solid monsters back?" Char glared at Sealyn, who waved at him from the carriage. "Unbelievable, it's like she's royalty or something."

*To give one's life
for a comrade,
is to give one's life
to a brother.*

*King Ryker Araelien
Entry 945*

Lord Marin

# Chapter 28

Months later, cold air flooded the landscape, and snow blanketed the ground. Ice sparkled in the morning sunlight. A large, warm fire crackled in the breakfast room. Sealyn sat in front of the cozy fire, sipping coffee. Maekel fluttered at the window, drawing stars with her breath as she blew on the cold glass. Sealyn held the scroll in her hand, rubbing her thumb back and forth across the broken seal.

Another clue. Another mystery. How many were there? Would this be an endless saga, or was this the last one? No one knew. Months passed with many sleepless nights. The arrival of Stoltland's royal fleet only complicated matters. Each day felt like another game the new Stoltland queen was playing. She still felt the shock of Lady Corentine stepping off the ship as Queen Corentine. She replayed Jace's confused expressions as his mother made him bow to her.

Elysium was just a day away from the Trundatta Ball, so the entire capital city was seasonally decorated. White and silver ribbons were tied to each pole in the market, adorned with white feathers. Ice sculptures of mystical creatures were in each corner. Fortunately, the weather helped prevent the ice from melting.

Sealyn opened the scroll again, just as she had done a hundred times since the night of Perdonair. She reread the words: "Where snow cannot fall." She repeated the numbers: two, four, seven, and one. How did these two pieces work together? Perhaps King Perdon moved the Heart of Elysium to their tropical lands. Snow couldn't fall there. What about underground? Snow most assuredly can't fall underground, but then those numbers.

Every time Sealyn thought she was getting close, the numbers would deny her access to the answer. Was it twenty-four and seventy-one? Was it two and 471? Was it 247 and one, or was it 2,471? Her brain ached for a break.

She saw the butler walk past the door carrying a tray. He wasn't heading to any of the bedrooms, so she decided to catch up to her butler.

"Good morning, Cidreek. Where are you taking that breakfast tray?"

"Good morning, Your Majesty. I'm taking this tray to Lord Marin. He's in the Historical Archives Room."

"I guess the conservatory has too much fog on the windows in the mornings for his enjoyment?"

"Correct, Your Majesty."

"Thank you, Cidreek. I will take the tray and have breakfast with him, just like a grandfather and his granddaughter should. Do you mind bringing me my usual breakfast in there?"

"At once, Your Majesty. I think that's a wonderful idea."

Sealyn pushed open the cracked door to the Historical Archives Room and saw surprise and delight on her grandfather's face.

Lord Marin said, "Well, now. This is quite an enjoyable surprise."

Sealyn placed the tray on the old wooden table, which was cluttered with dusty books and opened scrolls from the past. Candles in need of replacement lit the windowless room, filling it with the musty scent of mold and parchment.

"Good morning, Grandpa. I thought it would be nice to join you for breakfast. What are you doing in here?"

"I like to come in here and brush up on my historical knowledge."

Sealyn sat in the old chair, picking up one of the scrolls in front of her. She read a few lines of the Old Laws, wishing she knew more about them, especially the reasons behind their creation.

"You look troubled. Is there anything I can help with?" He scooped up his eggs and bacon, then sipped his black coffee.

"I just wish I knew where it can't snow."

"Can't snow? That's an odd desire, but there are plenty of places where it cannot snow."

"Name some." Sealyn sat back in her chair and folded her arms, almost daring him to solve the puzzle for her.

"Easy. There are the tropical beaches, the tropical oceans, the Waterfall of Fire in Stoltland…"

Sealyn chuckled. "Sure, sure, you've made your point. I was hoping there was a place here in Avondelle, but everywhere is covered with snow. Even the frozen lakes and waterfalls have inches of snow."

Lord Marin adjusted his glasses. "Yes, yes, everywhere but the graves of the martyrs."

Sealyn's eyes widened, and her stomach turned. "What? Graves of the martyrs? What do you mean?"

Butler Cidreek set down Sealyn's breakfast tray and exited quickly. The steam of freshly baked Puffin Pies filled the room.

"It's an old tale, my dear. Twelve warriors sacrificed their lives to protest against the king, who knelt to the curse. The families of the brave twelve buried them after the slaughter. The legend says that snow physically doesn't fall on their graves out of respect for their virtue. Only the purest form of flower grows on their graves: the white fantalaya."

Sealyn exhaled a laugh. "The white fantalaya? Now I know you're joking."

"Why do you say that?"

"Because that flower is a myth."

"So you've heard of it?"

"Yes, it's in a famous children's book called *The Hare and the White Fantalaya*. I'm sure you even read me that book."

"Indeed. I did, but that doesn't mean they don't exist. My dear, where do you think writers come up with their stories?"

"Wild imaginations?"

"From unseen realities."

"Unseen? You mean like invisible?"

"Sometimes, yes, but what is the past if not unseen to its future? We did not see our thousands-of-years-old past, but we've heard the stories."

She propped her elbows on the table. "Where would these graves be? I've seen the Avondelle graves. There's no ground without snow."

"What does the white fantalaya look like?"

"White stem, white leaves, and white petals with a light blue pollen center."

"Excellent memory. My darling, your desire is masquerading in plain sight. It seems as though your answer is camouflaged."

A strange feeling washed over Sealyn, as if she were on the verge of recalling something important but hadn't quite gotten there yet. "Gramps, do the numbers two, four, seven, and one mean anything to you?"

"Not that I'm aware."

Sealyn dropped her head. It was hopeless. How was she to find camouflaged graves and solve this number paradox?

Lord Marin cocked his head. "Although the year 2471 was the year the twelve were slain." Sealyn's head shot up. Lord Marin leaned in close to his granddaughter and placed his hand on hers. "I don't believe in coincidences. Do you?"

"Not the least bit!" She jumped up from the table, kissed Lord Marin's cheek, and hugged him. "I have to go."

"Where to?"

Sealyn paused. "Well, I've had such a vivifying conversation with one grandfather; now I must have one with my other grandfather."

Lord Marin scrunched his eyes. "Sealyn, your other grandfather is dead."

"Exactly."

Princess
Siany
Araelien

# Chapter 29

Princess Siany shivered as they halted the horses in front of the Avondelle graveyard. She rubbed her eyes, still reluctant to be awake and definitely not wanting to be out in the morning snow. However, she came because she recognized the urgency in her sister's voice.

Sealyn dismounted her horse, boots crunching on the snowy ground. "Tie the horses here. We have to walk without them in the graveyard."

"Can you finally explain what we're doing out here in the freezing snow?" Siany's breath swirled in the morning air.

"Have you ever heard of the legend of the twelve?" Siany shook her head. "Neither had I till this morning. Grandfather Marin decided to share the tale with me."

"Sealyn, what does this have to do with freezing in a graveyard?"

"The clue read, 'Where snow cannot fall.'"

"Yes, but look around, Sealyn. There's snow covering everything. Even our footprints are being covered up by the falling snow."

"Listen, Siany. The legend of the twelve tells of twelve graves that can't have snow fall on them because of the martyrs' deaths. Instead, white fantalayas grow on the graves, concealing them."

"Sealyn, do you hear yourself? White fantalayas? That's from a children's book." Snowflakes fell on Siany's lashes, adding a magical kiss to the mystery before them.

"Then explain to me why it was the year 2471 that the twelve were killed?" Sealyn raised her eyebrows.

Siany stopped walking and looked around with amazement. "Are you saying that the sequence of numbers from the Ever-Changing Mountain represents the year 2471, and we're supposed to find the graves of the twelve martyred men with mythical white flowers on them, and somehow those graves will lead us either to the next clue or the Heart of Elysium?"

"Excellent summation, dear sister."

"This is both brilliant and hard to believe." Siany shook her head, flakes of ice falling.

"It's more brilliant than anything. Brilliant that King Perdon would hide a clue in a legendary story. Most people wouldn't hunt myths."

"Good thing we're not most people, then, huh?" Siany rubbed her wool-gloved hands together and trudged forward through the snow.

They stopped in front of the large, dark iron gate that protected the royal graves. The frozen iron bars were twenty-five feet high and stretched for hundreds of yards long and wide. Sharp weapons were welded to the tops of the fence to deter intruders. Only the royals possessed keys to enter.

Sealyn opened the gate and locked it behind her sister. She gazed across the nonroyal graveyard to ensure they were not being followed. They paused at the grave of Graelynd's father, King Saven. They brushed snow from his statue and both wished he were still with them.

"Sealyn, what's the plan?"

"I keep wondering where the families of the twelve would have been allowed to bury them. If they were against the cursed king, then he likely wouldn't have allowed them to be buried in the same graveyard as everyone else, right?"

Siany nodded. "They would most likely be buried away from everyone?"

"Remember, this has King Perdon written all over the escapade, so he could have shifted graves to keep this secret." Sealyn rubbed her arms, studying her grandfather's snow-covered statue.

Siany nodded. "I didn't think of that. Let's fan out and look for anything that looks off. If he wanted the graves protected, then bringing them inside the gates would be the smartest move."

The royals strolled among the numerous statues of their ancestors, hoping something would reveal itself. Yet, nothing stood out.

"There has to be something we're missing." Sealyn tucked her hands in her pockets, scanning the countless grave markers.

"The only thing I couldn't get past were the boulders blocking the far corner." Siany pointed to the back left corner.

"Boulders? There aren't supposed to be rocks on this part of the land. That would prevent grave digging." Sealyn started walking toward the boulders.

"Oh, I thought they were there for the stonemasons to sculpt future statues."

Sealyn shook her head. "No. All stonework is first done at the masonry and then transported here. There's something not right about these boulders being here. We need to climb over them."

Siany threw her hands up. "Sure. Let's climb giant iced boulders with no one around."

"Where's that Feydom roamer courage now?" jeered Sealyn.

After several attempts, the royals surfaced on the other side of the boulders with minimal bruising. They stared in awe. Before them stood a giant oak tree with branches spreading over twelve unmarked graves. They smiled at the alluring white fantalayas covering each grave. Sealyn shook her head in disbelief. The flowers truly blended the graves with the snow.

The girls noticed a headstone that listed the twelve names, along with the year 2471. Sealyn bent down and pulled back a few of the flowers from the bottom of the short headstone, smelling sweet and wet. She read, "Here lies Hope."

"Hope? Why would a grave carry hope?" questioned Siany.

"Because hope is buried beneath us!" Sealyn started jumping up and down. "Siany, it's buried in this grave!"

"We must return quickly. We'll recruit help to dig up the grave. We've already been gone too long without being noticed." Siany looked worried. She quickly said a prayer, hoping no one had followed them.

"Not to fear. I have two roses with me to place on King Saven's grave. As far as anyone knows, we came to visit our grandfather."

As they rode their horses back to the palace, Sealyn wasn't sure whether the tears streaming from her eyes were due to the cold air or overwhelming joy. She was one step closer to protecting her kingdom and felt she needed to thank her grandfather. Apparently, knowing your history pays off.

With Drystan still having access to her military, Sealyn chose to keep the grave digging a family matter. Drystan and the recruits served penalties of trench digging and mucking stalls for five weeks, and Sealyn demoted Drystan's rank to that of a first-year recruit. They were allowed to return after signing a written statement assuring the queen that their mistakes would never happen again. This kept everything quiet. The biggest gossip was still Madilina flying the caelidon. Madilina had become the overnight sensation of Avondelle.

The majority of the queen's cousins accepted Sealyn's call for aid. Brandle, Tilmond, Jdru, Char, Rielen, Ezen, Cian, Kolt, and Brielin opened the grave. After hours of digging, they were finally able to tie ropes to the iron rings attached to the wooden casket. Everyone helped pull the casket out of its resting place very slowly. Sealyn dropped to her knees and pried open the casket.

The bones of one of the twelve lay before them, accompanied by his sword. Sealyn noticed that the bones appeared to rest on a raised platform. She signaled for her cousins to assist in lifting the edges of the dead man's bed. Once they set the bed on the ground, the secret covering revealed the secrets of Elysium's past, including not only the scrolls and books the king had hidden from the world but also strange flower petals. These were not the white fantalayas; instead, they were dried petals of a deep pink color.

Sealyn instructed them to pack everything from the casket into the saddlebags. They needed to sift through each item that was present. The petals were the one thing that stood out to her. She collected the petals in a special pouch and made a mental note to visit Lady Raquel about the flower.

After they dropped off all the articles at Sealyn's private natatorium, Sealyn stayed. She needed a moment to collect herself before diving into everything they had discovered. Her heart was ready for the findings, but her body ached for care. She changed into her water garments and decided to take a moment to relax. The steam hovered over the water, creating a welcoming atmosphere as Sealyn slipped into the aqua depths. Yellow and purple butterflies danced around the room, welcoming her mind to drift from the day's events to Jace's soft embrace. Jace. She missed him.

Since his mother had arrived, she rarely saw him. She was concerned that the new queen would persuade Jace to return with them. When they last spoke, Jace and Sealyn had agreed to announce their engagement at the Trundatta Ball. She hoped this was still the plan. Her bruises throbbed in the warm water, but her mind still wandered to thoughts of Jace. Trials awaited them; she could feel it deep within her bones. Somehow, Corentine would be their greatest foe.

Lady Adalina

# Chapter 30

# THE TRUNDATTA BALL

As part of tradition, Sealyn's Vinurs of the Court gathered in the upper foyer for a toast before the ball. They did this as kids after reading about it in one of their history books. They clinked their golden goblets together and drank to a magical evening. They walked to the edge of the banister, decorated with winter-white tree vines and white feathers. Over the years, the tradition had evolved into watching the guests arrive and rating the best costumes.

The guests loved the cheers they received from the queen's Vinurs. Bright and playful string music echoed throughout the castle. Sealyn could finally feel herself laughing and truly enjoying the moment. It had been so long since the stress of the mission didn't feel like a heavy weight. The clapping and laughter stopped once the Stoltlanders arrived.

The Vinurs gasped at the sight of their costumes. This was a direct insult to Queen Sealyn. The next few minutes would determine how the evening would unfold. Why did they need to test the queen's limits? Jace entered and smiled at Sealyn. He was wearing the appropriate clothes for the evening, so clearly his family knew what was required but chose not to follow suit.

Adalina whispered, "What should we do, Queen Sealyn?"

"The exact opposite of what they want. Let's go down now." Sealyn led Lady Vinurs down the left staircase while the men descended the right staircase.

Jace waited for Sealyn at the bottom of the staircase and reached out for Sealyn's hand, kissing it.

"May I escort you to the ballroom, Your Majesty?" Jace smiled.

"Certainly, Lord Jace." They walked in front of Jace's family and stopped. "Good evening to you all," Sealyn attempted to speak without sounding as if she had a mouth full of hornets.

"Good evening, Queen Sealyn. We have been eagerly anticipating this ball. The stories of the Trundatta Balls are, after all, legendary." Queen Corentine smirked at Prince Haedon.

"As are the customs of the ball," remarked Adalina.

Corentine's eyes twitched. "Oh, I'm sorry, is there an issue with our costumes? I figured you wouldn't mind if we wore black accessories instead of green. This way, we don't blend in with you, Elysians." She stepped closer to Sealyn.

Sealyn didn't budge, but her Vinurs and Commander Elmond stepped forward. "No issue. It's better for us to keep an eye on you. Enjoy the evening." Sealyn smiled and entered the ballroom without glancing back.

"That was epic," whispered Char.

"I just hope tonight's announcement sends shock waves to her onyx heart," Sealyn whispered back.

Sealyn pulled Jace to the side. She loved Jace's costume. Solid-white coat, shirt, and pants, with half of his face covered in a mask of green leaves and moss. She was proud of his first attempt at the Trundatta Ball's assignment, which was "Masks of the Forests."

She held his hand tight and whispered, "Are you still prepared for tonight's announcement?"

Jace blushed. "I was hoping you wouldn't want to back out." Jace had been nervous these past few months about where Sealyn and he stood. His family brought plenty of complications, mainly that they consumed most of his time. They wanted to be shown around the capital, the countryside, the mountains, and the lakes. He found it almost strange how interested they were in Elysium's lands.

Jace's gray eyes traveled from the bottom of her white ball gown, following the lush ivy vines that created a sinuous trail up her dress. The vines divided at her torso and formed a flattering silhouette of the bodice before vanishing over her shoulders. Her mask, adorned with ivy leaves dipped in silver sparkles, captivated his every thought. She was breathtaking. Of course, he wanted to marry her.

Sealyn blushed as she watched Jace's eyes ogle her costume. "Shall we make the announcement now?"

"Lead the way, my queen."

Heart pounding, Sealyn signaled the musicians to stop. The crowd backed up to give her room to speak.

"Welcome, my esteemed guests. I hope your evening has been a delight so far. You all look exquisite and did a remarkable job following the theme of tonight's ball." She clapped for them. "I, however, need to make an announcement, and I hope you all will share in my happiness. Lord Jace of Stoltland and I are engaged and will be getting married this Spring season!" Sealyn scanned the room with a joyful smile, but fear overwhelmed her like a ravenous lion. She noticed the stares and heard the whispers. A sense of anger and terror washed over her as she felt the eyes of those watching her.

Thankfully, Char burst through the shocked crowd and said, "Great news, our dearest queen! May I be the first to congratulate you both!" He hugged his cousin and made eyes toward all the queen's Vinurs to follow suit.

Once Char charmed the crowd, everyone clapped and came forward to congratulate Sealyn and Jace. A select few stood back. Drystan gulped down the last of his ale and shot a glance at Corentine. She looked as if she were about to implode. He needed to speak to her, but he didn't know how to orchestrate such a visit. Then he heard what he needed: a changing-partners song. Corentine looked at Drystan, and he nodded toward the dance floor. She took her husband's hand and stood beside Drystan and Pyry.

With each turn and transition to different partners, Drystan and Corentine were able to communicate.

"The mountain was a failure," whispered Drystan.

"Why?" Corenetine spun back to her husband.

Drystan side-stepped his wife and was back in front of Corentine. "Favien took the clue."

"Have they solved it?" Corentine twirled in front of a gruff gentleman who resembled a hairy tree. She scrunched her nose at the sight of the disgusting man.

Drystan smiled and guided a lady in what he could only describe as a dress made entirely out of bushes. He felt the branches scrape against him and winced. He spun her away and locked hands with Corentine. "I don't know. I'm out of ideas on how to get it from him."

Corentine stared into Drystan's jade eyes as he held onto her waist. "Who does Favien hold most dear?"

Drystan's stomach dropped. Of course, he knew the answer to that, but what was this woman capable of? If he said her name, would he be sending her to her death? Drystan could hardly bear to look at Pyry as they twirled in circles. Then he sidestepped one last time, and there were Corentine's inky eyes waiting for his answer. He sighed. "Lady Pinx."

After dancing five dances in a row, Jace needed a break. He saw the Vinurs gathered in a corner, laughing and clinking goblets, so he decided to join. As he approached, he could see the queen's infusions were on full display, but he noticed different names painted on the bottles. He picked up the bottle with the light blue, bubbling liquid and observed the mesmerizing sapphire flowers at the bottom. Painted in the center were the words *Blue Lagoon Magic*. He heard *her* chuckle and turned around, shaking his head. "Blue Lagoon Magic, is it, Your Majesty?"

Sealyn bit her lip. "Did you really think I would name my infusions those other names?"

"So you lied."

"Maybe I was 'name-testing,' or perhaps I needed good excuses to bring up such subjects we discussed. You sure you don't want a glass? I heard it's your favorite." She winked, and Jace melted all over again.

"Queen Sealyn!" roared Favien. "This is the best-tasting…uh…um…what's it again that I'm drinking?" Char rolled his eyes and whispered in his ear. "Ah, yes! This yellow liquid is the Courage of the Lion. No. I mean Lion's Courage." He hiccupped.

Sealyn shook her head. "Perhaps you've had a little too much courage already?"

"Nonsense!" slurred Favien.

"What's five plus two?" asked Char sarcastically.

"False!" shouted Favien.

"False?"

"No. It's nine!" Favien attempted to count his fingers.

Char laughed. "There you have it, Queen Sealyn. He's perfectly fine. Five plus two is false nine."

Sealyn noticed Pinx wasn't among them. Since Favien didn't have the slightest clue which way was up or down or how to add, she walked to Norella, Sorcha, and Adalina. "Good evening, ladies, have you seen Lady Pinx?"

Norella shrugged. "Last I saw her, she was laughing with Pyry, Lulana, and Drystan."

"Laughing with Drystan?" asked Sealyn.

Sorcha folded her arms. "That seems odd, right? Pinx isn't a fan of Drystan."

"But you know Pinx, she doesn't like confrontation," added Adalina. "Maybe she was just really enjoying herself? I did see her having a couple glasses of the Forbidden Romance infusion. She said she liked that one the best because it was pink." Adalina adjusted her eucalyptus leaf mask.

"If you're worried, Sealyn, we can check the ladies' powder rooms," suggested Sorcha.

"Yes, please make sure she's well. I don't want anything to be wrong."

The three ladies strolled to the ladies' powder room, fully expecting to find Pinx passed out on one of the pink and gold lounge chairs. Instead, they found nothing; Pinx was nowhere in sight. They scanned the room. One stone wall featured four gold-framed mirrors extending from the floor to mid-wall, facing the wall with the three indoor latrines. Each latrine included wooden walls and a door for complete privacy, and each enclosure was spacious enough to accommodate a small table with a wash pitcher and bowl.

Glittering, sheer, pink-tinted curtains divided the lounge area from the latrine room. The lounge area was filled with Zuri's fragrant candles and Raquel's musical plants. The ladies loved reclining on the pink velvet couches. It was a peaceful room from the loud dancing outside.

As they pushed the curtains aside, a crunch filled the air. Norella stepped on broken glass. To her left stood the mirrors, yet none were shattered. To her right were the latrines, which had no glass at all. All three ladies gazed at the wall opposite them, which featured large windows. Fear struck them like a fist to the chest. They dashed out of the powder room and quickly found Sealyn.

Sealyn tried to keep the broken windows hidden from most of the guests. Her Vinurs of the Court, along with Commander Elmond and some royal guards, gathered in the ladies' powder room. Commander Elmond ordered that the grounds be searched.

"Are we to assume Pinx is missing?" asked Tybalt. He put his arm around Norella, trying to comfort her.

Adalina gasped. "Let's not use missing yet. Can we just say we don't know where she is?"

"Adalina is right." Sorcha nodded. "We need to stay calm and remain positive."

"But this is the second lady to go missing," pleaded Tybalt.

"Second?" questioned Jashun, who looked more like a snake in his costume than he would admit.

"Lady Zuri. She hasn't been seen in months, and she's not in her shop. I've checked because I needed an elixir for… uh…my, well, food troubles." Tybalt cleared his throat.

"Lady Zuri isn't missing. She's on a special quest." Sealyn looked slightly at Finn, who had a frightened expression. He gave a small nod and looked away. "We have ordered all servants, including the Nichts, to scour the castle and the grounds for Lady Pinx. Commander Elmond is conducting interviews with everyone who saw her. If you have any information, please share it with him so he can create a timeline. In the meantime, Lord Favien will be staying in our guest quarters in the White Horse Suite. Lord Doebromir, Lord Tybalt, and Lord Jashun, will you stay with him?" The gentlemen nodded. "I have arranged for several beds to be added to the room for your comfort. For everyone else, as much as I know you would love to aid in the search, I need you to return to the ball and continue to at least appear to have fun. We can't let certain guests know there's an issue."

Sealyn remained in the lounge. She sank into the velvet cushions and dropped her head into her hands. A gentle hand rested on her back as her sister sat beside her. The sisters shared a tender moment. Allowing her to cry, Siany held the most powerful woman in the kingdom, and she realized the crown was heavier than it looked.

Lord Doebromir
Lord Favien

# Chapter 31

The next morning was eerily silent. What should have been a joyous time was instead filled with gloom. Pinx was still missing, with no clues to her whereabouts. The commander's forces discovered scuff marks on the ground and horse hooves beneath the broken windows, but the trail went cold miles away from Avondelle.

King Ryker set his freshly squeezed orange juice on the round stone table in the war room. He counted off with his fingers, one by one. "Let me get this straight. The spy, Drystan, whom we were supposed to arrest the night of Perdonair, is still mingling among our troops as if nothing has happened. The person responsible for Drystan becoming a traitor is now somehow the queen of Stoltland, and they're refusing to let the former queen leave their boats for health reasons. The night my daughter decides to announce she's marrying the son of our worst enemy is also the night that one of her ladies is kidnapped by who knows. But to top that off, you, Queen Sealyn, thought it was wise to dig up one of the twelve martyrs' graves with your cousins and sister, thinking that would lead to the next clue? Did I leave anything out?" He lifted his arms in question.

"So we're dropping the stolen mirrons part?" joked Char.

"Char, don't make me lock you in the dungeons!" growled Ryker. "Why are you even here?" He looked at Sealyn. "Why is he here?"

"Believe it or not, he comes in handy." Sealyn looked at Char, who mouthed, "Wow." Sealyn stood up and started walking around the table. "I'm not sure what more we can do. I've already sent for half of our northern troops to come to Avondelle. We've increased the number of spies monitoring the Stoltland ships, the Stoltland guests here, and Drystan. We have every soldier and recruit searching the lands for Pinx. The Council of Wisdom is working in rotating shifts, studying what we found in the coffin, while Faith Commissioner Herb is collaborating closely with Lord Favien during this challenging time." She paused and spun back to face the table. "I think we need to focus on the 'why.' Why would someone kidnap specifically Lady Pinx?"

Doebromir hobbled to his feet. "It's Drystan! I know it!"

Char threw his head to the side. "Seriously, Doebromir? Drystan can't be the bad man for everything. At *Liquid Courage* the other night, you blamed Drystan for Madam Yeel's garden fire; then you blamed him for your missing sword when it was Lord Jashun who had borrowed it. Fire?

Drystan. Thievery? Drystan. Volcano erupting? Drystan." Doebromir pounded his fist on the table, making a loud bang.

"Char, you've made your point," remarked Sealyn. "Drystan himself could not have been the one to take her because he was accounted for the entire time during the ball; so eliminate him from the list."

"Pinx is obviously a direct link to Favien, so if we look at it as someone trying to take a stab at Favien, then who would that be?" asked Tilmond.

"Favien is loved by all. Even among the soldiers, no one has an issue with him," said Max.

"If the kidnappers weren't from Elysium, then perhaps our Stoltland guests had a reason. I want to reiterate that I'm saying 'if.' I'm not accusing yet." Prince Adomin brushed his jet-black hair.

Ryker looked up with huge concern. "Didn't you say it was Favien who grabbed the clue?" Sealyn nodded. "What if Drystan shared that information with Corentine?"

"It wouldn't matter. Favien never saw what it said," replied Sealyn.

Ryker shook his head. "They wouldn't know that. What if they think Favien saw the clue, so they kidnapped his bride-to-be as ransom for the clue?"

Sealyn smacked the table. "Everyone, we need to guard Favien and show that we're guarding Favien. If we demonstrate the impossibility of contacting or kidnapping Favien, then perhaps they will release Pinx. I want guards under his window, guards at his door, guards at the end of the hallway, and guards inside his room. I want this spread throughout the kingdom. I want the talk of all of Avondelle to be how much Favien is being protected. Now, I have another meeting, and I'm late."

The wooden gate creaked as Sealyn pushed past it. She loved walking in Lady Raquel's garden. Northern primrose flowers lined the stone pathways through the vegetation. Their alluring crimson, azure, yellow, and orange colors dazzled everyone who walked by in the snow. Sealyn noticed that the deep purple violas were in full bloom, too. She loved picking their petals and adding them to her teas.

Outside the main garden house were large pink camellia shrubs. How did Raquel manage to grow such big blooms? Her gardener could only grow these flowers to half their size. She noticed that the ornamental cabbage and kale in the open space beside the garden house were almost ready for harvest. Even though the snow-covered flowers and plants outside were impressively lovely, such as the bright yellow winter aconite and the light purple crocus, the most magnificent features of the property were Lady Raquel's garden houses.

Completely constructed of glass panes, the garden houses were designed to grow plants that thrived only in spring and summer, even during the winter months. These plants required extra care, so Sealyn knew she would find Raquel inside.

Raquel was a petite woman with light brown hair and the most darling face, adorned with tiny freckles across her cheeks and nose. Despite her small stature, her personality was anything but diminutive. She was bold and fierce, which is why she and Sealyn got along so well.

"Good morning, Lady Raquel."

Raquel dropped a few strawberries at the sound of Sealyn's greeting. "Oh, Queen Sealyn. My apologies. I was not aware you were coming here today. I'm completely filthy."

"Not to worry. You look perfect."

"My Queen, may I offer you my special blend of strawberries? I call them red sugar berries. I mixed some of the special sugar cane into the soil, and each batch is sweeter than the last. Here, try one." She handed Sealyn a plump, bright red strawberry. Sealyn bit into the most juicy and sweet fruit she had ever had.

"Raquel! These are absolutely delicious! You must take some into the market. I bet *Mimby's Morsels* will want them."

"Oh, yes, Your Majesty. She does. I gave her a basketful before the ball. She wants them year-round." Raquel shifted her footing. "I know you didn't come all the way out here to gab about my tasty treats, did you?"

"You're right. I came to ask about these petals." Sealyn pulled out the pouch where she had kept the bright pink petals from the coffin and shook a few petals into Raquel's cupped hands.

Raquel's ivy-green eyes glowed. "I know exactly what this flower is, but I'm curious how you came by these petals."

"The less you know, the better."

"Understood, Your Majesty. Well, this is the blood passion flower. It only blooms during the spring season, but you can use the powers of the petals throughout the year."

"What do you mean by its powers?" She wondered whether these particular powers were what preserved the petals for these hundreds of years.

Raquel lowered her head. "This particular flower is one of Elysium's greatest secrets. Its petals can heal wounds and illnesses. The pollen can even revive other plants that are dying. The petals change colors throughout the blooming season, signaling which power is available."

Sealyn nodded her head, still trying to figure out how this flower could be linked to the Heart of Elysium. "Raquel, your family is legendary among the many generations who have grown up on these lands. I wonder whether any old stories were passed down about the Heart of Elysium?"

Raquel's eyes widened. "Your Majesty, why are you concerning yourself with such things?"

Sealyn stepped closer. "So you have heard of it then?" Raquel nodded uncomfortably. "Raquel, how would this flower and the Heart of Elysium be linked?"

Raquel's mouth gaped, and in walked her husband, Lord Aerrik. "Good morning, Your Majesty. I thought I heard voices. I didn't know whether my wife had finally gone crazy or whether that was just wishful thinking." He laughed.

Raquel shot him a mean look. "Can we offer you any refreshment?"

"Thank you kindly, Lord Aerrik, but your wife has already let me sample her delicious strawberries. Raquel was also about to finish telling me a fascinating tale."

Aerrik folded his arms. "Oh, really. What tale?"

Raquel looked nervous. She loved her husband more than words could express, and she didn't want to cause any trouble for her family. She thought of her two children inside, who were probably playing with her father. Her family held many of Elysium's secrets, and few knew that, but here was her queen in her garden house asking for her help. She had to be loyal to the crown, especially to Sealyn. Sealyn financially supported the growth of her garden. Whatever Raquel wanted to build or test, Sealyn always encouraged her and ensured she had a clear path to achieve her goals.

Raquel cleared her throat. "The Heart of Elysium." Aerrik dropped his arms. "Queen Sealyn, the Heart of Elysium is what gives Elysium its power. To be honest, all kingdoms have one. It's how the kingdoms live. A kingdom will flourish more without the hand of the curse upon it, which for our kingdom was weakened by your lineage. No one has seen it for thousands of years, though."

"Why? Why keep it hidden?" questioned Sealyn.

"Whoever has possession of it will control the country. It's called the Heart of Elysium because it acts as our beating hearts."

Sealyn held up her hand. "Wait, are you saying that this thing is alive?"

"Yes, but not the way you and I are alive."

Sealyn nodded. "Well, that cleared it up. What else can you tell me?"

Raquel looked toward Aerrik. He nodded. "My family was chosen hundreds of years ago to help protect it. They were very loyal to King Perdon. So, when the battles took place and he nearly lost it, he commissioned us to add more defenses around it.

Sealyn jutted her head out when she caught those words. "Around it? You mean you know the exact location of it?"

Raquel dropped her head. "Yes, My Queen. I do, but please don't ask me to tell you where." Tears formed in her eyes.

"Raquel, before I ask where it is, because I will be asking that, I will tell you why." Sealyn proceeded to tell them both what had transpired over the past months between Elysium, Stoltland, and Drystan. Their faces changed from shock to anger to fear to sadness. "This is why I need the location. I want to protect it too. We need even more defenses than what it currently has, so what does the blood passion flower have to do with it?"

Facing the destruction of her family's legacy, Raquel pondered how to avoid fully revealing the truth. She did not want to lie, but she aimed to protect the Heart of Elysium. She could trust Sealyn, but this secret surpassed them all. Sealyn always respected her, so perhaps she wouldn't make her tell all the details if she gave her just enough to satisfy. Raquel looked at Aerrik and then back at Sealyn. "Its roots are wrapped around it."

# Chapter 32

Weeks passed, and the snow began to melt. The rivers gushed with flowing waters. Spring flowers started to bloom in the fields and forests. With the snow melting, it was time for the Stoltlanders to return home. Jace breathed a sigh of relief when he saw the trunks by the front door. The servants were scurrying about the manor, trying to pack his family's things as fast as they could. Something was different about his mother. She seemed almost darker, or had she been like that his entire life, but he never noticed?

Corentine walked down the stairs, smiling. "Good morning, my son. How are you today?"

"Good morning, Mother. No complaints here. I see you are all packed?"

She waved her arms and rolled her eyes. "Well, we would be, but your servants are so incompetent."

"Mother, please. You can't say things like that in front of them; nor should you say that in general."

Corentine glared at Jace. "Are you daring to tell me what I can and can't do? Who's the parent, and who's the child? I raised you, Jace. Don't you forget your place in this world. You can't educate me, child." She snapped her head and walked into Jace's breakfast room.

Jace was ready for all the arguments and berating to be gone. He needed a long break. He needed to see Sealyn.

While she was eating her sugary breakfast, the butler brought Corentine a letter. She tore it open, recognizing the handwriting, and shooed the butler away. She read, "Our final attempt failed. More guards were stationed. Time to forfeit the package." She crumpled the letter in her palm, sitting in silence for several minutes. They needed to leave quickly and with great urgency if the package was about to be forfeited. She gulped down the remaining coffee and walked toward the fire. When Jace entered, she swiftly threw the letter into the flames, causing the coals to hiss.

"My son, something terrible has happened in Stoltland, and we must return with much haste. Order your servants to load the carriages immediately."

Jace hurried to his mother's side. "Is everything okay? What happened?"

"That's for royal ears only, Jace," Corentine pompously elucidated. She was halfway out the door when she turned back. "Something you might want to get used to hearing. You might be marrying the queen, but they won't allow you to be king."

"I care nothing about titles. My childhood taught me that much." He winced at the burning in his wrists.

Corentine slammed the door behind her. Jace turned to face the fire. He closed his silver eyes and gripped both hands on the mantel, trying to calm his rage. Feeling the fire's heat, he slowly opened his eyes and noticed a half-burned letter. He tried to grab it, but the flames kept him from reaching it. He squinted and read, "forfeit the package." What could this mean? What was the package, and who was forfeiting it?

Jace heard the carriages stirring. He raced out front to see his family climbing into their heavily packed carriages.

Jace approached his mother. "Mother, I need to ask you just one question."

Corentine squared her shoulders at Jace. "What would that be?"

"You wouldn't ever do anything against Elysium, right? I mean, you wouldn't hurt anyone, right?" A memory surged from his past; one of a dark cave, agonizing pain, and the sounds of death.

Corentine gasped. "Jace, I'm shocked you could ever ask me such a question. I want peace for our two kingdoms just as much as you do. Now, we really must start. Remember, your mother is always your first lady love." She kissed his cheek and stepped into her carriage.

Jace remembered the last time he didn't share information with Sealyn; she felt betrayed. He didn't want to hold on to something like this, but he also didn't want to add to Sealyn's distress. He figured if anyone would have an answer on how to approach Sealyn, it would be Char.

A loud crash echoed through the stone walls of the market. Shouts rang out through the alleyways. Jace was enjoying the Puffin Pie he had just bought, but then he heard what everyone else was hearing. The brothers were arguing again. Jace really hated interrupting heated arguments, but he needed to talk to Char.

"That's it! I'm leaving! You can deal with this on your own today!" shouted Char. Char stormed out of a *Brother's Bond* so heated that he bumped into Jace. "Jace? What are you doing here? Don't answer that. Let's go have a drink at *Liquid Courage*."

"But it's morning . . ."

"No. No. That wasn't a question." Char pushed Jace through the two wooden doors and pointed to a table in the corner, looking at Barm.

Char sat down with a hard thud and flopped his head over his folded arms on the table. He let out a long moan.

"Char, are you all right?" Jace asked.

"I'm never going back there! I'm so done working with my brother!"

Barm, the barkeep, shuffled over to their table with two giant ales. "Cheer up, me lord. Things will blow over, aye?" He patted Char on the back after he set the two drinks down. "Will you two's be wantin' any breads?"

"No, thank you, Barm. I want to feel this ale to my core." Char started chugging the ale.

Jace smiled at Barm with worried eyes. "I'm fine. Thank you." Barm shuffled back behind the bar to attend to the other weary morning drinkers.

"Char, slow down. I need you to be lucid for what I'm about to tell you." Char rolled his eyes and wiped his mouth with his sleeve. "This morning, I found a burned letter that someone sent my mother. I could only read a piece of it, though, because the flames were too hot for me to grab it. Char, promise me this won't cause a war between our two lands."

Char tilted his head dramatically. "You know I can promise no such thing. If your mother has her hand in treasonous situations, then that's her fault."

Jace sighed heavily. "You're right. All I could read was 'forfeit the package.'"

Char's brows pressed together. "What does that mean? What's the package, and who's forfeiting it?"

"I have no clue. I wasn't sure whether perhaps the palace guards had heard any news about a package or a deal gone bad?"

"Not that I know of. Everyone is still focused on finding Lady Pinx." Char spat out his ale. "Jace, I have a bad feeling. I know what the package is. Actually, not what but who."

Sakul looked at Siany and Pyry with weary eyes. Planning a royal wedding was becoming quite the task since Sealyn seemed completely uninterested. Her attention was on Pinx, and who could blame her? He watched Sealyn stir her tea despondently. It was as if her emerald eyes were attempting to locate the map to Pinx's whereabouts in the swirls.

"Queen Sealyn, did you hear what I said?" Sakul tried not to ask the question in a harsh tone.

Sealyn shook her head, snapping out of her trance. "My apologies, Lord Sakul. I know you're doing your best, but it just doesn't feel right planning a joyous occasion with one of my friends missing."

Pyry placed her hand on Sealyn's. "We completely understand. Why don't we give the planning a break, and we can try again tomorrow?"

They started packing up the parchments when they heard a loud scream coming from outside the palace. They rushed to the breakfast room windows and saw Aerrik riding a horse with a single wagon hitched to it. He was moving at an abnormal speed for a wagon pull. Sealyn noticed Raquel in the wagon, waving her arms and screaming for help.

Sealyn, along with several guards, ran down the front palace steps to the wagon. Lord Aerrik jumped from the panting black steed and ran to the wagon, sweat fell from his brow. He waved quickly to the guards. Sealyn's heart sank when she saw who Raquel was holding—Lady Pinx. She looked lifeless and pale, with dark circles under her almond-shaped eyes. Her eyes remained closed as the guards ran up the stairs with her.

Sealyn ordered the guards to take Pinx to her favorite room in the palace: the Rose Garden Room. Tapestries featuring pink and red roses of all types adorned each wall. The white marble fireplace made the pink rose quartz mantel shine brighter than anything else in the room. Two light green striped chairs rested at the foot of the bed, with a small white marble table in between them. Fresh roses from the palace garden were always picked for this room, displayed in a white and gold vase that sat on the table.

After five days of Pinx drifting in and out of consciousness, she finally began to keep liquids down. Sealyn entered the room with Maekel and Norella. Norella carried a new tray of both solid and liquid foods, while Sealyn brought the purple exiguum she had named Ella. Ella loved cuddling with Sealyn, so Sealyn thought the tiny fuzzy elephant would lift Pinx's spirits. Sealyn placed Ella on the bed beside Pinx, and she immediately curled up next to her, begging for affection.

As Pinx stroked the large, soft ears of Ella, Sealyn asked, "Pinx, I know this has been such a difficult time for you, but do you have any memories that may help us find your kidnappers?"

Tears formed in Pinx's eyes. She leaned her head back on the dark mahogany headboard. "Everything is a blur. I remember the Trundatta Ball. I remember dancing and laughing, but then it goes blank. How can someone wipe away a month of memories?"

Norella folded her arms. "They mind-poisoned her! I just know it! You saw the tests they did." Pinx looked confused.

Sealyn sighed. "Lady Zuri left a detailed journal about her many concoctions. One section was how to test whether someone was mind poisoned. The doctor cut the back of your finger and then mixed a special mineral blend of Zuri's. If the vial turned green, then there was no drug poisoning, but if it turned black, then yes. It turned the blackest black I have ever seen. This did help us save your life because the doctor could then treat you."

"I owe Zuri my life. Where is she so I can thank her?" asked Pinx.

Favien walked in. "I want to thank her, too." He had tears of joy in his eyes. Favien was beginning to gain healthy weight back. He finally had an appetite.

"I'm afraid your gratitude to Lady Zuri will have to wait. She is on a private quest." Sealyn rose from Pinx's side and let Favien take her spot.

Pinx smiled into Favien's eyes and felt safe. She loved him so much it hurt worse than her headache. "There's one thing you can answer for me," Pinx said. "No one has told me how I was found."

Sealyn leaned against the canopy bedpost, which was ornamented with a lush garland wrapped around it. "Oddly enough, Lady Raquel was in her garden when she looked across their fields and saw the black horse and wagon. The horse had stopped at a small watering hole in the middle of the field. She and Lord Aerrik investigated the scene. Raquel tried to give you water, but you coughed it up. I'm pretty sure the entire kingdom heard Raquel's screams for help."

Pinx looked at Favien. "Let's invite them for tea this afternoon and thank them properly." Favien kissed her forehead gently and stroked her long, black waves of hair.

Char, Sakul, Sorcha, and Adalina entered the room with Chocolate Jabbles, flowers, and royal playing cards.

"We came to see whether you all might be up for a game of cards?" Sorcha asked.

"Absolutely." Pinx squeaked. She grabbed her throat, not realizing how raw her voice still was.

Char saluted Lady Pinx. "You'll have to excuse me and Queen Sealyn. We're needed elsewhere at the moment."

Once outside the room, Sealyn whispered, "What's this about, Char?"

"Brace yourself, cousin, but I know who kidnapped Pinx, and I have proof."

Heated, Jace stood up from his seat in the music hall. His mind and heart were in conflict. How could Char accuse his mother of kidnapping Pinx, and how could he make such an accusation in front of his future bride? The evidence pointed toward his mother, but his heart told him to be loyal to his blood.

"Stop, Char. No. There's no way she did this!" Jace folded his arms and stared down at Char.

Sealyn tilted her head. "How can you be absolutely sure?"

"Because she's my mother! I think I would know my own mother! Don't you?"

"Listen, Jace. No one wants to be right about her being the culprit, but there are too many coincidences for us not to take notice. Do you see any possible cracks in your stance?" Sealyn tried to sound neutral, but she was shocked by how naïve Jace could be about his mother's capabilities. Would this pose a future problem for their marriage and her kingdom?

Jace buried his head in his hands. "I can't believe it. I just can't. She knows we are to wed, so why jeopardize our marriage with a kidnapping?"

Char shrugged and motioned for Sealyn to speak. "Jace, there's been so much more going on behind the scenes than you realize. I've had to keep certain subjects off the table with you because they dealt with your family. To be short, your mother has tasked one of our own with finding the Heart of Elysium, which is what empowers this kingdom. If she possesses it, then she controls our power."

Jace's mouth gaped, and his head started spinning. Could his mother be this treacherous? Could she really only desire to promote herself? Would she be willing to destroy his happiness to gain control and power? He closed his eyes and shook his head, not wanting his childhood memories to come alive.

Char looked at Sealyn with a strange expression. Sealyn shrugged. She wasn't sure if Jace believed her or not. His reactions were very conflicting, like an internal battle between two forces inside Jace's mind.

"If all that you say is true, even the possible kidnapping, then what? What happens between Elysium and Stoltland? What happens to my mother?"

Sealyn clasped her hands together. "Patience. I would like to ask you to limit your communication with her. I'm working on a plan that would hopefully prevent our two kingdoms from engaging in another war, but this is extremely delicate, and I'm afraid we're running out of time and options. Our conversations can never be repeated to her or anyone else. You can talk with Char and me whenever you need, but please, Jace, trust me. I've sensed something dark about your mother since the first time we met, and even more so when she returned as queen." Jace nodded his head. "Jace, I do have one more question for you," Sealyn smirked.

"And what would that be, My Queen?"

Sealyn grabbed his hand. "What song would you like to dance to for our first dance as husband and wife?"

Jace felt the tension melt. "Now that, my gorgeous Queen, is a question I definitely have an answer to."

# Chapter 33

Spring arrived, and the blossoms' perfumes danced in the air. Sealyn awoke to a loud thud in her room. Maekel was trying to keep Ella and Eldon, the blue exiguum, calm, but they kept running around the room, knocking into chairs. Sealyn laughed at the sight of Maekel chasing the two most adorable creatures. Today was her wedding day. It had finally arrived. She felt somewhat exhausted from the week-long wedding events, not to mention the awkward encounters with Corentine, but she was ready to marry Jace. She had insisted they return for the wedding, but security was on high alert.

Avondelle was filled with people from all regions of Elysium. The market bustled with the influx of guests for the royal wedding. White ribbons and flags adorned every inch of the open market. Sakul felt his sweat soaking through his shirt as he issued orders to the servants for their detailed tasks. He had never planned an event this grand.

The ceremony would take place in the royal gardens. Sealyn specifically requested the area by the swan pool. She loved the aqua pool that was home to numerous swan couples and the enchanting white water lilies. The path leading up to the large rectangular pool was a long and wide stone walkway. The walkway was shaded on either side by enormous oak trees. Sakul hung vines of white fire flowers and crystals from the branches of the oak trees. He placed several vibrating palms in white pots at the base of each oak tree to ensure the fire flowers remained lit throughout the entire ceremony. A large, round arch stood in front of the pool, garlanded with grapevines, green palms, eucalyptus, and pink peonies. Sakul had rows of light wooden benches on each side, with large white lanterns at the ends.

The weather was perfect, with a light breeze and warm spring air. The birds chirped the songs of the ancestors, welcoming the approaching sunset. Sakul hoped he had timed everything perfectly so that the ceremony would conclude just as the oranges and reds painted the sky. Sakul and Hueweyn also built portable doors and frames so Sealyn could have an indoor entrance to her outdoor wedding.

Sealyn clung to her father's arm as they waited behind the closed doors. Tears of joy filled Ryker's eyes. He loved his daughter more than his own life, both of his daughters. He felt joy, but he also felt loss. He had to hand over his daughter's life to another man, who became her first priority. He was now second. Parts of him felt relieved, but others ached for the small girl who would climb into his lap at the end of a long day and demand a story. How he loved telling his girls stories.

Lord Marin came around the outdoor-indoor doors, helped by Jdru. Jdru winked and left quickly. Marin looked at his beautiful granddaughter standing there with his son and froze. "Sealyn, you look stunning."

"Thank you, Grandpa Marin. I have a surprise for you."

"I was wondering why Jdru brought me back here." Marin chuckled.

"Grandpa Marin, you're in your nineties, and you've had four boys, so let's do something you've never done before and walk a girl down the aisle." Sealyn did her best to hold back the tears that her throat was eager to shed. Lord Marin collapsed into Sealyn's embrace, crying. No one had ever seen this decorated military man cry, but today, his granddaughter tugged at that heartstring and won the battle.

Ryker helped his father steady himself. Each father took an arm of Sealyn's, and the doors opened to enchanting music. Sealyn kept reminding herself not to cry, but with every step, it became harder and harder.

She had a thousand conflicts buzzing in her head. She tried to shut out the military strategies surrounding her wedding that they had devised earlier that morning, tried not to think about the rumors that Stoltlanders were planning something big during the wedding reception, and tried to block out the fact that she still didn't know the location of the Heart of Elysium. It was like moving through water while keeping focus on the light at the end of a long cave. She could sense the tension among the guests. A darkness lingered in the air. It felt ancient; it felt cold.

Her eyes met Jace's gaze. Those silver eyes made her weak. They were a source of light for her when everyone else saw chaos. He was her confidence in the storms, her lighthouse. She could sense the good he could bring to the world if he finally found himself. He just needed freedom, and she could provide that for him. She smiled as she saw him shedding tears of joy.

Jace was incredibly excited, and his expression brought smiles to everyone around him. When Ryker placed his daughter's hand in Jace's, the guests sensed a shift in power. Sealyn was no longer in King Ryker's shadow; she now had the option to rule individually as the Queen of Elysium or to reign together as King and Queen of Elysium.

As the ceremony progressed, glances around the seating area were exchanged. Drystan tilted his head toward Corentine, Corentine raised her red eyebrows at her guards. The Stoltland guards disappeared and then reappeared several times. Elysian treetop spies concealed themselves in the oak tree branches, observing all the exchanges taking place. Nichts quietly flew above, relaying messages to Commander Elmond from the treetoppers. Commander Elmond had never experienced a more intense wedding than Sealyn's.

As Jace escorted his new wife up the back palace stairs, he felt complete. It was as if he had been living in a dream his whole life, and it wasn't until this moment that he finally awoke. He felt reborn. They walked into the Garden Library for a private moment before entering the ballroom.

This was where he had met his wife. Jace held Sealyn's hands and stepped back, giving her a long look from head to toe. Her dress was immaculate with the intricate white lace sewn over the emerald silk underdress. The gold crown, adorned with large emeralds, sparkled in the candlelight. He stepped closer and stroked her cheek. He could smell jasmine in the long locks that draped over her shoulders, the ends perfectly framing the edges of her ample bust. His heart raced. How long did they have to remain in here? He wouldn't be able to contain himself for much longer. His blood needed her. His bones ached for her.

The door flung open. "My pardons, Your Majesty, but the guests are ready for you now." Sakul motioned for them to follow him. Jace was both grateful and angry.

The crowd clapped and cheered as Jace spun Sealyn around to their favorite song. They laughed when Jace stepped on her dress and cheered when Sealyn couldn't help but lean in for another kiss. The food was a massive feast with roasted chicken, steamed fish, and seared deer. Everyone was enjoying themselves, except the guests from Stoltland.

Corentine's wedding to Prince Svagon had been small and quiet. Queen Mother Phyre did not want a big spectacle due to Corentine's reputation. Corentine never let go of the fact that her wedding was not a royal affair. She watched her son receiving the royal treatment she had always desired for herself, and instead of feeling happy for her child, she felt bitter and angry. She was jealous that he was getting the life she wanted, and he was a silver-eyed outcast.

After one too many drinks, Corentine made another spectacle, trying to get Jace to focus on her. Jace was so tired of his mother's negativity by this point. "No, Mother! No! Stop! Leave me alone!" This sent Corentine over the edge. She walked away from Jace and channeled the dark mist. She closed her eyes and commanded the mist to move the feet of each Stoltlander out the doors. Within seconds, the black mist was beneath each Stoltlander's shoe, compelling them to walk out. No one noticed the mist; it was as stealthy as Corentine.

Jace felt bad for raising his voice to his mother, so he turned and walked toward their tables, but he found no one there. He dashed out the doors, sprinting down the front palace stairs, only to see the Stoltland carriages driving away. He expected more from them, but why should he? After all, his mother was involved in kidnapping Pinx. Now, he felt guilty asking the queen for a special favor to unlock a full investigation before any arrests were made. Sealyn granting his request was the only way his family could even attend the wedding. He was heartbroken on his wedding day. He wished at least one person from his family would jump out of a carriage and return, but none did. He was a man with an unaccepting family, but now he had married into a new family—a powerful family.

The next morning, Jace strolled briskly toward the breakfast room. Before he could make it to the door, he saw King Ryker.

"Good morning to you, Lord Jace."

"Good morning to you, too, King Ryker." Jace bowed.

"Feeling well this morning, son?"

"Ah, yes. Quite well, just very tired from the lack of sleep…" Jace paused and realized what he had just implied in front of King Ryker about his daughter.

Ryker's face dropped. "Let's move on, Jace. Enjoy your breakfast." Ryker hurried past Jace, trying to avoid making eye contact.

A loud laugh erupted from the large portrait of an unattractive, plump old woman wearing a pale dress. The painting was quite ancient, with many chipped sections. Could a painting really laugh?

"Is someone there?" Jace asked hesitantly.

Another laugh came, but this time, the portrait cracked open like a door. "Good morning, my husband. Do you find it funny to inform my father about our lovemaking?"

"Sealyn! What is this, and no, I found it rather uncomfortable."

Sealyn hopped out of the portrait hole and closed it. "Jace, today I get to show you my secret world, but first, we need sustenance."

Sealyn whisked Jace down the secret passageways while Jace chewed his Puffin Pie. He loved her opening up to him like this. It was so liberating. He felt it—freedom. This is what it felt like to be free. Sealyn had freed him from the bullying of his world. She freed him from the chains his mother clothed him in. She freed him from self-doubt. Now, he had his whole future in front of him.

Sealyn opened the door to the musty old war room. She and Char had repaired a few chairs to sit at the intact sections of the table. Jace was amazed by the ancient ruins.

"Take a seat, husband," Sealyn flirted.

Jace chuckled. "Yes, wife."

"Jace, I wanted to show you this room because this was where a huge battle took place. Our enemies tried to destroy us with fire cannons, but the warriors prevailed. At least, that's what I've read from these scrolls I've found in here."

"A great battle sounds interesting."

"Yes, but that's not why I brought you here. I believe we're going to face many hard battles in our future as well, but just like these walls, I believe we'll be the ones to remain standing. Jace, there was a rumor that Stoltland was planning something for last night, but as far as we know, nothing happened. Do you have any information about this?"

"Are you accusing me of treason?"

Sealyn lifted her hands in surrender. "No. No. I just didn't know whether you overheard anything. You spent a lot of time with them the week before the wedding, is all."

"Yes, because they're my family, Sealyn," Jace protested.

"Easy, Jace. There's no need for that tone. I just wanted to see if you had any news that might help solve this mystery. We've already received word this morning that your family plans on leaving tomorrow without saying goodbye." Sealyn saw the hurt in Jace's eyes.

"That doesn't make sense. Why would they just leave without seeing us first? I know the reception was heated, but surely she owes me or your family an apology for leaving—but to just leave without saying anything? Why? She's my mother! Doesn't she care that I just got married?!" Jace slammed his hands on the stone table, making a loud smack that echoed through the empty halls.

"How can I make this better for you?"

"I need to see them before they leave. Let's invite them over tonight to smooth everything out."

A bad feeling fell over Sealyn as if icy fingers had grabbed her shoulders. "Jace, are you sure you want to invite her here? You're sure you don't just want to let them go? After all, the investigation is still underway." She couldn't understand why he couldn't see the hurt this was causing her. His mother wanted Elysium's power, and she brainwashed an old friend for it. Her best friend had been kidnapped, and his mother was involved—the very woman he wanted to bring back to their palace.

"No! I can't. I have to see them before they leave. Ending a visit like this would be hard to recover from if there's ever going to be peace between our lands." Jace extended his hand to his new bride, and she clasped it.

They sat in silence, gazing at one another. Jace remembered every pleasure of their wedding night. He loved the simple pale nightsleep gown she was still wearing with her hair loose and unbrushed—vulnerable only to him. He picked her up and sat her on the edge of the broken table, making sure it was the smooth section. She wrapped her arms and legs around his body. How could they not give in to their passions in a dark secret chamber?

Sealyn tried to stay focused on each kiss, each touch, each sound, but her conflicting thoughts kept interrupting. How could she keep making compromises that hurt her kingdom—compromises that went against every fiber of her being? Did she marry the source of Elysium's destruction? Was this marriage now a danger to her people because she couldn't say no to him? All she could find herself saying was yes to everything about him.

An evil grin spilled across Queen Corentine's face. She read the letter Jace sent her inviting them over for a meeting. She tossed the letter in her husband's lap, then flipped her glowing red hair.

"See. I told you he would bend. I knew the silent treatment would make him reach out to resolve everything." She walked around the main guest room of Jace's manor and scoffed at the jade curtains hanging by the windows.

"I never should have doubted you. Is everything ready? This could turn bloody."

Corentine placed her hands on her hips. "I received word late last night that everyone is in position. We know the Heart of Elysium has something to do with that garden woman. Guards are headed there now. They've been instructed to search through every piece of land they own. We must get to the palace now. It's only a matter of time before someone spots our soldiers at Lord Aerrik's house. Our royal guards are in position as well for the castle plans." Corentine paused and looked out the window. "I've been waiting so long for this. I will be Queen of Elysium by tonight!"

Rocking back and forth while sipping his midday coffee, Aerrik felt the effects of the queen's wedding wine. Raquel giggled at the misery in her husband's eyes. She stoked the fire and then sat down in the other wooden rocking chair.

"I had a lot of fun last night. I'm so happy for Sealyn and Jace." Raquel beamed.

Aerrik rubbed his head. "I had a little too much fun, but yes, I'm happy for them, too. I'll be honest, though. I did have my doubts whether Sealyn could do this—be the queen we needed."

Raquel raised her eyebrow. "Oh, and what changed your stubborn mind?"

Aerrik chuckled. "It was that day she came here asking about the Heart of Elysium. You asked her not to make you break your vow, and she respected that. I will say that I blindly followed her mirron request. I pondered for days why she asked me to find out how to shave a mirron." Raquel laughed. "What a task that was! Thank goodness Lady Madilina knew. She really is something when it comes to animals."

Raquel raised her cup to Aerrik. "Cheers to you both because shaving those mirrons was no easy task!"

"Ha! Nor was sewing the blankets together! That was the turning point for me. Sealyn knew the only way to protect your vow and to add more protection to the blood passion flower was to make it invisible."

Raquel rocked gently. "A mirron coat fence. How brilliant is that? Hundreds of years go by, and no one else thought of that?"

They looked out their back window at their kids playing a game of chase in the garden. Suddenly, Raquel's heart dropped. She saw a Stoltland soldier in her fields, then another, and then another. Why were they here? Did they know? Did Sealyn betray them? No. Sealyn would never crack. They must have followed Sealyn, as they looked like dogs sniffing a rabbit trail rather than men with maps.

Raquel looked at Aerrik. "When did you say Temm and Stawyer would be here?"

Aerrik stood. "Any minute now. They wanted to come talk about the events of last night."

"You better hope they get here now because Stoltland has just invaded and is making a move for the Heart of Elysium. We're under attack!" Raquel pointed out the window.

"Quick. Get the children. Take them into the basement. Throw the blanket over the hatch." Aerrik grabbed his sword from above the mantle, where five swords were mounted over his stone fireplace. He hoped his friends had brought theirs, but if not, they would be covered.

Raquel hurried the children down the hatch. The young girl, with her braided hair, looked scared, but their youngest, a boy with bright red hair, seemed eager to join the fight. The freckled boy grabbed his wooden toy sword for good measure before descending the ladder.

Aerrik heard footsteps at the front door. He pushed Raquel behind him as she finished putting the blanket over the hatch. The door opened, and Aerrik raised his sword, ready to protect his family. Temm and Stawyer walked through the doorway with arms raised.

"Easy, Aerrik. What is this?" snapped Stawyer.

"Hush, Stawyer, and draw out your swords. Stoltlanders are trespassing on our lands. It's time to defend them!" Without hesitation, Temm and Stawyer drew their swords and seized the extra mounted swords as well. They hurried out the back door with Aerrik. Raquel's heart stopped. She knew she should listen to Aerrik about keeping the children in the basement, but the palace needed to be warned, and she couldn't abandon her kids. She swiftly uncovered the hatch and motioned for the children to come back up the ladder.

Raquel carefully opened the front door, ensuring no other Stoltlanders were in sight. Fortunately, Temm and Stawyer had ridden their horses that morning. She quickly lifted her daughter, Faith, onto Stawyer's white horse. The creature was enormous compared to the small child. Raquel swiftly followed by placing Finnley, their son, behind Faith.

"Faith, my darling girl, I need you to race to the palace as fast as you can. Tell Queen Sealyn and anyone who comes in your path what has happened here. Stay at the castle until we come to get you. Our queen will keep you safe." Faith's eyes filled with tears. She didn't want to leave her parents behind. "It's going to be okay. Finnley, you hold on tight to your sister." Raquel handed the reins to her tiny daughter and nodded. "I love you both so much. Now go!" She smacked the horse's rear, and it galloped off with intense speed.

She watched her children speed off into the distance, tears streaming down her cheeks. Her concentration broke as shouts and grunts interrupted her. The clanking of sword blades echoed loudly. She raced to the window inside to see what was happening.

After killing one of Stoltland's soldiers, Aerrik's sword collided with another tall, dark Stoltlander's weapon in a deafening clash. The black sword whipped around quickly, targeting Aerrik's head and missing by mere inches. Ducking under the strike, Aerrik thrust his sword forward, slicing his opponent's leg.

The Stoltlander cried out in anguish. With a jabbing pain, he lunged forward, attacking Aerrik from the front, but Aerrik jumped back. Aerrik slipped on one of Raquel's pots and fell backward, causing his sword to fall out of his arm's reach. The black sword came swiftly toward Aerrik's chest, but Stawyer swung his sword with force, sending the black sword flying across the garden.

Aerrik rolled toward his sword and sat up, quickly thrusting it through the Stoltlander's stomach. The tall man fell to his knees as crimson flowed from his lifeless body. Stawyer kicked the fallen enemy in the side and watched the life fade from his eyes.

"Thank you, Stawyer," Aerrik said, catching his breath. "Where's Temm?"

They looked around the gardens and into the fields. They counted four dead bodies, none of whom were Temm. They noticed movement toward the back of the field and saw Temm fending off two soldiers. They sprinted toward their comrade. As they leaped over the short stone fence that separated the garden from the fields, another broad Stoltland soldier charged forward, knocking Stawyer onto Aerrik. The broad soldier bounced up quickly. Stawyer threw Aerrick on the other side of him. The Stoltland warrior wearing all black didn't hesitate and, with force, plunged his black sword forward, piercing Stawyer's side.

Aerrik reacted as swiftly as he could. He wrapped his arms around Stawyer and barrel-rolled him away, dodging the black sword's intended killing stab. Stawyer moaned and held his side, where blood spilled from the deep cut. Stawyer was always saving his comrades. Why must it always be Stawyer? In one battle, he was stabbed eight times with forty-two cuts; no one understood how he survived.

Aerrik whispered, "Don't die on me yet, my friend. Stay strong." He jumped up, blocking the black sword with his. The two men stayed locked in a battle to the death. Both men's arms began to tire. Aerrik saw his friend in a pool of blood and caught sight of Temm falling and kicking away the enemy's sword.

Aerrik felt his wrist bend unnaturally, and it sent shocks of pain up his arm. He dropped his sword and stood frozen as his opponent held the bloody sword tip at his neck. The enemy's gruff voice snarled, "Kneel before your death." Aerrik stood without moving.

He would bow to no one but his queen. He saw the muscles tense as the black sword moved backward to gather momentum. He prayed for his family's safety; then he felt hot liquid splash on his face. He opened his eyes to another one of his swords sticking out of the broad soldier's throat. Aerrik stared in amazement as the man dropped to his knees, choking on the sword and his splattering blood. In shock, he saw his brave wife standing in front of him, trying to catch her breath.

With tears streaming down her face, Raquel embraced her husband. "I couldn't," she gasped, "I couldn't let the father of my children and"—she gasped again—"the love of my life die without trying to save him." She sobbed into his strong arms.

"Thank you, my love. Thank you. It's okay. I'm okay." With his jade eyes sparkling, Aerrik leaned back and cupped her cheeks. "We make a good team."

Breathing heavily, Temm came over to them and put his bloody hands on his knees. "I could have used some of that help." His bald head and bushy brown beard were covered in dark blood.

"Looks like you handled yourself." Aerrik patted Temm's back. "Wait! Stawyer!" They raced over to Stawyer and slid next to him.

Raquel felt his pulse and checked his breathing. "He has a pulse but is barely breathing. We need to get him inside to stitch him up."

They laid Stawyer's limp body on the kitchen table. Temm and Aerrik ripped open the bloody shirt and gasped at the large wound oozing blood. So many other scars covered his torso, each one a life he saved. Now, it was up to them to save his life. Raquel began cleaning and sewing the wound.

Aerrik yelled, "The children!" His heart sank as he saw the blanket not covering the hatch door.

"It's okay, love. I sent them to the palace. I'm sorry I did so against your instructions, but I knew the palace had to be warned. Sealyn will make sure they're protected."

Aerrik grabbed his chest. "You did the right thing. I'll ride out to the palace to make sure the children are safe. Temm, you stay here and make sure none of those bodies out there come back to life. Help Raquel with whatever she needs. Once Stawyer is stable, hook up our wagon to old Dover and get Stawyer to the palace doctor."

With the wind whipping over his face, Aerrik feared what he might find at the palace. Did his children make it safely, or were there other Stoltland soldiers stationed along the road? If Stoltland made this bold move at his home, what were they planning for the palace?

# Chapter 34

Sealyn wiped her sweaty palms on her gown. She felt nervous about the family meeting; something seemed off in the air. She could almost sense her bones urging her to be on guard. Swaying slightly, she tried to remain still so the artist could paint her and Jace's portrait. With Jace wearing the king's crown in this portrait, her kingdom would understand her true intentions regarding the crown. She wore the same beautiful feathered gown she had worn for her portrait, and Jace donned, for the first time, the Elysian colors.

When she saw the hour, she motioned for the artist to stop. They had to change for their meeting with Jace's family. Jace couldn't help but watch his new wife change clothes. Why did she need clothes? There should be no clothes ever!

"I see you decided to go with the pants dress thing," Jace teased.

Sealyn laughed. "Yes. Let's call my outfit the 'pants dress thing.'" She wrapped her arms around Jace and gave him one of their many passionate kisses. She stared deep into his swirling silver eyes and saw sadness. Sealyn felt as though battles were about to take place, but she couldn't quite picture what these battles would be. One battle would be for Jace's loyalty. Corentine would request that of him. She felt confident that Jace would stand strong beside Elysium, but something was tugging at her gut about Jace's loyalty. What did this mean? Should she fear Jace? Was their love truly prophesied against?

Sealyn didn't trust Stoltland, so she kept her northern army in Avondelle for added protection. Due to the meeting, she increased the number of guards on duty for the evening threefold. If anything were to happen tonight, she wanted her family and guests to be safe. Many of her family members and the Vinurs of the Court remained at the palace after the wedding. She wished she could join them in the banquet hall, but instead, she had to work on building a bridge between her kingdom and Stoltland's.

They chose to hold the meeting in the Garden Library to avoid seeming too formal since they were family, after all. Sealyn watched Corentine enter the room and felt a presence of darkness with her. Something was wrong. Sealyn tried to make eye contact with Corentine and her husband, but neither would look at her. They both focused only on Jace. She glanced at her sweet new husband with concern. His face and demeanor were different. His posture seemed odd; he slouched his shoulders and lowered his head.

"Welcome, King Svagon and Queen Corentine. Please have a seat. We wanted to have this meeting to clarify any misunderstandings and apologize if any wrongs were done on our part."

"An Elysian marrying a Stoltlander is a wrongdoing."

Sealyn's eyes narrowed. She could feel Corentine was trying to bait her, but why? Why push her like this? Did she actually want to start a blood war? "Corentine, a word of caution. Jace is my husband, whether you like it or not, so get over any prejudices you have."

"I've never been spoken to like this before in my life! Jace, you are going to have to learn how to control your wife. You're an annoying coward, you are! What kind of son doesn't stand up for his own mother?" Corentine stared down at Jace.

"Corentine, you are *not* allowed to speak to my husband like that in our palace!"

"Why, you disgusting witch! You are the most horrible little girl I know!" Corentine stood fast and walked forward toward Sealyn. Her husband ran toward Corentine, blocking her from getting too close to Sealyn. Rising slowly, Sealyn was ready to defend herself if necessary, but Jace jumped in front of her, staring down at his mother.

"Sit down, Mother! What are you doing? You dare approach the Elysian queen like this?"

Commander Elmond opened the door. "My Queen, I heard shouting. Is everything okay?"

"Corentine, I believe the commander needs an answer to his question," snapped Sealyn.

Corentine huffed. "Everything is fine, you old tree. Now get out!"

"He's my commander and will be treated with respect. Mind your tongue." Sealyn was growing tired of the prideful bullying.

Corentine glanced at her husband, exchanging a peculiar look. Sealyn also noticed them surveying the room before settling into their seats. Were they assessing what was in the room?

Sealyn heard loud voices outside the room. Something was definitely off. Commander Elmond opened the door again. "My apologies, My Queen, but there's someone who needs to speak with you on an urgent basis." Sealyn rushed to the door and closed it behind her.

"What is happening? Why are you behaving like this? I thought we were supposed to be working on peace, not starting a war!" Jace said.

"My boy, it's time for you to choose." Corentine smiled her evil smile.

"Choose?" questioned Jace.

"Yes. Choose Stoltland or Elysium. Your Mother or that child? Choose!"

How could she put him in this position? How could she ask to break his marriage? What would this cause if he chose Sealyn? What would happen if he chose his mother? Whoever he chose, he would hurt one of them tonight.

"What do you want, Drystan?" Sealyn said with annoyance.

"I merely came to tell you of a plot to overthrow the crown. I'm here to warn you!" Drystan knelt on one knee.

"Get up, you lying snake. You've been helping with this plot since its birth. Now, you're here for a different reason. I feel the curse upon you. You crave what they offered. You were envious of someone else. Guards, arrest Drystan for treason!" Three guards surrounded Drystan with their spears.

Tybalt came running into the ballroom. "My Queen! My Queen!"

"Yes, Tybalt, what is it?"

"The children. Aerrik and Raquel's children rode in on a horse to tell us that Stoltland soldiers invaded their lands. They said their father and friends were fighting them. My Queen, we're under attack."

Sealyn realized what was about to happen. A pang of guilt washed over her. She was the one who invited the Stoltlanders here, and now Avondelle needed protection from them. This would be her first battle as queen, and how she handled it would echo throughout her reign.

"Commander Elmond, where is Lord Char? I need him now!" Command Elmond sent a soldier to fetch Char from the banquet hall.

"My Queen, your family and guests are in the banquet hall. We need to move them to safer grounds," Commander Elmond urged.

"Of course. We must secure the next in line—my sister. She can't be in the same place as my father and mother." Char and the soldier came running over to the crowded area. "Char, I need you to escort Aerrik's children and all the party guests not in direct line to the crown into *our* war room. Next, Commander Elmond, I trust you with my life, so I'm giving you Elysium's life if I should fall in battle."

"My Queen?" questioned Commander Elmond.

"Take my family through the ugly woman portrait. This will lead to my bedchamber, but instead of taking the stairs, veer to the right. Walk until you come to an iron door. It will be unlocked. This is the room that will protect my family. Lock the door behind you until this is over." Sealyn looked at Char, who looked angry.

"The portrait, Sealyn? Seriously? Are there more secret passageways? I want a map, a detailed map!"

"Char, I really don't have time for your banter. You have your instructions. Now, go!" Char raced to the banquet hall. "Tybalt, I need your troops to take my sister down a different passage. In the banquet hall, behind the tapestry of the garden, you will find a door. Press the round emblem of the fox. Only the fox is very important. The door will swing open. The passage will lead to a *Brother's Bond* in the market. Keep her safe there. You all have your orders. It's time to defend your homeland."

Commander Elmond stepped closer to Sealyn. "You haven't said how we are to protect you, my Queen."

Sealyn paused and looked into the eyes of the men and women she was asking to defend the capitol. "Today, I am another member of the royal army. I will fight with my comrades."

Commander Elmond shook his head. "I was afraid you would say that." He motioned to a soldier. "Here, My Queen. I brought your bow and quiver along with your sword." Sealyn smiled and embraced her commander, who was like a second father to her, always prepared to protect her at any cost. She loved him dearly.

A heart-stopping screech echoed through the halls of the palace. "They're here! We're under attack!"

Sealyn and Elmond rushed to the windows only to see a large force of Stoltland's army charging the palace guards.

"Commander, how many do you count? I see maybe fifty or seventy?" Sealyn squinted.

"That seems right, but this is only the front. We have no idea how many others are attacking from the rear or elsewhere. My Queen, we are most likely surrounded."

Sealyn walked to the center of the room. "Again, everyone knows their orders. Protect the crown's line. Protect your home. Protect us from being cursed again."

Sealyn unclasped her skirt, letting it fall to the ballroom floor, wearing her battle leather pants. She readied her bow with an arrow and raced to the Garden Library door. Looking back, she heard a loud clashing of swords and the grunts of soldiers fighting. What would she find on the other side of this door? Surely, the Stoltland royals had left, and Jace would be sitting on the couch waiting for her. She hoped that's what she would find. Once she opened the door, her worst fear came into view: a dark Stoltland warrior was holding a knife to Jace's throat with the king and queen side by side.

"Choose, Sealyn. Your husband's life or your crown," Corentine hissed.

450

# Chapter 35

The spring air filled Sealyn's lungs as she sat on the balcony of her bedroom. She tried to lift the cup of tea, but her arm caused her too much pain. Her mother reached across and helped her raise the cup to drink. They sat in silence, gazing out over the gardens. How peaceful it seemed now. The sounds and scents of nature painted over the horrific and bloody battle that had taken place. You could no longer smell death in the air; instead, the lilies and jasmine wafted a sweet aroma to help ease the pain everyone was facing.

Maekel fluttered quietly to the stone table beside Sealyn. "Your Majesty, I hates to tells you this, but another two soldiers just passed aways, including Recruit Alon." Maekel sniffed her tears.

Sealyn did not make a sound, but a single tear slid down her bruised cheek. All the lives lost, and for what? Power? They wanted power. They wanted to control Elysium. She didn't understand this evil. Her heart felt as though it was breaking into pieces. How could she have let this happen?

"Also, Majesty, I wants to say again how sorry's I am for your loss," Maekel tried to say without bursting into a large cry.

Graelynd placed her hand on Sealyn's shoulder. "Thank you, Maekel. We, of course, appreciate your condolences and your help. Do you mind leaving us for a while? Once King Ryker returns, please send for us." Maekel nodded and flew off quickly. "My darling girl. You can't blame yourself for evil actions that weren't your own. The choices Stoltland made will forever be solely their responsibility."

"So many," Sealyn sobbed. "So many lives lost."

"You made the right decisions through the battle, though. There was nothing else you could have done." Graelynd knew the weight Sealyn carried. She and her husband had faced this same grieving after each battle. Fighting for what is right always comes at a cost.

"Did I? It doesn't feel that way." Sealyn regarded the landscape, trying to shut out the dark memories of the battle.

Graelynd walked around the balcony. "Sealyn, today's meeting won't be easy, but you'll have no choice but to show a strong front. They need a leader now more than ever. You can't succumb to fear or sadness. You must rise, my love, to greater heights than you thought you could. Believe in yourself. That is the first step: believing in you. You can do more than you think you can, even when you're in pain. Don't let the pain lie to you." Graelynd took her daughter's hands and helped her stand. She walked her to the edge of the balcony. They looked down and saw the servants still scrubbing blood from the steps. Graelyn gently cupped Sealyn's cheeks. "You are brave, and you are the chosen leader. It's time for you to rise, my courageous phoenix."

Even though Sealyn felt every bruise, every cut, every soreness in her body, she fell into her mother for an embrace she so desperately needed. With the sunshine sparkling on her wings, Maekel tiptoed softly on the stone banister and cleared her throat. "Majesties, the king and the others have gathereds in the war room. They are waitings on you."

Sealyn didn't want to confront what that room implied, but she repeated her mother's words in her mind. She had to do this. Elysium needed her to lead. Everyone was feeling pain, and it was her responsibility not only to share in her people's suffering but also to help heal the wounds, too.

An awkward silence enveloped the war room. Sealyn noticed all the visible injuries her trusted team had sustained. She wished she could erase the past three days. This was supposed to be the happiest time of her life. She should have been enjoying her honeymoon with her husband, but that was taken from her. The past couldn't be changed.

She tried to sense the emotions of the room, but all she could feel was death. Grief coursed through each warrior's veins. Men and women had given their lives so that each person present could uphold Elysium's purity.

Sealyn looked at her father. "The count?"

Ryker dropped his head and read aloud the battle report. "The total body count is 253 dead. This includes Stoltland and Elysian soldiers as well as civilians. We have scouted the lands along the shore and discovered several dead bodies, including Stoltlanders who succumbed to their wounds and civilians who attempted to fight against them." Sniffs were heard around the room.

Doebromir rested his elbows on the table and buried his face in his hands, attempting to conceal his tears.

With a lump in his throat, Max demanded, "How did this happen? I'm sorry, I have to ask this." He brushed away a tiny tear from his bruised eye.

"From the intelligence we have gathered," Sealyn began, "two of the Stoltland ships were filled with military units. They had secret compartments in their below-deck quarters that concealed them from our guards who searched the ships. They slipped off the vessels during the night until all warriors were gathered on land near Avondelle. They stayed in a deserted farmhouse on the edge of the border. Once they received word from their queen, they separated into several units to surround the palace. The unit that was supposed to steal the Heart of Elysium failed miserably thanks to Lord Aerrik, Lord Temm, Lord Stawyer, and Lady Raquel. Sealyn nodded to Aerrik, who had a wrapped wrist and a large cut along his right cheek.

The door opened, and Princess Siany walked across the stones with a large stack of parchments, her heels clicking on the floor. The air felt as if it shifted, dread encircling them. Siany took her seat and only looked at her sister.

Everyone knew why she was there, but this was the part Sealyn didn't want to face. "Don't give in to fear," Sealyn repeated her mother's voice in her head. She nodded at her sister. This was it. She, like everyone else in the room, would have to face that terrible battle again.

Siany regarded each pair of Elysian green eyes, reluctant to read what she needed to. "Greetings, everyone. As you all know, I've been interviewing everyone involved in the battle, and I've completed the final composition. I'm here to recount the events of what we are titling the 'Battle of the Betrayals.' We begin with Queen Sealyn facing the choice between her crown and her husband

# Chapter 36

The bow stretched tight as Sealyn held her position at the door, aiming an arrow at the dark soldier who had a knife to Jace's throat. She noticed a small trickle of blood slowly dripping from the blade. Her anger began to rise, and her mind started to cloud. She craved vengeance! She couldn't allow that to guide her heart. She took another step forward.

"Easy, child," Corentine growled. "Each step you take is more blood from your husband."

"Don't you mean your son!" snapped Sealyn.

"He made his choice. Now, make yours!"

Sealyn quickly glanced around the room. She noticed that the king and queen were now armed with swords, while the soldier had only drawn his knife. She could hit any target she wanted. Her gaze fell on the soldier's bent elbow, the only part of him directly in front of Jace. What a coward this soldier was to hide behind him. Sealyn realized that once she released her arrow, she would be at war with Stoltland forever. With a silent breath, she whispered, "I choose war," and released her arrow.

The arrow glided swiftly, slicing right through the soldier's forearm to the back of his tricep. The bloodied arm remained bent, but his hand dropped the knife. Instinctively, Jace pulled the soldier's sword from its scabbard, and as the soldier fell, Jace swung down with all his strength, cleaving through the soldier's neck. The severed head rolled in front of Corentine, with the black eyes looking at her. The headless body lay on the ground, spasming. Corentine screamed and charged at Sealyn.

Sealyn slipped the bow across her chest like a sling and drew her sword. With a loud clang, Corentine's sword collided with Sealyn's. Sealyn pushed Corentine backward, but Corentine lunged forward, stabbing toward Sealyn's chest. Sealyn blocked each stroke with force.

Jace stood before Stoltland's king, his bloody sword at the ready. He looked at Svagon with confusion. Svagon appeared frozen, as if his eyes were made of ice. Then, Svagon began to shake and dropped his sword. He fell to his knees and slid against the side of the fireplace. Svagon wrapped his arms around his knees and began to rock and sob. Jace recognized this as the soldier's mind wound. He chose to spare Svagon; it was the honorable thing to do.

The door banged open, and Drystan ran inside, carrying a sword dripping with blood. Whose blood? Elysian or Stoltland? He saw Jace standing over Svagon and watched his queen and Corentine engaged in battle, but the curse whispered to him, "Jace has everything you want. Kill him and take what he possesses." Drystan had a chance at redemption, but he chose envy—he chose to kill Jace. Drystan's blade sliced through the air, cutting Jace's arm as Jace spun backward.

Out of the corner of her eye, Sealyn saw Drystan strike Jace. His sleeve was soaked with blood. Sealyn knocked Corentine's sword aside and quickly swung her left fist, which collided with Corentine's jaw. Corentine staggered and spat blood; then, screaming, she lunged at Sealyn.

Jace was quicker than Drystan, but Drystan was the more skilled swordsman. Jace needed to outsmart his enemy's strength. He threw the sword at Drystan but missed. Drystan continued to advance. With no weapon, Jace resorted to throwing books at Drystan, but Drystan dodged each one.

A few of the books fell onto the fireplace, catching fire. The flames danced across the books and onto the rugs. Drystan dropped his sword and grabbed Jace's shirt; then, he swung his large fist at Jace's face, breaking Jace's nose. Blood poured over Jace's lips.

"I'll kill you without my sword, and I'll watch the life leave your gray eyes with my hands around your throat!" Drystan yelled.

Another punch to the stomach made Jace cough up blood, crimson dripping over his lips. Jace yanked the rug Drystan was standing on, causing Drystan to fall backward. Seizing the opportunity, Jace grabbed a large vase and smashed it over Drystan's head. The porcelain pierced Drystan's skin in several places, making his face resemble rain dripping on a window—except this was blood: traitor's blood. Both men stood, out of breath, circling each other. Jace broke the circle and sprinted for Svagon's sword, with Drystan right behind him. Jace leaped over the couch, then tucked and rolled, grabbing the sword and preparing to defend himself.

The flames continued to consume the Garden Library as battles raged outside. Commander Elmond had gathered the royal family, and, alongside his troops, he led them to the ugly woman's portrait. Before he could get everyone through the portrait door, Stoltland soldiers attacked. The men ushered the women into the doorway. Elmond, along with his troops, Ryker, and Tilmond, stood their ground and fought against the soldiers.

Ryker watched helplessly as each of his men fell. Blood splattered the walls, limbs were severed, and pools of blood formed under too many bodies. He felt his sword getting heavier, but he kept fighting. As he slashed his sword through another belly, he saw young eyes looking back at him, filled with fear. This was just a boy in front of him. Why did such a young life have to end? "I'm sorry," Ryker whispered. The young boy slipped from Ryker's sword to the ground, blood coursing over his uniform. Ryker stood with remorse, then looked up to see another enemy's sword coming toward his heart. There was nothing he could do; this would be his ending.

Commander Elmond couldn't get to his sword in time to save his king, so he did the only thing he could. Elmond threw his body in front of his king, allowing the enemy's blade to pierce his own heart. Ryker screamed in anger at the sacrifice of his dear friend. That blade was meant for him, not his comrade.

Tilmond delivered a final killing blow to his victim's throat and jumped over the bodies before thrusting his sword through Elmond's killer. As Ryker caught Elmond in his arms, the weight of what was happening pressed heavily upon him. Tilmond knelt beside them, both men carefully lowering Elmond onto the crimson-stained stone, a chilling reminder of the battle's brutality. Blood bubbled from Elmond's lips, and with a faint, trembling voice he whispered, "An honor, my king." Emotions surged within Ryker as he felt the warmth and life slowly ebbing from his friend, a heartache that would haunt him forever.

The light left Commander Elmond swiftly, far too swiftly. Ryker held onto Elmond and wept over his lifeless body. This man was like a brother to him. They fought battles together side by side and saved each other's lives on multiple occasions. Now, Ryker couldn't repay the favor. He pressed his forehead to Elmond's one last time and whispered, "The honor is all mine, my brother. Thank you. Go in peace."

Tilmond stood and reached out his long arm to Ryker. "Uncle Ryker, we have to go. Hurry." They hurried behind the portrait, secured the door, and then raced down the dark corridor. War didn't wait for grief; it only added it.

Char heard the soldiers gaining on them. The soldiers had spotted them escaping through the large vase. The old war room was stocked with plenty of weapons, which they would need. The soldiers in black rushed in and started surrounding them. Char was grateful for the military friends he had in the room, but he was terrified of what would happen to the ladies and children if they lost.

The Stoltland soldiers launched their attack. Char swung his rusty sword at his assailant, but the blade shattered against the enemy's weapon. His heart sank. How could they defend themselves with such brittle arms? The attacker returned for another swing at Char, but he was quick on his feet and kept evading the strikes.

Favien climbed onto the table and jumped onto one of the soldiers, knocking them both to the ground. Favien began pounding the enemy with two large rocks he had picked up from the rubble. When Favien stood up, the enemy's head looked like mush, and Favien's face was splattered with blood. Doebromir defended himself against his attacker using an old chair, while Sakul wielded old shields.

One of the soldiers smashed a chair over Favien's head, and Favien went still. Pinx screamed, vile rising in her throat.

Sorcha held Pinx back from running to Favien. The ladies clung to each other, keeping the children inside their gathered circle.

Doebromir twisted his protective chair, breaking the attacker's wrist. He kicked the soldier in the chest and picked up the sword that had been dropped. He swung with force, slicing diagonally through the soldier's neck into his chest cavity. Blood splattered on Doebromir's legs as the fallen soldier fell.

Once again, Char evaded the sword's strikes; then he noticed a soldier reaching for Sorcha. Sakul spotted the same soldier and panicked. He dropped his shield and felt a blow to his cheek. He fell to the ground, trying to shake his head to regain his composure.

Sorcha screamed as the soldier grabbed her. He held a sharp knife to her throat and yelled for them to surrender. Sakul felt as though he was drowning. Staring into Sorcha's tear-filled jade eyes, Sakul saw his love flooded with pure terror. His head still spinning, he crawled toward Sorcha.

Doebromir walked slowly toward the soldier to get his attention. Char snuck up from behind. With the soldier focused entirely on Doebromir and the crawling Sakul, Char leaped out from behind, but the soldier had another knife concealed in the palm of his free hand and stabbed Char in the stomach. A cold, nauseating feeling engulfed Sakul as he watched the sharp blade pressed against Sorcha's throat glide across her flawless ebony skin.

Sakul screamed in agony as he watched his beautiful love fall limp from the soldier's grasp onto the stone floor.

Doebromir swung his sword at the soldier, slicing across his stomach and causing his entrails to spill out.

Pinx ran to Favien. She began shaking him. "Favien! Favien! Wake up! I need you! You can't leave me!"

Doebromir, Adalina, and Brenna assisted in caring for the motionless Char, pressing torn strips from their dresses against the wound. The blood flowed from the small blade that remained in his stomach. Sakul sobbed while holding Sorcha. Norella and Madilina tore strips from their dresses to try to stop the bleeding from Sorcha's wound, but hope seemed to drain from the room like the blood flowing from Sorcha's neck.

Tears streamed down every cheek, a testament to their profound connection. They were more than just friends; they were family. They had spent countless days playing games and engaging in spirited pipscot fights, each moment a thread woven into the tapestry of their lives. The thought of this being the end of their cherished memories—an end to the smiles and laughter—felt unbearable. Who could help them now?

The couch toppled backward with Jace. Drystan seized the opportunity, but a large flame prevented Drystan from delivering his killing blow. The air was barely breathable and became nearly impossible to see through. Corentine was putting everything she had into killing Sealyn. She couldn't understand why all her years of sword training weren't overcoming an archer. With each blocked advance, Corentine's anger intensified. The dark mist began to rise slowly.

Another vase shattered against the burning bookshelves. Drystan quickly seized Jace by the throat. They both collapsed to the ground, exhausted. Jace felt the burning inside his throat, his body gasping desperately for air. His vision began to blur, and darkness started to close in. The fight was slipping from his heart.

Releasing his hands from Drystan's firm grasp, Jace's arm extended and landed on a broken piece of the vase. His fingers gripped the sharp porcelain tightly, and with one last desperate attempt to save his life, Jace thrust the sharp point into the side of Drystan's neck. An immediate rush of air filled Jace's lungs. He coughed loudly, the smoke-filled air burning even more with his desperate need for oxygen. Jace crawled to the window and pushed both windows open.

Jace wobbled toward the flinching Drystan, whose blood was spitting from the wound. Drystan tried to speak, but no words could form. Grabbing his neck, he propped himself against the door, begging for Jace not to approach him. Jace saw no reason to show mercy. Drystan was a traitor and would repeat the same actions. He never learned from his mistakes and had tried to kill not only Jace but also the queen—his queen—his wife. A life for a life. He had to protect his new kingdom and prevent Drystan from infecting them with the curse. Jace dragged Drystan's sword and raised it above his head. With both crimson-stained hands clasped around the hilt, he plunged the sword through Drystan's treacherous heart.

Jace stared only for a moment at the blood dripping from Drystan's lips. He took another life. This was his second kill. Would it be his last? He spun around quickly and squinted to see his mother and wife still in battle. One final swing, and Corentine's sword flew across the room. Jace blinked as Sealyn held her sword to his mother's neck. His mother's life now rested in the hands of the queen she had just betrayed. Jace rushed to Sealyn's side as they both stood amidst a pile of ashes.

Corentine wiped her bloody lip, her teeth stained crimson like her hair. "It doesn't matter if I lost this battle. What does matter is that you two will lose the war. Haven't you figured it out yet?"

"Figured what out, Mother?"

"The two curses on our lands: pride and envy. These are the most powerful curses placed upon all the kingdoms, so I don't have to defeat you in battle right now. I can simply watch you two tear each other apart because these curses are greater than either of you." She let out an evil laugh, then coughed against the smoke.

Sealyn stepped closer with her sword still pointing at Corentine. "Watch your words, witch. You have no right to speak them."

"My dear little queen. Allow me to educate your small brain." Corentine began to pace the burning room. "Stoltland was the original fall. Our curse was the reason everyone started falling in the first place, and who do you think was second?" Corentine stopped and pointed at Sealyn. "It was Elysium! Pride and envy can't exist together, so you see, my darlings, your marriage will destroy not only your kingdom but yourselves as well."

Sealyn dropped the sword, remembering reading the history scrolls, but something deep inside her spoke with a still, small voice. "We won't be held accountable for what our ancestors did. Their weaknesses don't have to be our weaknesses. We can be the ones to break the generational curses. Elysium already has the key to our curse. We must show kindness to those whom others deem unworthy and continue to protect them. We must be generous with our blessings and will continue to do so. We show mercy even when it hasn't been earned, and above all, we love unconditionally. With these actions reflecting the character of our hearts, the weaknesses of our ancestors have transformed into our strengths."

Angered, Corentine inhaled the smoke and embraced the darkness, yearning to be freed. Her onyx eyes glared at Jace and Sealyn. She raised her hands up. "It's time I fight with the old magic." She threw her head back and screamed, "Arise!" Black mist rose from the floor and spread throughout the library. The mist seized Sealyn's sword and hurled it through the window. Sealyn felt a wave of fear. What kind of darkness was this? How could such power exist?

The dark mist formed bindings around Jace's wrists and ankles, propelling him against a charred tapestry on the wall, encircling his throat and squeezing tighter and tighter. Sealyn had no idea how to combat this ancient magic. She crouched low to the ground near the ashes. In her fear, she remembered her grandfather's words: "My darling, just because you have a title, doesn't mean you are a queen yet. One day, you will know without a doubt that you are the true Emerald Queen." Was today that day? Sealyn raised her head and locked eyes with Corentine. The mist circled around her like a slow tornado.

Sealyn rose slowly, along with the ashes. "I am *not* afraid. Evil has no place here. We don't worship the curse."

The mist raised Corentine, forming a horse for her to ride. Corentine lifted her bloodied chin while seated on her black horse. Darkness shaped a spear in Corentine's hand, and rage flashed in Corentine's eyes. Sealyn braced for the worst but felt an electric sensation coursing through her body, like the static from rubbing wool blankets together.

She saw the ashes rising and what appeared to be a green flame beneath her feet. She should be burning, but she felt no pain. She should have felt fear, but instead, she felt confident. She watched as Corentine charged forward, throwing the spear directly at her. A gust of wind swept over Sealyn, and everything went dark. Sealyn blinked, thinking she was dead, but instead, she saw feathers.

Feathers? Why was she seeing feathers? She looked around, feeling the soft wall surrounding her. She was wrapped in two extraordinarily large emerald wings. Wings? Was she really seeing this correctly? Maybe she had inhaled too much smoke. The wings opened with a loud screech from the enormous beast behind Sealyn. She watched the black mist tremble at the sound of the creature's voice. The creature let out another deafening call that sent the black mist fleeing from the library. Jace dropped to the floor, gasping for air. Sealyn ran to Jace. Seeing he was okay, she looked back and saw the most glorious sight she had ever witnessed.

What had not been seen for thousands of years was standing tall and walking toward Corentine: the legendary Green Phoenix. He stood at least ten feet tall with an even larger wingspan. His bright, soul-piercing yellow eyes scowled at Corentine. Large, clawed feet sparkled like gold, and his long green tail feathers of emerald and white curved around the room, snuffing out the fires. He was truly breathtaking.

Sealyn and Jace walked slowly to stand beside the grand phoenix. Corentine's mouth gaped, and her body shook.

"Corentine, I wish for no further bloodshed." Sealyn looked at the mesmerizing phoenix and smiled. "We'll show you mercy even though you have shown us none." The green phoenix nodded in agreement. "You will return in only one ship—the one that carries Queen Mother Phyre. The remaining ships will be burned, and all captive animals will be released into the wild. You and your family are no longer welcome here. You will return to your land with the understanding that if you cross our borders without permission, I will destroy you. Do I make myself clear?"

Corentine nodded speechlessly, eyeing the creature of old.

Emerging from his hiding place, King Svagon joined his wife as they left the library. Too many bodies littered the floor. Blood was everywhere. Sealyn's heart sank. Jashun, Max, Aerrik, and Jem rushed into the room. Their mouths dropped open at the sight of the green phoenix, and they fell to their knees.

Sealyn ran to them. "Are you all right? Where is everyone?"

Aerrik spoke quickly. "We're fine, Your Majesty, but so many lives were lost."

Sealyn started pacing. "First, I need you three," she pointed to Jem, Jashun, and Max. "To take King Svagon and Queen Corentine to the dungeons." Jem and Max grabbed Svagon's arms, while Jashun took Corentine's arm, escorting them to the dungeons.

Sealyn turned to the green phoenix. She looked deep into his yellow eyes. "I don't know how I know this, but I know you can sense who needs help right now. I need you to help find those we can't get to who are in the most need." Like a light piercing through the dark night, the phoenix soared in green flames toward the old war room. Sealyn realized where he was heading. Death was coming. "Aerrik, I know you want to know about your children, but that's where the green phoenix just went. They'll be safe with him. I need you to take the passage to where Tybalt is keeping my sister. Bring them back."

Aerrik nodded. "Of course, Your Majesty, but Queen Sealyn, where are you going?"

"To find the rest of my family and then sound the bells for Elysium's healing." Sealyn grabbed Jace's hand, and they both raced off to the portrait, with death greeting them at every corner.

Queen Sealyn,
My dearest cousin, my deepest
condolences. My heart is with you
always. I wish I could be with you in
body, but I'm there in spirit. These
will be dark times you face, but
remember that the hardships we
face are only temporary.
Stay focused on your task. Like
your mother says, "You are
stronger than you think you are."
I'll be traveling back to Avondelle
soon. Until then...

All my love,
Lord Prince William Dovinus
"Will"

# Chapter 37

# THE EMERALD QUEEN

After finishing the reading, Siany paused and surveyed the room. Everyone had tears and anger in their Elysian eyes. She hated not being part of the battle, but knew she would have been a target for the enemy. She sighed. "The reading of the account has concluded."

"Thank you, dear sister. Perhaps over the next few weeks, more stories will need to be added because we are most assuredly praying for the recovery of all the victims of the Battle of the Betrayals."

Max shook his head. "They came out of nowhere! Why? Why did they attack in this way? You married one of their own peacefully." He slammed his fist on the table.

"Pride has a way of making one unsatisfied," Sealyn responded. "We believe that Queen Corentine wanted the Heart of Elysium to control Elysium's powers, but the fail-safe was to kill the royal family and occupy the throne."

Doebromir squinted. "How did they manage not to gain the Heart of Elysium?"

"They would have," Aerrik said softly, "if it hadn't been for Queen Sealyn's brilliant idea of shielding it with blankets of mirron fur."

"How clever!" Prince Adomin remarked.

"They walked right by it several times, even fought Lord Temm in front of the entrance, but they never figured it out. The angle of the reflections made it look like a patch of lush forest."

Max scratched his head, always full of more questions. "May I ask one more question, Queen Sealyn?" She nodded. "Legend says that the Green Phoenix rises not from ashes but from fire. Is the legend wrong? You weren't standing in fire, correct?"

Sealyn closed her eyes and allowed her mind to go back to that horrific moment. She remembered the ashes rising with her, but also the green flames beneath her. "He created his own fire." Sealyn opened her eyes, blinking in shock at her revelation. "We are of the great phoenix's powers, so does this mean that Elysians can create their own flames?"

Everyone's heads snapped to King Ryker. He blinked. "No. I believe that the old magic has been awoken."

"What does that mean?" asked Max.

"It means that the parchments found in that coffin are, now more than ever, the most valuable weapons we have. They contain the answers to the old ways. We're going to see more of these archaic powers emerge."

Graelynd entered with a somber demeanor. "Excuse the interruption, Queen Sealyn, but you're needed at the front gate."

Sealyn excused herself and greeted the soldier at the front. "Greetings, My Queen. I come with a message from Lady Zuri."

"Lady Zuri? She's back?"

"Yes, Your Majesty. She returned two days ago. She hasn't left the old Crystal Fort with the recovering people." He attempted to appear brave in front of the large green phoenix standing beside Sealyn. The phoenix paid no attention to the young soldier; instead, it preened its feathers, basking in the sunlight.

"Take me to her, please." Sealyn turned to the phoenix. "Follow me. It'll do the injured good to see you."

What a sight for the nurses and the injured to behold when their queen walked into the old fort with the legendary phoenix. Sealyn walked slowly among the injured and dying. For those who were awake, she would stop and offer encouragement, making sure to thank each one. Over the past week, dozens had died while she held their hands, and her heart was breaking.

She was glad that everyone agreed to turn the fort into a grand hospital once this was over. She had a nurse point her in the direction of where Jace and Zuri were. She opened one of the large meeting chambers and found Jace sitting beside Char, who remained unconscious. Seeing Jace alive and well made her heart feel as if it could be pieced back together.

She saw Zuri tending to Sorcha, who lay still, and beside her was Sakul, spilling tears with his hand clasped over Sorcha's. Sealyn let her tears fall as she watched Pinx brush Favien's hair. He lay still like a corpse.

Norella met Sealyn's gaze and shook her head, indicating no change. Sealyn dropped her head and looked to her other side, only to see Raquel and Temm sitting with Stawyer. She observed as her cousin, Brandle, removed Stawyer's bandages.

The wound looked swollen and infected. Zuri rushed to his side and poured what appeared to be purple salt onto the wound. Sealyn was relieved to see Stawyer stir, but his chances of survival were slim.

Zuri walked up to Sealyn and hugged her. "My Queen, I'm so glad to see you alive and healthy. I've missed you."

"I'm so glad you're back. I've missed you, too."

"I wish I could give you good news about your family and friends, but their fate is with Creator. I've done all I can do. Your Vinurs usually come in around this time and feed all the volunteers and patients. They've been so helpful."

"I'm glad. Let's speak in private before this room is filled with everyone." Sealyn motioned for Jace to join them.

They walked to the back terrace, which offered a wide view of the palace to their left and the lush landscape in every other direction. With the birds chirping and the scent of blossoms in the air, it felt peaceful despite the pain and suffering behind it. The large phoenix settled at the edge and gazed out over the stone banister. The gold feathers above his head moved gently with the breeze.

Keeping her eyes on the phoenix, Zuri said, "Many things have changed since I've been away."

"Yes, some are easier to explain than others."

Jace shifted his stance. "I've been in suspense long enough. Where have you been, Zuri?"

Sealyn nodded to Zuri. "The queen commissioned me long ago to go back to Len Nove. We had to be sure of the state that it was in."

"Be sure? Be sure for what reason?"

"We had to be sure it was ready for a power shift," Sealyn replied.

"Power shift to whom?" Jace questioned.

"To us, my love. We're going to break Len Nove's curse, and unfortunately, that calls for a shifting of the crown's power...to me."

"What?!" exclaimed Jace. "Why do you want more power? You sound like my mother."

"No, Jace! How dare you say such things!" Zuri's cobalt eyes flared.

"Easy, Zuri. Jace, we now know how to defeat the curses. Each one will be different, and none will be easy, but we must do this to end the evil and suffering in our world. Your mother's attack was no ordinary attack. It was a power launch."

Jace stepped back. "What do you mean by that?"

"Jace, we've studied your mother's moves over the past week, and her actions show that she wants to rule not only Elysium but all the seven kingdoms. She has allowed the dark magic to overtake her and lead her on a quest for control of everything and everyone."

"And yet you let her go," choked Jace.

Sealyn walked to the stone railing and grasped it, feeling the pain she had caused her people. "Yes, because vengeance is not for us but for Creator. He will deal with her, and if fate decides for us to have another battle, then mercy won't be on the table."

"I can't see my mother trying to overtake all the kingdoms."

"How blind are you? Can you not see the damage she's caused?" barked Zuri. The green phoenix snapped his gold beak twice at Zuri. "My apologies, Jace. That was rude of me."

Jace waved the apology away. "No need, Zuri. I'm just having a hard time wrapping my mind around my mother being a world-dominating dictator."

"She's dangerous. She knows right from wrong, but she willingly chooses wrong. She embraced her desires over the safety of others. This is a person who can't be trusted. Jace, I won't make you choose between your family and me, but I will ask you to make wise decisions for our safety in how you conduct your relationship with them going forward."

Jace reluctantly nodded. He was genuinely surprised that he was not forbidden from having any contact with them.

Zuri sighed. "So what happens next?"

Sealyn gazed across the evergreens of her land. It was difficult to envision how this place appeared under the curse anymore. With a fierce glimmer in his yellow eyes, the mighty phoenix snapped his beak, beckoning them toward untold adventures. Sealyn's lips curled into a determined smile as she faced the majestic creature. "Our next quest. The battle for Len Nove begins now."

# LIBRARY OF CREATURES

- <u>GREEN PHEONIX:</u> A legendary creature from the old magic; the protector of Elysium. Only one way to bring back the creatures of old—break the curse.

- <u>PHEONIX:</u> Phoenixes are native to Elysium. They come in all sizes; the smallest are the yellow feathers. Most have red feathers, but the northern ones have blue. Most Elysians own phoenixes as pets, and they wander freely throughout the kingdom.

- <u>NICHT:</u> Nichts have heads that look too large for their arms and legs, with beautiful wings, and are known to make words plural when not necessary. Nichts vary in size by their classification. Earth Nichts are the largest, growing to the size of a human toddler. Others are as small as a human's hand.

- HIRCUS GOAT: Hircuses are in the goat family, but they have two sets of horns. One set atop the head, facing behind him, and the other below its ears, curving below and following the jawline. Almost all are solid black, with a purple stripe down their back and purple hair covering their black hooves. Their milk is known to have healing powers throughout Elysium.

- CAPRAS GOAT: Caprases are in the goat family. They have solid white fur with icy white eyes and spikes running down their spines, along with horns that protrude forward. Their milk is poisonous to humans, but can heal every other creature in all seven kingdoms!

- <u>NEEDLEBOB</u>: They are in the spiny rodent classification. Most needlebobs are shimmering gold, but those found in Stoltland have black tips. Needlebobs love thick forests and spend their days under ferns' shade, hunting beetles. Needlebobs may look cute, but beware— their needles contain potent hallucinogenic poison. Once a needle pierces its victim's skin, the poison takes thirty seconds to release its effect. Hallucinations can last for hours and, in some worst cases, days. Needlebobs prefer to roll from one place to the next instead of walking. Their needles tuck and form around its body, allowing it to form a shell for easy rolling.

- <u>HORNED WHALE:</u> Horned whales look like sperm whales except they have horns protruding from their heads like a long-horned cow. They are extremely fast, but also submissive. Unfortunately, Stoltland has captured this breed and uses them for speedy trips across the ocean.

- <u>MIRRON:</u> Mirrons are an anomaly to the horse family. They are as tall as a camel, as wide as a rhinoceros, and completely covered in hairs that look like slivers of mirror. This is why they are referred to as invisible. Their fur reflects the scene around them, camouflaging them from enemies. Mirrons are highly intelligent and often understand humans. They're favorite vegetable is pumpkin, so be kind and bring them some.

- <u>MOON BUTTERFLY:</u> Moon butterflies are a rare sight, as most people are asleep when they emerge. They only displayed color after being exposed to moonlight for hours. They're attracted to heat and travel in large groups. Their colors range from red to purple and sometimes orange. They love drinking nectar from the pixie flowers and enjoy teasing nighttime predators.

- <u>EXIGUUMS</u>: Exiguums have a genetic code that prevents them from growing beyond their newborn size. They still mature just like normal elephants, but remain small for their whole lives. Exiguums have special colors. Mainly purple and blue, but sometimes grey. Exiguums are fuzzy instead of rough. Their eye colors vary from green to blue.

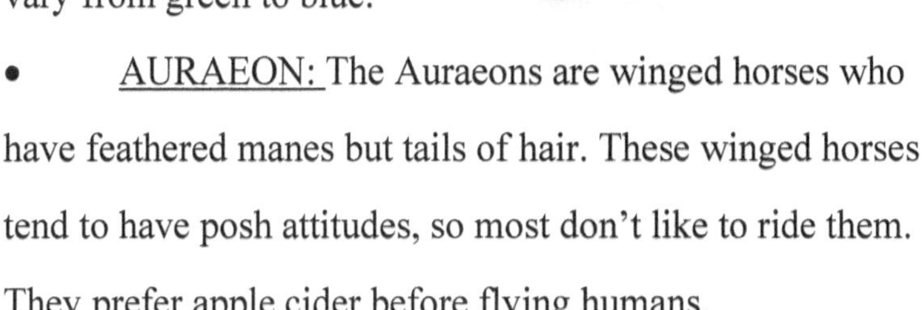

- <u>AURAEON:</u> The Auraeons are winged horses who have feathered manes but tails of hair. These winged horses tend to have posh attitudes, so most don't like to ride them. They prefer apple cider before flying humans.

- <u>NOMOSEV</u>: Nomosevs are winged horses who have tails of feathers and manes of hair. Nomosevs had the friendliest personalities, even engaging in laughter, understanding human jokes. They are the favorite to ride among the winged horses. Before riding, make sure to feed them Puffin Pies; that's they're favorite.

- <u>CAELIDON</u>: Caelidons are winged horses with their manes and tails composed of feathers. Fastest of the winged horses, very dangerous to ride. They're stand-offish toward humans, but if you're lucky, you might be able to persuade one to come close if you have Chocolate Jabbles with peanut butter.

# ACKNOWLEDGMENTS

What a joy it is to have this completed novel, but I must recognize certain people who may or may not have realized their spark in making this book come to life.

My incredible husband, Kyle Massie, stood by me in all the ups and downs a self-publisher faces. You spoke life into me when I needed it most and gave grace on those many work nights. I love you as much as Sealyn loves Jace.

My supportive parents, Rhett & Gwen Salley, who I'm sure are still in shock that I wrote a book, I want to thank you for your inspiration. Thanks, Papa Bear, for teaching us capture the flag, which inspired Feydom. Thanks, Momma Gwen, for teaching me that the paper on the desk is just as important as the paper in the bathroom.

Mindy Salley, my sister, is the one who kept asking questions and kept asking when I was going to finish. Your persistence always reminded me of what you told me during my freshman year at NGU: "We aren't quitters."

I could not have had a better team to discuss my creative ideas than Amanda Barnett, Sarah Sanchez, and Ashley Davis. I appreciate you all for being willing to hear my thousands of ideas and reading my first painfully unedited chapters, drawings, etc. Thank you!

I must thank Brad Barnett for his expertise in jujitsu and for giving me the correct wording for fighting scenes. Thank you!

To the Clear Pond Book Club, I cannot express my gratitude enough to each of you. Being willing to read my manuscript and give feedback with edits was everything I needed to keep moving forward. You all have become another family to me. I'm eternally grateful.

Caleb Wygal for telling me, "Just keep writing!" Thank you, my friend, because of that statement, I finished my book. You energized me to keep going and gave excellent advice on where to start self-publishing.

Susan Welch for being willing to read my first seven chapters and use her famous red pen for editing. Thank you for being a great English teacher to me.

Special thank you to Jesse Winter with Duo Storytelling for the in-depth editing. I'm beyond appreciative.

Thank you, Casey Kaiser, for teaching me the difference between American English vs. British English. I appreciate your hard work!

Miblart for an excellent book cover. Thank you for your patience in working with me and for all the edits.

Of course, Chris Salley, for being wonderfully you. Remember, the world is a much better place with you in it.

And above all, the entire credit and glory go to the good Lord above. Thank you for giving me a creative mind and so many blessings. All praise to you.

# ABOUT THE AUTHOR

MAEGWEN SALLEY-MASSIE is the author of *The Emerald Queen Rises* and its forthcoming sequels. She grew up in the Pee Dee Low Country of South Carolina with her loving parents and sister. Her childhood was spent mainly outdoors building forts, riding horses, playing capture the flag, riding ATVs, and playing volleyball. She began writing *The Emerald Queen Rises* during the pandemic as therapy. She is a woven polypropylene specialist by day and a fantasy fiction author by night. Her favorite food is sushi, and she loves to travel the world. Maegwen currently lives in Myrtle Beach, SC, with her husband, Kyle, and their cat, Khaleesi.

For more information about Maegwen and her books, please visit:

www.greenfernspublishinghouse.com
www.theemeraldqueenrisesbook.com
www.maegwensalleymassie.com

Or follow her on Instagram and Facebook @MaegwenAuthor

www.ingramcontent.com/pod-product-compliance
Lightning Source LLC
Chambersburg PA
CBHW030332010826
48973CB00004B/971